BASIC
LAW

BASIC LAW

A Mystery of Cold War Europe

J. Sydney Jones

MYSTERIOUSPRESS.COM

OPEN ROAD
INTEGRATED MEDIA
NEW YORK

Cover design by Mauricio Díaz

978-1-4976-9047-9

Published in 2015 by MysteriousPress.com/Open Road Integrated Media, Inc.
345 Hudson Street
New York, NY 10014
www.mysteriouspress.com
wwww.openroadmedia.com

To Tom—he knows why.

BASIC
LAW

The Grundgesetz (Basic Law) is the Constitution of the Federal Republic of Germany.

PROLOGUE

But in the end, none of it matters.

Not what went down in Prague a quarter century ago. Not Gorik's secrets or Vogel and his goons. Not even Father.

In the end, sleep is all that matters.

Realizing this as she lies on the unmade bed, she smiles as if she has discovered great wisdom and looks to her left to the red numbers of the digital clock on her bedside table: 3:03.

Then the room begins to spin crazily around her; her prized Klimt print, *Judith I*, leers at her from the wall opposite her bedstead. She shivers as sudden fear and panic grip her. She does not want to die. Not now. Not like this. What if he doesn't follow the trail she's left?

But it is too late. The blonde woman on the bed dressed in faded jeans and a black turtleneck cannot keep her eyes open. A blood vessel pulses erratically at her right temple. Her breathing is ragged, a loud wheeze that is labored as if she has a bronchial condition. She is beyond fighting the sleep; yet suddenly her entire body flexes and she forces a final word: "Sammy."

No one is there to hear.

CHAPTER ONE

She'd think it was a lark, Kramer tells himself. Playing got-you-last. Reni thumbing her nose at all of them for one final time. Even had herself planted in consecrated ground. What a joke that was. Kramer would love to know how many marks out of Herr Müller's hefty wallet that took.

Renata Müller, queen of the German Left, one-time head of the Green coalition in the German Parliament—Red Reni the press loved to call her—laid to rest with full Catholic honors despite committing suicide.

But that just didn't compute to Kramer. Reni was not a suicide type of woman.

And there was the melon-faced priest at the rain-soaked interment with the sack of dirt in a blue plastic shopping bag to keep it dry, sprinkling it on her coffin like pepper on a steak. The same priest who'd gone around twenty some years ago muttering about the evils of their cohabitation. Jesus, what a lovely last laugh.

"They serve an excellent pike here, Sam," Herr Müller says, not lifting his eyes from the hand-printed menu he's scrutinizing.

"Great," Kramer replies. He's seated across an expanse of blue-and-white checked tablecloth from Müller, playing at studying his own menu some more, but actually eyeballing a waitress in a dirndl that shows way too much cleavage.

Kramer's also trying to figure out Müller's post-funeral invite, but not spending too much time on it. He never turns down a free meal. His shoes are sodden from the rain, and his stomach sour from too much single malt the night before. A man in that condition does not ask why, just when.

"And the white wine is tolerably good as well." This time, Herr Müller fixes Kramer with penetrating blue eyes; the nares of his hawk nose quiver. "But I seem to recall you being a beer man."

"No. Wine is fine." The words are out before Kramer can stop them. He suddenly remembers Reni's warning about her father: *He can charm a snake, Sammy. He makes you want to please him.*

Herr Müller smiles, with lips only, then beckons the waitress and orders for both of them. After she leaves, they sit listening to the clink of cutlery at other tables.

Kramer finally ends their silence. "Sorry about your daughter."

Herr Müller's jaw muscle works, like a stage direction for grief. Kramer has trouble taking him seriously with his health club tan in November and his white hair freshly coiffed for the occasion. But maybe he's just trying to keep his mind off the body in the coffin, too.

"Renata will be missed by us all," Müller replies. "But let's be honest, Sam. She was very hard on friends. She could be a difficult person, demanding at times."

Kramer says nothing as the wine, salad, and rolls are delivered.

"Lord knows, we had our differences," Müller says, filling the wineglasses. "Lately, we called a truce, but in the years you knew her, Sam, Renata and I had a rift between us. I assume you were aware of that."

Kramer nods and thinks to himself, More like the Grand Canyon.

"Yes," Herr Müller continues, "we eventually overcame our differences. Some never did, I am afraid to say. Gerhard, for example . . ."

Kramer perks up at his mention. "Yes. Where is he? I expected to see him at the funeral."

"Gone. Taken himself off somewhere." Müller munches desultorily on the salad and swallows. "The male syndrome of the late twentieth century, Sam. Chaps who cannot stand to be hidden by the much larger shadow their mates cast." Herr Müller looks at Kramer appraisingly, with a touch too much interest. "You haven't stayed in touch with him?"

Bells go off in Kramer's head. So this is why the lunch, he figures. "No, I haven't seen him in years."

Müller shakes his head. "One would think he would at least return to pay his final respects. She was his wife, after all." Müller pauses momentarily, smiling at the waitress as she brings the main course. Then his eyes lock again on Kramer. "But let's speak of more uplifting topics, Sam. You, for instance. What have you done with yourself all these years?"

Kramer shrugs. It's his experience that when people ask such questions, they don't want real answers. It's easy for him to put the mask on; years of being the anonymous interloper and interviewer have prepared him. So for the next few minutes, as they both attack the meal, he regales Müller with tales of the life of a foreign correspondent: the trail of stories that led him from Belfast to Kabul to Sarajevo.

"So you've settled in Vienna," Müller suddenly interrupts. "Not a bad city. It's where you all met, isn't it?"

"Yes." All of us, Kramer thinks.

Suddenly, Herr Müller's smooth facade cracks. He bows

his head in his long, tanned hands, and a sob escapes his lips, partly choked off.

"God, how awful. Dead all those days and none of us even caring. Left to her neighbors to find her."

He looks up, eyes red-rimmed but still piercing.

"It was the smell, you see. There was this powerful stench, and they thought perhaps a gas line had a leak."

"I don't get it." Kramer can no longer play the disinterested role. "It's just not like her. Why the hell would she do it?"

Müller shakes his head abruptly, as much to steel himself as to indicate *I don't know*. "She left no note."

"Could it have been an accident?"

Another shake of Müller's head. "Not likely. The coroner thinks she may have ingested the better part of a bottle of sleeping pills. Though it was difficult to tell after so much time had elapsed. She was depressed."

"About Gerhard leaving?"

"Hardly." Müller has control of himself again. "It was bigger than that. Since being out of Parliament, she felt useless—that the best part of her life was past. I cannot understand such pessimism, myself," he quickly adds. "There is always something to live for. Always a new day to present itself. She could have done so many things with her life. But you younger people seem to want things easily, instantly."

Suddenly, the idea seems ludicrous to Kramer. "You're saying she killed herself because she was no longer in Parliament? Come on."

Herr Müller lifts his hands shoulder height, stretches them palm upward. An uncharacteristic shrug for such a verbal man.

"Who knows what thoughts arise at three in the morning?"

They get through the lunch and exchange addresses, though neither has the faintest desire to see the other again. Herr

Müller honks once as he departs from Bonn in his silver Mercedes. Standing in the gasthaus parking lot, Kramer wonders if Müller got what he was looking for out of the lunch meeting; he knows that he himself did not. A viable explanation for Reni's suicide has yet to be offered.

The rain has let up some, but the afternoon is dark and somber. Kramer returns to his room at the Hotel Bad. It is functional: a pine-veneer single bed and meager comforter along with a matching faux-pine wardrobe and nightstand. A tiny dormer window looks out on the steeple of the Catholic church. Beyond it is the greenery of the cemetery where Reni was buried this morning.

Kramer has no plans; he's not scheduled back at the paper until tomorrow. He expected old friends to turn up for the interment; that they might wake the dead. Now, this room seems a silly expense. He could catch the afternoon flight back to Vienna; be in the office first thing in the morning.

Instead, he slumps onto the edge of the bed, elbows on knees, rubbing his eyes, feeling sudden exhaustion. Early this morning, he caught the red-eye from Vienna to Bonn; that and the effects of the heavy lunch and wine are catching up with him. He yawns, kicks off his damp shoes, and stretches out on the bed, pulling the comforter over him.

Sleep comes effortlessly; and suddenly Reni is hovering over him, on him like a glove, her bushy blonde hair tossed about her face, teeth biting into her lower lip as if to hold off the moment of climax. The only position she knew—on top.

She moves slowly on him, minuscule rotations of her hips and fluttering interior caresses, as he holds back, too. He stares into her face that looks in pain, feels himself joining her, part of her, so much in love with her that it hurts. And when she comes, she opens her eyes in surprise, looking at him, looking into him, her mouth formed in a silent scream of pleasure.

But the scream turns into the chirruping of a cricket, and Kramer slowly crawls out of the dreamscape to hear his telephone ringing. He grapples for it clumsily and finally gets the receiver to his ear.

"Yes?" His voice low and thick from sleep.

"Mr. Kramer? Have I disturbed you?"

"Yes and yes."

Silence at the other end.

"Who's speaking, please?" Kramer finally asks, rubbing his face to wake up, to wipe away the vision of Reni.

"Sorry. Walther here. Dieter Walther of Schnelling and Walther."

The caller pauses as if that is supposed to mean something to Kramer. It doesn't.

"We telephoned you in Vienna, but your office said you were here in Bad Lunsburg. I must have missed you at the funeral today. Handy that you are in town, though."

"Why is that?" Kramer says, beginning to feel annoyed.

"Because of the will, you see. Renata Müller's. I am her lawyer, and you have been mentioned in the will. Perhaps you could stop by sometime before leaving Bad Lunsburg."

It's the best offer Kramer's had today. He glances at his wristwatch: a little after four in the afternoon.

"How about in ten minutes?" he says.

CHAPTER TWO

The office is where the voice on the telephone said it would be: opposite the half-timbered town hall. The firm of Schnelling and Walther is in a new three-story building with a long glass facade to catch the reflection of older "quaint" buildings. It has no character of its own. The offices are on the third floor; Kramer takes the stairs instead of the elevator.

It's all palms and leather couches there; a secretary sits at the mahogany desk with a phone to her ear. She smiles at Kramer as he enters, nodding to a couch, and continues the conversation. Kramer sits, picks up an art magazine from the glass table in front of the couch, and leafs through reprints of abstractions, nudes, and graffiti before the secretary finally hangs up the phone, reattaches a clip-on earring to her left lobe, and smiles again.

"Sorry to keep you waiting," she says in English. "Mr. Kramer?"

He nods.

"You're to go right in. The door to your left." She gestures in back of her.

He gets up and goes to the door, knocking lightly before

opening it. A small, thin man sits behind a massive desk and looks up with owl eyes as Kramer enters.

"Have a seat," he says, not bothering to rise.

Kramer crosses to the desk. Behind the little man is a view of the old town hall and rolling green hills in back of it. Kramer takes a chair in front of the desk.

"I spoke with you on the phone, Herr Walther," Kramer begins.

"Schnelling, actually," the little man interrupts, placing two pale hands on the green desk blotter in front of him. "Herr Walther had an urgent meeting to attend. But we both dealt with the unfortunate Frau Müller's estate."

Kramer takes an immediate dislike to the man without really knowing why. His size makes Kramer, at six four, feel rather ungainly. But it is more than that. There is an air about the man, a pomposity that rankles. *Frau* Müller. The Germans have never found an equivalent for *Ms.* Never even tried.

A gray file folder sits on the desk to Herr Schnelling's left, and he opens the front cover.

"I believe Herr Walther explained that you are mentioned in Frau Müller's will."

"He said that, yes."

"You were a friend of Frau Müller's?"

"Renata Müller and I go way back."

"Friends?"

"Lovers, if it's any of your business."

The owl eyes blink; the pale hands thrum fingers on the blotter.

"Quite," he says. "There is no question of inheritance, you see, Mr. Kramer. A *re*quest rather than a *be*quest."

He smiles, pleased with the turn of phrase.

"That's why I was interested in your connection to the deceased. Professional rather than prurient interest."

"Just how am I mentioned in the will?"

Schnelling refers to the pages in the file now. "As executor, I believe her phrasing was . . ." He shuffles pages, comes to the passage. "Yes. She has named you executor of her literary estate."

It is the first Kramer has heard of it. "What literary estate?"

"Let me read the paragraph, and I quote: 'I do hereby name Sam Kramer of Vienna as executor of my literary estate. In case of my untimely death, it will be up to him to dispose of notes, interviews, and finished manuscript for my memoirs as he sees fit.' End quote."

Kramer sits forward in the chair. "She was writing memoirs?"

Schnelling shrugs. "I was merely her lawyer, not her confidant. But if she was engaged in any such activity, then the results must surely be stored at her home. All safe-deposit boxes are listed with us and the contents already accounted for. No mention of memoirs in any of that."

Kramer thinks: Young to be writing memoirs. Then a second thought, "When did Ms. Müller name me her literary executor?"

"Really, Mr. Kramer. I don't know . . ."

"Oh, come off it. She's dead. I was her friend."

"Yes." Schnelling says it grudgingly, as if he means *no*, and examines the clause. "It was appended October the second of this year."

Kramer makes the calculation. "Several weeks before her death?"

"Yes," Schnelling says. "Is that significant?"

It's Kramer's turn to shrug. "I don't know."

They sit staring at each other for a moment; another blink of Schnelling's round eyes.

"I assume you will want to take possession of the materials

in question before your return to Vienna, Mr. Kramer. I am prepared to accompany you to Frau Müller's house at your convenience."

They meet the next morning at Inheritance, Reni's name for the farmhouse she purchased with the money her mother left her. Kramer is bleary-eyed after anesthetizing himself the night before with several bottles of Dortmunder beer. The day is as featureless as he feels; Herr Schnelling is checking his watch, leaning against a purple Porsche as the taxi drops Kramer off.

"Am I late?" Kramer sidesteps a mud puddle in the unpaved drive as he approaches Schnelling.

"A trifle." Tight, humorless smile. He is wearing a homburg and a pinstripe double-breasted suit that makes him look even shorter than he is today. In the light of day, his skin looks almost translucent, Kramer decides.

"After you. Mr. Kramer. I believe you know your way?"

Kramer does. He and Reni lived here for several months before moving on to Greece. The outside looks much the same as it did more than twenty years ago: a low, white-walled structure in the shape of a U. The barn and stalls at one end of the U were long ago converted into a solarium and study. One difference: there are neighbors now. The farmland on the edge of the town has been developed; Inheritance is now ringed by small, tidy bungalows with small, tidy gardens. They enter the door in the middle wing; it is locked, but Schnelling produces the key. Kramer has an eerie feeling as the lawyer opens the door, like someone unlocking his own past.

There is a strong smell of disinfectant as the door opens, and a shiver passes over him as he remembers Herr Müller's comments about the stink.

"There we are," Schnelling says with false goodwill.

Kramer takes a moment to orient himself; nothing in

here is as it was when he lived here with Reni. The entryway has been knocked down so that the door opens immediately onto the living room. It's all hardwood floors and white walls, a far cry from the linoleum and shoddy wallpaper that used to be here. All ladder-back chairs and pine cupboards instead of cheap aluminum and Formica. The walls are a photo gallery. Kramer gazes briefly at them as Schnelling leads him to the study. Reni and her father in endless variations: first step, first bike, first graduation. There are only a few of Gerhard and Reni. Who photographed them? Gerhard is heavier than Kramer remembers him. Also clean-shaven—which is, surprisingly, an improvement. Reni does not look happy in those few shots with Gerhard; she reserves the smiles for her father.

"Any papers or memoirs that exist should be in the study." Schnelling leads Kramer past a closed door that was once their bedroom.

Kramer stops, turns the knob, but the door is locked.

"The body was found in there," Schnelling says, and Kramer jerks his hand away as if burned. "Nothing of interest, I assure you. The police surveyed it thoroughly at the time."

Kramer nods and feels his stomach flip-flop. He wants to get this over with, get away from the smell of disinfectant, the black-and-white memories on the walls. It is claustrophobic; it is her life since leaving him, and he wants no part of it. He is a stranger to it, an interloper.

"I suspect the papers will be in the file cabinets," Schnelling says as they reach the study.

The first room to be converted after Reni bought the old farm, this study has not changed over the years. The old rolltop desk is still there along with the Olivetti portable he wrote some of his first stories on. He immediately determines to take this with him: a reminder of better days. The Schiele nude they bought in Vienna still hangs on the wall along with a red-and-black woven bag from Crete. Memento of their first visit there.

On impulse, he reaches into the bag and feels at its bottom the rough edges of pottery shards they gathered at Phaistos in 1972.

Schnelling is squinting at him from the wooden file cabinet, and Kramer sheepishly withdraws his hand from the bag, palming several of the shards as he does so. More keepsakes from a forgotten time.

"Perhaps you could check the drawers, Mr. Kramer."

They go about their searches for several minutes, neither speaking. For Kramer, the contents of the room are like a leap into the past: this was the Reni he knew and loved, not the collector of rustic housewares.

In the second drawer of the desk, under a rubber-banded collection of tax returns, he finds an old photo. He and Reni at the ruined palace of Phaistos, snowcapped Mount Ida behind them repeating the silhouette of the palace ruins. They look so young in the photo, young and trusting. The world is theirs as they squint into the strong winter sun, arms around each other. Kramer's hair is worn long, and his beard is just filling in. Reni wears her blonde hair braided and coiled on top of her head. The Cretans loved her hair; the children in villages would come up to her to touch it, giggling and frightened.

Kramer remembers the day this photograph was taken. They stayed at the government-run Xenia Hotel the night before, walked in the ruins under a full moon, collected shards in its shadow, and told each other stories of what life must have been like four thousand years ago. And back in the room, they had made love with the moonlight streaming in the open window, caressing their naked skin with its blue light. Afterward, they lay in each other's arms, reading D. H. Lawrence by the strong moonlight.

A perfect moment; Kramer realized it even then. He wanted to stop time, to keep them forever encapsulated in that perfect moment.

"There's nothing here." Schnelling closes the last file drawer. "Have you had any luck?"

Kramer quickly slips the photo into his coat pocket, remembering now something else about that perfect moment. Gerhard came to join them the next day at Phaistos. He was the one who took the photo.

"Nothing yet," Kramer says.

Another half hour of looking turns up nothing. If there are files for a memoir, they are not in the study. Kramer finishes with the scattering of papers on top of the desk. Jottings for a proposed newspaper article on skinhead violence, a shopping list, some scratched-out figures of a failed household budget. But no memoirs.

"Lumber room next, I guess," Kramer says.

Schnelling looks confused.

"A storage room off the kitchen. At least it was when I lived here. Maybe it's been turned into an herb room by now."

Kramer leads the way toward the far wing of the house away from the study. More improvements here: the kitchen floor has flagstones now, covered in rag rugs. More pine and country kitsch. But the lumber room remains as it was, a larder never used as such by Reni. Here boxes are piled on top of one another like the skyline of a miniature city.

"Oh my," Schnelling says.

Kramer nods in agreement. "None of these are labeled. I guess we just start digging through them."

The lawyer checks his watch.

"Late for a very important date?" Kramer says.

"I do have other clients."

"Take off, then. I can handle this alone."

Schnelling seems mightily relieved. "You're sure?"

"Absolutely." Kramer shoots him his competent, likable grin.

Schnelling departs, giving Kramer the keys to the house and an admonition to be sure everything is locked up upon leaving.

It takes him two hours to sort through the boxes of old clothes, books, and memorabilia. Most of it is Gerhard's. No sign of memoirs, but another photo to add to his collection: the Magnificent Seven taken in the courtyard of the Palais Forster in Vienna, where they all went to school together in 1968. Unbeatable, unstoppable they had declared themselves. He, Reni, and Gerhard form the center of the group in the photo. Then Randall in back, clowning as always, fingering rabbit ears over Kramer's head. Rick, the artist, with paint-smeared jeans kneeling in front. Helmut, with his Trotsky glasses and notebook in hand, the Wittgenstein buff, standing a few feet separate from the rest. And Maria, the refugee from Prague. God, how he has tried to forget Maria over all the years. How he has wanted to erase all memory of her. She is fragile and beautiful like a pre-Raphaelite waif, a flower in her hand as she stands on Kramer's right. Reni is in the middle, as always; the focus of the picture, so sure looking, so in control.

A sudden noise from the front of the house jolts him into the here and now. A heavy footfall or something being tipped over. He freezes for a moment, then calls out, "Anyone there? *Wer ist da?*"

No answer. He leaves the tiny lumber room and crosses the kitchen. Another clunk, like a heavy footstep coming from beyond the living room.

Schnelling's come back, he tells himself, taking a deep breath. You're just spooked by being in Reni's house alone.

He keeps going toward the study and, as he passes the locked bedroom, he hears a distinct sound coming from inside. As if somebody is blundering around in there, knocking against the walls. A cold fear grips him.

Don't be an ass, Kramer, he tells himself. Just check it out. Find the key and open the door. He pulls out the ring of keys Schnelling left with him, tries three before finding the right fit, then turns the lock. He looks around momentarily for a weapon, something to wield. Nothing is handy, and he forces himself to open the door.

A rushing in his face almost knocks him over: the beating of wings and a frantic clawing at his cheek. He throws his arms up over his face, and the bird flies back into the bedroom. Kramer looks quickly into the room: the lace curtains billow in from an open window, and a large crow finally manages to find its way out again.

Kramer's heart is pounding. Someone obviously left the window open to get the smell out, allowing the bird in. Mystery solved. He looks at the bed, at the pink mattress with no sheets. Is that where Reni was lying dead all those days? he wonders. Is that where they found her?

The cross draft caused by the open door suddenly blows the window shut with a bang. He goes to it, bolting it closed. There is no more of Reni's spirit in here to set free.

She has gone.

Taking her memoirs with her.

CHAPTER THREE

"I'm not sure this is a job for the criminal police, Herr Kramer. After all, we have no proof such memoirs existed."

Kommissar Boehm of the Bad Lunsburg Police Bureau leans back in his desk chair, making the springs groan. He is a large man, taller than Kramer, and thick-set. A caricature of a New York Irish cop, Kramer thinks.

"It is a long shot, I agree," Kramer says. "But you found no signs of illegal entry at the Müller house?"

"Oh, there were signs, all right. The neighbors, after being alerted by the mailman, had to force their way, remember? Through the solarium, I believe."

"I mean other than that."

Boehm shakes his head, pouting his lips as he does so to show how stupid the suggestion is.

"I suggest you contact Frau Müller's friends. Perhaps she deposited the memoirs elsewhere. If they ever existed."

Kramer says nothing, beginning to feel a damn fool for wasting Boehm's time. But his instincts tell him something is wrong. He has made a living from following these instincts for the story. Why the addition of his name to Reni's will if there was no literary estate to execute? And why a full month before her death? If she was feeling despondent, suicidal, wouldn't the addendum have been closer to the actual time of her death? A small thing to others, maybe, but Kramer knows the way Reni thinks . . . thought. And even more, if she were suicidal, why would she care about such worldly matters as memoirs?

He says none of this to Boehm: A police Kommissar, Kramer figures, does not make his living from following instinct. Boehm is obviously the empirical sort; give him hard and fast clues to follow, not a tingling of the hairs at the base of the neck, which motivates Kramer.

"I spoke with her father after examining the house," Kramer says. "According to him, Reni once mentioned memoirs, but he never saw them."

Boehm squints at him perceptively. "And?"

Kramer reassesses the man's acumen. "Yes, there was something more. Herr Müller also says that Reni, Frau Müller"—he grits his teeth as he uses the title—"was under considerable strain. That she increasingly invented reality of late."

Boehm folds massive butcher's hands over his blue suit coat. "There you have it, then. Perhaps these memoirs were merely in Frau Müller's mind. Something she intended to do one day, but never got around to. You'll excuse me for saying so, but she was a rather eccentric sort."

It is the logical conclusion: a woman prepared to take her own life was far from what one would call stable.

"As I said," Boehm goes on, "ask her other friends. Check further. If something turns up, feel free to get in touch once again."

Kramer, a professional at interviewing and better at ending interviews, is impressed with the ease with which Boehm hands him his hat. He feels like an hysteric, running to the police at the slightest bump in the night. But if there are memoirs . . .

"Herr Kramer?"

Boehm is standing, waiting for Kramer to do likewise. He gets hurriedly to his feet.

"I am sure it has been a shock for you. Your friend's death and the responsibility laid upon you by her will. She would certainly appreciate how seriously you are taking that responsibility. Perhaps too seriously?"

Kramer leaves the police station and heads for his hotel. There is nothing more to be done in Bad Lunsburg. Kommissar Boehm is probably right, Kramer decides. I am taking this too seriously. The curse of the newspaperman: always looking for the hidden story. Sometimes there just isn't one.

Kramer arrives at the hotel just as the day clerk is putting a note into his box. He sees Kramer and looks relieved.

"This is for you, Herr Kramer. It is already the second message from this person today."

There is only one man he knows who could answer to the description "this person."

"He sounded somewhat impatient," the clerk continues.

Kramer can just imagine.

"Thanks. I'll place the call from my room." Kramer takes the note, opens it. Blunt, to the point: Call Marty.

Kramer gets to his room, splashes some water on his face, then sits on his bed and places the call. It's lunchtime, but Marty, with all the restaurants of the Latin Quarter available to him, usually takes food in his Rue Vaugirard office. The call is answered on the third ring.

"Hey, Marty."

"Jesus, Sam. Where are you?"

"You know where. You called me here twice."

"I called some number that secretary of yours gave me. You could be in Outer Mongolia for all I know."

"She's a reporter, Marty, not a secretary. Just happens she answers the phones, too."

Marty chooses to ignore this. "Where's the goddamn Belgrade story, Sam?"

"I got involved in Germany. Kate didn't tell you?"

"She tells me your number. I'm supposed to interrogate her?"

Great. Kramer asked her to make excuses. Excuses aren't in Kate's fine print, obviously.

"An old friend of mine died, Marty. Renata Müller."

Quiet for a moment. Rumination from Paris. Then: "The German peacenik? Somebody kill her?"

"Suicide. Reuters carried it. You must have seen the clips."

"I see lots of clips. There a story in it?"

"She was my friend, for God sake."

"Great. How was the funeral? Over? Fine. You get flowers, put 'em on her grave, and get back to Vienna."

"I've been named her literary executor."

"Sam, I don't give a shit what they call you. I need you back in Vienna. Now."

"There were supposed to be memoirs, but I can't find them."

He knows it sounds weak, but it's all he can think to say.

"Sam, this Müller. She might have been a friend, okay? I'm truly sorry she's dead. I grieve, okay? But she's not news. You understand. She's olds. She's from the dark ages of the 1980s. I need your ass back in Vienna."

Kramer says nothing for a time, thinking one day he would like to stick a kosher dill in Marty's mouth and shut him up, friend or not.

"Sam. You still there?"

Kramer tells him he thinks so. Hard to tell anymore.

"No haiku today, Sam. Okay? I got a belly on fire up to my ears. People crawling all over me from head office in London, and you're not helping any, you know that?"

"How can I help you, Marty?"

From the other end, Kramer hears the clatter of antacid tablets being shaken out of a plastic bottle. A pause as Marty chews a couple. "You can get me that fucking story out of Belgrade, is what you can do for me."

"These things take time. You want quality or quantity?"

"Quantity, for shit's sake. Or haven't you figured things out yet? This isn't the old days, Sam. Not the old foreign correspondent in a trench coat pounding out the story on a portable Underwood. Today, you don't have a laptop computer and a fancy mobile phone, you're out of luck. We're competing with the TV, Sam, with this new Internet, too. We've got a TV on paper, for Christ's sake. Four-color, upbeat stories. You get it? I don't need quality when I got four-color. I went to bat for you when you wanted out of the field a couple of years ago. Fine, I said. Take the Central Europe desk. Our man in fucking Vienna. But I need product, Sam."

"It takes time."

But Marty's not interested in excuses.

"Look, I'll get you the story," Kramer says to Marty's sudden silence. "I got to go now. There's a call waiting. It could be from Belgrade."

"Don't bullshit me, Sam. You can do that to the others, but we go back. There's no call waiting. Hell, I don't even know if you've got an angle on a story. But you just get me one. Quality or not. Or start looking for gainful . . ."

"Good-bye, Marty. Hope the fire abates." Kramer hangs up, stopping Marty mid-sentence.

The rain has turned to snow flurries by the time Lufthansa Flight 382 lands at Vienna Schwechat Airport. It's a polka-dot dusk, and the heavy smell of snow is in the air as Kramer and the rest of the passengers on the half-full plane descend to catch the ground transport into the terminal building. They gather their luggage—Kramer's got only his carry-on and the Olivetti he rescued from Reni's—and pass through bullet-proof glass, past elite Cobra antiterrorist troops with machine pistols strapped around their necks. A plump hausfrau in an out-of-fashion Loden coat is waiting with three blond boys. The kids run to their dad, the guy who was sitting in front of Kramer on the plane sneezing nonstop into a filthy handkerchief. He gathers them up in his arms. Suddenly, he's a hero, not a sniffling businessman riding coach.

It's too late for the office today. Kramer catches the Schnellbahn into the middle of the city, to the Landstrasse, and takes the number two line underground from there to the Josefstädter Strasse. He prides himself on using public transport, keeping an old Deux Chevaux garaged on the Lenaugasse only for the occasional outing to the country.

Through the glass in the front door to his building, Kramer sees Frau Kulahy lumbering up the stairs. He waits outside, not wanting to have to exchange pleasantries with the old porter.

Viking, her Alsatian, has obviously just finished adding another pile of his crap to the city streets, for he moves sprightly up the stairs. But the dog senses Kramer at the door and turns his head to growl at him as he always does. The Frau jerks his lead and labors up the last two stairs on heavily wrapped legs. Kramer got a look at those legs unwrapped one day and still regrets it: a tortured relief map of blue varicose veins from a life of too much pork. Kramer is convinced that all of Austria will one day succumb to pork fat clotting up various veins in their bodies. The piggies' revenge.

He waits like a criminal until she and the dog go into their apartment, then unlocks the large front door and quickly passes along the tiled entryway. He does not bother to check his mail in the row of brass boxes to the right of the door, hurrying up the stairs before Frau Kulahy can take up position at her sitting room with its curtained windows letting off onto the landing.

The stairs are another point of pride for him, something to keep the pig's revenge from his own veins, and he is breathing hard, the carry-on and portable typewriter feeling twice their weight by the time he reaches the third floor.

But he stops halfway to the lock with his key: the door is already open a crack. He looks quickly right and left in the dimness of the hall and sees nothing. The radio is on in Frau Bechmann's flat next door: opera. Otherwise no sign of life on the third floor. He gets the same eerie feeling he had at Reni's farmhouse yesterday and is tempted to simply retrace his steps downstairs and fetch Frau Kulahy and her dog.

But there are a thousand explanations for my door being ajar, he tells himself. Maybe I didn't lock it properly before leaving.

But he knows he did, knows he always double-checks locks and gas burners before leaving the flat.

Or Frau Kulahy had to check on something while I was away.

Which is another crock: Frau Kulahy never checks on anything.

Kramer is still doing mental calculus when suddenly the door opens inward, and he jerks into an approximation of a combative posture, holding the key like a stiletto.

The person on the inside comes into view finally, and Kramer lets out air like a punctured tire. "Randall! What are you doing here?"

Randall, too, is startled to come face-to-face with somebody at the door and drops the string bag he is carrying, then immediately embraces Kramer. Kramer allows the embrace but does not return it. Randall hugs some more, then finally notices the lack of response from Kramer.

"It's nice to be wanted," he says, letting go of Kramer and

bending down to retrieve the shopping bag. "No 'How you doing, buddy?' or 'Where you been?'" He glances at the key in Kramer's hand, still gripped like a knife. "Put that away, Sam, before you do someone harm."

Kramer pockets the key and grins at his old friend, still sporting the signature shaved scalp and thick ginger beard like an upside down head. Still the lanky down-at-the-heels appearance that oddly wins the most beautiful of women for him. They want to protect him, feed him. Randall ends up sleeping with them as if he's doing them all a favor.

"I was just going out to the local pub to get some beer. You used to keep it by the case, Sam. What's the deal?"

"You've got money to buy beer with?" It's news to Kramer. "What have you done, joined the great working washed?"

"Ha-ha. Take that as a laugh. Actually, I found a few schillings around the flat." Unembarrassed, no contrition. The most natural thing in the world to go poking around another person's belongings and pocket any money you can find.

Which gives Kramer another idea. "How did you get in here?"

An impish grin from Randall. "The porter. She remembered me from last time. I told her I was invited. Nice woman. She needs work on her legs, though. Painful." He shakes his head. "Could have been attractive in her day."

Kramer can think of many adjectives to fit Frau Kulahy, but attractive is not one of them. Another Randall conquest.

"I brought a bone for the dog," Randall adds. "She seemed to think that made me okay."

Kramer stands on the landing a moment longer, saying nothing, wondering if he can deal with his old friend now, feeling as low as he does. He finally decides that, in fact, Randall may be the perfect tonic to his experiences in Germany.

"You heard about Reni?"

Randall nods, raising his eyebrows. "Couldn't come to the

funeral, Sam. Don't believe in them. Too damn sad. Like hospitals. But I thought maybe you could use a little diversion when you came back. A little of the old arm-bending at the local pub?"

Another smile from Kramer: he has cut down on the booze in the last two years. Told himself the old hard-drinking days are past. But Randall—the global village idiot with a network of friends around the world whom he visits on a nonstop basis—is right. A little therapeutic drinking may be in order. A little of the old *Wirkungstrinken*, drinking for effect, as the Austrians say.

"Funny thing is she called me only a few weeks ago."

This surprises Kramer. "Reni?"

"Yeah. I mean, didn't call me. No one knows where I'll be day to day. Not even me. But she called my dear old mom in Boise. Only address Reni had for me, I guess. I finally got the message a couple of days ago at the *Poste Restante* in Pisa. Just after I saw the notice in the papers of her death."

"What did she want?"

Randall tugs at his thick beard, squints incomprehension.

"No idea. Just wanted to find out where I was, according to the Mater. But was very particular that the old girl get her name right. Spelled it out *R*-for-Richard style at long distance rates."

They continue standing in the gloomy corridor for several moments, the faint strains of opera coming from Frau Bechmann's.

"Why the suspicious look, Sam? Maybe she just wanted to say good-bye to old friends. Maybe she already decided on ending things and just wanted to tie everything up."

Kramer is sure of very little in the world, but knows for a dead certainty that Reni was not the tying-up sort.

"Maybe," he says. "Maybe."

CHAPTER FOUR

Kramer awakens with a headache of monumental proportions, fumbles with the sliding off-button on the clock radio before it has a chance to jangle his nerves, and then suddenly swings his legs out of bed.

Fight the pain with movement, he figures, sitting upright abruptly.

By the time his head stops spinning, he has decided that speed is not a good idea. Take it slowly this morning: slow and easy.

Randall is still snoring on the couch, the floor in front of him littered with empty green and brown bottles of Gösser beer, a nearly empty bottle of not very old slivovitz menacing from the marble-topped end table. Kramer makes a cross with his fingers to ward off evil as he passes by the scene of carnage, hurrying to the bathroom.

A shower and shave later, with a cup of coffee in hand, he feels a little more human, but very little. Randall is still snoring; morning ablutions do not disturb him, so accustomed is he to sleeping on other people's couches.

Kramer forces himself to eat dried toast, to get something

in his stomach to soak up the bile, and thinks about last night. Dinner at the local gasthaus accompanied by several beers until closing time at ten, then more beers to-go and sitting up till two in the morning blathering on. Randall discovered the slivovitz somewhere in between, in the hidden recesses of the old Tyrolean hope chest Kramer uses as both liquor and record cabinet. He refuses to upgrade to CDs; just one more ploy to keep people consuming. Just as he refuses to give up the Underwood at the office; let the bright young kids fresh out of school click away on computers. He'll stick to forefingering the old typewriter, thank you very much.

By the time the schnitzels arrived last night, Kramer had told Randall about the missing memoirs, or the memoirs that never were, and about the general bad vibes he had in Bad Lunsburg. By the time they got onto the slivovitz back at the apartment, Randall had convinced him that it was all paranoia.

"Reni's dead, Sam. That's the bad vibes you're getting. Gone. Out of your life forever. Not just out of the picture. So maybe now you can get on with your own life."

Kramer acted like he didn't know what Randall was getting at, utterly clueless. But it was Randall's old message: "You fuck up your marriages, Sam, because you're still half in love with Reni. A woman needs more than half a man."

"Lovely advice coming from the perennial bachelor," Kramer would generally counter on these occasions, but not last night. He knew Randall was right. Finally right.

Kramer goes into the living room, puts the pot of coffee and places an empty cup on the floor by the couch for Randall when he awakens, clears away some of the bottles, and then gets his Barbour oilskin from the hall wardrobe. Randall's beat-up old leather pack rests in the bottom of the wardrobe: it contains a change of clothes and a book or two, Kramer figures. That's called traveling light through life. No home, no job. The last twenty or so years spent on the road, crashing with friends.

Kramer leaves a message on the hall table for Randall to meet him at Koranda's in the late afternoon, one of the few inner-city taverns not to have gone all modern and glitzy. No ferns, no postmodern frills. He picks his cap off the benedictory hand of the fifteenth-century, four-foot wooden Madonna standing by his door. He was lucky enough to find her at a flea market outside Budapest; now she has become his good luck totem. He touches her cheek coming and going from his flat. Today, he gives her a double rub.

Kramer walks to the office under a sky showing blue once in a while between high, scudding clouds. Brisk wind, not cold but bracing. Last night's snow has turned to filthy slush in the streets, leaving a white blanket in the parks and on tree limbs. The air is therapeutic.

By the time he gets to the office of the *Daily European*, he wishes he carried a hip flask, but fetches a coffee from the stand-up bar on the street level instead. Lots of cream; he leaves a brown lace collar of residue on the lip of his cup after he drains the coffee.

Kate is at the front desk when he enters.

"So he talked to you?" she says looking up from the copy she's editing.

Kramer chooses to ignore this, knowing the implication is that Marty ordered him back.

"We got any stringers at the Belgrade conference?" he asks.

She's gone back to copyediting, shaking her head at his question.

"Marty called yet this morning?"

Another shake of her head.

"Good." He heads to his office and sags into his desk chair.

Kate has arranged the last two days of wire service clippings on his desk. The rip sheets of today's are there, as well.

He glances at these, gets a feel for terrain from a Reuters story datelined Belgrade and another from AP. Then he remotes the small TV in the corner on to the CNN channel, volume down low until a story comes up from Belgrade, and he gets pad and pencil out, taking notes.

Two hours later, he's got five hundred words on a conference he hasn't been to in the flesh. There's a snappy one-graph lede, extensive quotes, a second-graph exclusive in the form of doubts from an unidentified source that the conference will succeed, and a zinger of a wrap that resonates of Hemingway at the Paris peace talks in the 1920s.

He pulls the last of three double-spaced sheets out of the carriage of the old typewriter, scrawls a pound sign at the bottom of the page to note the end, and then straightens the three pages together by sliding them through his hands, clacking the bottom of the pages on the desktop.

Kate is checking her eye makeup in a compact mirror as he opens his door, and she quickly puts the mirror away. She does not like people to know she is vain: her good looks are supposed to come naturally. Kramer knows that she actually eats meat if it is disguised well enough, though she professes the strictest vegetarian diet. It's the sort of intimate knowledge that makes them enemies. He hands her the story, and she looks at the pages quizzically for a moment, as if it is a pastrami sandwich. She flips through the pages, and her look changes to one of outrage.

"Oh no you don't, Kramer. I thought I heard the TV on in there. This is called plagiarism."

"Nonsense. Simply the highest form of flattery. Creative journalism."

"Like creating something out of nothing. Who the hell is this anonymous source in graph two?"

Kramer shrugs. "He refuses to be identified." Kramer is having fun with her; Kate is always so easy to shock.

"You made that up, didn't you? That's illegal. You're faking the news."

"No legalities involved, Kate. I assure you."

"Unethical, then." She scowls at the pages.

"More accurate. But since when have ethics had anything to do with journalism? Marty will love it. Our little scoop. Now do a quick edit and fax it off to Paris, please."

He says the last like a command, not a request, and she stops protesting.

Kramer is happy with himself. For once, he's won a battle with the high priestess of ethics. He turns to go back to his office, but she gets the parting shot, "If you insist on using that Stone Age typewriter, at least change the ribbon periodically. You do know how to change ribbons, don't you?"

After lunch, Kramer does penance for the night of debauchery, for the faked article—there's a laundry list of sins—by editing a backlog of "when" pieces—articles supplied by stringers throughout Central Europe, which can be used on slow news days *when* there is space, or *when* Kramer just doesn't feel like coming into the office.

A couple of good pieces among the detritus: one on preparations for the fortieth anniversary of the 1956 Hungarian uprising, still three years off; another on the former communist mayor of Bratislava, now a garbage man in Vienna.

Three hours of good work; rewriting, rearranging, almost like doing real writing. Kramer loses himself completely in time, a good feeling, but by four thirty, the lazy part of him is beginning to nudge and insinuate itself. Thirst and indolence set in.

He leaves his desk as is, goes out into the front office, and is surprised to find Randall there, chatting up Kate.

She reddens when she sees Kramer and looks down to her desk, as if she's been talking about him.

"Didn't know you two knew each other," he says, going to fetch his cap and coat.

"Koranda's is closed," Randall says, perched on the edge of Kate's desk. Her desk is the least perchable place in the world, Kramer thinks. "I thought I'd meet you here, the navel of news production, as it were. The nexus of the information empire."

He is being the grand Randall, Kramer notices. The transatlantic schizophrenic with his phony accent somewhere between New York and London. His wise-guy routine sure to please the girls.

Randall turns his gaze on Kate now. "And Miss Ferguson and I are only just now getting acquainted, no thanks to you. You've been hiding her. Not nice, Sam."

She smiles at this, a blush. A flutter of mascara-free eyelashes.

Coquetry! Kramer is aghast.

"I thought Koranda's was only closed on Mondays." Kramer throws on his coat, wraps a Kelly-green wool scarf tight around his throat as if the warm scarf will protect him from a virus—he's felt a tickle there all day, and the last thing he wants is a sore throat.

"Closed as in closed down," Randall says, and hops off the desk, looking pleased with himself.

"No," Kramer says. "Don't tell me. Another groovy coffee shop opening? A boutique for infants and Afghan hounds? I liked this frigging city better when it was stone-cold poor. When having a camera was a big deal. Shit."

"Easy, Sam. We'll go somewhere else." Randall smiles at Kate to show how unconcerned he is. "It's just a restaurant, after all."

"Just a restaurant! You know Heimito von Doderer had a *Stammtisch* there? Even wrote part of his last novel there?

That Girardi himself used to tipple there after walking the boards at the Burgtheater?"

They are both looking at him in incomprehension.

"We're talking about tradition," he goes on, knowing he's sounding like an old fart ready to embark on the one about the younger generation having no morals. "About the soul of a city rooted in its public places. But this city is going all private on us, all consumption-oriented. Might as well be in the States."

Randall rolls eyeballs at this. "Yikes, Sam. Not the old expatriate's lament, please. We'll be after boring the pants off Miss Ferguson here." He looks her up and down lasciviously, "Which would not be a bad idea, come to think of it."

She laughs at this. Well, actually giggles. Giggles! For Christ's sake, Kramer thinks. Had anybody else said this, she would be suing for harassment.

"Come on, Randall. Let's be off. You're embarrassing the woman."

"Oh, not at all," she says, looking all business once again.

Randall smiles at Kramer; his 'didn't I tell you so' grin. But it is soon wiped away.

"I think he's cute," Kate says. "In a retro sort of way. An aging Don Juan with a definite Peter Pan thing. Anthropologically interesting."

Kramer suppresses a laugh. Two minutes later, they set off into the late afternoon. It has already gone dark and streetlamps glow orange, snow gently whorling around the orbs of light. Pedestrians bustle along the Kärntner Strasse, shopping bags in hand, hats pulled down, collars up. The lights from shops spill out onto the busy street, and for a moment, everything is okay with Kramer. This is the old life he has come to love; this is the heart of Europe that he feeds on, this scene like a set piece out of a movie.

———

By the end of the week, Kramer is feeling liverish. Too much booze; too many late nights. He can't face an entire weekend of more of the same.

Late Friday afternoon, home from the bureau, he's about to give Randall the fish-and-friends speech, ready to be on his own again. Ruin his health in his own good time, not in Randall's. But Randall's already packed and at the door when he arrives. No good-byes for him.

The phone sounds from the kitchen before either of them can speak. Kramer lets it ring for a moment.

"Get it, Sam. It might be my ride."

Kramer reaches it on the sixth ring and identifies himself by his phone number.

"Herr Kramer?"

The voice is tentative, young-sounding with that softness of tone he usually associates with the Left or New Agers.

"Speaking."

"This is Klaus Pahlus from Real Editions in Berlin."

A pause for Kramer to pick up on it. He does not recognize the name or the publishers.

"Yes?"

"I was notified by Renata Müller's solicitors that you are her literary executor."

Kramer's nose twitches. "That's correct."

"We have not yet received her memoirs, Herr Kramer. Our publication deadline is drawing near, you see, and . . ."

Kramer feels blood rush to his head. "Hold on. What publication deadline?"

"For the memoirs." Pahlus's voice on the other end of the line no longer sounds so gentle; exasperation is setting in like a low front. "For Frau Müller's memoirs."

"But there are no memoirs," Kramer says. Randall has

come into the kitchen now and gives Kramer a what's-up look. "I found no notes or manuscript at her place. Nothing."

The other end is silent so long that Kramer thinks they have been cut off.

"Herr Pahlus? You there?"

"Yes, I am still here." A weariness to his voice. "Just as I feared."

Kramer does not like the last word. "Feared?"

"Herr Kramer. You were a friend of Frau Müller's, of Reni's, weren't you?"

"Yes."

"A good friend, as I understand."

Kramer says nothing; his mind is racing.

"Did you really believe the story of her suicide, Herr Kramer?"

CHAPTER FIVE

No, Kramer thinks again as the Mercedes taxi takes them into the city from Berlin Tempelhof Airport. Deep down I don't believe the suicide story. Not Reni's style.

They pass along a freeway once resplendent with checkpoints. Now there are no barricades to slow their progress, no border guards to point machine pistols at them while checking passports. High-rise buildings jut out of the cityscape ahead.

"You must have an idea about what kind of interviews Reni was conducting," Randall says. He sits next to Kramer on the cold leather of the taxi's backseat.

Pahlus's call did more than intrigue; it also changed Randall's travel plans.

"Not a clue," Kramer says as the taxi exits toward the Bahnhof Zoologischer Garten.

"But I thought that was why we were paying this visit. Not a social call." Randall sits forward in the seat, all tension and nerves.

"I guess so," Kramer says, trying to rein in his own nerves. "Why don't we wait and hear what he's got to say?"

"And why wouldn't he tell you over the phone? Who's he afraid was listening?"

Kramer looks sideways at Randall. "The bad guys." He feels laconic today and does not want to draw conclusions before the evidence is presented.

"I thought they lost. The Wall's down."

"There are always bad guys. Wall or no."

They sit in silence while the taxi completes its journey, slowing to park in front of a building that looks like it belongs in south central Los Angeles. Graffiti covers the entire facade; slogans for and against the skinheads, the Parliament, foreigners, God.

Despite the chill air, kids and adults are hanging out on this Saturday morning in baggy jeans, oversize shirts, sneakers, and baseball caps. Kids with boom boxes under their arms, high-stepping, jerking around. Slumped figures in doorways, nodding out; a speeding Camaro that squeals around the corner. It could be the States.

They get out of the taxi, pay the driver who looks nervous in this neighborhood, and then ring the bell at number 15. The brass plaque announcing Real Editions in the vestibule has been spray-painted to read "Red Editions." A voice comes over the intercom: *"Wer ist da, bitte?"*

"Kramer," he says, and a buzzer sounds, the front door opening momentarily.

Inside, it's dark and damp. A sign by the stairs points them up three floors to the publishing offices. Mostly businesses in the old building and mostly closed today. Pahlus is out in the hall of the third floor to greet them; tall and plump, hair worn in a ponytail and two rings in his left ear. Old jeans and a baggy sweater.

"You survived our street?" He speaks English in an easy colloquial manner and gives them no time to answer. A sudden smile. "It's not as bad as it looks. I mean there are druggies out there, but our government doesn't force them to crime for their next high. Not yet, anyway."

His face is surprisingly animated. Kramer figured from the telephone voice that he would be languid, cool, and laid back. But he's almost hyper.

"Come into our meager office, Mr. Kramer," he says grabbing Randall's arm and ushering him through a door. Kramer follows with a faint smile on his face.

On the other side of the door, they enter a different world. Gone is the gloom. Walls are missing here also, opening a huge space articulated by rows of planters built from glass bricks with all sorts of greenery flowing out of them: ivy, palms, philodendrons, ficus, and all sorts of other plants Kramer has no name for. The office is on the top floor of the building, and sky lights have been knocked through the roof to make the space bright, even in the winter darkness. Walls are painted vibrant greens and blues; a diagonal red stripe bisects one, purple another. Furniture is a hodge-podge of flea-marketry; computers on each desk have also been personalized: painted to individual tastes and decorated with photos, plastic toys, worry beads, and other jewelry so that they resemble small shrines.

Pahlus leads them to a large art deco desk in the furthest corner of the open office space. No one else is about on Saturday, but there is nothing creepy about the place as with other offices when the employees are not there. This space has animation, almost a life of its own, Kramer thinks.

Randall and he sit on a long, low sofa to the right side of the desk, a window to their back, and Pahlus takes a straight-back chair that does not match his desk.

"It is good you came," he says to Randall. "Reni spoke of you."

Randall looks amazed.

"I'm Kramer," Kramer says. "This is my friend, Randall. He knew Reni in the old days."

Pahlus shifts his attention, as surprised as Randall.

"Sorry." Checking Kramer up and down as if expecting someone as flipped out looking as Randall to be the friend of the great fem radical Renata Müller.

"Tell me about the memoirs," Kramer says.

Pahlus regains composure, leans back in his chair, fiddles with a wooden puzzle in the shape of a duck on his desk.

"Reni came to us about six months ago, saying that she wanted to publish memoirs of a different sort. A blend of the past and the present. Of course we were interested. Though her name does not have quite the cachet it once did, we at Real Editions are committed to supporting the political Left. Stalinism may have failed, and rightfully so, but Marxism has yet to be tested."

His eyes sparkle as he says this, reminding Kramer of Reni. He suddenly takes a liking to the pudgy editor.

Pahlus continues, "I, in fact, was personally honored that she should come to us instead of one of the bigger houses like Fischer or Rowohlt. She was one of my heroes when I was growing up."

Another smile as he opens a desk drawer, pulling out a half-empty bottle of Jim Beam. "Care for some?"

Randall and Kramer nod approvingly, and Pahlus fills a couple of cloudy marmalade jars from the same drawer and passes the drinks around.

They toast one another and Pahlus continues. "I'm sure the bigger houses would have been glad to take on her book, but Reni was adamant about having Real"—he pronounces it with two syllables—"bring it out. She was not prepared to compromise over content, she told us. No punches pulled, I think you say."

He looks inquiringly at Kramer.

"An exposé?" Randall says.

Pahlus shifts his gaze, smiling at Randall. "Partly. I mean she had many years of political involvement behind her. Knew everybody there was to know in Bonn and the European parliament, and had some pretty interesting things to say about certain of these people. Even some fascinating stories about her years before getting involved in politics—student radicalism and that sort of thing."

Kramer feels Randall seeking out his eyes, but looks straight ahead at Pahlus, ignoring the attempted communication.

"It wasn't going to earn her any friends," Pahlus says, "writing about these people from an intimate and critical angle, but Reni didn't care. She was absolutely the most honest human I've ever come into contact with. The truth was all that mattered to her, no matter how uncomfortable that might be for others."

Kramer takes a long sip of the bourbon, feels it burn down his throat. "And the interviews?" he prompts, for it was the mention of them over the phone that has brought him to Berlin.

"Yes, of course. Her contemporary history. They were to form the second part of the memoir. Sort of a state of the state address to the German people. They would prove to be every bit as inflammatory as the other material."

He stops, beaming at Kramer.

"And?" Kramer says.

"And nothing. Reni would not share anything about these. Only that they were political dynamite. She was going to name names, she said." Pahlus looks down reflectively, then suddenly lifts his head. "It was the way in which she said this, you see. So self-assured. So on top of things. Do you know what I mean?"

Only too well, Kramer thinks. "What names?"

Pahlus shakes his head. "*Big* was all she would say until publication."

"And you never got a look at any of this political dynamite?" Kramer asks. "Never saw that part of her memoirs?"

Another shake of the head. "I never saw any of the memoirs."

Kramer and Randall exchange looks.

"I know what you're thinking," Pahlus says. "That's why I wanted to see you in person, to explain to you. I know the memoirs existed. She spoke of them so clearly and in such detail. I refuse to believe I was deluded simply because she was an idol. I trusted her."

"You paid for them?" Kramer asks.

Pahlus goes red. "Eighty thousand marks."

Randall whistles. "There's that kind of money in this operation?"

"We would have earned it back in the first printing. From the way she described the memoirs, careers would be made and broken. It would be a bestseller."

Kramer finishes the bourbon. "Is that what you're afraid of? That someone got wind of the memoirs, one of those names that would be named?"

Pahlus nods. "Maybe I'm being paranoid."

None of them bother to define what that someone might do to suppress the memoirs: it is like white noise in the background.

"And without the memoirs?" Kramer asks.

Pahlus laughs. "I know one career that will be ruined, anyway. It was on my say-so that so large an advance was made. But Reni said she needed the money as a lubricant. Her interviewees were not all public-spirited." His expression changes, mouth turned down, eyes squinting. "It will ruin Real Editions, Mr. Kramer. That's the long and short of it. We'll go bankrupt without those memoirs."

If there are memoirs, Kramer once again reminds himself.

What will Kommissar Boehm say if I go to him with this new information? he wonders. Simple: Where's the proof the memoirs ever existed? Maybe she just ripped off Pahlus for the eighty thousand marks. Then another thought: absence of proof is not proof of absence. And Reni was not the ripping off sort; not with a show like Real Editions, anyway.

"Like I said on the phone, Herr Pahlus, there was no trace of memoirs at Reni's place or in any of the safe-deposit boxes she kept. No evidence at all they existed except in her mind."

Pahlus smiles winsomely. "That's where you're mistaken, Mr. Kramer."

He digs into the top drawer of his desk, finds a red-covered address book, and leafs through it until he finds the page he is looking for. Then he runs his index finger down a list of names.

"Yes. Here it is. One of the men Reni was interviewing. I had to call her once at his flat about the delivery of the advance, so she gave me his number and address."

The address of Herr Peter Gorik is in one of the more fashionable neighborhoods off the Kurfürstendamm. Neoclassical buildings along a quiet tree-lined boulevard that miraculously escaped the bombs of World War II. The home of someone with a tidy little sum in the bank, Kramer thinks as he checks the name register next to the doorbell.

No Gorik.

"He must have moved." Randall double-checks the names.

"Or never existed," Kramer says.

"What is it with you, Sam? It's like you don't want these memoirs to exist."

"Truth is, I don't know what to believe."

"Let's just buzz the super and find out if the guy ever lived here."

But they do not need to, for at that very minute a middle-aged woman in a white coat comes out, a stack of string-bound newspapers in her arms. Randall helps her with the door; she drops the papers at their feet: recycle day today.

Kramer smiles at her, "Excuse us, but would you happen to be the porter?" His most polite, stilted German.

She looks at them both with momentary suspicion; it goes with the job.

"I might be."

"We were looking for a friend of ours. Herr Gorik. Peter Gorik."

This makes her look even harder at them.

"Close friends, are you?"

Randall smiles winningly; it does nothing to soften her expression. The sun comes out again, brightening the broad, tree-lined street.

"You might say colleagues." Kramer hedges his bets.

She shrugs. "Think you'd know by now if you were colleagues."

Kramer has an evil premonition. "Know what?" he says.

"Herr Gorik is dead. Killed by a hit-and-run driver ten days ago."

CHAPTER SIX

"So what do you think this proves, Herr Kramer?" Kommissar Boehm sits like a pontiff in back of his desk in Bad Lunsburg, wearing the same blue suit he had on the first time Kramer met him. It's Sunday afternoon, but Boehm is the kind of cop whose home is the office.

"Seems to be a lot of deaths," Kramer says.

"Two," Kommissar Boehm quickly replies. "And no evidence to show they are related. One a suicide; the other an auto accident."

"Hit-and-run," Kramer says. "And Reni, Frau Müller, was interviewing Gorik before her death. Gorik himself gets knocked down and out after Reni's death but before her body is discovered. Don't you find that indicative?"

Boehm sucks in his cheeks, working his lips like a bass breathing.

"And you say the flat was empty already."

Kramer nods. "The porter said that relatives came the day after the death and cleared everything. Not a scrap of paper or the tiniest evidence of former occupancy. I checked on

Gorik in Berlin. He had no relatives. A retired bachelor and only child whose parents died in the war."

Boehm puffs his lips skeptically. "Everyone's got relatives. Cousins come in all shapes and sizes. Especially when there may be something to inherit."

Boehm casts a glance at Randall who is busy looking at the maps on the walls as if they hold secrets other than geographic.

"He doesn't speak German," Kramer says by way of excusing Randall's nosiness.

Boehm slowly nods his massive head, then turns back to Kramer. "You seem to have done your homework."

"I think we're on to something."

"You've thought that from the beginning," Kommissar Boehm says, slowly rising to pace the floor in front of the door. Randall turns to watch, slightly amused. Kramer looks straight ahead at the vacated chair, not knowing how to respond, not knowing what Boehm means by his statement.

"In fact," Kommissar Boehm suddenly stops, "you seem determined to make this case bigger than it appears."

"Not true," Kramer says. "I let it go, moved on to other things. It was Pahlus in Berlin . . ."

Boehm cuts him short. "I'm not criticizing, mind you. Merely observing. An average citizen off the street comes in with your story, I might listen more dispassionately. But a journalist, and one named literary executor of the deceased's estate . . . That's a bit different now, isn't it?"

Kramer feels himself losing his temper; tries to hold himself back.

"Kommissar, I hope you're not implying that I want to distort the facts for some personal gain, just to get a story out of all this."

Boehm does not respond, but begins pacing again. The floorboards creak under his feet.

Kramer continues. "What I believe this shows is that lots of people might have wanted to suppress Reni's memoirs."

"If there were memoirs," Boehm reminds him.

Kramer ignores this. "Say that our friend Gorik knew something big. Something that a powerful person in Germany would not want to come under public scrutiny."

"Vague, Herr Kramer. Vague, vague, vague. 'Somebody,' 'something big.' All conjecture."

But he stops pacing, sucking in his cheeks again, deep in thought.

"Easy enough to check on, though," Boehm says. "Let's ask Guinness if it's ever heard of Herr Peter Gorik."

Kramer's face shows incomprehension.

"Our online database." Boehm nods at a computer in the corner set on a specially designed table. "It's the national registration. Everyone's listed here," he says, going to the machine, sitting down in front of it, and hitting the space bar to awaken it. "We're quite up-to-date, you see?"

His tone is humorous, but he is not smiling. The Kommissar deftly enters codes to access the database, and then enters Gorik's name and address. The amber screen tells them the computer is working on the request, then pulls up a list of names beginning with *Go-*. Boehm hits the function key to see the next screen. Three screens later, Gorik's name is highlighted smack in the middle of the list.

"Interesting," Kommissar Boehm says.

Kramer reads over Kommissar Boehm's shoulder. "So he was for real."

Boehm ignores this as he keys something else and up pops a new screen, an ID sheet on Gorik, including, at the bottom, the news of his recent death.

"It reads accidental," Boehm says, facing the screen.

Randall has come to the computer now and looks over the man's massive shoulders along with Kramer. Facsimile fingerprints are included on the screen, as well as dates of birth and initial national registration.

"So he first registered on January 22, 1990," Kramer says, reading the screen. "Where was he before that date?"

A grunt from Boehm as he hits the function key again to call up the next screen.

"I'll be damned," Boehm mutters.

Kramer, unfamiliar with the layout of the screen, has trouble deciphering the information at first, but two words leap out at him: *Praha* and *Nachrichtendienst*.

"Jesus," Kramer says.

"What?" Randall says. "What's it say?"

Kramer glances sideways at him, "Seems Mr. Gorik was with East German intelligence, stationed in Prague."

"Yes!" Randall fists his hands, thumbs pointing up, as if winning a prize.

Kramer speaks German to the Kommissar's back, "A retired spook, right?"

Boehm nods, escapes out of the database, keys into another, and spends the next few minutes in a profitless search for more evidence of Gorik's doings. Kramer notices pockmarks at the base of the man's hairline and cannot remember seeing such scarring on his face.

"Nothing more," Kommissar Boehm finally says, spinning around in his chair to face Kramer. "No warrants on him. I wonder what interest Frau Müller would have had in him."

Kramer can think of a million. One comes immediately to mind, and it is sufficient. "Pahlus said her informant had political dynamite. Something to make and break careers in Bonn. It doesn't take much of a stretch to figure out the kind of information Gorik could share."

"Such as?" Kommissar Boehm says. "Conjecturally speaking, of course."

"Such as double-agent networks that were run in the former Federal Republic of West Germany. Traitors to the state who no one but men like Gorik know about. That sort of nice spy thing that died with the Cold War."

"Interesting." Boehm says it with all the conviction of a bored priest listening to the hundredth confession of the day.

"Can you come up with a better explanation?" Kramer says, beginning to feel pissed off.

"I don't have to, Herr Kramer." A smile. He turns to the computer again and calls up the original record on Gorik. "It says here he retired in 1989. I like that. Not much of a job left to retire from, I'd say."

He taps the screen with a thick forefinger, underscoring the date.

"So what's our friend been doing the last years?" Boehm says, as if to himself.

"By the looks of his apartment building," Kramer offers, "one thing he wasn't doing was worrying about money."

Boehm swivels in his chair to face them again, "I wonder how he was living, then. An interesting question. Perhaps I should get on to our tax friends and see if he ever filed a return."

Kramer doesn't care about Gorik's financial arrangements; the man is dead. Reni is dead. The memoirs are gone. That is the story, not Gorik's tax status.

Randall nudges him, "What the hell's going on, Sam?"

Kramer fixes his eyes on Boehm, answering Randall sotto voce in English, "He's interested in Gorik's tax record."

"For shit's sake," Randall sighs.

"What does he say?" Boehm asks.

Kramer feels like he's at the UN. "Nothing. Just wants to get some dinner."

"An excellent idea. I can suggest the Restaurant zum Bad."
Then Boehm refocuses. "Leave this to me. I'll let you know
the progress of my inquiries."

Kramer stays put. "It's not Gorik, you know. He's only a
pathway, not the destination."

"What are you getting at?"

"This: I believe Renata Müller was killed by someone who
had a lot to lose if her memoirs were published."

He has not said this out loud before. The sound of the
words, their finality, send a chill through Kramer. Murder.
Homicide. They're not his beat.

Kommissar Boehm says nothing for a time, just looks
down at the paperwork on his desk. When he finally does look
up, his eyes meet Kramer's. "Interesting theory. I'll let you
know if I discover anything about Herr Gorik. The restaurant
is opposite the town hall, by the way."

"He's an insufferable ass," Randall says over a dinner of sau-
erbraten and wheat beer that has a heavy yeasty taste. "But at
least he knows good restaurants." He forks a piece of meat
into his mouth and chews contentedly.

"Kommissar Boehm is dancing with us. God knows why,"
Kramer says.

Randall swallows. "Do you think he believes in the memoirs?"

Kramer shrugs. "Hard to tell. He's seen it all. Cynics are
hard to read. I think he's a professional . . ."

"But?"

"Who knows? Police are part of the bureaucracy. Maybe
he doesn't want to rattle any cages."

"You really do believe this, then? The memoirs. Murder.
The whole nine yards."

"After the revelation about Gorik, yes. Don't you?"

"Oh yeah. I'm a great believer in mysteries, in the darker

side of life." Another fork full of meat, more mastication. "Where to from here? Let the police handle things?"

Kramer has wondered this himself. *Will the Kommissar do any more than file a report to sit in some file in cyberspace? Does he really care? Do I? I'm a journalist, not a private detective.*

"Someone has to care." The words are out before he realizes how he feels.

Randall smiles with thin lips. "Watch out, Sam. You're beginning to sound like an inspirational speaker."

Kramer says nothing.

"Someone like us?" Randall says after a moment's silence. Kramer thinks about this. "Yes."

A head nod from Randall. "In that case, I think we need to do some evaluating." He takes a long draught of beer.

"Such as?"

Randall wipes foam from his beard with his cuff. "Such as suspects. Who might have wanted the memoirs?"

"Good luck." Kramer fidgets with his food; he has no appetite tonight. "Without the memoirs or Reni's notes and tapes, there's no way to know who Gorik named or in regard to what."

Randall finishes his food, looks longingly at Kramer's.

"You not going to eat those potatoes?"

Kramer pushes his plate across. "Take it all. How the hell do you manage to eat so much and never gain weight?"

Randall sets the plate in front of him, sighing. "All in the genes," he says. "And irregular meals."

He moves aside the half-nibbled portions of Kramer's meat, cuts into the untouched bit. They sit silently for a time as Randall disposes of Kramer's meal, making a contented belch as he sets fork and knife at four o'clock on the plate.

"So, what about the evaluation?" Kramer prompts.

Randall wipes his mouth with the linen napkin. There are candles on the table, well-heeled customers speaking in undertones, beer served in tulip-shaped goblets. Let the plastic pay for it, Kramer thinks.

"There's nothing we can do about Gorik's information," Randall says, settling back in his chair. "Let Boehm tackle that one. He might just come up with something from the tax angle. After all, finances are important in this. Remember the eighty thousand marks from Real Editions? How much of that do you think went to Gorik? How much would it take to keep up a flat like he had? More than eighty thousand. How much do retired spooks get for a pension, especially when their former employer and country aren't around anymore?"

It's an angle Kramer has not seen until now. "Blackmail?"

Randall shrugs. "Could be. A guy like Gorik's got to know a lot of secrets. Some might be for sale for publication, others for privacy. But there are other leads beyond Gorik."

Kramer has thought of these. "Reni's former political opponents in Bonn."

"Colleagues, too," Randall adds. "How about some coffee?"

They order two mochas from a waiter who is dressed better than either of them, and Randall has a piece of *Schwarzwälder* cake to fill any vacancies his stomach might be feeling in the next twenty-four hours.

"Delicious," he says through a mouthful of cake. "Try some?" He holds a fork full at Kramer who shakes his head.

"The way I see it," Randall says, "there are two angles here. Pahlus said Reni was writing memoirs about her own past and about the German present, which is Gorik, as far as we know. But there's lots of past to deal with. Years and years."

Kramer thinks back to Reni's funeral: a dripping yellow aspen at the grave site; the tight little group of mourners with umbrellas over their heads like so many mushrooms; the priest clutching a plastic sack full of consecrated dirt; Müller, hatless, in a black vicuna overcoat. And next to him in a Persian lamb coat and Italian boots was Eva Martok, one-time Green Party stalwart along with Reni, but now a top adviser to the conservative CDU chancellor. No more jeans or leftist politics for Martok, but at least she came to the funeral.

"I guess we could start with Eva Martok," Kramer says. "She knew Reni in Parliament, and I saw her at the funeral."

"Yes," Randall says tentatively. "There's a deeper past, too."

Kramer pretends not to understand. "Before Parliament?"

"Come on, Sam. We've been skittering around this since learning of Reni's death. Pahlus said it himself. Reni was going to come clean with all sorts of secrets, all sorts of skeletons out of the closet. Even from her radical student days. That's us, Sam. That's bloody well us!"

His voice has gotten louder and more strident; diners turn toward their table at the last word.

"What do we have to hide from back then? Who gives a damn?" But Kramer is lying to himself; he gives a damn and he's been hiding from that time for a quarter century.

Nothing is said for a moment and finally Kramer reaches into his jacket pocket; the photo is still there, the one he found among Gerhard's effects at Inheritance. He pulls it out, setting it on the table in front of Randall.

"Where did you find this?" Randall says, looking at the picture with amazement.

Kramer explains.

"Amazing. What a geek I was back then. Look at Maria."

Kramer has no wish to.

"You ever hear from Rick or Helmut?" Randall asks.

"Never. Not since 1969."

"Then maybe it's time we do," Randall says.

"For what?"

Randall squints at him. "Sam, we either play this open options or not at all. You don't remember Prague Spring? You don't remember what happened to Maria?"

CHAPTER SEVEN

Monday morning is fresh and clear, as if last night's decision to treat Reni's death as murder and not a suicide has quite literally cleared the air.

Kramer gets up early, dresses, and goes out for a walk, leaving Randall snoring lightly in the other twin bed. It feels good simply to be moving, to be breathing air sweet and tangy off the nearby Rhine.

Not much activity in town this morning. Time was when merchants would have their shops open by seven; the local farmers would be in town unloading produce at the central market; shoppers would be out for early bread; smell of coffee and diesel in the air; voices chattering; wooden crates full of cauliflower booming to the ground as they were thrown off the ends of mud-splattered flatbed trucks.

But no more. Now it's still quiet at nine in the morning. The central market has been replaced by a couple of chic food boutiques. The town makes its living off tourists and commuters who have bought up the old freeholdings and converted them into quaintly rustic homes—part of a seamless suburbia from San Francisco to Singapore.

Kramer liked the town much better in the 1970s, when living here with Reni. It was real then, pimples and all. A gritty little market town that had *Bad* in its name only by accident.

The Romans found some natural hot springs here once, but the mineral waters dried up long ago and exist now only in the minds of the tourist board. A poor replica of the ancient baths has been recreated in the form of a fitness spa with weight machines, mindless aerobics, and mud baths—the mud imported from Pomerania.

Kramer walks idly along the freshly cobbled pedestrian zone, his eyes free to look up rather than down, for there are no piles of dog crap littering the pavement as in Vienna and every other European city. Which means people have yards here, space. Blue sky overhead; a sudden covey of doves wheels in the sky toward the river. The old bakery is still in the Hauptplatz, its large front window steamed over, but now they serve croissants instead of cinnamon *Schnecken*—"snails"—baguettes instead of heavy black rye bread. Kramer recognizes no one from the time he lived here, not one shop owner or innkeeper. All retired to Portugal and the Costa del Sol.

Kramer remembers when Reni settled here. Some money was left to her by her mother, Alice. Kramer met the woman only once and took an instant liking to her, so American in the old-fashioned, midwestern way. All honesty and no-nonsense. She'd been with the Red Cross in Germany just after the war and had met Karl-Heinz Müller as a result of shared work. He had been in a resettlement agency then, vetted and cleared by the First Army of any Nazi tendencies. Just another young soldier drafted into the Wehrmacht toward the end of the war. And the sensible American woman, daughter of a powerful Illinois banking family and saddened by the loss of her fiancé in one of the final bombing raids over Tokyo, took to the somewhat younger Müller, to his ambition and eternal optimism. Her money helped create his own banking empire and, when she died in 1970 of stomach cancer, she made sure to leave Reni a bit of independence. Reni promptly sank part of the money into the Inheritance, an old farm with, at the time, a few acres surrounding it.

Remembrance of a better time, Reni explained then. This was when she and her father were at odds politically, and the old farm was where he had always brought the family to stay in the summer, renting the house every year. It was here that Reni had felt like a real kid, away from the Bonn scene, away from the center of power. And it was here that she and Kramer spent their first years together.

Inheritance.

Kramer's mind clicks through several shutter openings: Reni mucking out the old stall, rubber boots on up to her knees, faded denims and a baggy sweater, hair worn braided and up, wisps of golden blonde hair curling at her neck, her face so intent with the manual labor, so determined. Or playing tag that one midsummer night, frolicking naked in the orchard, running from tree to tree, the incredibly sweet smell of apricots in the air. Or stoking up the old wood-burning stove in the kitchen, trying to get the five-gallon pot of water to boil for the noodles they were preparing for the reunion, watching it and watching it and then shouting for joy when finally the water surface broke with the first roll of boil.

Pasta for the reunion. The Magnificent Seven joining up again, except that only Gerhard and Randall showed. No sign of Rick or Helmut. Maria lost to them all.

Another flurry of mental shutter openings and Kramer is once again back in Vienna in early November of 1968 and Reni is asking the same question Randall asked last night, "But what about Maria? What happened to Maria?"

Helmut cannot look them in the eye. He is haggard and filthy. He had to walk the final seven miles to the border in the middle of the night. There is a smell of terror on him like stale cigarette smoke.

"Where the fuck is Maria?" A scream this time; an animal sound.

Kramer pulls her away from Helmut who places his hands around his head, squeezes his eyes shut.

"Let him rest," Kramer says.

"We should never have sent her." Rick, the artist among them, stands looking out the front window to the street below, careful not to let the curtain swing when he turns back to them. "Never."

Like a movie, Kramer flashes. We're all characters in a bad spy film.

"It's too late for self-recriminations now," Gerhard says. "The plan didn't work. We begin from that point and move on."

Reni shakes off Kramer's hands from her shoulders. "It's my fault. It was my plan."

They're at Reni's place in the Jasomirgottstrasse; everyone else lives in the *Internat* dorm. It's a tiny flat with furniture from the 1930s, but it's private. Randall sits in the broken-down armchair, shaking his head.

"You can't plan for accidents like these. There's no way."

"I should have thought. Western license plates. Christ, they're like an invitation to vandalism." Reni sucks in air like a tired swimmer.

Helmut finally looks up, his eyes red-rimmed and bleary. "It was uncanny," he says in his *Gymnasium* school English. "Even before we could begin throwing out the leaflets, we could see the smoke. We had no idea what it was. Maria looked down. She said, 'That's our car, Helmut. It's burning.' And then all hell broke loose up there. Security personnel, militia. Jesus." He shakes his head.

"What about Maria?" Reni insists, her voice less strident now.

"They took her," Helmut says. "The police. I escaped down the fire stairs. But they took Maria."

Kramer is dragged into the present by a hand grabbing his arm, jerking him back onto the sidewalk. He feels the brush of a car as it flies past him; his jacket is caught in the jet stream of its passing. By the time Kramer looks, he can only see the back of the car fishtailing around a corner and out of town. He cannot make the style or brand, but is sure of one thing: its color is purple.

The man who pulled him out of danger still grips his arm. Kramer looks back at him, "*Danke.*"

"Goddamn stupid drivers these days," the man says. He is one of the old Bad Lunsburg crowd. Kramer thinks he recognizes him from the time he lived here. A small-time farmer he was then. Now he wears a business suit with the collar unbuttoned and tie loosened. A thick-set, short man with a red nose and a hand like a vise. He lets go of Kramer's arm.

"Sons of bitches use the roads like their private race track." He looks more closely at Kramer. "Do I know you?"

Kramer's heart is pounding; he tries to smile to show how little the near-accident affects him. "I think so. I once lived here. You farmed next door."

The guy opens his mouth in an ah-ha of recognition. "Renata Müller's friend. That's it, isn't it? But you had a beard then."

Kramer nods. This is like a benediction, being recognized.

"In town for the funeral, I'll warrant. Too bad about that. Too damn bad."

Kramer agrees; his mind begins to wonder about that car. About how much it was an accident.

"She was a funny sort, but a good woman. I don't care what they say here, she was good at heart."

"What do they say here?" Kramer asks.

The man looks uncomfortable. "Oh, you know how people are. Jealous and spiteful. Anybody got more than them, they just can't wait to bring them down. I can't believe it's true, anyway."

Kramer waits, not wanting to push the man into silence. Then as a prompt, "Reni had some odd ways. It was what made her interesting."

This seems to help, for the man smiles broadly. "Exactly. Peculiarities, I call them. But warm at heart she was. That's why I don't credit any of those stories about the skinheads and neo-Nazis."

Kramer tries not to show too much interest. "What stories might those be?" he says.

"Old Frau Gruber who lives across the road. Remember her?"

Kramer does, and immediately. The name calls up a sour-faced, mean-spirited woman who was forever complaining to Reni about their chickens ranging free and getting into her lettuces.

"Well, Frau Gruber's the one likes to tell about the visit. In the dead of night, a carload of them comes and stays a few hours, then leaves before dawn."

"How did she know they were neo-Nazis?"

The man snorts to himself. "You know how nosey the lady is. And this car parked on her side of the road. She goes out to it brazen like and looks in the front seat, shining her flashlight all over the place. There are swastika decals and copies of *Mein Kampf* in the front seat. That's enough for Frau Gruber."

Kramer suddenly remembers the man's name. "Herr Spalcke. Right?"

He beams. "Quite a memory there, lad." He puts out a hand. "Sorry to say mine's not up to the same level."

"Kramer. Sam Kramer." The name does not seem to register

with Herr Spalcke, but he cracks a couple of Kramer's knuckles as they shake just to show how well he remembers him.

"Still farming?" Kramer says as they are about to take leave of each other.

Spalcke shakes his head, spits into the gutter. "Sold off the acreage five years ago. A housing development." He waves his hand around them, and only now does Kramer realize that he is in the midst of what used to be Spalcke's grain fields. Small brick houses fronted by blue-green lawns now occupy the land.

"I'm a man of means," Spalcke says ironically. "Which means I collect rents and interest instead of working honestly."

Daydreaming, Kramer has let his feet lead him; he is only a few hundred yards from Inheritance.

"Between you and me," Spalcke says, drawing so close that Kramer can smell the yeasty sweetness of wine on the man's breath, "I think I made a mistake. Should have kept farming until I died. But the wife wanted an easier life. Wanted to be respectable and wear furs. Look at these cracker jack houses."

Then a bright smile. "But people got to live somewhere, I guess. No looking back, is there?"

Kramer does not answer, only smiles. Looking back is what he is best at.

They part and Kramer heads toward Inheritance, thinking about that near miss by the car, about the rumor of neo-Nazis visiting Reni in the deep of night. The air is filled with damp smoke, he suddenly notices, as if someone is burning leaves. Bit late in the year for that, he thinks as he rounds the curve and Reni's farmhouse comes into view. He sees a bulky removal van parked outside. Drawing near, he notices a hand truck leaning against the back left wheel. The double rear doors are open; pink sponge, protective coverings, and thick blankets hang out. Down the drive, he sees a purple Porsche parked by the front door, and suddenly remembers the lawyer Schnelling's car. As he passes by the car, he places his hand on the hood: it is warm.

There is activity inside, and he knocks on the partly open front door. No one responds and he enters, bumping directly into a tall, thin, stooped man with a hawk nose. There is a large mole next to the man's nose and, as Kramer excuses himself, he cannot take his eyes off the mole. The man notices where Kramer's eyes are focused and this seems to erase any civility he might have had.

"Who are you?" he says brusquely, pulling on the lapels of his gray suit.

Before Kramer has a chance to respond, a high voice comes from in back of the thin man, "Ah, Herr Kramer."

Kramer sees Schnelling approach.

"What brings you here again?" Schnelling says as he approaches the door.

The thin man continues to glare at Kramer; then a sudden thought changes his expression.

"Kramer?" the man says. "Right. I spoke with you on the phone last week."

"This is my partner, Herr Walther," Schnelling says, joining them in the doorway. Two workers in blue jumpsuits are busy in the living room taking all the photos off the walls and sticking them into cardboard cartons.

"Clearing her things out?" Kramer says. "Sort of quick, isn't it?"

Walther becomes fulsome, ingratiating. Kramer liked him better gruff. "Our client is anxious to clear matters up here. Such a painful time. I am sure he wants to put it behind him, to get on with his life."

"Your client?" Kramer says. "I thought Reni was your client."

"We are family solicitors, Herr Kramer." Walther smiles

indulgently at him. Kramer has a great desire to put a fist into that smile.

"Was there something you were looking for, Herr Kramer?" Schnelling speaks this time, wearing the same gormless smile as his partner. Mutt and Jeff. "Any luck tracking down the elusive memoirs?"

Kramer shakes his head. "No. No luck. I was just visiting again, wandering around town."

The firm of Walther and Schnelling did not need to know of his discoveries or of his new belief that Reni was murdered. "Thought I'd look at the old place one more time."

"Oh, it's not going away," Walther says. His voice is low and sonorous; as distinctive from Schnelling's as is his appearance. "In fact, we have managed to lease it. We'll use it as a home and office. After some improvements of course. I do think these old farmhouses have character. I hope it reassures you to know that the house will stay in the family, so to speak."

Reassuring like an enema, Kramer thinks. "You been here long?" he says. "I mean, there must be a lot to do overseeing the move."

Schnelling rises to the bait, "Enormous quantities. Well, we know that from last week, don't we, Herr Kramer? We simply closed down the office for the half day. We and the boys here have been at it since eight this morning."

Kramer looks quickly to the two men packing the crates; they return his look, smiling as if finding Schnelling a ripe joke. But there is nothing in their look to disavow the man's statement.

"Herr Walther was just on his way to get us a midmorning snack. Would you care to stay and share it with us?"

"Nice of you to ask," Kramer says. "But I should be getting back to the hotel."

Walther stands at the door as if to show him out. "Don't

worry about the old place, Herr Kramer. We'll take good care of it."

Kramer smiles wanly. "I'm sure you will." A sudden thought comes to mind; Schnelling's mention of their searches has triggered it. "Have your men cleaned out the study yet?"

"That's where we began this morning," Schnelling says happily. "Quite a mess in there, I assure you."

"I suppose it's all packed away?" Kramer can remember the litter of papers on the desk in there; the proposed article on skinhead violence among them.

"The books, yes," Schnelling says. "But Herr Müller told us to burn the rest. No time to sort through all those papers."

Kramer remembers the smell of smoke upon approaching Inheritance—so much for the article. Coincidental that Reni would be planning to write an article on neo-Nazis when there is the rumor around town of her being visited by them in the middle of the night.

"Herr Kramer? Is there anything else we can do for you?" Herr Walther stands like a bent willow waiting for him to leave. "Could I give you a lift into town?"

"Sorry. Just thinking. I'll walk, thanks."

"Ah," Schnelling says. "Exercise does one good."

Kramer takes his time going back out to the road; Walther delicately revs up the Porsche and grinds gears into second going past him, driving the car like a retired schoolteacher. Kramer glances across the street and sees the flutter of a curtain from Frau Gruber's. Looking back at Inheritance, it seems no one is watching his movements. He crosses the street, goes up to Frau Gruber's front door, rings the bell, and waits.

She'll have to play like she was out back, he figures, and not snooping on her neighbors. It takes time to get to the front door. And all the while she's probably standing right next to it.

Kramer listens closely to see if he can hear her breathing, then rings the bell again and smiles to himself. Finally, she answers the door, small and pinched and as mean-looking as ever. She feigns breathlessness, her clawlike right hand held dramatically to her chest as if to still her pounding heart. Some people look and seem old at forty and thus, when they approach some greater chronological age, they appear to have not aged one whit. This was so with Frau Gruber.

"Good day, Frau Gruber," Kramer says brightly. "Do you remember me?"

She squints at him through the screen door. Her face is long and narrow, sitting on tiny shoulders like an obelisk. She is about five feet tall and the long head does not fit. She wears a housecoat, and her hair is wrapped in a yellow turban.

"You're that American, aren't you? The special friend of the Müller woman." She says it as if it is current gossip, not twenty years old.

"That's right."

"She's dead."

"I know, Frau Gruber. That's why I came back."

"You're too late. They buried her last week. I always said no good would come of her living here."

Kramer resists the temptation to slap the old biddy up the side of the head.

"I'm not here for the funeral," he says. "There are some questions I have."

Her face pinches up even more; a contorted mask of suspicion. "What questions?"

Kramer smiles at her reassuringly. "I've heard around town that Frau Müller might have had some connection with neo-Nazis. I know it sounds bizarre, but I was wondering if you might know anything about that?"

Her face relaxes; cunning comes into the eyes. She won't

be blamed for the rumor, and will be free to elaborate on it. The perfect situation for the loose-mouthed.

She suddenly holds the screen door open, almost knocking Kramer off her narrow front porch.

"Won't you come in?"

Kramer feels like a spider beckoned by the fly, but goes into the stuffy old house, keeping his dislike for Frau Gruber at bay.

If Bad Lunsburg has gone upscale, Frau Gruber's home stubbornly resists any such modernizations. It could be a movie set for a postwar home, with paint-on wallpaper in a floral design, faded now to light brown on dirty white, a chipped deal table, embroidered homilies on the walls, even a picture of Adenauer over the gas heater. Kramer guesses that this honored spot once held a photo of Hitler instead.

She sits him in a rickety straight-back chair at the deal table and proceeds to bend his ear about how that "Müller woman" was bound to a bad end. It's only after twenty-five minutes of the harangue that Kramer is able to get the conversation around to the visit by the supposed neo-Nazis. But she is sure about it, she swears. They even had a couple of baseball bats, the weapon of choice for skinheads, in the front seat.

"You saw no one?" he asks.

She shakes her head as if this is one of the great disappointments of her life. "But I did write this down." She pulls out a filthy white notepad from the side pocket of her housecoat. "I like to keep track of things, you know. Who is coming and who is going. One cannot be too sure of people these days. There are bad ones out there, you know."

Kramer nods in agreement and takes the proffered sheet from the note pad. On it is an eight-digit number. A car license and, from the initial letters, one apparently registered in Bavaria.

"May I copy this?"

She thinks for a moment. "Why not? You're interested in who's coming and going, too, aren't you? I can tell a kindred spirit."

Kramer copies the number and returns the grimy slip of paper.

She beams at him, a fellow conspirator. "Want to know something else?"

"Sure."

"The local police didn't care, but I bet you will. It was parked out there the night she died."

Kramer does not show his emotion, instead goes into the journalistic role of doubter. "But how could you know which night? I mean she was dead over a week before anybody discovered her."

"Before *I* discovered her, you mean. I was the one to sound the alarm, finally. Not seeing her for all that time, and then when I went to the house, I could smell. You know? It was obvious."

Kramer shudders; he does not want to think of that part.

"So you kept track of Frau Müller's comings and goings?"

She looks proud of herself. "In a way, yes. And I distinctly remember the last time I saw her, she was tying back the fuchsias at the front of her house. I waved, but she pretended not to notice me. Always haughty." Anger shows at her face; a green line to each side of her nose. "Well, we all see what comes of being haughty."

"Yes," Kramer says, steering her back on course. "She was tying back fuchsias?"

"That's the very night I saw the car. It must have been two, three in the morning. I hadn't heard it arrive, fast asleep I was. But I had need to get up in the middle of the night."

Suddenly, she is all primness, not wanting to mention a late-night visit to the toilet.

"And that was when I noticed it. Parked right in front of my house like it owned the place."

"How long was it there?" Kramer says.

She shrugs. "How should I know? But I double-locked all my doors after seeing what was in that car, I can tell you. Finally, I went back to sleep. It was gone in the morning."

They sit in silence for a long moment.

"What do you think they would want with the Müller woman?" she finally says.

Finally, Kramer manages to take his leave of Frau Gruber, thankful for the lungful of fresh air he sucks in once out on the road. He heads back for the center of town; the day is still bright, but no warmer. Walking, he thinks of something Frau Gruber has said: Reni was tying back the fuchsias on the day she died. Is someone planning suicide that very night going to worry about the fuchsias? One more piece of evidence that she was murdered, he thinks.

Once back in the center, Kramer does two things. First, he drops off the license plate number he got from Frau Gruber to Kommissar Boehm, who fumes but agrees to run a trace on it in the end—the Kommissar seems even less interested in the near miss Kramer had, merely admonishing him for daydreaming on the streets. Secondly, at the post office, he sends a short fax to Paris:

> *Marty, gone fishing for a few days. I have vacation due.*
> *Kate will hold down fort. Love and kisses. Kramer.*

Back at the hotel, Randall is sitting on the small terrace off their room sipping on a cup of coffee. Crumbs of a lately deceased breakfast roll are scattered on a white plate with a Hotel Bad logo.

"The prodigal returns," he says when he sees Kramer.

"Just up?" Kramer says, joining him. There are two cups, but the coffee is gone.

"Sorry," Randall says. "Didn't know when you were coming back, and I hate to waste food."

Kramer tells him of his discoveries that morning, of the near miss by the purple car, and his visit to Frau Gruber. Randall appears not to be listening, gazing instead into the main square where a young and well-endowed girl is setting up a roasted chestnut stand. But when Kramer finishes, he looks up.

"I don't like that bit about the car. Reminiscent of Herr Gorik in Berlin."

"That's what I thought, too," Kramer says. "But maybe it's just paranoia."

They smile at each other; this is their new code word. Paranoia in an evil world is a normal condition.

"And the neo-Nazis?" Randall asks.

Kramer shrugs. "It might be important. But there's no telling if the occupants of the car were at Reni's or not."

Randall considers this for a moment. "You've had a busy morning," he finally says. "Not to be outdone, I've been poking through German phone books while you were gone. There was no sign of Rick . . ."

"If he's got any sense, he'll be back in the States. The new Germany is no place for him."

"I don't know," Randall says. "I remember hearing he'd settled here. Years ago, though."

"There must be some address for him in the States. If he's still in art, maybe he belongs to an artists' association."

Kramer stops, realizing that Randall never finished his initial statement. "No sign of Rick, but . . . ?"

Randall nods. "Bingo with Helmut. He lives in Hamburg.

On the Elbchaussee, no less. Profession listed is *Kaufmann.* Good old Helmut, a businessman."

"So?"

"Hamburg?" Randall says.

"Hamburg, it is."

CHAPTER EIGHT

At Randall's insistence, they rent a car in Bad Lunsburg; a fire-engine red Mercedes 380 SL. Childlike, Randall is infatuated with things mechanical and demands to do all the driving, which is okay with Kramer in principle: he hates things mechanical. Driving for him—unless it is in the American Southwest late at night under a full moon with the Beatles' *White Album* in the tape deck—is one of life's miseries to be borne only when absolutely necessary.

After thirty miles with Randall at the wheel, however, Kramer begins to wonder if there are not worse things than having to drive. Like being severely dead, for instance.

They have taken narrow country roads north and east, bypassing Cologne and its heavy traffic, heading straight for Dortmund. A countryside of rolling hills, glistening under the sun; of pruned-back rows of vines in every direction; farmers on tractors doing God knows what errands now that the harvest is in. Peaceful, bucolic. Randall, however, does not believe in slowing for other vehicles; does not seem to understand the elemental truths of driving, such as you don't pass on blind curves or on the right. He likes to use the horn, as if this makes up for all sorts of practical and moral infringements.

"Where did you get your license, Randall?" Kramer finally says after their second brush with eternity. Randall pulls them back into their lane just before a twelve-ton truck makes hash of them. "They selling them at Woolworth's now?"

Randall is whistling an aria from Verdi with great vigor. He stops the music, unpuckers his lips, and smiles quite insanely at Kramer. "I don't have a license, my friend. This is on-the-job training."

He emits a gleeful laugh and floors the accelerator, sounding the tires as they take a sharp curve marked fifty kilometers.

"Either slow down or I drive," Kramer orders.

Randall looks hurt, but slows down.

By the time they hit the little town of Hückeswagen, they have made a truce. Randall is allowed pedal to the metal on the straight stretches if he takes it easy around curves. By Dortmund, they are on the E3 Autobahn and fairly flying over the placidly rolling landscape of Münster.

"What's the speed limit here, Sammy?" Randall yells at one point. His voice can hardly be heard over the rushing of wind against the car.

"There isn't one," Kramer says without thinking.

"What're we ditzing around for, then? Time's a-wasting."

Randall stomps on the accelerator, sending the tachometer into a dizzying spin.

Kramer leans back, making sure his seat belt is fastened, and lets Randall have his fun. Leave it in the lap of the gods, he figures. Time was when he felt invincible; accidents do not happen to tourists.

Randall's driving has one plus: it leaves little time for Kramer to mull, to second-guess, to wonder what the hell he's doing away from his Vienna desk chasing ghosts from the past.

Exit signs to Osnabrück flash by. Randall is whistling his aria again. Clouds have gathered. The shimmering landscape is now dull brown and sodden. Forest to the right and hills like a rake turned on its back.

Bremen is a flurry of industrial parks and high-rise buildings, and soon they are onto the Lüneburg moor to the south of Hamburg.

"Car handles like a dream," Randall says. Then, "Damn, I'm hungry. We didn't stop the whole way. Maybe I've got a career, Sam. Truck driver. There's power for you."

Kramer manages a smile, says nothing.

The autobahn crosses the marsh before Hamburg, the roadway raised on stilts. Kramer tries to keep his attention on the scenery. Dockside industry begins to build up until they hit the first bridge across the Elbe. As they cross the river, Kramer looks down at all the paraphernalia of a busy port: piles of brightly colored containers fresh off ships; dock basins hectic with activity; quays, sheds, tall cranes like erector sets against the sky; ships bearing flags from around the world, one moving so slowly back out to sea that at first Kramer thinks it is docked and the land itself is shifting. To the right is the center of the city, a spire here and there; tall business complexes dwarfing these. To their left, a slope runs west over the far bank of the Elbe. Along its ridge is the street they are looking for: the Elbchaussee.

"Next exit," Kramer says.

Disappointment showing in his face, Randall puts on the turn signal. It clicks the end of his joy ride, like a second hand running down.

Kramer looks at the address Randall has copied from the phone directory: Nienstedten. Turning onto Elbchaussee, Randall is finally forced to reduce speed. It's a broad, busy avenue with the villas and parks of the fashionable and wealthy to their right. Classical architecture full of columns and architraves. They've been living on this street for a century and a half, those with money and power. To the left is the Elbe with its shipping traffic, fish restaurants, bathing strands. By the time they reach the little suburb of Nienstedten, it has begun to sprinkle. Randall turns on the wipers; their *slap-slap* punctuates the rest of the ride. Kramer cranes his head to see the house numbers, does a double take, rechecking the address on the notepaper from the hotel in Bad Lunsburg, then lets out a low whistle.

"Find it?" Randall says.

"That's it." Kramer points out his window.

"Where? All I see is a park."

"That's it. The house is way up the drive."

"Helmut's house? Business must be good."

Randall finds a parking space, cutting over two lanes in front of an Audi whose female driver honks furiously at them, and rubs tires against the curb as he pulls to a stop.

"He's not going to be there," Kramer says. "Probably still at the office."

Randall cuts the ignition, puts the keys in his pocket, and hits the automatic switch to pop open the door locks.

"I checked that," he says, smiling to himself. "Didn't tell you in Bad Lunsburg, but I found his business number first. They told me Helmut would be home in the afternoon. Something about a birthday party."

Kramer surveys the well-maintained grounds surrounding the villa. "He's going to love us crashing his party." Then he looks at Randall. "What business, and why the hell are you smiling like a drain pipe?"

"It's interesting," Randall says. "Not indicative, only interesting." He looks at Kramer out the corner of his eye.

"Out with it," Kramer says.

"The German-Czech Trade Alliance. That's the name of Helmut's business. Cute, huh?"

Kramer thinks about this for a moment. It's surprising enough that Helmut is a successful capitalist; stranger still he's doing business with the Czech Republic.

"I bet the boys in Prague never heard of Helmut's trip there in 1968," Randall says.

Kramer shakes his head, feels a shiver of realization pass over him. "And I don't suppose he wants them to know, either."

Randall nods in agreement.

Kramer finally says the unspoken, "Another person with motive?"

"That's what I was thinking."

They sit in the car another moment watching the rain fall steadily, coursing down the windshield in rivulets.

"Shall we?" Kramer finally says, and he and Randall get out, lock the doors, and go to the iron gate at the head of the drive. There is a bell and speaking grill built into the concrete post on one side of the gate. Kramer rings it once, and a voice comes on immediately.

"Yes?" Expectant.

"We're here to see Herr Pringl."

"Finally." The male voice sounds relieved; it also sounds familiar: low and precise with harsh gutturals.

"We've been expecting you," the voice continues. "Come up to the main house."

The gate is rung open, and the intercom buzzes off before Kramer can identify himself. He gives Randall a look and gets a shrug in return.

"Word gets around, I guess," Randall says.

It's far enough to use the car, especially with the rain falling as it is, so they return to the Mercedes, get in, and pull into the gravel driveway, staring amazed at the bushes clipped into shapes of zoo animals on both sides of the lane.

"Think there'll be gnomes on the lawn?" Randall says.

There aren't, but there is an elephant's foot umbrella stand in the entryway when they are admitted by a maid who looks like she belongs along the Mediterranean. She tells them to wait, that Herr Pringl will be right with them. From a room deeper in the cavernous house, they hear the sounds of children's laughter. Steps echo toward them, reverberating in the high-ceilinged entryway. The main stairs face them, leading up to a bank of stained-glass windows twelve feet high on the first landing. Blue and golden light is cast down the stairs through glass irises and dahlias.

The resounding footsteps draw closer, and Helmut comes into view from the rooms to the left. He is dressed in white flannels, a pearl-gray sweater, and burgundy leather slip-ons whose tassels bounce as he walks. His hair is slicked back like a Hollywood smoothie of the 1930s, and he wears round mock tortoise-shell glasses. He stops dead in his tracks, does a double take on Kramer and Randall, glances over his shoulder back to the sound of the voices, now more petulant sounding than before, and then looks back to the two of them.

"My Christ!" he says in his stiff school English. It always sounded funny coming out of his very German throat. "What are you two doing here?"

"We're happy to see you, too, Helmut," Kramer says.

"I am sorry," Helmut says, suddenly remembering manners. "It is such a surprise." Another guilty glance over his shoulder. "We were expecting someone else, to tell you the truth."

"I had that feeling," Kramer says.

"So how's it going, Helmut?" Randall goes up to him and gives him a hug that is returned with a stiff upper body by Helmut and quickly broken.

"Haven't seen you in more than twenty years," Randall continues effusively. "And it looks like you're doing all right for yourself."

"It really is terrific to see you fellows again," Helmut says flatly.

Another glance over the shoulder and this time there is the clicking of high heels coming toward them. A blonde woman, perhaps mid-twenties, with a beauty mark painted on her upper lip and breasts that could keep her afloat in case their yacht capsized, does the same double take Helmut did earlier.

"But this isn't the clown," she says.

Kramer gets the feeling they should have used the trade entrance.

"No, dear," Helmut says. "These are some old friends of mine."

She looks Randall up and down and raises her penciled-in eyebrows.

"How nice." Then, turning to Helmut, "And what about the clown? Herr Pavel's child is getting impatient."

"Look, I'm sorry we came at a bad time, Helmut," Kramer says. "How about we get together after the party?"

"Well, naturally . . ."

"It will be a very long party, Mr. . . . ?" the woman interrupts.

"Kramer," he says, extending his hand to the lady. She takes it limply; hers is cold as a dead fish. "You're Helmut's wife?"

She nods and Helmut gives her a hug, which she tolerates just as Helmut earlier allowed Randall's embrace.

"Katia Felsen-Pringl." He beams at her like the owner of a fancy car. "We've been married just a year."

"Great," Randall says, looking straight at her breasts under the mohair sweater she's wearing.

"And this is Randall," Helmut says to his wife. "We knew each other in Vienna."

Kramer senses Helmut almost warming to them. Then the maid returns.

"Herr Pringl, the party agency just called. The clown is sick. They fear it's pneumonia."

"Oh, lovely," Frau Pringl says. "Now what do we do? The children are expecting him."

She looks like a child herself, Kramer notices, in spite of all the silly attempt at vamping. Like a child who got into her mother's makeup kit. Her lips pout; her eyes water.

"Well, we'll get out of your way," Kramer begins.

"Have no fear," Randall says, pulling three umbrellas out of the elephant's foot, throwing one aloft and then balancing it head to toe on the other two like Chinese sticks. "One clown, at your service." The suspended umbrella falls to the floor with a clatter.

"I do better with oranges." He smiles engagingly. "Just get me some lipstick for my nose, and we're in business."

"I couldn't presume on old friendships," Helmut says, but his wife is more pragmatic.

"Can you really juggle?"

"Madam, I have been juggling all my adult life. It is the one thing I can do." Randall's eyes never leave her breasts.

"Here, then." She has an evening bag handy in the wardrobe by the door, fetches out a lipstick from it, and hands it to Randall. She doesn't hide the fact that she's doing this under duress, almost as if she is doing Randall the favor. "Hurry!"

And she is gone, strutting back on her clicking heels over the parquet, her tiny ass firm and high.

Helmut sighs and then smiles at them. "Really, this is awfully good of you."

"Think nothing of it, Trotsky," Randall says, lapsing into their old nickname for him.

Helmut blushes and swallows hard. "I would appreciate it if we could forget the past for the time being. You see, I have some very important guests here. Important to my business, I mean. Fellows from Prague who have absolutely no sense of humor. In fact, it is the birthday of the child of one of these men whom we are celebrating."

"Don't worry, Trots . . . I mean, Helmut, old chump." Randall pats him on the back as he applies the lipstick to lips and nose. "Mum's the word." He looks in the hallway mirror, leaning against a mahogany letter table, puckers his lips, adds another touch of red to the tip of his nose, then shrugs.

"Showtime," he says.

Helmut is all nerves as they approach the room where the kids are. Kramer is impressed not only by the size of the villa, but also by the quiet taste with which it is decorated. Either the Pringls had the good sense to hire a fine interior decorator, or Helmut's wife is not as ditzy as she appears. Either way, it proves they are not complete nouveaux.

"Look, I'll just sort of hang back here," Kramer says as the kids' voices grow louder and more insistent. "No introductions necessary, okay? We leave when Randall's done his shtick. But I do need to talk to you. Soon."

Helmut looks into Kramer's eyes, and for an instant the old Helmut is there behind the glasses: the old intensity and empathy. Then his wife grabs his arm, dragging Helmut into the room.

"Tell them the clown is here," she hisses in his ear.

Helmut talks directly to the portly man seated in the largest armchair in the room: Herr Pavel, Kramer figures, peeking through the open door.

"Sorry about the delay," he says. "But here he is, the man we've been waiting for, Randall the Magnificent!"

Randall chuckles to himself and makes a stumbling entrance into the party room, coming within an inch of sticking his bright red nose into the ornate birthday cake. Instant laughter.

J. Sydney Jones

For the next ten minutes, he juggles everything in sight: oranges and apples, cake plates and cut-crystal juice glasses, even eyeglasses, which he gathers from the adults, including Herr Pavel, who laughs in spite of himself. Kramer loves it, watching Randall do what he does best: making people laugh.

Randall finishes with a flourish, juggling the poker, shovel, and brush from the fireplace, and the kids are on their feet clapping for an encore. But Randall takes his leave like all good theater folk; making them want more.

In the hall again, Randall uses a towel supplied by the maid to wipe off the lipstick. He's beaming, hyper, ready for more.

"Maybe I won't be a truck driver, after all, Sam."

Kramer shakes his head. "You could be a Zen truck driver. Look, no hands at all."

Randall makes his lips turn upward; it cannot be classified as a smile.

"Do me a favor, Sam. You're the straight man, okay. Jokes are my territory."

Helmut stops them at the door. "That was marvelous, Randall. Herr Pavel loved it."

"How about the kids?"

"Oh, they did, too." Then catching himself again. "Okay, so I've changed."

"We all have, Helmut," Kramer says. "Nobody's making judgments."

"You've come about Reni, haven't you?"

Kramer nods. "But you get back to your guests now. We'll talk later."

"What is it?" Helmut says. "Collecting for some sort of remembrance?"

"No," Kramer says.

"Well?"

"You got a minute?"

Helmut looks back toward the party room. "They're open-

82

ing presents now. Come into my study." He leads them in the opposite direction from the party, through further groups of high-ceilinged rooms rich in Oriental carpeting, fine oils, and museum-quality furniture. There is a smell of wood polish to it all: the smell of wealth.

Helmut's study would serve as the library for a small liberal arts college in the States, Kramer figures. Several thousand leather-bound volumes fill the floor to ceiling built-in bookcases. Red and green leather club chairs in front of a river-rock fireplace; Kasimir prints of Vienna on the free wall space.

No drinks are offered. They sit and Helmut gets directly to the point. "Tell me," he says.

Faced with it, Kramer does not know where to begin, what to tell Helmut and what not to tell him.

"Did you know Reni was writing memoirs?" he finally says, looking for a reaction.

Helmut's face is a blank. "No. As with you fellows, I have not seen Reni since, well, since those days."

Kramer looks to Randall for help, but there is none there. Clowning is Randall's job; interviewing, Kramer's.

"You see, I was made her literary executor," Kramer goes on.

"So you remained friends, then?" he says. "I mean I read long ago that she had married Gerhard. You two were always thick as thieves. One imagined that you and Reni would have . . ."

"I haven't seen Reni since 1974."

"Oh," Helmut says. "But then, I don't see what this has to do with me. Will you be publishing her memoirs? Are you looking for sponsorship? Is that it?" He thinks a moment, and suddenly the color drains from his face.

"She didn't write about Prague, did she? Christ, Sam, that could ruin me."

Kramer and Randall exchange glances.

"I don't know," Kramer says. "I was hoping you could tell me."

"You're the executor, you said." Then he looks from Kramer to Randall. "Something's wrong, isn't there? This isn't just a friendly visit, old friends getting together once again. The Magnificent Seven!" He says it with an anger and a derisive passion that breaks through his smooth, at-arm's-length demeanor. "We were such children then."

"Agreed," Randall says.

"Playing at revolution," Helmut adds. "Playing with fire and getting our hands burned."

They sit quietly for a moment; the shrieks of the children can barely be heard in this solemn room. A clock on the mantle ticks loudly.

"So what is it?" Helmut finally says.

"Her memoirs seem to be missing," Kramer says. "She was interviewing some pretty freaky people before her death. And there are people who might not want the memoirs to see the light of day."

Helmut considers this, in control of himself once again. "Such as me?"

Kramer lifts his eyebrows at this.

"I think somebody killed Reni," Kramer says. "Made it look like suicide, then stole the memoirs. All traces of them."

"Obviously, the police do not concur," Helmut says. "That explains why you are going it alone."

"We're trying to trace down any leads. People in Reni's life who might not have wanted the memoirs to be published. People in her past and her present."

"So what do you want from me?" Helmut says. "A confession? You think I killed her to keep my connection with Prague a secret from my new trading partners?"

"I don't know what I expect from you," Kramer says. "Information, I suppose."

"I have no information, Sam. I didn't even know about the memoirs. I surely wouldn't have killed to stop their publication. Bribed, perhaps." An attempted smile that dies on his lips. "Somebody killed her?"

"That's what we think."

"There's more to it, isn't there? You're a journalist. I don't suppose you go jumping to conclusions without more evidence."

Kramer nods.

"I don't want to know, Sam. I'm not really part of this anymore, you see. I've got something to lose now. Too much to lose." He looks around the library, glances back toward the voices. "But maybe it is good you came. I mean about information. You see, I've been thinking about Prague lately. I go regularly, see the old department store where it happened. And the more I think of it, the more I know it wasn't vandalism."

"What do you mean?" Kramer says. "The car?"

Helmut stands suddenly. "Cold in here, isn't it. I should have laid a fire." He walks toward the fireplace and then turns. "Oh, well. Yes, the car. We all were contented with the idea of a vandal, even when the Czechs themselves were calling it a car bombing, a Western provocation. Or maybe *because* they were calling it a bombing."

Kramer thinks back to the meeting where they drew straws; each of them relieved in turn to pick the long ones, until only two were left in Reni's hand and there were only Maria and Helmut remaining to draw. They accepted the responsibility without even looking at their straws. Kramer did later that night, after Reni went to sleep: the straws were all the same length. Reni playing her little games; Reni who devised the scheme to throw the antigovernment leaflets off the tallest building in downtown Prague to protest the Soviet invasion and suppression of the Prague Spring.

"And what have you been thinking, Helmut?" Randall asks.

"That it wasn't an act of vandalism, after all. No blind coincidences. We all know there is no such thing as coincidence in the universe; yet we deluded ourselves all these years into believing in that incredible one."

"Just a feeling?" Kramer asks.

Helmut shakes his head. "My firm does more than import Czech beer," he says. "In fact, we deal in what the Czechs do best, armaments. I've seen these things close up—incendiaries, land mines, plastic, the lot. Back then, I didn't know gelignite from alum. I just saw the car burst into flames on the street below. But there was a sound. I heard that same sound again a few months back when our field men were testing a shipment of incendiaries. A sort of hissing growl preceding a bright flash and then flames. Odd that a sound can bring up memories from more than twenty years ago."

"What are you saying, Helmut?" Kramer says, but he feels he already knows.

"That a bomb was planted in our car. Probably in Vienna, set to go off in Prague. We could have been in it. But it was planted to do exactly what it accomplished: to cause an incident in Prague; to be something bigger than a couple of idealistic kids throwing leaflets off the top of a building."

"But that means . . ." Randall begins.

"Yes," Helmut says. "No one else knew of our plans. So it means that one of the seven of us planted the bomb. There's reason to suppress Reni's memoirs, if she discovered who it was. Assuming, of course, that it wasn't Reni herself who did it."

The door opens and Helmut's wife stands on the threshold, pouting her lips. "We were wondering where you went."

"Just coming, dear," Helmut says, going to her and giving her a peck on the forehead.

"What have you men been talking about? Former conquests?"

"Don't worry, Frau Pringl," Kramer says, rising. "Helmut led a very monastic life when we knew him."

"Poor boy. We'll make up for that, won't we?" She pats him on the cheek and then looks at Kramer. "Sorry to drag him away." She does not look one bit remorseful.

"We've got to be going anyway," Randall says, on his feet now. "Hope the kids liked the juggling."

She smiles, leading Helmut back to the party. "You can let yourselves out, can't you?" she says over her shoulder.

Helmut stops, whispers in his wife's ear a moment, then comes back to shake hands.

"One of us," he says. "Not a nice thought in the middle of the night. I'm actually glad to share it finally."

Back in the car Randall looks at Kramer hard, "Lying?"

"I don't think so. It sounded way too real. Even for a good actor. I would not call Helmut a good actor. Not by any stretch."

Randall starts the car, and they drive down the lane to the street once again. The rain has stopped; an occasional drop splatters on the windshield. Back on the street, they turn left toward town.

"I'm ravenous," Randall says. "I hope you've still got room on that piece of plastic."

They don't talk about Helmut's revelation. It's the sort of thing that needs to soak in. Near the docks, Randall pulls in at a seafood joint with graffiti spray-painted on the wall: *TV ist Gerhirnwaesche.*

"Can't be all bad if they call television brain-washing," Randall says.

Kramer is amazed. "How'd you know what that says?"

"Intellect, Sam." Randall thumps his right temple with his forefinger. "It's the stuff of evolution."

It's a rough neighborhood, but Randall's instincts about the restaurant turn out to be correct, and they have a hearty meal of cod, salad, fried potatoes, and beer. There is none of the salty taste fish gets if it's been lying around a cooler for days; the potatoes are crisp, not greasy; the beer, cold and plentiful.

They have no plans for the night. It is late to be driving back to Bad Lunsburg; dark by the time they finish their meal. About all Kramer knows of Hamburg is what any ten-cent tourist does: the shows on the Reeperbahn, which do not interest him in the least. They return to the car, trying to decide if they should hit the road or not, when from a nearby alley they hear a scream, then the unmistakable crunching sound of knuckles meeting cartilage.

Kramer moves to the alley cautiously, Randall following. From the mouth of the dead end, they see two youths dressed in black leather pounding on an inert body at their feet. Their black jeans are cut off at the ankle, revealing lace-up black boots. The skinhead on the right draws a boot back and kicks viciously; the body twitches and groans.

Kramer does not take time to consider the situation, but runs toward the thugs. "Stop it, for Christ's sake!"

The two turn as Kramer and Randall approach.

"Fuck off," the one on the right says. Kramer sees a chain dangling from his right hand.

"You'll kill him," Kramer says, still sprinting.

"That's the idea, prick." The skinhead slides the chain back and forth to get momentum for a swing.

Kramer stops and Randall bumps into him, panting hard.

"Look, we don't want any trouble," Kramer says. "The guy's down. Leave it."

Chain Man smirks at him, his chain glistening in the light from a streetlamp in back of Kramer. Kramer is close enough to see swastikas tattooed on the knuckles of the hand holding the chain. The body groans again, catching Kramer's attention. The victim is curled in a fetal position, arms around his head, leaving the kidneys wide open for kicks. The hands protecting the head are coal black.

"You sound foreign, fucker," the other skinhead says now. He is shorter than the one with the chain, but stocky. Thick arms and thighs on him like tree trunks. Kramer checks it out quickly, looking for other weapons. No bats, no guns. Just the chain. And the one swinging that looks anxious, his breath coming in rapid puffs like a junkie high on violence, needing another fix.

"Maybe we should fix you like we did the nigger here."

Kramer knows there's no use talking; it's past that. But he buys time.

"We just don't want to see anyone hurt," he says, stepping to his left, bringing the chain man with him, closer to his buddy so that he won't be able to swing the chain in a wide arc.

"Shouldn't we maybe go for the police?" Randall says in an urgent whisper.

Kramer can feel the adrenaline pumping now, feels the tension in his guts like he hasn't since he was a kid in Golden Gloves competition. No more observing, he tells himself. No more taking notes about violence, reporting on it dispassionately.

"You take the shorter one," Kramer says to Randall in English, never taking his eyes from the chain. "At least keep him off me until I handle the guy with the chain."

"Sam," Randall begins, but then stops. "Okay."

The two skinheads look at each other at the sound of English.

"Americans?" Chain Man says. "I haven't killed an Ami yet this year."

Kramer makes his move as the last word is spoken. He leaps on the bottom links of the chain dragging on the wet asphalt, and drives a right upper cut into Chain Man's gut, digging in deep, knocking wind out of him and sending him onto his ass. The chain is ripped out of his hand and Kramer picks it up and throws it clattering into an open dumpster. Out the side of his eye, he sees Randall and the stocky one squaring off, circling each other. That's all he has time for because Chain Man is on his feet again, raging like a stuck bull. He's young, good at beating up defenseless people two on one, and cocky.

Kramer can taste blood; can feel it like a white-hot need. He lets the kid come in close, throw a wide blow that he ducks underneath, then jabs twice into the soft gut again, and circles out of range. Kramer's heart is popping like an engine; he's on the balls of his feet. It feels good. The kid comes in again, throws a left, then counters with a kick that catches Kramer in the thigh, just missing his balls. The muscle knots and Kramer stumbles as the kid grins wildly. He senses motion to his right, bodies grappling, but the kid is coming in again, all legs and a long reach. The kid throws the left again and counters with his leg, but this time Kramer kicks out, too, from a solid base leg, tearing into the kid's knee joint, and crumpling him like a marionette with his strings cut.

The kid rolls on the ground and Kramer wants him to get up, wants to work on his face. Randall is knocked into him and Kramer turns toward the other goon now, snapping his head back twice with two sharp left hooks, but this stocky one is unfazed; his head's as thick as quarry rock. He charges in past Kramer's punches, taking three to the head like mosquito bites and grabs Kramer around the chest, squeezing air out of his lungs and lifting him off the ground. Kramer feels light-headed, cannot get his breath, knows his eyes are going bleary, his mouth gasping for oxygen. He forces his thumbs into the skinhead's eyes, pressing and pressing until the youth roars, dropping him. Kramer moves in for close body work as the stocky one holds his hands over his eyes; two in the solar plexus, spinning him with the force of the punches, then a jab to the kidneys, buckling him over, and a kick to the seat of the pants sending him head first into the side of the dumpster.

"Look out, Sam!"

Kramer spins around at Randall's warning. Chain Man is up again, with a stiletto in his hand.

Kramer's eyes dart back and forth, looking for some shield, some weapon. He whips his oilskin jacket off and wraps it around his left arm as the other circles closer and closer, swiping at him in wide arcs with the gleaming blade.

Kramer doesn't know about this; Golden Gloves never gave him much instruction in knife fighting.

"Hey, dickhead!" Randall yells, but Chain Man pays no attention.

"Hitler prick, I'm talking to you," Randall screams.

Both Chain Man and Kramer look this time. Randall is spinning a long piece of piping he's picked up from a heap of rubble at one side of the alley; twirling it like a baton, like a weapon in martial arts. The pipe's a blur as it spins and spins from hand to hand, and Randall assumes an attack pose; bent left leg, right leg jutting straight back.

"*Hai!*" Randall shouts, a loud explosion that startles even Kramer.

He circles with the swirling pipe, his face all intensity. "I'm going to give you an eight-foot enema, fucker." Randall's face is bleeding at the nose and mouth; his eyes are completely lucid.

Chain Man looks at his buddy, just getting to his knees by the dumpster. The stocky one peers up at Randall wielding the pipe. "Shit."

"Split," Kramer says, "and maybe we'll let you live."

Chain Man glances once down at his knife, then charges between Kramer and Randall down the alley and away. The stocky one's eyes are big as saucers as he inches along one wall toward the open street.

"*Hai!*" Another feint with the pipe sends him scuttling like a fat pig after his friend.

Kramer looks at Randall, amazed. "I didn't know you were into that shit."

Randall drops the pipe, wiping his hands together. "I'm not. But don't ever be telling me juggling is a useless art."

"You silly son of a bitch."

"And what are you? Bleeding Rambo? Rocky Ten? I'll be your manager, Sam. A new career for both of us."

Another groan from the inert body cuts short their rejoicing. Kramer leans over him. "It's okay now. Can you walk?"

He rolls the guy over; his face is a purple welt where the chain cut him.

"Jesus," Randall mutters. "We better get him to a hospital."

This makes the man come to life. "No hospitals," he says in a clipped Nigerian accent. "I'll be okay."

"Can you walk?" Kramer gives him a hand, and he stands unsteadily. "We should get you out of here. Your friends could be back."

The man allows Kramer to help him to the car, his eyes staring down at his feet all the while.

"Really, Sam," Randall says once they reach the car. "That was pretty fancy fisticuffs. Wish I had a video. I thought you were a pacifist."

Kramer feels the rush of the fight now; he could coast on

it. He once came to love that feeling; that's why he quit box-
ing. He needed the rush, just like Chain Man.

Randall unlocks the car door and props the front seat forward to get the African in back, but the man hesitates.

"No. I live here. Just around the corner."

"We'll give you a lift, then," Kramer says.

"No. You've done enough." He lifts his eyes now; there
are tears in them. "Why couldn't you just mind your own
business? They weren't going to kill me. Just rough me up a
bit. It's like an initiation. Then they leave you alone. But now
they'll kill me if they ever see me again. I'll have to move. And
it starts all over again. Why couldn't you just stay out of it? It's
no business of yours."

Kramer wasn't expecting thanks, but the words hit him
like Chain Man did not. They take the wind out of him; send
nausea into his bowels.

"Fuck me running," Randall says in a moan, looking down
the street.

Kramer follows his eyes. From around the corner in front
of them, come a dozen youths in black, wielding chains and
baseball bats. Kramer checks the other way; another group
flanking on them from that end of the street.

"Move it," he says, shoving the protesting African into the
backseat, jumping into the front himself, slamming and lock-
ing the door. Randall is in the driver's seat fumbling with the
key in the ignition when both groups start racing for the car.

"Start the son of a bitch!" Kramer needlessly yells.

The engine turns over when both groups are converging on the car, ten, maybe fifteen yards away. Randall's eyes
hold the same lucidity as in the alley. A brick lands on the
hood, rattling up to the windshield just as Randall puts it into
gear and burns rubber in reverse. The others aren't expecting backward motion; the rear group is caught off guard as
Randall smashes into one of them, a body flying up and over

the top of the car. He hits the brakes and spins the wheel, fishtailing the car to head in the opposite direction. There are blows on the trunk as Randall throws it into first. Suddenly, the windshield in front of Kramer explodes in a shower of fragmented glass as a bat crashes into it. Kramer feels hot liquid flow down his face and realizes he's been cut. Randall smokes tires, his back wheels swerving right and left, as they speed out of the dockside.

From the back, the African groans again, "You've done it now. Ruined it all. Why couldn't you just mind your own business?"

"Can it," Randall says in English and, as if understanding him, the man sinks into stillness. They bump over cobblestones; fly around curves toward the city center.

CHAPTER NINE

"I thought a smart journalist like you would know when to keep his ass covered." Kommissar Boehm snicks the last piece of croissant from the plate, examines it as one would a dog for fleas, and then plops it into his mouth. Quick mastication; slow swallow.

"You want me to order more? Some coffee?" Kramer nods at the full pot. They are sitting on the glassed-in terrace of the Hotel Bad midmorning after spending most of the night in Hamburg; first at the central police station and then at emergency getting fifteen stitches in Kramer's forehead. He is in no mood for Boehm's critique.

Boehm wags his head at the offer. "On a diet." He pats his broad middle. "The wife says I need to drop twenty pounds."

Kramer begins to wonder what all this hail-fellow stuff is about. *I couldn't give a damn about your diet*, he wants to say.

"You look fit enough to me," he says instead.

"What were you doing in Hamburg?"

Kramer sips coffee; it stings tiny cuts inside his mouth. He wonders where he got them. The punks never laid a hand on his face. Were they self-inflicted, grinding his teeth and biting his gums while sleeping on the way back to Bad Lunsburg this morning?

"Visiting," he says.

Boehm glares at him across the table. Randall is asleep upstairs in their room, having done all the driving, looking like a pugilist who lost the fight: a swollen, purple eye and puffy upper lip.

"Look, Kramer," Boehm says, "I don't want to play games with you. If you're stirring up nests, I should know."

"They were just punks. Skinheads. Unrelated to Reni or her memoirs. They were pounding on some poor bastard, about to kill him. Randall and I stopped it. Then they brought in reinforcements."

"That's not exactly the way Hamburg reports it."

"You keeping tabs on me, Kommissar?"

"You bet your ass I am. Loose cannons make me nervous."

"I'm just looking for the truth."

"I don't know what kind of truths you expected to find dockside in Hamburg. You might as well walk Harlem at midnight."

"Are you a traveler, Kommissar Boehm?"

"I've been to New York. Interesting, good music, but I carried my PPK with me." He pats the bulge under his left arm, then eyes the coffeepot. "Maybe just a half cup. No cream."

Kramer pours out some of the rich coffee. It gives him the jitters, and sometimes the runs, but he loves it.

"What do they say in Hamburg?" he asks.

Boehm sips the coffee daintily. The demitasse looks like a child's toy cup in his massive hand. He smiles at the taste, puts the cup down.

"According to your African friend . . ."

"I never met the guy before. I just didn't like to see him get killed."

Boehm ignores the interruption. "He fell down. Tripped

over some piping in an alleyway. These two guys were helping him, and you and your buddy jumped them. They naturally ran to get help after you cleared some cobwebs out of their heads. Then you proceeded to kidnap said African."

"Get real, Kommissar. You believe that scenario?"

"Nobody likes a good Samaritan, Kramer. You save a guy's life, he owes you. What is it your boy Shakespeare says? Neither a borrower nor a lender be."

"Have you come to arrest me?" Kramer finally says.

"Hell no. You're my entertainment center. Watching you chase all over Germany after phantoms is better than a Chaplin film."

"So to what do I owe the honor of this visit?" Kramer says.

Boehm spins the tiny cup on the table, sniffs once, and then casts a wry smile.

"I traced that car number you gave me. I guess that's why I'm a little interested in your fracas last night."

He pulls a sheet of yellow memo paper out of the inside pocket of his worn blue suit coat and hands it to Kramer.

"Ever hear of him?" Kommissar Boehm asks.

Kramer reads the name on the paper: Reinhard Vogel. He nods.

"I interviewed him a couple of years back for an article on the rise of the right. He's slick. The man who makes Fascism chic."

Boehm nods. "How'd you get his license number?"

Kramer hesitates, decides he has to trust somebody, and tells him Frau Gruber's story. Kommissar Boehm listens without interruption, sucking on his lower lip.

"So he was a buddy of Renata Müller?" Boehm says when Kramer finishes his explanation. "Strange company."

"I'm not sure how he figures in with Reni," Kramer says. "When I was going through her effects, I came across a page of notes for an article on neo-Nazi violence. I didn't give it much thought at the time but, after hearing Frau Gruber's story, I went back to look for it. Schnelling had burned it along with a bunch of other papers."

"Advokat Schnelling is a very thorough man," Boehm says, smiling.

Kramer eyes the policeman, sensing something else at work. "You're interested in Vogel, aren't you?"

Boehm finishes the coffee and looks Kramer square in the eye. He then takes a wallet out of his jacket pocket and opens it in front of Kramer's face. On one side is his Kriminalpolizei identification with his mug shot, on the other side is a photo of a lovely young woman in shorts and halter top, with a bushy head of red hair and freckles on her nose. There is strong sun in the picture, and she is squinting and smiling into the camera. The kid next door, but with that extra special something.

"She didn't take after me for looks," Kommissar Boehm says, flipping the wallet shut and returning it to his inside jacket pocket. His eyes fix on Kramer's again. "Sweet kid. A real beauty. She was only twenty when she died."

Kramer knows the rest of the story; he doesn't need to be told.

"Vogel?"

Boehm shrugs. "His group of thugs. Same thing. Magda was her name—after her mother's best friend. She thought it was cute to run with the tough boys, the rebels, the skinheads. You know kids; they figure they're immortal, invincible. Nothing can touch them. She started doing designer drugs at first, and then she got hooked big-time. But that was the setup, wasn't it? Her so-called 'friends' suckered her. She began selling her body for needle money like it was a big joke, like she was just doing anthropological research. Like she was above it. Munich cops busted her once for soliciting and gave me a buzz when they found out whose kid she was. I dragged her home, but she only ran away again. Last time I saw her, she was under a gray sheet at the Munich morgue."

"OD?" Kramer asks.

Boehm nods. "A belly full of crack." He says nothing for a time, then continues. "So you got business with Vogel, I'm interested. He uses the skinheads for drug dealing to help finance his cause. If there's anything can be pinned on him regarding Müller's death, I'm your partner. So we share, okay?"

Kramer thinks of the picture: Boehm's daughter had the same invincible, naive look on her face that Reni once had.

"Okay," Kramer says. "We share."

Randall wakes up shortly after one. This is no day to be traveling; Kramer has a task for them nearer at hand than Munich.

They take the local train to Bonn instead of driving; Kramer's good customer rating with Avis has sunk after returning the battered Mercedes this morning. Eva Martok's flat is a short tram ride away from the station. It feels good not being encumbered by a car; not carrying a bulky metal shell around with you, forever on the lookout for a parking space.

Randall grabs a hot wurst from a stand outside the station and munches it on the tram, much to the disgust of other passengers. Nobody says anything, though. He and Kramer look like desperadoes with their bandages and bruises.

They get off at the Prinz-Albert-Strasse and take their time getting to Martok's building at number 43, pausing before ringing the bell so Randall can finish the last bit of sausage, heavily coated in hot mustard. He tosses the paper plate it was on into a garbage can stuck inside an ornate bit of green-painted circular grillwork.

They're in the heart of Bonn's Old Town; buildings on this street were old when Beethoven was a boy picking his nose. Renovated now; cheery pastel facades, cream-colored lintels.

There is no intercom on number 43; the house door is open. It's a tiny baroque house with a corbeled, vaulted entryway once used for horse and carriage; the stone steps in the stairwell are grooved in the middle from years of wear. Kramer called from Bad Lunsburg before coming. Martok sounded suspicious, but agreed to meet with him. Tuesdays are her day to work at home.

She's on the top floor, the third. There's a brass clapper on her door in the shape of a hand. Kramer knuckles it to wood and the door opens on the second rap. No dead bolts, peepholes, or door chains. Martok's the trusting sort, he figures. Crime has not yet found its way into this quarter of Bonn.

"You're Kramer." She says it like an accusation, then notices his bandaged forehead and checks out Randall, whose head increasingly looks like a swollen purple balloon, standing in back of him.

"What the hell happened to you?" She speaks English like she's studied in the States, and wears Levis that fit her waist and thighs snugly, and a faded black Grateful Dead T-shirt. Barefoot; no nail polish on her toes.

"We had a difference of opinion with a baseball bat." He jerks his head backward. "This is my friend, Randall. He knew Reni, too. We're not as desperate as we look. Honest."

Standing in the entrance, she looks as if she's reconsidering her invitation for a meeting. She's got one of those strong faces that would look equally good on a man, but that's all that is masculine about her. She's wearing some subtle scent that Kramer remembers from his college days, triggering adolescent hormonal memories.

"Don't let these bruises alarm you, Ms. Martok," Randall pipes up. "I am a deeply nonviolent person. I only fight when they're smaller than I am."

Her face brightens at his comment; a double row of very human teeth appear, neither straightened nor overly white.

Her nose wrinkles perceptibly as she smiles. "Come on in. I don't know whether to offer you a beer or a raw beefsteak."

It's not the apartment of a CDU official. Nothing upscale but the address. Simple, clean, uncluttered. Oversize pillows on the floor, Japanese prints on white walls. There's a low, black, varnished table in the middle of the sitting room to eat from, Japanese style. The place is airy, bright, and warm.

One piece is out of place, endearing like Martok's imperfect teeth, because it makes the place more human. Next to two woodblock prints by Ikato is a kitschy cuckoo clock with a female hunter poised for the bird to come out so she can take aim and miss.

"I don't force guests to take their shoes off," Martok says, "but it's kinder on the downstairs neighbors. I'll put your coats in the wardrobe."

They take off their coats and hand them to her. Kramer tries to remember if he's got yesterday's socks on, then figures what the hell. He and Randall both kick their shoes off in the vestibule, leaving them by the door, and follow her to the black table, sitting on the floor around it. Kramer hopes she'll bring up the offer of a beer again; he can use one to counteract his coffee jitters. She is looking hard at Randall, and he is returning the stare.

"Do I know you?" she says suddenly.

Randall shakes his head. "But it could be arranged."

Kramer sighs to himself, but Martok lets it go and turns to him.

"So what do you want to know about Reni, other than that she was a complete bitch?"

Kramer feels heat rise, waits for it to abate, then speaks. "You had a falling out several years ago."

She pulls out a pack of spiced Indonesian cigarettes and lights one, filling the room with the smell of cinnamon and cloves. She exhales a blue flume of smoke from her nostrils.

"You might call it that. Why the interest? She's dead. Let it rest."

"What came between you?" Kramer says.

"You doing her biography or you just nosey?"

He tries on a bright smile; it pulls his stitches. "A little of both."

"Let's just say you didn't bend to pick up your soap if you dropped it around Reni."

Randall snorts.

"I don't read you," Kramer says.

"Perhaps it's because I'm so coarse. Don't tell the chancellor. He thinks I'm a virgin. What I mean is she was a lying, self-serving little harpy who made a Hollywood starlet seem scrupulous by comparison. She swung both ways in bed and in the Parliament. You could never trust her vote or her fidelity. I should know. I was her ally in politics and lover in bed."

It takes a moment for this to sink in. Kramer refuses to believe it. Spite talking.

She jabs the cigarette into a clay ashtray, extinguishing it.

"You loved her, didn't you?" she says to Kramer. "Reni mentioned you."

He says nothing, merely nods.

"Lots of us did," Martok continues. "She was the kind of person who made you want to love her, to please her."

Like her father, Kramer thinks. Just like her father.

"I'd never been with a woman before Reni. You know how it was in the seventies '70s and early '80s. All great feminists together. Push the boundaries to the limit. One time through, might as well experience it all. Except that it became more than bed games for me. More than playing doctor with each other's bodies. You see, Kramer, I loved her, too. I'm just like you, except I finally saw her for what she was. She'd cut any deal, lay any two-legged anthropoid, to get her way. To stay in the limelight."

"But she was true to her ideals," he says.

Martok clucks her tongue. "Sometimes. Especially when the votes were there. Other times, like with the deployment of cruise missiles, she would suddenly come down with bronchitis. She voted for her own fame and succeeded in splitting the Left apart in the process. All that remains is a fragmented bunch of prima donnas in the Greens and Socialists, while the Right grows stronger daily."

"You're no longer on the left, as I understand it," he says. Tacit implication being: You're as hypocritical as the others; as divisive as you claim Reni to have been. It's the only way he can think of hitting back.

"So you buy it, my conversion?" She smiles knowingly at Kramer, then at Randall.

"You're telling me you're a mole inside the opposition? Come on."

"You come on. There's more I can do as a close adviser to the majority party than I could ever do as a minority critic. Those are the realities of the new Germany. You do what you can, where you can. You don't see me living the high life, do you?"

"No," Randall chimes in, looking about the apartment. "I certainly don't."

They exchange a long look and Kramer feels cut out. He also feels a hollowness, as if a piece of Reni has been carved out of him, for he knows that at least part of what Martok is saying is the truth.

"And what about Gerhard?" Kramer says. "What was he doing while you and Reni were having it off under the sheets?"

"Watching, probably. But I'm being crude again. Sorry. They were married in name only, like a cover for Reni. A safety net. And he was always there to catch her when she fell. I'll give him that. With arms outstretched. She called him her pillow. 'I left Pillow at Inheritance,' she would say when coming here to stay overnight."

Kramer stifles the desire to ask her if Reni ever talked about him. He looks up to see her peering into his face, compassion in her eyes.

"You *still* love her, don't you? You poor sod."

He flexes his hands under the table. Skepticism, Kramer, he tells himself. It's the first tool of a good journalist. She's managed to take the interview away from you. Worse yet, you've allowed it. So pull it together, suck up your self-pity, and get on with what you know best. "Did she ever talk to you of memoirs?"

"She never talked to me, period. Not since '89."

But she doesn't offer what happened then to rip them apart, and he has the feeling she won't tell, either. He remembers the gossip columns talking about a possible love affair between Reni and a close personal friend of Martok's, but put it down to small-mindedness and the urgency to sell papers. The sort of story Marty would love. Did Martok have her "pillow," too? Someone Reni wanted?

"So you had no personal contact whatsoever with her after that time. Is that right?"

"You're beginning to sound like a cop, Kramer," Martok says, lighting another fragrant cigarette. "There's something you're not telling me. Something big. Why do you think there are memoirs, anyway?"

"Because she made me the literary executor of them."

"What? Don't you have a regular job?" Which remark draws a traitorous laugh from Randall, and Martok exchanges glances with him once again. "So what about the memoirs?" she says.

"They're missing," Kramer replies.

"Maybe they never existed."

Randall butts in, "That's what the police believe."

Her eyes get big. "So you've already been to the police about this?"

"Yes." Kramer has a sudden need to lash out, to hit her with information as she's clubbed him. Infantile, but he allows it. "She had a publisher in Berlin," he says. "I believe these memoirs were so explosive that somebody killed her to suppress them."

The body blow takes its toll. Martok visibly winces, and Kramer plunges on.

"One of Reni's informants for the book, a former East German intelligence officer, died just before Reni's body was found. A hit-and-run accident, the police are calling it. I think that's too much of a coincidence to ignore."

She is shocked, slumping over the table suddenly as if in pain.

Finally, she hisses, "The bitch. Can't even allow me to hate her in death." She looks up at them. "I mean, a suicide you can be disgusted with, right? Even hate. But the victim of a murder? That's different. You've got to feel for someone who's been killed."

Her eyelids begin to flutter; a sudden thought. "So you're not just looking for these memoirs, are you, Kramer? In fact, you're looking for Reni's murderer."

"I'd like both," he says. "But I figure the memoirs will lead to the killer."

"Guess again," she says. "Reni's list of enemies was long and long. I could name a dozen possibilities in Bonn alone. She cut a wide swath."

"Why did you go to her funeral?" he asks suddenly.

She considers this for a moment as a muscle twitches in her jaw, a thick vein on her forehead pulses. "Just to make sure," she says. "To see the coffin and know she was out of my life for good."

"Just for the record"—Kramer stretches his leg under the table to work out a cramp in his right hamstring—"you didn't kill her, did you?"

She smiles. "I could have at one time. It would have felt good. And I'm what I'd call a pacifist." She shakes her head at Kramer, glances quickly at Randall. "No, I didn't kill Reni. But there are lots of people with less peaceful natures than mine."

"Such as?"

"Gerhard, for one. How long can you be a human pillow? I think he actually loved Reni, and that could be dangerous. She had to destroy love. It was like a warped sense of survival in her. She felt trapped by love. She hated it."

She says nothing more, and Kramer figures that's all there is for the time being. He pulls his legs out from under the table and stands, then Randall does the same, both of them making departure noises.

"But I've been a lousy hostess," she says. "Didn't even offer you a beer."

"It's not too late." Randall smiles broadly down at her.

"Would you really like one?"

"Not for me," Kramer says. He's not sure he wants to share a beer with someone full of so much hatred for the person he loved for so long. He's had enough debunking of myths for one afternoon.

"I'd love one," Randall says, sitting back down across the table from her. "You go on, Sam," he says, not taking his eyes off of her. "You've got other calls to make, but I've had enough for today." Then looking up at Kramer, he says innocently, "See you back at the hotel, okay?"

She makes no protests when Kramer goes for the door; and neither of them bother getting up from the table. Kramer slips on his shoes, laces them up, gets his coat from the wardrobe, and humps it on.

Randall and Martok are still staring at each other across the polished expanse of the table.

As Kramer leaves, he hears Martok saying again, "I'm sure I've met you before."

By eight o'clock that evening, there is still no sign of Randall. Kramer has a light dinner in the kitschy gasthaus where he lunched with Reni's father after the funeral. Over coffee, he pulls out his leather-covered notepad and an HB pencil and begins making notes. Events and people are rapidly mushrooming; he is losing sight of his path.

Reni's Death and Missing Memoirs, he writes at the head of the page. Then strikes out *Death* and inserts *Murder*.

The memoirs and murder are contingent upon each other, he knows. If there were no memoirs, there would be no motive for murder.

But there is corroboration for the memoirs: Pahlus in Berlin staked his career and publishing house on them; the mysterious Gorik seems to have paid with his life for participating in them; Reni's father had at least heard his daughter speak of memoirs, though he had never seen them himself. Martok knew nothing about them. Any other leads to follow in order to verify the existence of Reni's memoirs?

No. Kramer is a believer. He takes this first ladder and disposes of it.

So who stood to lose? he wonders. If Gorik fingered somebody who was a former agent for the East, say someone powerful in the West, and that person got wind of the memoirs . . . Clear enough, Kramer thinks. The penalty for treason, even with the game of the Cold War long over, is still death.

Kramer scrawls *Gorik's Information* on his list.

Then there is Martok's surprising revelation from this afternoon. Sexual politics can make for bad blood, but bad enough to murder for? And why now? Like Martok says, there was a time when she could have killed Reni, but not now. It's been several years since Reni was in Parliament. Or did she have secrets about those days that someone in Bonn wanted kept secret? Illicit affairs might be enough to ruin political careers in the USA, but in Germany? *That's if I can trust Martok's story*, he thinks. A big *if*. Could Gerhard have taken a final revenge for years of cuckolding?

But you have no proof of that yet, he reminds himself, finishing the coffee, which has now gone cool.

He closes his eyes. *But you know it's true, don't you? You know she was capable of everything Martok told you this afternoon.*

Kramer writes: *Martok's List*; *Gerhard?* He would need to talk with her further; get more names from Eva Martok of other people Reni was on the wrong side of. Were there people locally that would fit on such a list also? he wonders. Isn't crime most often a neighborhood affair? What about that near miss yesterday; the purple car? Who stands to profit from Reni's death? His mind races with mundane possibilities here. Is her property so valuable to someone like Schnelling and Walther that they would want to get her out of the way? Or did Reni offend some wacko like Frau Gruber who sought revenge? Village life is often claustrophobic enough to result in murder.

He writes *Local Angle?* but is not too excited about that. Then he taps the pencil against the pad like a drumstick, suddenly reverses it, and writes another two words: *Magnificent Seven*.

That's where Helmut's information takes him. He seemed convinced that somebody planted the bomb in the car, one of their group. Had Reni come to that conclusion as well? Or was she the one, and did Helmut figure that out? Lots to lose for him with his Prague business connection. Was yesterday's visit just elaborate theater for them?

Three more names on the page: *Helmut, Rick*, and *Gerhard*.

He does not bother with Maria. She is lost to them all. After a bogus trial in Prague, she was sentenced to twenty-five years in a maximum security prison. Years later, Kramer tried to trace her through a source in Charta 77. According to this man, a writer of political satire, Maria had died during her third year in solitary confinement.

Stupid, stupid children, he thinks. All just to throw some meaningless leaflets off a building: Down with tyranny. Down with the Soviet aggressor.

He looks at the list of names and subjects: Gerhard gets two entries.

And one final entry: *Reinhard Vogel—Neo-Nazi Connection?*

CHAPTER TEN

Still no Randall in the morning and Kramer goes ahead with plans to fly to Munich. A call to the Germany United offices is all that is needed to arrange an interview with Vogel for that afternoon. The guy loves publicity, negative or positive.

Kramer talks with Vogel's press secretary, a youngish-sounding woman with a sultry voice, a difficult task in German, and is as amazed as ever with how normal the new variety of Nazis are. That's the scary thing about them: they've learned how to package themselves, how not to scare off the border-line Fascist with rantings and ravings about extermination. But that stuff is still there, like a basso continuo, underlying their entire credo: racial purity; German nationalism; xeno-phobia, sentimentalizing the old days and the goodness of the land before godless machines ruined everything.

Germany United, with their computer banks, fax machines, and fleet of BMWs and Mercedes are hardly preindustrial.

Kramer packs up, pays the bill, but keeps the room in Bad Lunsburg, and leaves a note for Randall telling him he'll be back the following day. Just as he is handing the day clerk the message, in strolls Randall with a grin on his face so wide that his brown-stained front teeth show. He checks out the carry-on thrown over Kramer's shoulder, the paperwork on the counter.

"Ditching me?"

"It's in the note. I'm on my way to Munich. Want to come?" He booked two seats just in case.

"Is there time for breakfast?"

"On the plane, Randall. On the goddamn plane."

He takes Randall's arm and moves out to the taxi line in front of the hotel.

"Easy, Sam. Don't worry, be happy."

"Randall, you're an amoral cretin sometimes, you know that?"

"Whoa, now." Randall shakes his arm loose. "You're not serious, are you?"

Kramer goes to the lead taxi in the rank, a blue Opel, and pokes his head in the passenger's window, *"Flughafen, bitte."* Then turning back to Randall, "Just get in. We'll talk about it on the flight."

"Munich?" Randall asks.

Kramer nods, opening the back door, throwing his carry-on bag on the floor, and sliding across the seat to the far side to allow Randall space.

"But I haven't got my bag," Randall says.

"It's okay. Just get in. You never change your underwear, anyway."

Randall gets in, closing the door. "So what's eating you? Last night? You missed me? Or did you want her for yourself?"

"Piss off, Randall. You know what's bothering me."

"Sleeping with the enemy? Well, don't worry. I didn't, and she isn't. Turns out, I remind her of some swami dink she knew in the '70s."

Randall looks around, realizes they're on the freeway headed for the Cologne-Bonn airport.

"Christ, Sam, you made of gold? Don't they have buses that go to the airport?"

"I was waiting until the last minute for you." Which isn't exactly true; all the midday flights were booked by the time he called this morning, and he had to settle for one that would make him scramble to catch it. But why tell Randall that? he thought. Let him feel guilty.

You can be such a prick sometimes, Kramer.

"You know, Sam, you're not as bad as they say." Randall curls his feet up on the seat, crowding Kramer, getting cozy, hands behind his head leaning against the door. "The cushy life of a foreign correspondent." He yawns hugely.

"So how is our friend?" Kramer says, looking out his window at a low gray-white sky with crows gathering over wheat fields full of stubble and mire. The suburbs of Bonn approach to his left: neat white row houses with black-tiled roofs.

"I didn't say she was our friend," Randall replies. "Just not our enemy."

"Domestic or international?" the driver suddenly says, looking in the rearview mirror.

"Domestic," Kramer says to him, not bothering to add which airline: inside Germany there is only one. He turns to Randall, "Why do you say she's not our enemy?"

"'Cause she's still hooked on Reni. Beneath all the blather and out-front protestations of hate, she can't let Reni go any more than you can. And she's hiding something. I know that pretty sure. That's why I stayed."

"So what'd you find out?"

"That she sleeps in the nude."

Kramer shakes his head impatiently.

"I mean, I was sleeping on the couch," Randall hurriedly says. "It got late; we were talking. She cooked a nice omelet. We listened to old Stones albums. Like a time warp.

"Anyway, she was good enough to give me a berth for the night, and I was sleeping happily enough until sometime in the middle of the night I hear movement in the flat, pop an eye open, and see her bare-assed in the sitting room, fetching her mobile off the charger and taking it into her bedroom. Now who the hell would she be calling in the middle of the night? I was wondering."

"Who?"

"I never found out. By the time I tippytoed to her door, she was talking in a murmur. I couldn't hear shit; no names, no nothing. Maybe it was her swami friend."

"Swift work, Watson."

Randall shoots Kramer a smirking grin. "But I did get a chance to rifle her purse first thing in the morning while she was in the shower."

Kramer says nothing, checking the digital clock on the dash in front: 10:49. The plane leaves at 11:30.

"Want to know what I found?" Randall says.

Kramer does not reply, examining his cranky spirits, wondering how much they're the result of possible indiscretions on Randall's part, how much jealousy. *Why didn't she pick me?*

Grow up, Kramer.

"Eva's little black book," Randall says, ignoring the silence. "Appointments and phone numbers. Know what was written in the square under October twenty-eighth?"

Another smile; he's enjoying this. Kramer does not show impatience on his face, but he's interested.

"Phone Reni, 18:30."

This catches Kramer's attention and Randall nods vigorously at his surprise.

"As in October of this year," he adds.

"But she told us . . ." Kramer begins.

"That's right, Sam. No communication with Reni in years. I wonder why she'd tell a lie like that?"

They make Lufthansa Flight 181, but just barely. It's a race to concourse 22 for them, and Kramer is sweating and sucking air by the time they get there. The tickets are waiting for them at the door and a sour-faced stewardess, annoyed at late arrivals, inserts their seat assignments, before they are ushered into and through the connecting causeway to the waiting jet, its engines whining. More stares of business types as they board and find their seats in economy class on the port side, just under the middle exit.

The good news is that once above the clouds, it is a clear day, a sky as blue as a dream; the bad news is that it's a beverage-only flight, no food. Kramer is forced to listen to Randall's laments and growling stomach all the way to Munich.

Upon arrival, Randall devours three Mars bars at the first shop he sees. Once the rail link delivers them at the main train station, they walk fifteen minutes and then he's got to have a late lunch of kraut and wurst at a tourist trap just off the Marienplatz, dead in the center of the city.

Kramer's appointment is for four; there's no hurry. Vogel's office is nearby, according to the address the secretary gave him this morning. Last time he interviewed the man, it was in the apartment of one of his followers, a well-off architect. Now Germany United has offices three blocks from the main cathedral, the Frauenkirche. Coming up in the world.

"This shouldn't take too long," Kramer says as Randall mops up the meat juice on his plate with a caraway roll. "Where do you want to meet?"

Randall swallows hard. "I'm not going with?"

"No way. These jerks generally like press attention, free publicity of any sort. But they lump us into three categories.

There's the sensationalist boys from the illustrated mags who they charge for interviews and manipulate with bogus stories. There's the in-depth people who never pay for interviews, and who try to give balanced coverage of the neo-Nazi scene. And there are those who have an agenda, who guys like Vogel figure are only out to trash them. The Antifas, they're called. Anti-Fascists."

"Let me guess," Randall says. "You're in the middle category."

"So far. And I don't need you to blow my cover."

"But I'm a skinhead."

"Not with that beard, you're not. They get one look at you, they read punk or, worse, a *democrap*."

Randall picks another roll out of the basket on their table and wipes at his plate some more. "So what'd you write about Vogel before that's made him love you so much?"

Kramer ignores the attitude and tells him straight. He needs to refresh his memory before he visits Vogel, anyway.

"The truth. That he's part of a Nazi resurgence that is larger than anyone gives it credit for. An estimated half million members in three right-wing parties that are loosely affiliated. That they say out loud what most respectable Germans feel, but are afraid to express—Germany for the Germans; Germany as the leader of an ethnically cleansed Europe. Welcome to the fourth Reich."

Randall considers this. "So why bring me along? Comic relief?"

"How about we meet at the west door of the cathedral at six? It's important they know I've got an appointment afterward. That somebody knows where I am."

"I thought they loved you."

"Just as long as they believe I'm in one of the first two categories."

J. Sydney Jones

Kramer walks out into the main square, heavy with traffic and pedestrians. He's always liked Munich, for it's a city much like Vienna: slow, central European, Catholic. He passes by the Mariensäule, appreciates its baroque playfulness for the hundredth time. A city that worships Mary can't be all bad. Ahead of him, over the soot-blackened buildings at the far end of the square, he sees the twin golden onion domes of the Frauenkirche and smiles despite himself. Never a devout anything, Kramer can appreciate the art and architecture of Christianity without being burdened by its attendant baggage.

The afternoon is chill and damp; he feels it bite at his nose and cheeks, and digs his hands into the felt-lined, hand-warmer pockets of his oilskin. Got to put the jacket liner in when I get back to Vienna, he thinks as he leaves the square by the northwest corner.

In ten minutes, he's at the building where Germany United is housed. Perfect PR, he thinks, looking up at the fanciful late-nineteenth century creation with its turrets and sharp gables. A Mad-Ludwig pastiche in the heart of the city. From a window on the second floor, the red, black, and gold flag of the old German empire ruffles in the breeze, flanked on either side by long red and black banners from the Third Reich.

Pedestrians on the street look up as they pass, but seem unsurprised. Neo-Nazis are a way of life in the new Germany; part of the legitimate political scene, it seems. Kramer finds himself almost longing for the good old Cold War days when the Superpower rivalry kept such aberrations at bay. Or did it only focus our attention elsewhere, while the Right continued to build? After all, the Cold War was only a continuation of the Nazi war on Bolshevism, according to Neofascist ideologues.

Vogel's headquarters have the second and third floors all to themselves. Kramer was directed on the phone to go to the third. The stairs are blocked off, and he is forced to use a rickety elevator whose grillwork door closes with effort. Red-plush bench seat and beveled glass windows in the elevator cabin.

Kramer soon sees why the stairs are blocked. On the third floor, he is greeted by two men in brown shirts, black pants, and boots, sporting Nazi armbands. They are one step up from the skinheads in Hamburg; look as though they may have graduated from those very ranks. Short hair, heavy brutal faces with eyes that look right through Kramer; Heckler and Koch 9 mm submachine guns at the ready. Behind them stands a third man, huge and uncomfortable-looking in pleated pants, a polo shirt, and a sports jacket. He's the sort of no-neck who needs to be in a uniform of some sort—athletic or military—to look right. He does the frisking while the other two look on.

Security is up with the neo-Nazis ever since the shotgun slaying of the head of the National Front last year. Now every leader of every right-wing party has his own bodyguards; his own private militia, just like the good old days of the '30s.

Once they determine that Kramer is clean, they nod him toward a massive desk in the middle of the long corridor. More stage scenery: the corridor is a miniature nave from a Gothic cathedral; red banners are draped from the high vaulted ceiling; photos line the walls. A Nazi Hall of Fame: Hitler, Goebbels, Goering, Hess, even one of Röhm, for whom Vogel, Kramer remembers now, had glowing words during their previous interview. Much more fond of the SA than the SS, in fact. A point he made several times, as if that proved his ideological credentials.

"After all, Herr Kramer . . . may I call you Sam? After all, Sam, one cannot dismiss the Nazi state simply for presumed excesses of one kind. You must remember the historical situation. Germany was the bulwark against godless Communism. Ours was a defensive war against Bolshevism. Hitler had no wish to fight the West. Didn't Hitler create one of the first truly modern states, eradicating unemployment and instituting an annual ten percent growth rate in the economy? Find any state in today's world to match that record."

Chilling words when Kramer first heard them, but easily discounted, sitting in a private apartment with them decked out in their silly brown shirts, empty beer bottles littering a low coffee table. Playing at being Nazis.

But now the words take on power, backed by all this show. The movement obviously has money in back of it, Kramer figures, approaching the desk where a female secretary in white blouse and black skirt is seated. They obviously have police connections as well, he thinks, if they haven't been raided for illegal possession of firearms or for displaying all these Nazi artifacts. Advocacy of a return to National Socialism is still a crime according to the German constitution, the Basic Law.

The secretary is not the one Kramer talked to this morning; this one's voice is hard and dry. After getting his name, she uses the phone, announces him, gets orders, and then directs Kramer to a room at the far end of the hall. More guards are posted along the corridor leading to this door, their eyes never meeting Kramer's. He suddenly feels very alone and very vulnerable. Red carpet, red banners, limestone walls black with age, massive oak doors at the end of the hall. A guard, this one a cartoon reproduction of a Hitler youth with flaxen hair and cornflower-blue eyes, raps on the door for him.

From inside: "Enter!"

The young guard opens the door, ushering Kramer in.

"Sam. It's good to see you again."

Vogel is standing near the door in what is apparently a

reception room; both he and the room are a universe apart from the corridor outside.

"That'll be all," he says in German to the young guard. "I shall call if I need you."

"Very well, Führer," the kid says and closes the door reverently.

Vogel turns to Kramer, smiling, knowing the effect he's creating. Decked out in a light-green, double-breasted designer suit that costs easily what Kramer makes in a month, wearing an air of proprietorship in the midst of the huge corner room with originals of David Hockney and Willem de Kooning on the walls. Chrome and leather furnishing, deeply woven carpeting with earth-tone geometric designs, a view out the turret window to the Marienplatz and the spires of the cathedral beyond.

Vogel follows Kramer's eye, still smiling.

"We've come a long way. That's what you're thinking, isn't it?"

Kramer turns his attention to Vogel, nods and sits in the leather armchair offered him. "Quite a little dukedom."

"It looks as though you had an accident," Vogel says. "I hope it was nothing serious."

Kramer shrugs it away. "Slipped in the bathtub."

"Yes. One does not realize how much greater is the death rate by domestic accident than by violence. Reading some newspapers, however, you would not know that. One would assume that every broken nose in Germany is due to our overzealous cadres."

Kramer has the unpleasant feeling that Vogel knows about the incident in Hamburg the day before.

"But accidents in the bath are surely not what you have come to discuss, Sam. How can I help you? And by the way, thanks very much for the even-handed presentation in your article."

"It's called objective journalism."

Vogel catches the defensive tone in Kramer's voice, and raises his eyebrows. He sits in a low chair opposite Kramer, fastidiously straightening the crease in his slacks.

"I understand," Vogel says, crossing his legs. "Believe me, I understand too well. You don't much like me or anything I stand for. You're a liberal, of course. Most of the press is. That is why I thank you for not playing advocacy journalism despite your own feelings. It was an honest account, fair to all sides."

In other words, Kramer thinks, *I was used somehow by Vogel.*

"Planning a follow-up series?" Vogel asks. Like most of the world, he is conversant with media lingo. "It might be the propitious moment, after our recent stunning victories in Schleswig. Eight of our members elected to the state legislature. Not bad for a party once called 'fringe' and 'aberrational.'"

A trim thirty-eight-year-old, Vogel looks the part of an ad-exec rather than the leader of the strongest right-wing party in Germany. His presentation is upscale, as well. The threat has been delivered by the trappings in the corridor. In this inner sanctum, it's all reason and modernity by comparison. The effect has been intentional; you're meant to be drawn to Vogel in his business suit and Kennedy haircut, if only in reaction to the hysteria of the Nazi paraphernalia on the road to Oz outside the door.

Clever, Kramer thinks. *It almost worked with me.*

"There are a lot of good journalists covering the neo-Nazi scene nowadays," Kramer says. "They're taking you boys seriously."

"They should. We are very serious people."

"But I've come about a different matter. Renata Müller. Did you know her?"

Vogel does not blink; picks a bit of lint off his slacks.

"Of her, yes. The old Left is dying off. Her death is a metaphor, I should think. The old, useless liberals of the Federal Republic making way for the revitalizing strength of the Right."

"Yes. Nice metaphor. She was a friend of mine."

"I'm sorry."

It's unclear if he's sorry she was a friend or that she died. Kramer knows it is a calculated misunderstanding.

"What has she to do with me?" Vogel says.

"I was hoping you could tell me that," Kramer says. "Your car was reported parked outside Müller's house near Bonn around the time of her death."

"Sam, you disappoint me. I thought we were having an interview, not an inquisition. What story are you working on?"

"The murder of Renata Müller."

Still no reaction from Vogel. Kramer stays quiet. A tick plays at Vogel's left eye; he focuses harder on Kramer to stop it. Traffic noise sounds from outside; footsteps clack in the hall. Finally, "I read that it was a suicide. Have you become a private detective in middle age?"

Kramer ignores this, pressing on. "There are some loose ends to the case, you might say. Your visit is one of those."

Vogel sits absolutely still for a moment, not saying a word. Kramer can hear his own heart pounding; he did not mean to push it this far, this fast. It's a stupid move; he meant to go at it indirectly, to tease information out of Vogel under the guise of new articles. Perhaps get his opinion on various politicians, right and left, Reni being one of those.

But Vogel's glowing words about Kramer's article stung; he feels like a dupe. Simply covering the neo-Nazis gives legitimacy to them, makes them newsworthy. He feels part of the problem rather than part of the solution. So he struck out like a hurt animal.

J. Sydney Jones

"Sam," Vogel finally says, "any other reporter I would have my friends outside escort downstairs to the street. Understand?"

Kramer suddenly realizes he has failed to play his ace, neglecting to let Vogel know someone is waiting for him.

I've broken every goddamn rule there is, he tells himself, a sudden chill of apprehension passing over him.

"I don't know what you're after, but I feel obliged to help you as much as possible. This one time. No more. You say my car was parked outside Renata Müller's farmhouse. I will not even go into how you might have come across this information or why I, a private citizen, should be hounded for it, if it is true. Freedom of movement is, I thought, a fundamental right. I will only ask you what car and when."

Kramer locks eyes with Vogel; they return stares for a moment and Kramer is the one to finally look away. He pulls out his notebook, turns to the relevant page and reads the date as well as the license number of the vehicle.

Vogel shakes his head, smiling once again. "But, Sam, whoever traced that license for you neglected to tell you one thing. That car was stolen from me two months ago. Ask the police.

"And the date? I'll have to check, but I'm almost positive that I was attending an important party meeting that very night here in Munich."

He rises, "Is that all?"

Kramer flips the notebook closed. "I guess so." He stands and is taller than Vogel. They look at each other for a silent moment and then Kramer goes to the door.

"Sam," Vogel says as Kramer begins to open the door, "stick to journalism. I don't think there's much of a future for you in investigation. And watch out for that bathtub. Looks like a nasty cut."

Kramer says nothing, going back out into the corridor, past reception and to the elevator. He feels sweat down the back of his shirt as he presses the button for *Erdgeschoss*, ground floor. The assorted guards stare at him blankly as the elevator jerks into gear, taking him back to another world.

Once out on the street again, he takes a deep breath. If evil has a palpable form, it is inside that building.

So the car has been taken care of, he thinks. Handy that; a stolen car can beat all sorts of registry traces. Provides a neat little alibi.

Kramer walks down the street, taking more deep breaths, liking the feel of the cold air on his skin.

Vogel was there, Kramer knows. He wonders if Vogel caught his own slip, for Kramer had made no mention of what kind of house Reni lived in. Yet it was Vogel himself who mentioned it: *You say my car was parked outside Renata Müller's farmhouse.*

Neither did he mention the time of day, but Vogel offered the night meeting in Munich as proof he wasn't there.

Yes, Vogel was at Reni's all right. So why not admit it? What's to hide?

Kramer arrives at the cathedral well before six; no sign of an early Randall. He goes in, his head jerking upward to the incredibly high vaulted ceiling of the main nave, just as the architect intended him to. Simple lines in the nave; dazzling white, flanked by columns; stained-glass windows shedding warm light from the side aisles. Kramer takes a pew, sits amid the polyglot visitors, their guidebooks in hand. A few old girls are at the side altars praying, lighting candles, keeping tradition alive. But mostly it's tourists and the curious.

The visit to Vogel has chilled him; he sits huddled in his jacket trying to figure out what the connection between Reni and Vogel was. Something that he might kill for?

A tap at his shoulder. Kramer looks up to see a pleasant-faced Japanese tourist nodding and smiling at him.

"Please. Picture." He pokes his camera at Kramer, nods at a smiling Japanese woman standing ten feet away.

"Sure," Kramer says, getting up and taking the camera. The man shuffles to join his wife, and Kramer fixes them in the viewfinder, the space between their faces bisected by the crosshairs of the viewfinder. They stand there so trusting, so open and smiling that for an instant Kramer forgets Vogel and his insane form of pseudo-politics; forgets even Reni. He depresses the shutter button and the camera makes a healthy, tight click. It's an old metal-bodied camera, very little plastic. Sensible and practical, like its owners. Kramer takes an instant liking to both of them, and they bow at Kramer in thanks.

Just then, Randall strolls into the cathedral, peering myopically about. Kramer sees him, waves, and Randall joins him at the pew. Kramer has no opportunity to tell him of the visit to Vogel's, for Randall has his own news.

"I've found him," he says, his face pink with the cold. "The weirdest bloody coincidence."

"Found who?"

But Randall ignores him, "I was just strolling around the little streets of Schwabing, digging the scene, you know. Like the old days there, with college kids aping hip garb. Bell bottoms have made a comeback. You know that?"

"Found who? Gerhard?"

"And there's a shitload of galleries now. Munich's a Soho with pretzels. Most of it's crap, but there was some representational stuff that had a feel to it, you know? Life. Passion. Somebody spent some spunk over its creation, not just cold-blooded construction."

"It's Gerhard, isn't it? Where is he?"

But Randall ignores this. "One of the galleries had a whole series of nudes. I liked them, reminiscent of Lautrec, but then that's not a bad comparison. Reminiscent of someone else, too."

Not Gerhard, Kramer suddenly realizes. "Rick!"

Randall traces his hand over the cupid's head carved into the side of the pew in front, not looking at Kramer. "So I go in and check these out. The proprietor's a tough old bird in tweeds and brogues straight out of an English garden. In fact, she is English; been running the gallery for twenty years."

"Randall."

"I'm getting there. Turns out the paintings are a series about prostitutes. Just like Lautrec. Intentional. 'Postmodern pastiche,' she called it. I take a closer look at the paintings, at the lower right corner, and there it is. RF."

"Rick Fujikawa," Kramer says. "It's got to be him. Did you find out where she got them?"

"He lives right here in Munich. Has for the past fifteen years."

"You're kidding." But he notices a sudden gloom come over Randall.

"Only thing is, the old girl said something about an accident. He almost died."

They look at each other quickly. No more accidents, Kramer thinks. We've had enough of them.

CHAPTER ELEVEN

Rick's flat is on Thiemestrasse, not far from the Englischer Garten. Kramer can see the leafless elms and horse chestnuts in the park down the street as they get out of the taxi; can smell the heavy mulch aroma of green space in the midst of city. He's had time during the taxi ride to tell himself there are all kinds of accidents in the world; that Rick's doesn't necessarily have anything to do with their searches.

"Maybe we should call first," Kramer says as they approach the door to the apartment house. The building is postwar, square; not much imagination to it, thrown up in a hurry to accommodate a population sick from years of battle and death. A brick facade with occasional terraces jutting out of the uniformly flat surface.

"He's not listed, remember?" Randall tries the front door; it's unlocked and they enter the tiny vestibule with stairs leading directly upward.

Low ceilings, narrow hallways, the sound of televisions coming through thin walls. Not the sort of place an artist would rent, Kramer thinks. He tries to remember Rick, his tastes, his dreams. But all he comes up with is the face from the picture he found at Reni's. For having been such great friends, there is little remaining. Prague erased most of it.

This is Randall's show; Kramer lets him track the apartment down. It's on the fifth floor at one end of the corridor. An engraved card lit up under plastic on the door holds the same initials as the paintings: *RF*. Randall rings the bell. Kramer looks around the dim hallway. No one about. Randall rings it again; there is a shuffling sound from inside finally.

"Did the woman from the gallery say if he was up and about?" Kramer says. "I mean, we don't want to be dragging him out of bed."

The fish-eye peephole is covered from the inside for a moment; someone is checking them out.

"Hey, Rick . . ." Randall says. But he has no time to say more, for the door is suddenly kicked open against his head, knocking him back into Kramer. They stumble, but the corridor wall keeps them from falling. Getting his balance, Kramer looks into the double barrels of a shotgun pointed straight at his head.

"What do you want?" The woman aiming the gun is tall and scary looking with nostrils flaring and blonde hair teased impossibly high. Short leather skirt and thigh-high boots. The finger gripping the trigger has a black-lacquered nail. She speaks German with a southern accent, almost Austrian.

"We're here to see Rick," Randall says from in back of the door, and the shotgun tracks right to include him. He peeks his head around the door that has wedged him against the corridor wall. She jerks her head to the left for him to come out.

Kramer sizes her up, checks the distance, her hyper state, his chances of making a play for the gun without having his insides sprayed all over the walls.

She continues to glare at them both, and Kramer can sense she is losing it.

"We're friends," he says quickly in German. "We're not

here to harm anybody. We have no weapons." His mind races. *Reassure her*, he thinks. *Tell her anything to make that right forefinger ease off the trigger incrementally.*

Her jaw muscles work furiously as she stands between them and the flat; her breath comes in rapid bursts.

"You're the cocksuckers did it to him, aren't you?"

"What's she talking about, Sam?" Randall tries out his most winning smile on her, but she only squints her eyes at him, jabbing the barrels toward his stomach.

"I should blow you both in half."

Kramer thinks he knows the lay of the land, now. "We're friends of Rick. From long ago. Americans. We're not here to hurt him. Is that what you're afraid of?"

His words reach her, but she doesn't lower the gun.

"Maybe you could just ask Rick," Kramer says. "He'll tell you." *If he's here at all*, Kramer thinks. *Please be here, Rick. Please remember us.*

She looks at Randall, then back to Kramer. There is doubt in her eyes.

Good. Kramer takes a long breath.

"Look, goddammit," Randall says, waving the gun away. "I don't like having that thing pointed in my direction."

Maybe she does not understand the words, but Randall's tone comes through loud and clear. She instantly flexes again. Kramer has an insane desire to strangle Randall, feeling like one who has talked a suicide back from the edge, only to have a bill collector come to the window and begin hectoring.

"Honestly, miss," Kramer hastily says, "we are not your enemy. My friend's just nervous with that gun pointing at him. And we're not thugs, despite these bruises and bandages."

Another tense moment and finally she jerks the shotgun toward the door, gesturing them to go in front of her. "Hands on your heads!"

Kramer does as she says; Randall follows his lead. "She nuts, Sam?" he whispers.

Kramer says nothing. The flat is in darkness, all shades drawn, only a faint glow from under the door of one room. Kramer bumps into the edge of a couch, loses his balance for a moment, and feels the twin metal circles of the shotgun barrel dig into his back.

She directs them toward this one strip of light from under the door. "Open it," she hisses at Kramer. "Slowly. Keep your hands in plain view."

He feels the barrels at his back again, prodding. He does as he's told, twisting the metal knob and quickly raising his hands over his head once again. The door opens inward, and they enter a room full of mirrors, which make it appear there is an entire symphony orchestra of men with hands on their heads and blond Valkyries toting shotguns.

A circular bed is to the right, built partially into the wall. A figure lies there quietly. The light comes from a small bedside lamp that looks like a giant arachnid.

"I found these scum outside," the woman says. "They say they know you."

The form slowly sits up in bed, bandages on face and hands. Two eyes peer out of the bandages, deep brown and almond-shaped.

"Rick?" Kramer says. "It's me, Sam. Randall, too."

The eyes blink once, twice. Silence.

The barrels dig into Kramer's back.

"Rick?"

The figure slumps down again. Then a muffled voice speaks, "You silly sons of bitches. You almost got yourselves disemboweled." Then to the woman, in German, "It's okay, Margit. They're friends. Relax."

The barrels are removed from his back and Kramer has to

stop himself from turning on her and grabbing the gun out of her hands.

"What the hell's going on, Rick?" he asks.

A bandaged hand waves them toward the bed. "Have a seat. There's plenty of room on the bed."

But Margit gets there first, taking the front-row seat, laying the shotgun to her side on the black satin sheets and cradling his head in her strong arms. Kramer and Randall sit uneasily on the edge of the bed on the other side of Rick.

"What happened to you?" Randall says.

"He shouldn't speak too much," Margit says suddenly in passable English. *Playing linguistic possum before, apparently,* Kramer thinks. "He's got stitches," she adds, again in English.

"It's okay, babe," Rick says. Then to Kramer and Randall, "You are looking at a statistic, gentlemen. Another incident of violence against foreigners."

He tries to laugh, but the bandages choke off his mirth.

"They did this to you?" Kramer says. "Neo-Nazis?"

"They thought I was Chinese." Another muffled laugh. "Is that funny, Sam, or what? We all look alike to them. They can't tell the difference between a Vietnamese and a Japanese."

"Not so much talk, Rick," Margit says, now opting only for English. Then to Kramer, "He likes to paint in the red-light district. It's where we met."

"Don't believe a word she says, Sam," Rick says, but his voice comes from a distance, like listening to someone on a bad international phone connection. "She's the love of my life. Margit is a scholar, not a whore."

Margit raises her eyebrows at this, but it clearly pleases her. She strokes Rick's bandaged head.

"I was there the day it happened," she says. "A bunch of rowdies and skins came into the district."

She looks at Randall's shaved head, and Kramer now understands why she was so jumpy when she saw them through the peephole.

"They were out to carve any foreigners they found there soiling lovely German maidens. Jesus, as if it's not a job and as if I wouldn't rather have an Asian between my thighs than one of those fucked-up little kids who cry for their mommies when they come."

"Didn't I tell you, Sam?" Rick says. "A scholar."

She ignores this, and continues, "Well, they see Rick there painting and they go crazy. There were three of them who cut him. If not for the girls, they would have killed him."

"They love me there," Rick offers. "I've painted them all."

"We saw," Randall says. "It's how we found you. The lady at the gallery gave me your address."

"You were looking for me? Why?"

Kramer's mind is functioning again. "When did this happen? How long ago?"

Rick looks at Margit, shrugging. "Three, four weeks ago?" he asks.

She nods.

"How bad is it?" Kramer asks.

Rick hesitates. "The witch doctors say I'll be able to work again."

"They cut his hands badly," Margit says. "One tendon was severed."

"I won't be much to look at, I guess. Bandages come off in ten days."

"Don't worry, lover." Margit hugs him. "You'll be beautiful." She looks up at Kramer with tears in her eyes.

More silence, and then Rick's muffled voice, "Why were you looking for me? You hear about this? I wanted it kept quiet. It wasn't in the papers, was it? No names, no follow-up visits from the skinheads, I figure."

"No," Kramer says. "It wasn't in the papers." He decides on the direct approach. "Reni's dead. Did you know that?"

Rick sits up suddenly. "Reni? No way."

"Yes," Kramer says. "I'm afraid so."

"How? What happened?"

"They say it was suicide," Kramer says.

Margit looks at him warily, a wolf bitch protecting her pup. It's as if she knows they are bringing complications into Rick's life. Kramer senses loyalty in her; a loyalty so strong it will destroy anyone she perceives as Rick's enemy.

"I didn't hear," Rick finally says, slumping back down in bed. "I haven't got much news lately. Shit. Reni dead. She seemed so percolating last time I saw her."

Kramer exchanges glances with Randall. "You make it sound recent. Did you two stay in touch?"

Rick nods his bandaged head. "Just lately. I mean it must have been twenty years since I saw her. But she caught my exhibition, just like you. Came up to the studio one day like no time had elapsed since sixty-eight. Like it was just yesterday we talked last."

"When?" Kramer says.

"The first time? Maybe three months ago." He does not look at Margit for confirmation this time, and Kramer can see jealousy playing on her face.

"So you saw her quite a bit lately?" Kramer says.

"Every time she came to her meetings. Maybe once a month."

"What meetings?"

"Good old Reni. Up to her usual tricks. Scamming and being *sehr engagiert*. Told me she'd infiltrated some group of right-wingers. Became the trusted new Fascist in their midst, acting as if she'd given all the old leftist bullshit up for good. What a lark she was having! Last time, she was laughing out her ass about how she was gathering all this terrific information on the group. Sponsor lists, friends in high places in Bonn, all that kind of stuff. Even mention of connections in the skin trade."

Kramer sees Margit blush at this bit of information, but Rick does not notice, continuing with his story. "I thought Reni was going to pee her pants telling me about it. That's how I'd like to remember her: laughing at the world. She sure didn't seem suicidal at the time."

"She didn't mention the name of the group, did she?" Kramer says.

"God, I don't know. They all sound like something out of a bad World War Two movie. Besides, I only half-believed her. Reni loved to fabricate. That was what made her fun to be around. She talked about memoirs, too. 'Jesus,' I said, 'they're for old farts.' But she only smiled. Great smile she had. Wish I could have painted that some time. You know one side of her mouth was lower than the other? She cut it when she was a kid."

Kramer nods, remembering her lopsided smile. "Did you see her after you were attacked?"

"No," Margit says. "There were no visitors."

"So what's the mystery, Sam?" Rick says. "Why all the questions? You don't think her death had anything to do with me getting cut?"

Margit looks at the bandage on Kramer's forehead; examines the bruises on Randall's face. She does not like what she sees.

"You need to sleep, lover," she says.

"Sam?" Rick says. "You didn't answer me."

"I don't know, Rick. There just seems to be a lot of violence coming down lately."

"It's a violent world."

"Yeah," Kramer says. "I guess so." Then, "Someone killed Reni. I'm pretty sure of that."

Rick does not reply; his eyes blink at them some more.

"She always played it close to the edge," Rick says finally. "It was only a matter of time before somebody finally gave her a shove."

The old hotel in Bad Lunsburg is beginning to look like home away from home. The potted palms cheer Kramer as he enters the lobby; the look of recognition from the desk clerk is reassuring.

"Morning, Karl."

The clerk nods. "He is calling again. The one from Paris."

Turning, the clerk plucks a sheaf of notes out of Kramer's pigeonhole. "Five times yesterday. Three times already this morning. Is he a relative, Herr Kramer?"

"Worse," Kramer says, taking the notes from Karl. "He's my employer. Thinks he owns my soul."

"Employers are *dreck*," Karl says, then feels he has overstepped himself. "If you don't mind my saying so."

"My sentiments exactly." Kramer looks at the notes briefly. Pretty much the same message in all of them: Get back to Vienna or else. One of them, however, is not from Marty. The rest Kramer tosses in a wastepaper basket on his side of the counter and then goes to the row of phone booths in a far corner of the lobby.

Randall, meanwhile, has taken himself off to the breakfast room. Another rotten trip on the plane back from Munich this morning as far as Randall was concerned: rolls and coffee only. No real nutrition. Randall suddenly seems to need nutrition all the time. Like cheese; like meat. Funny thing about that, Kramer thinks, entering a vacant booth and placing the message in front of him on a tiny plastic tabletop. When he's being bankrolled, Randall forgets about being a vegetarian.

Kramer slides his Visa card through the magnetic strip

reader and dials the number on the message. Three beeps later, Pahlus is on the line in Berlin.

"You called?" Kramer said.

"Aah, yes, Mr. Kramer."

His voice sounds up today, Kramer thinks.

"I just wanted to thank you."

"For what?"

"Well, for taking care of things as you did. Very honorable of you. We at Real Editions are most grateful."

"Hold on, friend," Kramer says, watching the cost of the call tally on the red digital display in front of him. "I don't think I follow at all."

"The advance," Pahlus says, becoming impatient. "To thank you for returning the advance."

"You got your money back? The eighty thousand?"

A pause from the other end. Then, "It was from the Müller estate. I thought that you must have . . ."

"Hey, I'm only the literary executor. I don't schlepp marks around."

"I see. Then I am sorry."

"Don't be. When did you receive this little windfall?"

"Yesterday. The cover letter says from the estate of Renata Müller, et cetera, et cetera."

"That'll be her father, then. She must have left a stipulation in the will."

"That explains a lot, doesn't it?" Pahlus says.

Again, Kramer feels one step behind. "Like what?"

"Reni providing for us. Not leaving us in the lurch. I mean, if she was going to kill herself, the honorable thing would be to somehow cover her debts. I told you she was the most truthful person I ever met."

"Yeah. I'm very happy for you."

Talk to Eva Martok if you want to know about Reni's honesty, Kramer thinks.

"Mr. Kramer?"

"I'm still here."

"Maybe it's as the police there say. Maybe she really did commit suicide. Maybe there were no memoirs, after all. Why else would she make such a stipulation in her will?"

Kramer thinks a moment. "I don't know there was such a stipulation. Only a guess. And why appoint me literary executor for memoirs that never existed?" he counters. "You can't have it both ways, Pahlus. Either she was honest about everything, or not."

Silence from Berlin for a time. "I suppose you're right," Pahlus finally says. "But this money could not have come at a better time for us."

"Answer me one thing, Pahlus. If I find the memoirs, you still interested in publication?"

"Well . . ." His voice sounds pained, like the mention of memoirs gives him a stomachache. "I would have to confer with my colleagues."

"So it was the money," Kramer says.

"Look, without Reni to back them up, any allegations made in the memoirs would be meaningless, wouldn't they?"

"And you alone would be responsible for any libel charges," Kramer says. "That's what you really mean, isn't it?"

More silence. Then, "We've come a long way from our initial meeting, Mr. Kramer. I felt quite cordial toward you then. But suddenly, you are combative. Suddenly, you are only interested in finding fault. I tell you: find the memoirs and I'll talk with the publisher."

"You have a contract," Kramer says.

"With a dead person, Mr. Kramer. Hardly valid. Has something gone wrong? You sound out of sorts. Unbalanced. Perhaps you're too close to this matter to investigate it objectively."

"Thanks for the advice. Invest in government bonds," Kramer says, and hangs up.

"Dickhead," he says to himself. "I'll give him objectivity."

Then he wonders, *Am I too close to this? Am I pushing too hard, looking for connections where there aren't any? Is that why the world is full of coincidences lately, because I'm manufacturing the connections in my head?*

But Vogel isn't a manufactured coincidence, he reminds himself. He was at Reni's farm. He as much as admitted it.

And was Rick a coincidence? Kramer wonders. Perhaps some of Vogel's goons traced Reni to Rick. Maybe they wanted to teach Rick a lesson for messing around with the purity of a German woman. That sort of thing. It's happened before. It's the reason for the deaths of more than one Turk or Vietnamese lately.

And if Reni made off with names of donors and secret members of Vogel's party, would that be reason enough to eliminate her?

A knocking at the glass of the phone booth brings him out of this analysis. Randall is munching on a sandwich. White fat of smoked ham hangs over the edges of a poppy seed roll. Kramer looks more closely at the sandwich: actually it's Westphalian ham, much moister than prosciutto, more like raw bacon. He shudders watching Randall chomp contentedly.

Randall says something, but Kramer cannot make it out and opens the door. Randall continues to mouth more silent words, then grins broadly and laughs at his stupid joke.

"Piss off, Randall."

"Come on, Sam. Enough with the Hamlet stuff. Who'd you call?"

"Pahlus. Seems Reni's will must have provided for the return of the advance."

"No shit."

Kramer says nothing, getting up from the bench and exiting the tiny booth.

"But that means . . ."

"I know what that means. Or indicates. That she suspected she was going to die."

"Which makes it look like suicide again."

Kramer considers this. "Or that she knew she had enemies."

Randall squints to show how little he thinks of this theory, then takes another bite of the ham sandwich.

"We don't even know if Reni was the one who provided for the money," Kramer says.

Randall swallows, picks a string of fat from his teeth, looks at it appreciatively for a moment, then flicks it off his fingers like nose-pickings.

"Right, Sam. So you're saying Herr Müller just decided to lay eighty thousand on a leftist publication because he's such a public-spirited guy."

"Could be."

"Not in this life. What's in it for him?"

"Who knows? But it's worth checking on."

Randall has the courtesy not to ask him how he intends checking on it, but merely follows him out of the hotel and through the main square to the old town hall. They enter the building opposite this and go straight up to the offices of Schnelling and Walther. The secretary is filing her nails today, looking as pretty as ever, but surprised to see him.

"I'd like to see Schnelling," he says.

"Do you have an appointment, Herr Kramer?"

He smiles at her. "No. But they're expecting me." He heads for Schnelling's door.

"But you can't go in now, Herr Kramer. They're in conference."

Randall shrugs his hands at her as if to apologize for

Kramer's manners, and they enter the office to find Schnelling bent over the desk. Walther is standing next to him and has his arm draped over the smaller man's shoulders. They are examining an architect's model of what appears to be a housing development. Schnelling looks up angrily at the intrusion, the skin around his mouth red and raw-looking.

"What is it, Fräulein . . ." He stops when he sees Kramer in the doorway. "Herr Kramer." A false smile from Schnelling. Walther smiles at him, as well.

Kramer feels loved.

"I wasn't aware we had an appointment," Schnelling says, turning his back to the desk. Walther does the same.

The trained seals, Kramer thinks. "We *don't* have an appointment. But I have an urgent question and didn't want to have to wait until next week. I didn't think you'd mind."

Schnelling does not move from the desk. "Well, if it is important. How can we help you?"

"Renata Müller's will. Was there a stipulation in there for eighty thousand marks to be paid to Real Editions in case of her untimely death?"

Schnelling and Walther exchange glances. Randall hovers behind Kramer, half in and half out of the office. No polite have-a-seat today.

Finally, Walther answers in his deep radio announcer's voice, "I'm afraid that is privileged information, Herr Kramer. We cannot divulge it."

"It's a matter of public record," Kramer says.

Walther shakes his long head. "No. It is made known to the federal bureau of taxes, perhaps, but not public."

"Look," Kramer says, attempting to be reasonable, though he does not feel that way at all. "I'm an executor in her will. She had a contract with Real Editions. I should be able to know these facts."

Another shake of Walther's head. "Why not ask Herr Müller? Maybe he will tell you. But I am sure you understand our position, Herr Kramer. The professional restrictions . . ."

Kramer tries to get a look at the architectural model in back of them on the desk and both Schnelling and Walther follow his gaze.

"What you got there?" Kramer says. There is something familiar to the layout.

"Oh, nothing," Schnelling says, folding his hands together in front of him. "A little project of ours."

Kramer approaches, and Walther sits on the desk as if to hinder his view.

"More row houses," Kramer says, getting closer to the desk. "More suburbia. I thought you boys were lawyers, not developers."

"Really, Herr Kramer," Schnelling finally protests. "I don't know what business it is of yours. Now if you do not mind, we have a lot to do."

But Kramer is close enough to see why the model looks familiar. The core of it is Reni's farmhouse; what's left of the acreage around it has been subdivided into five other kitschy-looking farmhouses for tired execs.

"Nice," he says. "I bet Reni would have loved that. How long have you gentlemen been waiting for her to die, anyway?"

"Really, Herr Kramer, I resent that," Schnelling splutters.

Walther gets off the desk now, standing eye-to-eye with Kramer.

"I think it's time you left, Herr Kramer. Before we are forced to call the police."

Kramer nods, but does not move, staring at the desecration of Inheritance. It was the one thing Reni wanted never to change; the one thing that held meaning for her in an ever-changing world.

"You seem desperate to impute improper intentions, Herr Kramer," Walther says. "I don't know what your problem is. Do you believe the whole world is in a conspiracy against you? That everyone held a dagger hidden under a cloak to kill Frau Müller? I assure you, nothing could be further from the truth. Renata Müller killed herself. The property reverted to the inheritor whose representative found worth in the housing scheme you see before you. That is his concern. Not yours. And surely not Frau Müller's, for she is dead and gone. Now, good day."

They walk for a time along the town's newly cobbled streets, Kramer saying nothing, hands stuck in his pockets, seething. Finally, Randall taps him on the shoulder.

"How about we eat lunch, Sam?"

It is all Kramer needs to set him off. "Christ, Randall! Is all you can fucking think about is your stomach?"

An old lady dressed in chic country clothes leading a long-haired dachshund on a leather leash crosses to the other side of the street at the sound of Kramer's angry voice.

Randall squints at him. "No, I can think of lots of other things, Sam, since you ask. Like why you're as tight as an overwound watch. Like why you're beginning to see killers in every closet. Like how maybe you could use a beer and some food to bloody well slow down. But I'm sorry to be such a bore for suggesting it."

Kramer feels the heat leave him to be replaced with shame.

"You're right, Randall. Sorry. Okay?"

Randall shrugs. "If you say so."

"No sulking, please. I say I'm sorry, you say that's okay. That's the way it's supposed to go. Get the drill?"

"I mean we can't just go bursting into lawyers' offices, Sam. Even I know that. You might as well have accused them of killing Reni for her property. You can't believe that."

Kramer is not sure what he believes anymore.

"I think you're right," Kramer says. "It is time for lunch. Then we'll have a talk with Herr Müller."

CHAPTER TWELVE

Karl-Heinz Müller doesn't come into the office anymore, according to the secretary at the International Development Bank. He's semi-retired, she tells Kramer over the phone.

"Besides, with fax and a modem, your office is anywhere."

Which makes Kramer wonder if the person he's talking to is even at the bank offices, or is tucked away in a neat little bungalow with her fax and modem plugged in and the afternoon soaps from the United States turned down low on the television.

He knows the address in the Bad Godesberg section of Bonn. He and Randall take the local train and walk from the suburban station. It's villa land here; not as swank as Helmut's Elbchaussee, but you couldn't touch one of these villas for under a million marks, Kramer reckons. Yards large enough to be called parks; two- and three-story structures in styles from neoclassical to flat-roofed international; here and there, the conical roof of a gazebo amid beds carefully mulched in leaves and pine boughs.

Müller's is on Fleischauerstrasse, Butchers' Lane, a rather downscale name for this upscale neighborhood. The house is very much like the ritzy villas in Vienna's wealthy suburbs, Kramer thinks. Pale yellow with forest green trim on the door and shuttered windows. There's a tall spiky wrought-iron fence around Müller's grounds and an intercom at the gate. Kramer pushes the black button and announces himself. There is no verbal response, but the gate buzzes unlocked, and he and Randall enter onto a cobbled drive leading up to the massive front door intended for the passage of carriages. A smaller door is cut into this, and it opens as Kramer puts a hand to the ring knocker, revealing a stooped, gray-haired woman who is old and old. Her right hand resting on the latch bears knotted blue veins like the roots of an oak.

"Traudl," Kramer says, as surprised as the woman herself is. "You're still . . ." he stops himself from saying *alive*, "with the family."

The old woman's eyes light up as she slowly focuses on him; recognition comes with a smile. "Mister Gerhard. You've come back."

Kramer shoots Randall a glance. "No, Traudl. Not Gerhard. It's Sam. Sam Kramer." He takes her frail hand in his, smiling into her wrinkled face.

"Sam?" She says it like a foreign word. "Miss Renata's Sam?"

He nods, squeezing her hand.

She looks confused. "But Miss Renata isn't here any longer. Haven't you heard?"

"I know," Kramer says. "We've come to see Herr Müller."

At the word *we*, she glances at Randall, visibly wincing. He is obviously not her idea of an ideal visitor in the afternoon, or any time of the day.

"I wonder if you remember Randall," Kramer says. "He knew Miss Renata in Vienna."

She shakes her head. There is a fleck of white spittle in the corner of her mouth; a pink tongue darts out to clean it.

"It must be . . . what? Twenty years?" Kramer says.

"All of that." She looks at him keenly; she must be in her eighties but, despite the fact she mistook him for Gerhard, it is obvious she retains all her faculties. Faithful Nanny, Reni used to call her. Surrogate mother, filling in the holes Reni's father could or would not.

"And you're still working?"

She laughs at this lightly as if it were the silly question of a five-year-old.

"Do I look like a worker?" She peers up at him. Permanently stooped over, she has to crane her neck to speak to him. "I've been an official leech on the state for the past fifteen years. Retirement is shit, if you don't mind my saying so, Sam. I've just come over to help Herr Müller sort through Miss Renata's things. He doesn't know what to do with them all. I suggested he burn them, move on with what's left of his life. But he is stricken, Sam. Stricken. He insists we go through everything with a fine-tooth comb, separate the effects into piles of save, toss, give away. Tedious man."

She takes her hand out of Kramer's, wiping it on the housecoat she is wearing like someone determined to get down to work.

"But what are we doing talking out here? Come in, come in. Have a cup of coffee. Bring your friend along."

Kramer smiles at Randall. "Come on, friend. You're invited, too. Just don't track in any dirt."

They follow Traudl into the entryway and up the back stairs that lead to the kitchen. He remembers his first visit here with Reni; that was in 1969, after the year in Vienna, and she wanted to bring him home to meet her family. Her mother was still alive then, but failing already, and Traudl had obviously run the domestic scene for some time. Herr Müller had been distantly polite, but upon that first visit, Traudl asked only one question, "May I wash your clothes for you?"

Kramer smiles as he remembers this inauspicious beginning; it took him several years to win the old lady, not that he had cared or tried, but they became real friends by about the time Reni decided to leave him.

She takes them into the kitchen, sits them at a table built into a nook in one corner with a window looking out to the back garden. There is a glass enclosure below, steamed over.

"You will have coffee," she says, turning on the stove under the kettle and filling a filter cone with ground coffee. *She never did wait for answers*, he thinks.

"Is Herr Müller available?" he says finally.

"Swimming." She inclines her head toward the window. "An extravagance, I told him when he was putting it in."

Kramer looks back out the window. The glass enclosure houses a swimming pool; he can see movement inside.

"But he does enjoy his swim. Keeps him fit, not like me. He still stands tall. Likes to wear them skimpy trunks, too, so that everybody can see how tall he is down there, as well." A cackle, like leaves burning.

She bustles about the kitchen, putting cups and several slices of coffee cake on the pine table. The water comes to a boil, and she pours it over the grounds. The faint smell of skunk comes from the coffee, then a richer, fuller aroma. Kramer keeps his eyes on the indoor swimming pool below. Müller is doing nonstop laps like self-abuse.

Traudl sets the coffeepot on the table, sitting across from Kramer, cocking her head to one side so as to get a look at him. Otherwise, because of her stoop, she'd be staring down at the table. Her eyes are a pale blue, like shallow water, and he has always been aware of them. They are liquid now, a tear builds up and leaks from the corner of her right eye.

"Why did she do it, Sam? Why?"

Kramer thinks a moment, wondering if he should tell her of his suspicions.

"She talking about Reni now?" Randall asks, not waiting to be served but tipping the white ceramic pot over his cup and filling it with deep black-brown brew.

Kramer nods, then looks back to Traudl. "I have no idea," he says. "But I'm trying to find out."

"Everything to live for," Traudl says. "Her whole life before her."

Or thirty-plus years of it, anyway, Kramer tells himself, if you go by insurance actuary tables. But to a woman of Traudl's age, mid-forties must seem like youth.

"Did you stay in touch?" Kramer asks her, pouring coffee for himself.

Traudl daubs at the tear with the sleeve of her housecoat, sniffs defiantly, then attempts to square her bowed shoulders. One of life's battlers.

"At Christmas and Easter. That sort of thing. She was a busy woman."

"When was the last time you saw her?"

She thinks about this; normally, her entire head would have looked upward, as if that was where thought originated. Now only her eyes can roll up, the cornea half hidden by her upper lid, revealing half-moon slices of yellow-white below.

She blows air through her lips finally, making a plosive, despondent sound. "I'm not sure. Isn't that awful? An old lady losing her memory. Maybe three months ago. Or two." She shakes her head, annoyed.

"What was she like when you saw her?"

"Like?" Her eyes go up again. "Tired. I think she had been playing tennis that day. Her wrist hurt, she said. Complained like an old person about the way her body was slowing down."

Kramer gets more direct, "I mean, did she seem despondent to you at the time? Depressed?"

She shakes her head. "Sore muscles, maybe. But my Miss Renata wasn't the depressed sort. Never played the role of

the hothouse plant. She was too busy giving the world hell."
Another mirthless cackle. "Two kinds of people in this world,
Sam. Those who get depressed and those who make others
depressed. We both know which one Renata was."

Kramer sips the coffee; it's warm and full of flavor.

"That's pretty much what I was thinking," he says. "She
wasn't the suicide type."

An eye blinks at Kramer, turns down to the table, then
peers back at him, squinting. "What are you saying, Sam? She
didn't kill herself?"

Kramer takes another sip, not responding.

There is silence in the kitchen for a time. Kramer sees
boxes stacked here, some of the same ones he saw the movers
packing at Inheritance. A Black Forest clock hangs from one
wall with a tiny wooden man perched outside the hole, stick
rifle in hand, waiting for the bird to pop out at the hour. This
vaguely reminds him of something, but he does not know
what. On the wall opposite, sits a massive credenza, its open
top filled with blue-and-white onion-pattern Bavarian por-
celain.

"You're saying someone maybe killed my Miss Renata?"
Traudl asks again. The clock ticks loudly in the ensuing
silence. "Is that what you're saying?"

"I don't know," Kramer says. "I'm trying to find out."

"If that's true, if somebody killed her, you let me know.
You let me know and I'll find the bastard. You let me know."

Kramer gets up and moves around the table to her, putting his arm around her brittle, bent body. She is all bones and
angles, and is trembling under his touch.

"Easy now, Traudl. I'm sorry I upset you. I don't know.
There were supposed to be memoirs and I can't find them.
But I don't know. Okay? Maybe it was a suicide, after all.
Maybe there were no memoirs. Maybe she was sick."

It's the first time this possibility has entered his mind. *Smooth move, you idiot*, he suddenly thinks. *You haven't checked that angle out yet. Haven't even tracked down her doctor.*

Traudl jerks away from his half-hearted embrace, squinting a rheumy eye at him again.

"Well, of course there were memoirs," she says, treating him once again like a silly five-year-old. "That's what she was doing when I visited. Working on the memoirs."

Kramer feels his heart race. "You saw them? I mean she was working on them when you were there? She didn't just tell you about them?"

"Yes, I saw them. A stack of paper this high." She pinches thumb and forefinger together, then opens them a good inch and a half apart. "That big. I told her it was ridiculous for a young person like her to be doing her memoirs already. That was something for old age. But then she said a funny thing. It all comes back to me now that I think of the stack of papers. 'Traudl,' she said, 'I feel old. Real old.' She always was a silly girl. Just a puppy and talking about feeling old."

Moisture builds up in her eyes again, but Kramer does not try the comforting embrace this time.

Before leaving her, he looks again at the clock.

"That was Reni's?" he says.

She follows his eyes to the wall, and then lets out a little snort of amusement.

"Hardly. One of Herr Müller's passions, collecting those stupid things. He has one room that does nothing but click and cuckoo nonstop, there are so many. Funny, though. I recall a matching one hanging there when I worked for the family. With a female hunter instead of male. I wonder what he did with it? Herr Müller was always so particular about his clocks, wouldn't allow any of the help to dust them, but had to do it himself up on a step ladder, looking a right fool."

Müller is still doing laps when they go below to the pool. The smell of chlorine is coming off the heated water. Kramer slides the glass door open, but Müller does not notice their presence for two more laps, catching a glimpse of them out of the corner of his eye as he dips his head underwater, his stroke smooth and strong, his body gliding through the water like it was made for that medium. He slows now that he knows he is no longer alone and, reaching the far end, he pulls himself partly up on the ledge, resting on his elbow. He isn't even breathing hard, Kramer notices. There is not an ounce of fat on his tanned torso.

"Sam," he says. "I was just thinking of you. Care for a swim?"

Kramer shakes his head.

"How about closing the door in back of you?" he says in English to Randall. "That's a good fellow."

Randall does so. It is warm inside, and the chlorine clears Kramer's sinuses. White plastic chairs are grouped around a table at Müller's end of the pool, and Kramer heads for these as Müller pulls himself out, water pouring off his back and thighs in thick rivulets. He sees what Traudl means about the bathing outfit: a bit of bikini that goes up the old man's ass and bulges around his sagging balls in front. Kramer notices a puckered angry circle of flesh near the top of Müller's right leg as the man dries off with a large white towel. Müller catches his gaze, looks down at the scar.

"My war memento," he says, staying in English for the sake of Randall. He drapes the towel over his shoulders and joins Kramer and Randall at the table. As Müller brushes his wet hair back, Kramer notices what seems to be another scar under his left upper arm close to the armpit: a wrinkled bit of gray like a tiny sand dollar.

"Sorry to disturb your workout," Kramer says, waiting for

an invitation to sit. None is given; Randall sits anyway. Müller's cold gray eyes glance at him momentarily. No recognition.

"This is an old friend of Renata's," Kramer says. "Randall, Mr. Müller."

Randall rises and offers his hand; Müller takes it momentarily.

"She had so many," he says. "Old friends, that is."

"Like Pahlus?" Kramer says.

Müller finally sits, waving a hand at the other chairs in silent invitation.

"I know nothing about Herr Pahlus, but that he is now a somewhat richer man than he was yesterday."

"Reni's will?" Kramer says, and Müller nods.

"It was a stipulation," Müller says. "Like you were." A wry smile.

"He gave her an advance against her memoirs," Kramer explains.

"It is no business of mine."

Kramer persists, "But she did say in her will that he be left eighty thousand?"

Müller is busy drying between his toes and looks up. "Was that the figure? I don't concern myself with such things. I merely followed the directions of my daughter's will."

"Didn't it seem odd to you?" Kramer says.

Müller looks up at this. "Odd? Everything my daughter did for the past twenty-five years seemed damned odd to me. Should I be keeping track? No, Sam, what seems odd to me is that you're coming around here asking questions. That you're coming around lots of places asking questions. That seems odd to me. Damned odd and impertinent."

Kramer finds the choice of words interesting. "I'm a journalist, Herr Müller. I think there's a story here. I think the police have missed something."

"And I'm her father, Sam, I'm asking you to keep your nose out of where it does not belong. Renata killed herself. Isn't that enough for you?"

"There was no note."

"To hell with the note." He rises, the towel falling away from his shoulders. His body is one tightly wound coil of tendons; his fists curl and uncurl spasmodically.

"She is dead, Sam." He makes a great effort to calm himself; it shows on his face as if he is smelling feces. "Let her rest in peace. She was tormented enough in life."

"How tormented?"

But Müller is completely in control once again; the chink in his calm facade repaired.

"Her politics, her ruined career. Perhaps *tormented* is too strong a word. But she was not a happy person. She became too inward-looking. As a girl, she was so full of life, full of movement and activity. But then after that year in Vienna, she was no longer the Renata I knew. She changed."

"It's called growing up, Herr Müller," Randall adds. "We all do it."

Müller stays standing and ignores this comment as if it is a pesky mosquito in the periphery of his life. Goosebumps stand out on his tanned flesh; his body is completely hairless as if he shaves himself.

"What are you saying?" Kramer finally asks.

"To forget it. My daughter, your former friend, is beyond us all now. Nothing can bring her back. Your inquiries only sully her memory."

"Bad for business, is it?" Randall says under his breath, and Kramer shoots him a sharp look.

The comment goes unnoticed, apparently. "I'm asking you as her father," Müller says. "Leave it. She killed herself. There were no memoirs."

Kramer waits a moment, then delivers the parting shot, "That's not what Traudl says."

Müller takes the information without a blink. "Traudl is an old woman of unreliable memory. Is that all you have managed to discover for your trouble?"

"Who told you we've been asking questions?"

But Müller does not field this one, staring at Kramer like a piece of meat at the butcher's. "I don't think we have anything further to discuss, Sam. I'm disappointed."

"Yeah," Kramer says as he and Randall get up and move toward the sliding glass door. "Life is a pretty disappointing place."

They leave Müller standing alone on the white tiles surrounding the pool, the black strip of bikini at his groin like a soiled tourniquet.

"What's he hiding?" Randall says as they shut the gate behind them.

Kramer looks back at the house and sees Traudl at a window. She waves a good-bye from the parlor upstairs, her hand moving like a broken bird. Kramer grins up at her, then turns to Randall.

"Maybe it's like you said. Reni's bad for business. He just wants her dead and gone so he can get on with life."

"So why's he going over her effects like an archaeologist in search of a Rosetta Stone?"

Kramer says nothing; something else is preying on his mind. They continue walking along the quiet residential street.

"Hello, Sam? Remember me? Randall? The guy who asks questions that you ignore?"

"Sorry," Kramer says, stopping suddenly. "I need to get to a phone."

Reaching a main intersection with shops and banks, Kramer finds a phone stall, a little half-bubble of plastic just big enough to cover the phone and a caller's head. Once his head is stuck underneath the hood, it begins raining. Light at first, but steady, building up into rivulets on the plastic hood. His call is transferred and he's put on hold, listening to canned Mozart for a time. Then a woman's voice comes on and gives him information, and he hangs up.

Randall, meanwhile, has found cover in the doorway of a lingerie shop and is busy ogling the merchandise and the fashionable women coming and going.

"We're in luck," Kramer says. "She's home sick today."

Randall rubs his hands gleefully. "Oh, happy fucking day. She's home, she's home." He stops rubbing his hands, drops the phony grin. "Who's home, Sam? And why are we in luck?"

"I'll explain in the taxi." He waves one down by the pharmacy. By now, cars are sloshing through standing water on the wet pavement, umbrellas are bobbing along the streets. The sodium lamps flicker on, making the afternoon seem surreal and stage-lit.

They put up a last-minute fight for the cab with a blue-haired matron who's been on a shopping spree, her hands filled with bags from boutiques. She wins, but a second taxi stops and they take it. Once inside, Kramer gives the address to the cab driver.

"We're going back there?" Randall says, recognizing the address. "What's up?"

"Time on our hands," Kramer says, and sits back to enjoy the luxury of the taxi ride.

Twenty minutes later the cab drops them at the corner of the Prinz-Albert-Strasse and Königstrasse. The rain has not let up and is falling in fine lines of moisture, almost unbroken drops. No dawdling for them today. They head straight for number 43 and its house door is once again open. Up on the third floor, Kramer has to use the brass knocker several times before there is any sound from inside. The door finally opens a crack: the chain is latched today. Eva Martok peeks at them through the crack.

"Hello," Kramer says. "I wonder if you have a minute. I forgot to ask you something the other day."

Her eye encompasses Randall, but does not blink. The door shuts on them. Almost a minute elapses, and Kramer is about to use the knocker again when finally it reopens, unlatched. She looks flustered today, fiddling with the chain. Unable to insert the bolt end into its holder, she finally lets it drop, dangling free against the door. She's in an oversize tartan wool bathrobe, its sleeves rolled up at the cuff. Her hair is a mess, falling out of a hastily made bun, drooping into her face and over her ears. There is the strong, sweet smell of booze to the place, intermingled with the sickening aroma of her Indonesian cigarettes. He looks at her red eyes and figures the color's not from crying. On the low table is an empty bottle of Johnny Walker Black. One glass.

"I'm sick," she says. "Can't this wait?"

Her voice is not slurred. The drinking must have taken place last night; the hangover today.

Randall wraps an arm around her like her old buddy, leading her to one of the pillows on the floor. Her bedroom door beyond is open, the bed rumpled and unmade.

"How about some coffee?" Randall says, giving her a hand to sit down.

"I couldn't keep it down," she says. Her shades are pulled, and her face looks pale green in the dimness of the room.

"The questions won't take a second," Kramer says, all smiles, sitting on the floor next to her. Then his eye goes up to the wall decorations, her Japanese prints, and the out-of-place cuckoo clock.

"You lied to us last visit," he says, suddenly going very cold and monotone. "You told us you didn't hear from Reni after 1989. In fact, you called her just last month."

She puts her head in her hands. "This can wait," she says, clearly in pain. "I'm sick."

"Self-inflicted," Kramer says, glancing at the empty bottle. "Don't expect pity for a hangover. What's wrong, having trouble living with yourself lately?"

"Sam . . ." Randall begins, but Kramer shoots him a steely look that shuts him up.

"This is hardball, Eva. You know what I mean."

She focuses on a space between her knees and nods slowly. "Okay, so she got back in touch with me after all these years. How'd you know?"

Kramer says nothing and Martok's eyes go to Randall for an instant.

"She got in touch with you?" Kramer finally prompts.

Martok sighs. "She tried to. Left a couple of messages at my office to call her. I didn't want to talk to her. Didn't want to think about her anymore."

"But you finally did?" Kramer says.

She shrugs. "I finally tried. I had to write myself a message so I would place the call. But nobody was home."

"And you didn't try again?" Kramer asks her.

"What was the use?"

But he counters with his own question. "Why did she call?"

Martok looks at Kramer through an oily strand of hair. "The messages she left said it was something important she had to tell me. You don't think it had anything to do with the memoirs you're looking for, do you?"

Kramer does not reply. He knows that Reni didn't answer Martok's call because she was already dead by October 28, sprawled out on her bed with a belly full of barbiturates.

"In fact," Kramer suddenly says, "you've lied to us right

down the line. Why didn't you wait for the morning to call Müller?"

She looks up again. "I don't know what you're talking about." She turns to Randall. "What's up with you guys? I thought we were friends."

Kramer gives Randall no chance to respond. "We can be. If you start leveling with us. What was so urgent that you had to phone Müller in the middle of the night after we visited you?"

She glares at Randall, wipes the hair out of her face, suddenly realizing where Kramer has got his information. "You prick," she hisses.

Randall says nothing; the cuckoo comes out of its hole, singing four o'clock. The hunter lifts her gun, but the bird slides back in before she has a chance to aim it.

"You told him about our investigations, didn't you? About Pahlus in Berlin and how he was out eighty thousand marks."

Kramer includes Randall in this accusation. If he's right in his assumptions, Randall must have continued to fill Martok in on the particulars of their investigation during their little slumber party. And by the look on Randall's face, he sees he's hit the target.

Martok sits huddled on the floor now, saying nothing.

"Was anything you told us the truth?" Kramer asks with a harsh edge, cutting at her. She winces at the sound of his voice. Randall is no longer making noises to ease up on her, seeing the lay of the land for himself now.

More silence; suddenly her body begins to shake and tremble. She is sobbing, head bent into her hands.

"You and Reni probably weren't even lovers," Kramer says.

She sits upright, wiping at her eyes with the rolled up sleeve of the bathrobe. Her jaw sets, tiny muscles like iron couplings twitching there. "Oh, we were lovers, all right. Not something I'm overly proud of now, though."

"What happened?" Kramer asks, his voice softening, his manner less in-your-face.

She shrugs. "We grew apart."

"And that's why you phoned Karl-Heinz Müller in the middle of the night to warn him about us?"

She pats the pockets of her bathrobe. There is nothing there.

"I need a cigarette." She looks around the room. "They're in the kitchen."

Kramer looks at Randall, and he gets up to fetch them.

She sniffs once, rubs the sleeve of the bathrobe across her nostrils.

"You're his lover, aren't you?" Kramer says suddenly.

She doesn't react, only hugs her knees to her chest, rocking with her butt on the pillow.

"Was," she says finally. "It's been over for a couple of years. But Reni couldn't deal with that. Underneath her great revolutionary role, she was a fucking prig."

"In fact, he came between you two?"

She sniffs at this, seeming to honestly consider it.

"That's what she said, too. Funny. Accused him of stealing every friend she ever had. But it wasn't that way, you know. He's an interesting man. Older than a coot, but still vital and fun to be with and knowledgeable about all sorts of things."

"Such as Black Forest clocks?"

She looks up at hers on the wall, and her eyes blink in understanding. She nods.

"So that's how you guessed? Because of a clock."

"Partly. So why the call in the middle of the night if you're no longer lovers?"

Randall comes back in with cigarettes in hand just in time to hear about lovers and almost drops the packet.

She shakes her head, reaching for the cigarettes, and lights one up. She is one of those smokers who seem to actually eat the smoke, to ingest it like protein. She sits back against the wall, luxuriating, her lungs filled with smoke, and then finally exhales.

"You wouldn't understand."

"Try us," Kramer says.

Another drag. A sigh. "Okay. Because he's so sad. Because he's an old man all alone with no wife and no daughter. All that's left to him is his business and Reni's death, even more than her life, is damaging that."

"I'm weeping for him," Randall says.

"See, I said you wouldn't understand."

"This is the same pitiful old man," Kramer says, "whom you had an affair with only a few years ago. Right?"

"So I've got a father fixation. So arrest me. What's it to you if I tell him about your investigations or not?"

Kramer weighs this one. "Because now we'll never know about the eighty thousand. That editor in Berlin got his money back. Did you know that? Reni supposedly left it to him in her will, just in case. And if that's true, it means she may very well have been planning suicide."

"That's what everyone keeps telling you, asshole."

Kramer lets it go. "But you told Müller about the editor, didn't you?"

After a hesitation, she nods.

"So we'll never know if Reni's father sent the money to avoid a scandal, or if Reni actually stipulated it," Kramer says.

"What's he say?" she asks.

Kramer rolls his eyes. "Come on. What do you think he's going to say?"

She considers this as the ash tumbles off the end of her cigarette onto her robe.

"I still don't see what it matters," she says after a moment's silence. "God, I could use a drink."

Kramer and Randall rise in unison; it is as if they both

realize this interview can go no further. There have been no significant looks today between Randall and Martok; like they never met before.

"You want my opinion?" she says as they go to the door. "I think you fellows are sniffing at the wrong pile of shit. I think you're afraid to look at what's staring everyone square in the face."

"And what is that?" Randall says.

"You keep saying Reni didn't kill herself. Okay. Assume murder. Who stands to gain? You keep chasing some Mr. X who was in some mythical memoirs. But get simple. Get direct. Who inherits? Reni was a wealthy woman, or didn't you know? Her mother left her well off, and Reni invested wisely. Someone stands to make a tidy sum off her death."

Kramer thinks of the housing project he saw at Schnelling and Walther.

"That's her father, then," he says.

She blows smoke at his suggestion. "Think again. That's Gerhard. Reni told me he would get the house, the stocks, the whole shitaree. Karl-Heinz is only the executor. He's already got enough money of his own, anyway. No, you find Gerhard. Ask him how it feels to be a cuckold; see if he has fond memories of his dead wife."

Two messages await Kramer back at the hotel in Bad Lunsburg: another threat from Marty, though this one gives him a date four days hence by which he has to return to work or Kate takes over, and one from Helmut in Hamburg who has tracked him down through the Vienna office, requesting him to call, no matter how late he gets in.

He puts the first on hold till the morning, and dials Helmut's number. It is picked up on the second ring by Helmut himself.

They make polite noises of hello and how are you, and then Helmut gets down to business.

"Look, Sam, when you were here, there's something I failed to tell you."

"What's that, Helmut?"

"About the Prague trip. About the car bomb. You remember who rented the car? Who got it gassed and ready to go?"

It's not something Kramer has spent much time considering over the years. "Who?"

"The way I remember, Reni delegated the job to Gerhard." There is a muffled noise off the phone, and then Helmut's voice speaking away from the mouthpiece, "Just a second honey. I'll be right there." Then back to Kramer again, "You hear me, Sam?"

"Did he?"

"What?"

"Did Gerhard rent the car and get it serviced?"

"That's the way I remember it."

"So he was the last one to touch it before you and Maria headed for Prague?" Kramer asks.

"I thought you'd want to know."

CHAPTER THIRTEEN

Kramer awakens the next morning to a gnawing anxiety that has nothing to do with Reni's death, Vogel and his goons, or Gerhard's whereabouts. As he lies on his back in the single bed listening to Randall snore and smelling the sharp bite of late fall coming from the open window, Kramer discovers the anxiety is all about filthy lucre. His finances. Or lack thereof.

Up to now, he's been playing it fast and loose with Marty, with his desk in Vienna, with such mundane aspects of life as how one earns a living if thrown out of their job at forty-five years of age. Wordsmith for hire: a bit tarnished and frayed, but some good mileage left on the chassis. Fucking marvelous, that prospect.

Kramer gets up, not waking Randall. He showers, dresses, and slips out of the room. Over coffee in the palm-filled solarium, he reviews the money front. In the week he's been on this investigation, he's clocked four air fares and six nights of lodging at a hundred plus a night—thank God for off-season rates. Not to mention restaurants and rented cars. For two. Well more than three thousand dollars and all on plastic at twelve percent. He doesn't even know his credit line; they'll tell him when he reaches it, he figures. He takes a quick drink of coffee, like it's a bourbon up, and wonders how the hell he'll ever pay it off.

Next comes the bank account. At last reckoning, he had about twelve hundred in savings. The checking account is a joke, filled up on the first, empty by the second. *Hand-to-mouthing it, Kramer*, he tells himself. *At your age. You miss one paycheck and you're on the street.*

He finishes the coffee, swallowing pride with it.

If you're one paycheck away from the street, you don't play fast and loose with the employer, Kramer. You don't tell him to bugger off in a million silent ways.

He takes out his pad and pencil and begins composing a fax; no, two faxes, he decides. He's not going to do any talking this morning; rather he'll approach it the way he knows best, by the written word. One for Marty and one for Kate.

One good thing about Friday: no weekend editions, so the coming two days are free, anyway. Marty's fax is easy: he just promises him the world. Back in Vienna by Wednesday at the latest—though he hasn't got a clue when he will return—with a story on neo-Nazis and government collusion in Germany that will knock his socks off. Besides, I have vacation due. The ace in the hole. But conciliatory; not telling, asking.

Kate's is harder. He needs to convince her to keep the office afloat without bellyaching to Paris. With her, he simply tells the truth; that this is a story he cannot let go of. Trust me, just this once. Pull the extra weight; I'll pay it back.

So Kramer finishes these messages, sits back in his chair feeling pious as hell and orders another coffee. The two slips of paper in front of him hold the tiger of anxiety and financial panic at bay. But for how long?

He looks about the glassed-in terrace, redolent of wet soil in terra-cotta pots, starched linen, and the late nineteenth century. He expects to see an aristocratic Russian family enter at any moment, children neatly decked out in sailor suits, nanny bringing up the rear; all bustles and sun umbrellas and a consumptive older sister.

Instead, Kommissar Boehm saunters through the door, hands in pockets and a porkpie hat on his massive head. He is wearing his ubiquitous blue suit, moisture at the shoulders. Kramer looks up; rain is washing off the glass dome overhead.

"We've got to stop meeting like this," Boehm says, drawing back a chair and seating himself without waiting for an invitation.

Kramer smiles wanly. "I was going to come and see you later this morning."

Boehm takes off his hat, shaking beaded water onto the floor. "The wettest damn fall I remember in years. I'm growing webs between my toes. So what were you going to see me about?" Boehm says, shaking his head at the waiter who is approaching their table, shooing him away. "I thought maybe you'd have come in yesterday."

"I was busy."

Boehm rubs the end of his nose with thumb and forefinger. "So I heard. He called this morning."

"Müller?"

A nod from Boehm.

"What'd he want?"

"Cooperation." Boehm smiles with his mouth, not his eyes.

"Such as?" Kramer says.

"I tell you to lay off private citizens. To mind your own business. Let the police do theirs. That a person might have recourse to a harassment suit. That sort of thing."

Kramer feels the back of his neck go red, feels the heat of it in his throat. "Hold on here, friend. I hope to hell you're not telling me to lay off."

Boehm stays calm, picking at a cuticle on his left thumb.

"That's what he wanted me to tell you," he says. "So I'm telling you. What you do about it is your business. You sure pissed him off. Maybe he doesn't like your bandage."

"He's afraid of publicity. Bad for business."

Boehm considers this with a pinched mouth like he's sucking a lemon. "He sounded angrier than 'bad for business' this morning."

"An old woman who once worked for the Müllers actually saw the memoirs at Reni's. That's what I told him. He didn't like that much."

"So the memoirs are for real?"

"What have I been telling you for the last week?"

"Kramer, this line is boring me. I delivered my message. Now you deliver yours. What'd you find out in Munich?"

Kramer spends the next few minutes detailing the events of his visit to Vogel and his denial of any personal knowledge of Reni, of how the car in question was supposedly stolen from him. He also tells of the discovery of his old friend, Rick Fujikawa, and of Reni's visits to him after her monthly meetings and of her bragging about seeing membership and donor lists. Finally, he relates the fact that Rick was beaten by skinheads four weeks ago.

Boehm's face shows interest at the mention of membership lists momentarily, then freezes into an impassive mask again as he lets the information settle in for a time, considering it, piecing it together.

"So he was beat up when Müller was still alive?" Boehm says.

Kramer nods.

"And he can't remember the name of the group Müller was visiting?"

"No," Kramer says. "But I figure Vogel's goons followed her when she left . . ."

Boehm nods impatiently. "Yes. You told me what you figure. Not something that holds up in court, though. This Rick.

J. Sydney Jones

You say he hangs out in the red-light district. His live-in is still in the trade?"

Kramer nods again.

Boehm takes out his own pad and pen now and begins making notes to himself. Kramer listens to the scratch of writing for a time, then Boehm flips the pad closed and returns it to his drooping breast pocket.

"You should have come in yesterday," he says.

Before Kramer can reply, Boehm pushes on.

"I'll look into the assault on your friend. Who knows? There may be a connection to Vogel. Maybe Müller *was* followed by Vogel's boys to this Fujikawa. Dumber things have been done. But I don't want to roll Vogel over for simple assault. No. I want him on the big stuff."

Boehm's face suddenly goes dark, his eyes narrowing into slits like crossbow apertures in a fortress. Kramer feels uncomfortably like he's in the sights.

"So we trade," Boehm says, casting off the evil mood. "I've been looking into the Gorik case. Tracking down witnesses in Berlin. That was a sloppy job of investigation. If I didn't know better, I'd think my comrades in arms at Berlin central don't give a shit about the death of an ex-intelligence officer from the East. I'd think they figured however he died, whoever got him, it was good riddance to bad rubbish. So I picked back through the people who saw the accident, and one thing I came up with was the car."

"You got a make?"

"No such luck," he says. "But one old girl did remember something interesting about it. It was big and fast and didn't even stop after knocking Gorik into next week."

He looks at Kramer shrewdly for a moment, pacing himself.

"And," he adds, smiling, "it was purple. The old girl was sure of that. When do you ever see a purple car anymore?"

This information sets bells ringing in Kramer's mind, making him recall the car that came close to hitting him earlier in the week.

"So I ask the next question," Boehm continues. "This time, it's closer to home. Your Frau Gruber. I'm curious about that car parked outside her house one night. I talked with her this morning."

Kramer feels himself tense up, guessing at the rest.

"It was dark, she tells me," Boehm goes on, folding his massive hands on the table in front of him. "But the flashlight lit things up for her. No swearing on a Bible for her, but she's pretty certain the car parked that night was dark blue or purple."

"It doesn't say on the registration?" Kramer says.

Boehm shakes his head.

"And why wasn't there a tag on the registration when you looked the license number up?" Kramer asks. "Some note about the car being stolen."

"There wasn't, but that means nothing. We're just getting our records computerized; there's no cross-referencing yet. But if Vogel tells you to ask the police about it, then he must have filed a report. He's got himself covered. We've got some linkage, though. And now it's a *stolen* car, so it allows me to do some checking, to be interested in it without people getting suspicious."

"People such as other cops? Have the neo-Nazis gotten that powerful?"

Boehm shrugged. "My old grandmother always told me better safe than sorry."

"Am I getting a message here?" Kramer says.

Boehm flexes his meshed fingers, cracking a knuckle. "Maybe. You're a smart journalist, Kramer. You must have other leads to follow."

"I thought you wanted to nail the bastard."

"Oh, I most fervently do, Kramer. But not for killing you. I mean, I could let you bumble around some more until you make yourself such a nuisance to Vogel that he has you eliminated. Then maybe, just maybe, I'd turn up some more traces, something to connect him to your death. But it's not a sure bet. You're not interested in long shots, are you?"

"I know how to take care of myself."

Boehm nods sideways skeptically. "It's time you let me take the lead with Vogel."

"What? You don't want an amateur mucking up the traces, is that it? Christ, man, you wouldn't even be on Vogel's trail if it weren't for me. You don't give a damn if Reni was murdered or not, do you? It's only important that you might be able to pin it on Vogel."

"He had motive," Boehm says. "If, in fact, Müller infiltrated his cell. The neo-Nazis are very reluctant for anybody to know where their money comes from. And the purple car that killed Gorik teases me." Boehm looks down at his hands, then up at Kramer. "But no, you're right. I don't give a damn about Müller. I figure she was a big girl, able to look out for herself. I'm still not convinced her death wasn't plain old suicide. But I'd be a fool to do a pass on anything that could trip up Vogel. Especially homicide. So I tell you, follow your other leads. Shake other cages for a while. Who knows, they may lead us back to Vogel in the end." He leans back in his chair. "It's called division of labor."

Kramer looks hard at the Kommissar, trying to read his face for motivation and honesty. It is a blank; a solid chunk of granite staring back at him.

"If I find out you're running a cover-up . . ."

"Don't even finish it, Kramer. We want to part company today as friends. I don't cover up, okay?"

They sit across the table for a silent moment, eyes locked like newlyweds who failed to get it off the night before.

It makes sense to Kramer; a crazy kind of logic. A purple car in common is nothing to go on. Suggestive only. Let the cop sniff around for a while.

Kramer has other leads to follow.

"How about some help tracking a guy?"

Boehm squints at the suggestion. "You got a reason?"

"There's a husband who stood to profit from Reni's death. He's suddenly very nonexistent." Kramer says nothing about the pull of the past, the search for who is responsible for what happened in Prague in 1968. It's light-years away from what Boehm cares about, Kramer figures. Money is a tidier motive.

Boehm is nodding. "I know about him. Didn't even come back for the funeral. He a friend of yours?"

Kramer has no idea how much Boehm knows about Reni's background; decides on limited honesty.

"Sort of."

Boehm laughs, breaking the tension between them. "Sort of. Like the sort of good old friend who stole your girl, in fact."

"You've been doing your homework."

"I try. You settling old scores with this, or do you really believe Gerhard Schwarz could kill someone? He lived here, you know. I used to see him in the shops. Husband of the local celebrity. He didn't look like the killing kind."

"I thought they never did," Kramer says.

"That's from detective books. Take it from me, most murderers look like murderers. Especially with something like this. We're not talking the heat of the moment. If Müller was killed, we're talking about a well-planned operation. Somebody sat up nights working it out."

"So, how about it?" Kramer says.

"The trace? If he's the big winner with Müller's estate, her lawyers should know where he is."

"Something tells me they're not going to be cooperative."

Boehm smiles. "Rattling their cage, were we? Not smart. The only thing those two have to hide is their love."

"Schnelling and Walther?" They seem so cold and lifeless to Kramer that he is surprised they have any sex life, homo or hetero.

It might explain things, though, he thinks. Like the other day when I burst into their office. Was it the housing project they were trying to hide, or the fact that they were making out in the middle of the afternoon?

He smiles to himself. It actually makes them more human. He's no homophobe. For Kramer, the only sin is having no one to love.

"Something funny about that?" Boehm says, misunderstanding Kramer's smile.

"No, nothing. Maybe I was pissing on the wrong fire with them. Like I say, they're not likely to be very helpful."

Boehm gets up suddenly, hitching at his waist band with his elbows. "I'll see what I can do about Gerhard Schwarz. This is a trade, right? You keep out of Vogel's way for the time being. I don't want him running for cover just yet."

After Boehm leaves, Kramer goes to the post office and faxes his messages. It has grown cold suddenly and the rain has stopped. To the east are herringboned clouds scudding high and fast. Snow, he tells himself. He can smell it in the air.

Back at the hotel, Randall is finally up and finishing off an English breakfast in the solarium, the local paper open to the entertainment section on the table in front of him.

Randall looks up as Kramer enters. "Sam, old boy. You eaten?"

"Hours ago." He sits across from Randall. "You look the shits. What's up?"

"Not my pecker, thank you." He finishes his coffee, closes

the paper, and rolls it into a baton, which he sticks into his jacket pocket. "What's on the agenda for today?"

His good humor is forced, Kramer knows, but lets it go.

"We're put on hold," he says, then tells of Boehm's visit.

Randall nods as Kramer finishes. "Just as well. I have a feeling about this, that the past holds more secrets than the present. *Cherchez les temps perdu*, not the frigging Nazis. This Vogel cat's a geek, a sideshow. I think it all comes back to Prague, like Helmut says."

"What about the car, then?" Kramer counters. "The late visit the very night Reni died?"

"There are lots of purple cars, Sam. And we don't know exactly when Reni died or even if the occupants of that car were visiting her or some other fruitcake in town. And maybe, just maybe, the car really was stolen from Vogel."

Kramer says, "Mmm."

Kramer spends the next hours not thinking at all, just walking, walking. He follows a graveled road out of town into the vineyards. The vines have been cut back: small white circles against the aged brown wood mark the amputations. The sky is lowering and the smell of snow grows heavier. He climbs to a rise over the Rhine and watches cargo barges glide along the river, their decks spanned with washing hung out to dry. He wishes he were aboard one of those, just floating along through life. The water, thick and sluggish, looks a better medium than the hard pan of conflicting stories he's plowing his way through.

A red-nosed farmer drives past him on a spanking new tractor, waves a friendly hand, tops the crest of the hill, and is gone.

Kramer wanders idly on, forcing his mind off thoughts of Reni, memoirs, Rick, or neo-Nazis. He wants a clearing cut in the vegetation to allow some light in. He follows the track down and up through the vineyards, liking the pull of muscles in the back of his legs, the thumping of his heart in his chest, and the pound of it in his ears. His city shoes hurt and he wishes he had his old hiking boots. They're sitting in the hallway wardrobe back in Vienna. Suddenly, he's almost nostalgic for his flat, for the routines of the life he's built in Vienna.

But his thoughts are cut short by the whine of a car engine behind him. He's meandered down into a gully where the lane narrows to the width of a single car and threads between high hedgerows. The thick branches of the hedgerows allow no passage through them. Only a few feet from a blind corner, Kramer decides it's a good idea to put some space between him and the approaching vehicle. Suddenly, the pitch of the engine whine grows louder, higher.

The car is speeding, and Kramer walks more quickly at first. Then, as the sound of the car gets closer and closer, he begins to run along the dirt track. He stumbles over a clump of grass in the middle and, as he is picking himself up, sees the car turn the tight corner into the gully. It's purple, and that's all it takes for him to push himself to his feet and race forward blindly, searching the shrubbery to both sides for a way through. He feels like a trapped animal forced down a chute. One way out, and that is straight ahead with the car gaining on him every second.

Breath catches in his throat; his heart is pounding wildly. The track climbs out of the gully, and he sees a break in the hedgerows ahead, but the car is gaining on him. It shifts into a lower gear as it too begins to climb the incline. The break in the hedgerow is getting closer and closer, but Kramer knows he will not make it; feels the car on his heels. No place to hide.

Suddenly, the car stops in back of him; a voice calls out, "I didn't know you were a jogger, Herr Kramer."

Kramer stops in his tracks, sweat pouring down his face. He knows the voice. Turning, he sees Walther grinning at him, his head sticking out the driver's side of his Porsche.

Kramer breathes deeply, his entire body feeling relief.

"This is private property, you know," Walther says. "It's posted."

"Then what are you doing here?" Kramer asks, keeping his distance from the car.

"Examining my property," Walther says. "Real estate is such a fine investment, don't you think?" Walther revs his engine once again, like a threat. "You really should be careful where you go running, Herr Kramer. All these narrow lanes and blind curves. One could have an accident so easily."

"I'll remember that." Kramer edges against the prickly branches of the hedgerow as Walther puts the car into gear once again, slips past Kramer, and gives him a wave in his rearview mirror.

Back at the hotel a note from Boehm is waiting: *No sign of Gerhard in Germany.* A Swiss bank is managing the inheritance for him; no trace on that end, either. But Boehm has been busy on the computer and has come up with recent credit-card purchases. One stands out for Kramer: a one-way ticket to Athens purchased two months ago.

It's the lead he's been searching for.

Three hours later, he and Randall board an Olympic flight to Athens.

Seated at the back of the plane are two men with newspapers open, covering their faces. One is a large man with a neck so short and thick that his head appears connected directly to his shoulders. He is massive in width, taking up arm space well into the second man's area. This second one is smaller, and his lips move as he reads the sports section of *Bild*. The larger one is not reading. He moves his newspaper slightly aside as Kramer and Randall stow their carry-on bags into the overhead compartment. Watching them, he smiles to himself, then adjusts the paper once again to conceal his face.

CHAPTER FOURTEEN

After an overnight in Athens, they catch the early morning flight for Crete, arriving in Iráklion. The day is clear and the orange groves surrounding the city are in blossom. It is all lush and golden under a high sun; they have left Europe behind.

Iráklion is only a stopover; the bus for the south coast leaves in half an hour, long enough for Randall to seek out a souvlaki stand and gorge himself on greasy mutton, washed down with a Fix beer.

Their bus is new and flat-nosed with wide panoramic windows, a million light-years away from the old rattletrap buses that once crisscrossed the island. But boarding with the other twelve passengers, Kramer is pleased to see that the driver has not been overwhelmed by luxury. The dash and front window are still the miniature shrine they have always been for Greek bus drivers, festooned with worry beads and sacred cartoons, decked out in plastic flowers and pictures of smiling kids. Kramer is reminded momentarily of the computers in the Real Editions office in Berlin.

The driver jumps aboard and starts the engine, glancing

at the passengers briefly and frowning because there are so few: such a paltry audience for his performance. He is still young enough to be in love with speed, letting them all know what they're in for before reaching the outskirts of Iráklion: honking through intersections with the door open to be able to gesticulate at drivers to his right; screeching rubber around corners and speed clutching down instead of braking; jacking up the volume on his miniature boom box and filling the bus with bouzouki music and a wailing male voice that symbolizes the eastern Mediterranean for Kramer.

Randall lifts an eyebrow at Kramer and promptly drifts off to sleep. But Kramer watches it all: the passage through small villages surrounding the capital, through lush groves of orange trees and into the more arid hill country, climbing, climbing; the country beginning to look more and more like the American Southwest; the meager farms, houses freshly whitewashed houses under a sparkling sun. Still climbing, they pass wooden trellises laden with grapes, drying into raisins, on both sides of the road. Off to the right now, he sees the snowcapped tip of Mount Ida. The driver uses his horn around tight curves; the music blares, unchanging, as if it is one continuous song. Kramer nods off for a time despite his best intentions, and when he is jolted awake by a sharp application of the brakes and a rocking, swerving motion, he looks out the window to see a wide-eyed farmer in a small HiAce pickup that the bus leaves behind as if stationary.

They are descending now, out of the highlands and into another verdant agricultural plain, the Messara, around the market town of Timbaki, their destination.

Behind them, following at a discrete two hundred yards, is a blue, late model, four-wheel-drive Suzuki; its front seats are occupied by two men, obviously from northern Europe. The inside of the vehicle smells of leather and gun oil. In the backseat, protected by cowhide slipcovers, are two bolt-action Mannlichers the men bought at a certain hunting shop in Iráklion. Next to the leather cases are five packages of cartridges. They will score the lead themselves, so that the bullets will spread more easily upon impact. To purchase hollow points would be to call attention to themselves. These two men are cautious; they are pros.

Dr. Alexandros Kariakis is just finishing his afternoon surgery when Kramer and Randall arrive at his office. The doctor still has no secretary; patients simply take a seat in the waiting room until he calls them.

Kariakis pokes his bearded satyrlike head out into the room and calls out automatically in Greek, "Next." Then he squints more closely, smiles, and bounds into the waiting room, arms outstretched.

"Kramer! Is it really you?"

Kramer rises and meets the bearish-looking doctor; they embrace, and he feels the man's ample stomach against his. They've both put on weight over the years. Kariakis digs his fingers into Kramer's shoulders, holding him at arm's length.

"Where have you been all these years, barbarian?"

Kramer smiles, shrugs. "Around."

Kariakis begins to laugh; it is deep and rattling, and ends in a coughing fit. He is a friend from Kramer's days in Crete; he tended to Reni once when she had a bout of food poisoning and became much more than a doctor to them.

"Come in, come in," Kariakis says, leading the way into his office and lighting a cigarette to stifle his cough before sitting behind a scarred old desk.

Nothing has changed here: the same eye charts on the wall, the same ancient examining table, perhaps even the same sheet covering it. A medical degree on the wall from the University of Delaware. Ash tumbles down the front of

Kariakis's white coat as he looks expectantly from Kramer to Randall. Kramer makes introductions and the doctor indicates two chairs.

"Sit, sit. You must be tired from being *around* so long. You never wrote, barbarian."

Kramer sighs, "I sort of put all this out of my mind."

"Is it in the air, then?"

Kramer smiles incomprehension at him.

"Reunions. Everybody returning to the omphalos."

Good, Kramer thinks. *I was right*. "Who else has been back lately?" he says.

Kariakis suddenly looks at the cigarette with disgust, as if only now realizing he is smoking, then stabs it out in a glass ashtray on the corner of his desk. It is filled with other such shredded butts.

"Your friend," he says. "The Chameleon."

Bingo.

The hills shimmer and ripple in the heat; the fragrance of mountain thyme is heavy in the air. Sweat drips into Kramer's eyes as he proceeds up the hill, the unfamiliar boots on his feet pinching with every step. Randall is in back, whistling what sounds like an aria from a Puccini opera. Kramer does not know which one. Gazing up at the snowcapped peak ahead of him momentarily, he stumbles over a rock in the path, kicks up dust, and then looks down at the trail like it was the rock's fault.

The whistling stops. "How much farther, Sam?"

"Why? You gotta pee? Stick it out anywhere."

"You get funnier the longer I'm around. What're you going to do for straight men after I'm gone?"

"I don't know," Kramer says, answering the previous question. "I've never made this climb before."

He stops, adjusting the weight on the old backpack he borrowed from Kariakis. The back of his shirt is drenched with sweat. A thick line runs down the middle of the front as well, dark against the khaki. He unfastens the canteen at his web belt, unscrews the cap, and takes a long swallow. It's warm and tastes of aluminum. He passes it to Randall.

He squints again at the top of the mountain. The snow there looks golden under the high sun. Bees are busy in the thyme bushes to both sides of the goat trail they're following; black desiccated goat pellets are underfoot. From a distance, he hears the clanging of a bell around a buck's neck. High overhead, a hawk circles in an updraft; a sudden breeze cools Kramer as it breathes on the wetness of his shirt.

Despite the heat, the pinching boots—which he purchased in Timbaki this morning before departing—the canteen—which has no canvas sheath to keep wet for insulation—and Randall's off-tune whistling, Kramer is loving this. His mind is clear, his body throbbing with exertion, his feet itching to get under way again. Give him a path to the horizon and walking boots on his feet and he's a happy man.

"I don't get the thrill of it all," Randall suddenly says. "This is work, not recreation. Recreation means having fun, means having other people do the work for you."

Kramer looks back at Randall who is gazing over the groves of huge-boled olive trees on the Messara Plain below, a red handkerchief tied over his shaved head.

"It's something we always planned to do," Kramer says. "Follow the old Minoan routes across the island, up Mount Ida." He looks again at the snowy saddle ahead. "The birth-place of Zeus, home of rebels and brigands. It's where the resistance held out during the German occupation."

But Randall is still unconvinced. He grunts once, takes a swig of water, and spits it out.

"It's tepid. Stout is the only drink that should be served tepid."

Kramer takes the canteen back, caps it, and says nothing.

He clips it to his belt, takes a deep breath, hitches up the pack, and starts out again.

They've been on the path for four hours already, leaving their rented car at the tiny village of Lourakia at the base of the mountain. According to Kariakis, Gerhard has been walking the ancient paths for the past two months, wherever they still exist, wherever they have not been paved over by highways. Kramer came up with the notion more than twenty years ago, after discovering a map of the routes as well as descriptions of their lengths in a book by the archaeologist Pendlebury. On a later visit to Vienna's National Library, he had searched out the only topographic maps available to the island in sufficient scale for hiking—1:50,000—drawn by the Wehrmacht in 1940. Thirty sheets of them copied and folded neatly in a waxed cotton sleeve and left behind with other detritus of the Cretan chapter of his life after the island had become too much for him to bear; after Reni's defection had ruined it for him. Kariakis had magpied the maps and given them to Gerhard when he returned to the island earlier in the fall.

Kramer thinks of Kariakis's nickname for Gerhard: Chameleon. It is apposite. He slaps at an insect on his neck, smiling at the name.

Gary Black.

"You ever ask him why he changed his name?" Kramer suddenly calls back to Randall.

"You mean Gerhard?"

"Right."

The squeak of leather straps and the glugging jostle of the canteen flapping against Kramer's hip punctuate their conversation.

"No. Never mentioned it. Too weird to mention."

Kramer laughs. Exactly. Everyone was changing their names in the '60s and '70s: Tipi and Sunset and Rainbow.

But Gerhard for Gary? Schwarz for Black? *Give me a break,* Kramer thinks. Yet nobody ever questioned it. It was too weird to deal with. The Yank gone native in Kraut land.

Kramer has no idea what to expect when he catches up with Gerhard; is not exactly sure why he has come all this way to find him. According to Kariakis, Gerhard has been hiking the country for the past two months, not back in Germany dosing Reni with barbiturates so as to inherit her small fortune. But who's to know? Kramer wonders. Who's to say where Gerhard's been? Traveling alone; no set itinerary. He could have taken a break for a spot of homicide. Using the walking tour as his alibi.

The Pillow. Gerhard's other nickname, but not quite so kind. How much does being the cuckold hurt? Kramer thinks back to 1974, when he received word from Reni that she was not coming back to him. That she was staying in Germany with Gerhard instead. Being the cuckold hurts a lot, he knows. A hell of a lot. And revenge is a powerful motive.

A hawk calls overhead, the ends of its wings tipped upward like feathery fingers.

They say nothing for a solid hour, until they come on the opening of a cave that beckons them out of the heat. They sit close to the mouth in the cool shade, with the moist-dirt smell coming from the darkness at their backs, and eat lunch. Kramer has brought several loaves of bread and wax paper–wrapped chunks of feta. There are also mild yellow onions, a jar of olives, some lemons, and in Randall's pack, a bottle of raki. They squeeze lemon juice on the bread, slice onions and cheese, and make open-faced sandwiches, sipping lightly from the raki between bites. From the cave mouth, they look back down the side of the mountain. The day is so clear that the view extends all the way to the coast, an indistinct blue line in the mid-horizon, darker than the sky.

They eat in silence for several minutes; then Randall burps contentedly, rises, and starts examining the cave.

"You might want to play Ariadne," Kramer calls to him, his voice echoing in the cavernous space. "Put a string on your finger if you don't want to get lost."

Which is enough to bring Randall back into the light of day.

"I don't think I've got the spelunker spirit in me, Sam. It's black as night in there."

"Some of these go for hundreds of yards underground," Kramer says. "Branching all over the place so you never know where you've been. Ancient religious shrines."

"I think I prefer Gothic." Randall tosses another olive in one side of his mouth, spits the pit out the other. "How far up do you think he'll be?"

"No idea," Kramer answers him. "He left Timbaki a day before we did. It's a couple of days up there, maybe more. Depends on how much you dawdle. Kariakis said he was coming back to Timbaki after the climb. There's only one path on this side of the slope. So he'll either be going up or coming down. We'll find him somewhere, I guess."

"Very reassuring." Randall tosses another olive into his mouth. "Why don't we just pitch camp here then and wait for him?"

Kramer gets to his knees, repacking the lunch things, stabbing his old Swiss Army knife into the earth to clean it off, then closing it and sticking it in his pants pocket.

"You stay, if you want. I'm enjoying the climb. We'll meet you back here."

"I'm not staying here alone, Sam. There are bats and all sorts of wild animals in the night. Why do you have to be such a masochist?"

Two hours later, they are well above the tree line; the terrain is a jumble of boulders and thyme bushes half a man high. An occasional black pine survives on the dry slopes and lizards dart past them on the path, making Randall start. The sun is past its zenith, a fact to be grateful for. Kramer feels sunburned on the neck and face. He has no hat with him, no sunscreen. It's almost winter, isn't it? Weather like this makes a man a believer in global warming.

The saddle of the mountain comes in and out of view as they drop down ridges cut by narrow cols and ravines; the goat trail twists like a snake up the side of the mountain, following the path of least resistance. On one such ridge, they come upon a shepherd with a small flock of goats feeding placidly on dusty scrub brush on the steep uphill side of the track. The bells on the goats clang softly in the warm afternoon. The man is seated on a rock midway along the exposed ridge, looking down the ravine that borders the other side of the trail. He is decked out in mountain wear: tall black boots, wide pants, a black vest with red cummerbund, a tasseled black scarf on his head. He sports a rakish mustache, greased and twirled upward at the ends. He has a lean hawk face and startlingly blue eyes, which turn from the ravine to watch them with suspicion.

Kramer is happy to come across him. It is the first of the traditional Cretan dress he's seen and he's been afraid that it, like so much else of traditional island life, has passed away with the coming of the tourists and the joining with united Europe. Homogeneity as the great killer.

"*Yassou,*" Kramer greets the man as they approach.

The Cretan says nothing, merely nods his head as they pass. But Randall has not been fooled.

"What the fuck are you in that get-up for, Gary?"

Kramer turns, startled, and now he too sees beneath the disguise. The blue eyes; the sharp nose.

"Hi, guys."

"Christ," Kramer says. "Twenty some years and that's all you can come up with?"

183

Gerhard gets up from the rock, shrugs shyly and puts his hand out to them.

"I thought I was seeing things," he says.

His hand is cool and hard as Kramer grips it. Not the soft fish it once was.

"I mean, what the hell would you two be doing on a goat trail in Crete? It was too bizarre to contemplate." He takes his hand back, twirls his mustache and squints at the thought. "What *are* you doing here?"

Randall hums the theme from *Twilight Zone*, flashing wild eyes at him. "We are in cyberspace, old chum. A blip on somebody's computer screen."

Kramer shakes his head at Randall, then turns to Gerhard. "Kariakis told us where you'd be. I need to talk with you."

Gerhard laughs dryly. "It must be pretty important to track me all the way here. I thought you were living in Vienna."

Kramer nods. "How'd you know?"

Gerhard takes a wad of gum from his mouth, examines it like a diamond merchant counting facets, then chucks it into the brush.

"Reni told me. She kept track of you, Sam." He looks at the feeding goats for a time, his lips pursing, eyes unblinking. Then he turns to Kramer again, "I figured we'd have to do this one day. You still hate me?"

Kramer thinks about it momentarily; it deserves an honest answer.

"I did for years," he finally says, shaking his head. "But no more. Life's too short to be pissed off all the time."

"Then this isn't a vendetta journey?" Gerhard says. There is laughter in his voice, but an edge of fear as well. "It would have been very in-scene, very apropos, tracking me down in the mountains of Crete, where vengeance is a way of life."

Kramer does not want to come to the point just yet; looks for other small talk.

"What are you doing with a herd of goats?"

Gerhard looks at them fondly again. "Not mine. I'm just following them. Have been for the past day. We could learn a lot from the ruminants."

"Such as?" Randall says, taking off his pack and sitting on the rock Gerhard just vacated.

"Such as patience," Gerhard says. "Infinite patience and total concentration. You need both to survive on the side of this mountain. But you didn't come all this way to talk about goats. It's Reni, isn't it? What's wrong? Did she send you after me?"

"You really don't know, do you?" Kramer says, and suddenly wishes he had not come looking for him; wishes that it would not have to be him to tell the story.

"She's dead," Randall says, looking not at Gerhard, but at Kramer. "They're calling it suicide in Germany, but . . ."

Gerhard looks at them with incomprehension for a moment.

"Is this some kind of stupid joke, Sam?"

Kramer shakes his head, looking at the ground. "No joke."

Gerhard stands for a moment wide-eyed, jerking his head between Kramer and Randall.

"It's true," Kramer says, looking into his eyes now. "I'm sorry."

Gerhard says nothing, then suddenly crumples to the ground, moaning as if in pain. His shoulders heave as he sobs.

Randall looks at Kramer and they walk a few yards away for a time, looking down the col as it winds treacherously beneath them, the result of some old run-off. Scree covers most of its length; a scattering of dusty blue-green bushes cling to the bottom tract. A splashing sound catches Kramer's attention: Randall is peeing onto the rocks.

Turning, Kramer sees Gerhard is still huddled in the trail, but his shoulders are heaving less violently now. He has taken the black scarf off his head and is using it to wipe his eyes. Thin wisps of his hair float above his head in a light breeze.

They walk back to him and Kramer swings his pack off, setting it on the ground next to Randall's, and then pulls the bottle of raki out of Randall's pack and uncorks it.

"Drink some of this," he says to Gerhard's hunched shoulders, to the bald spot on top of his bowed head.

Gerhard looks up, red-eyed and pained, takes the bottle and tips it up, swallowing twice, three times. The liquid splashes out the neck of the bottle as he lets it down and hands it back. He wipes his eyes and stands.

"Sorry. I'm being a melodramatic baby. People die all the time, don't they?"

A sudden determination crosses his face as he looks at Randall, "You said it was a suicide?"

"The police say that," Randall says, leaving the rest implied, and sitting again on the rock.

Gerhard looks at Kramer, now alarmed. "But what do you think?"

"I think somebody killed her."

"What! Why would anyone . . ." But he cuts himself off. "She *did* make enemies. No use denying that."

Kramer says nothing. The day is deadly still but for the rhythmic sounding of the goat bells.

Gerhard thinks some more, then sits down next to Randall.

"So, did you come to tell me about Reni's death or to see if I'm the killer?"

Kramer smiles. "A little of both."

"Sorry to disappoint you," Gerhard says, slapping the knees of his jodhpurs and raising dust. "But I've been busy trudging the Minoan way, old friend. Besides, why would I want to kill Reni?"

"Eva Martok says you inherit her estate. Plus you might

have been left at home one too many nights." There are better ways to phrase it, but Kramer does not want to search for them. He wonders if, in fact, he has forgiven Gerhard; if he is not, in fact, trying to inflict pain with his questions.

"That bitch," he hisses, but offers no particulars.

"Why did you leave, Gerhard?" Kramer asks.

He shrugs. "There was nothing there for me anymore." Another dry laugh. "Never really was, in fact. I was her companion, Sam. Not much more. There were times when she felt some pity for me, the loyal dog, and conferred connubial gifts, but mostly I was her campaign manager and general factotum. Even dogs get tired of being kicked eventually."

"Come on, Gerhard," Kramer says. "You two ran off together. There must have been more to it than that."

Gerhard looks up at Kramer, amazement on his face. "Is that how you read it? That we ran off together? Bolted to Gretna Green like a couple of young lovers? Jesus, Sam, how strange the world is and how much simpler it was once, huh? Just a bunch of proto-hips freewheeling around Europe, not giving a shit for anything but having a good book in the pack and enough money till the end of the month. I liked me better then."

Kramer does not respond, but he knows the feeling. Remembrance of things past. But it doesn't make the present any easier to get through.

"How should I have read it?" he asks, taking a swig of the raki now himself and handing it to Randall.

"I was handy, Sam. That's all. Reni hated to be alone. I was her buffer. It helped that I was crazy in love with her anyway. But that had nothing to do with it. I was just handy."

"You went to Germany together," Kramer says. "There were lots of handy men there."

Gerhard shakes his head, squinting with a grin. "Don't you get it, Sam? She wasn't running from you. She was running from herself. She didn't mean to leave you. In ways, she never did."

Kramer and Randall exchange glances. "I don't follow," Kramer says.

Another shake of the head from Gerhard, but this time it means finality rather than frustration. "I can't get any clearer, Sam. I promised Reni I'd never tell. I don't think it's a promise her death can alter. But you should know that she didn't want to leave you. She always loved you. That's all that matters."

"No, it isn't," Kramer says, suddenly angry. All those years, all that lost love and emotion. Was it all the matter of a misunderstanding?

"Look, Sam. Reni was one of those people who didn't belong in the real world. She set herself a strict code of moral conduct and was screwing up all the time. No one could toe her party line, not even her, and she was the biggest loser. She just couldn't face you anymore, is all. Not after what she learned."

"What the hell did she learn?"

"I've said too much, already."

"Look," Kramer says, "maybe this has something to do with her death. With her killer."

Gerhard considers this for a moment, then shakes his head. "No way."

"Did she tell you she was writing memoirs?" Randall asks.

Gerhard takes the bottle from his hand, thinks better of it, and fishes out a stick of gum from his vest pocket.

"That was all she cared about anymore." He slowly unwraps the gum, rolls it into a coil, and plops it in his mouth.

"Did you read any of it?" Kramer says.

"She wouldn't let me near her precious papers."

"Did she ever mention a man named Vogel? Reinhard Vogel?"

Gerhard tries the name out like a taster washing his mouth with wine. No bouquet.

"She never mentioned him. I know the name. Who doesn't? Our new Germany's answer to Adolf. It's jerks like him who made me leave that country. I mean, I've loved Germany like only a convert could all these years. Forgiven her all her sins."

Randall makes a sour face. "They call it the Fatherland now. It's a male country, Gary."

But Gerhard ignores this, warming to his theme as he would in the old days.

"I became more German than American, for Christ's sake. And then you know what some skins tell me one day in the street in Bonn?" But it's rhetorical; he has all the answers himself. "I should get my sorry ass out of their country. I'm a miserable foreigner stealing their jobs. Me, who speaks German better than any of those shaved-headed Cro-Magnons, and who's never drawn a day's wages in all the years I've lived in Germany."

He rises suddenly, pulling down the vest where it has ridden up.

"I loved that country, Sam. I gave up America, never went back. And now Germany's turned into a cesspool. You can't live in a cesspool. Reni loved it, though. Gave her something to fight against, she was always saying. Me, I don't want to fight. I want to blend. What a wish, huh? Just to blend. Not stand out in any way. What's wrong with us, anyway?"

It's oblique, but Kramer understands the question. The generation of 1968, all those brainy talented dropouts who stayed dropped out, who distrusted success like it was Nixon in drag, afraid of achieving, like it was compromising values.

"Did Reni mention seeing Rick?"

The suddenness of the question catches Gerhard by surprise. He has to process the name.

"You mean Fujikawa? Rick, the painter? Where?"

"In Munich."

"No. I didn't know she met up with him again. What's he doing?"

"Painting," Kramer says. "And recovering from a beating the skinheads gave him."

"See? A cesspool. He should get out of there."

Kramer wonders why Reni would not have told Gerhard about Rick, or about Vogel. Unless she did, and reasons he's lying for his own reasons. Or unless she thought she would be protecting Gerhard by not telling.

"But it's funny you mentioning Rick," he says. "'Cause Reni did track down another of the Magnificent Seven."

"Helmut," Randall says, nonchalantly, as if to one-up. "We saw him in Hamburg."

Gerhard smiles, interested. "Did you, now? Old home week. But it's not Helmut I'm talking about."

It's an easy calculation to make for Kramer: process of elimination. "But that means . . ."

"Yeah," Gerhard says, grinning broadly. "She found Maria. She's still alive."

CHAPTER FIFTEEN

Kramer feels the blood hum in his head. "Where is she?" he finally says.

"Prague. She's working at some publishing house. At least she was when Reni last saw her," Gerhard adds.

"When was this?" Kramer asks.

Gerhard twirls the ends of his mustache, twists his mouth in concentration.

"Wasn't long after I came down here. You lose sense of time on the trail. The letter came to the *Poste Restante* in Athens, so it couldn't have been long after I arrived. Six weeks ago, maybe?"

"What did Reni say exactly?" Kramer says, trying to fit this new bit of information into the burgeoning mosaic.

"Not much. Just that she'd met Maria again, and that she had news. You know Reni. It was always what she didn't say that mattered."

"What didn't she say, Gerhard?"

He counts them off on his long fingers, "Well, number one, what news? Number two, how she found Maria after all these years." Then he angrily fists his hand. "Jesus, Sam, I could go on for hours with what was left out."

"You remember the name of the publisher?" Kramer asks.

Gerhard ponders this for a while, shaking his head. "I threw the letter away, too." More squinting of his eyes. Then, "Hold on. It begins with a *K*. Something like Kareesia." He rubs his beard. "Didn't seem important at the time. The address was a bunch of Czech words full of acute accents and those upside-down chevrons."

"Hačeks," Randall says.

Gerhard turns to him. "Say what?"

"Hačeks." Randall smiles. "That's what those upside-down chevrons are called."

Gerhard looks puzzled for a moment. "Right." Then to Kramer, "Anyway, that's where Reni ran her down."

"No address?" Kramer says.

"No. I would have forgotten it by now, anyway." He goes to the edge of the ravine, stares off into space for a time, and then focuses at the scree far below. "Looks like a car down there," he says. "See?"

Kramer goes to the edge and follows Gerhard's pointing finger to a trail of dust far in the distance.

"Didn't know there was a road up that side of Psiloritis."

Just like Gerhard, Kramer thinks, to use the Greek name for the mountain instead of the much simpler English: Mount Ida.

Gerhard turns to look at Randall still sitting on the boulder. "But you said you visited Helmut." Then to Kramer, "And Rick. Then me. What's up?" His eyes widen momentarily and a slight smile crosses his lips. "You think it's one of the old gang who killed Reni. That's it, isn't it? One of the Magnificent Seven. But why?"

"It keeps coming back to the memoirs," Kramer says. "Someone didn't want those memoirs to be published. Her editor in Berlin called them 'political dynamite.'"

"But why one of us?" Gerhard turns toward the ravine

again, shaking his head, taking in large gulps of warm wind funneling up the col.

Kramer looks at Randall, "You want to explain about Helmut?"

Randall shrugs. "Sure."

As briefly as possible, Randall fills Gerhard in on their visit to Hamburg, their initial suspicions of Helmut himself because of his new trading partners in Prague, and then relates Helmut's own theory about the car bombing in Prague and the fact that he, Gerhard, was the one to rent the car, to deliver it to Helmut and Maria.

Gerhard spins around, his face red with anger. "But that's not true. I mean, I rented the car, all right. But I wasn't the only one to have it before Helmut."

Kramer squints an eye at him. "Who else?"

Gerhard controls his anger, looks down at his dusty boots. "I can't say."

"It was Reni, wasn't it?"

Gerhard's eyes stay focused on the scuffed tips of his boots.

"Come on, Gary, for Christ's sake!" Kramer wants to shake him. "She's dead. You can't protect the dead."

Gerhard looks up. "Yeah, okay. It was Reni. She took the car that Friday before I delivered it to Helmut. She said she wanted to drive it across a border or two just to confuse the police. Reni the Conspirator. It was something about getting the plates on lots of different border police blotters so that we could say it had been lifted if the shit hit the fan in Prague. No traces back to us."

It doesn't make sense to Kramer, but he lets it go.

"So Reni took the car for a joy ride," Kramer says. "Why didn't you say so before?"

Gerhard shrugs his shoulders, then shakes his head. "Who was asking? We all bought the idea that it was vandalism. Some red-hot Red who went berserk seeing Western plates."

He pauses, looking hard at Kramer. "You don't think Reni set the bomb, do you? I mean what good would that do anybody?"

What good, indeed? Kramer thinks. "It would help if we knew where she went that day."

"Overnight, actually," Gerhard says. "But then you should know that. You and she were lovers by then, weren't you?"

"Working up to it," Kramer says. "But we didn't get strong until after Prague."

He thinks about that comment for a moment, about the timing of their relationship, and wonders, for the first time, if there is any significance to it. Once you open the doors to doubt about another person, there are infinite corridors to follow. A maze with no way home but blind trust.

In fact, he had not been with Reni just before the Prague fiasco; she had thought it better that none of them be seen together for a time before and after the mission.

"So we're looking for somebody who planted a bomb under the rented car," Gerhard says, "over a quarter of a century ago. Great."

"That's one avenue we're pursuing," Randall says. There's a heavy formality to his voice, and Kramer remembers that he and Gerhard were never the best of friends. Too much alike for that.

"There's a possible neo-Nazi connection, as well," Kramer explains.

"Vogel?" Gerhard asks.

Kramer nods. "Rick says she managed to infiltrate his organization. To get her hands on sponsor lists and Fascists in Bonn who haven't come out of the closet yet. Sympathizers in high places."

"Rick says this?"

"She visited him after the meetings."

"Extraordinary." He twirls his mustache again. "I can't believe this is actually happening. Reni dead. Murdered. You're sure of that?"

"It smells like it," Kramer says.

Gerhard squints his eyes, sets his jaw: a bad caricature of John Wayne.

"I've got to go back with you, then. Help catch the bastard."

Kramer waits for Gerhard to finish his dramatics before pressing him on the secret that Reni learned in 1974 that could drive her from him, that was so terrible she could no longer face him.

"Look," Gerhard says, facing Kramer, and searching out his eyes. "I know I'm a comical sort of prick to you, Sam. Always spouting off dramatically, going native wherever I am. Never finishing my great American novel. Hell, never even starting it, if the truth be known. But I loved Reni. Loved her so much it was like a constant ache. I wouldn't harm a hair on her head. I just couldn't stand to be around her any longer. It hurt too damn much being ignored. I don't need her money. I've been clipping coupons from Daddy's wise investments lo, these many years. And I didn't plant a bomb under the car I delivered to Helmut. I don't even know how to light a firecracker, for God's sake."

He lets out air, his chest sagging with the effort, then turns, looking back down the scree. Suddenly, he waves; an automatic gesture, as if he has just seen someone he knows.

Kramer is about to look when Gerhard continues, "But Vogel. I don't like that connection. Too much coincidence. I've got to go back with you. Got to talk with . . ."

Suddenly, a crimson mist explodes out the back of Gerhard's neck, wetting Kramer's face. The whack of a rifle shot echoes up the ravine. Gerhard stands paralyzed for a moment and then is spun around when another shot tears a ragged hole in his back, exiting just above his heart. He crumples to the ground at Kramer's feet just as the second report sounds.

Kramer leans over him, cradling his head in his arm. A quarter-size hole seeps blood from his neck; another from his chest. He feels the carotid artery: nothing. It's no longer Gerhard he's cradling, but a corpse. Blood leaches onto Kramer's shirt sleeve. A *thwump* sounds to his right and stops him from any thought. Dirt kicks up at his feet. Flies buzz overhead, followed by more cracks and echoing reports. Except they aren't flies, but bullets.

"Get back from the edge, Sam!"

Randall is hiding behind the boulder and bullets ping off it, ripping white scars in its dusty cowl, sending showers of rock powder and chips flying. Kramer looks quickly down the ravine. There are two of them standing in plain sight, rifles to their shoulders, shooting and climbing. Despite the difference in elevation, the shooters have a firing angle on him and Randall, both exposed on the bare ridge. Kramer flattens himself on the ground as a bullet pounds into Gerhard's body. His mind turns off as he crawls back to cover, pulling himself with his hands. He wants to be one with the soil, to play the lizard. He hears the bullets overhead, but does not panic. His reactions are cold and automatic. There is no time for fear: that will come later.

A hand grips his and pulls him the last yard to the relative safety of the boulder. Relative, Kramer soon discovers, because the shooters have an angle on the entire bit of exposed ridge where they are hiding. He and Randall are midway along the ridge; twenty yards or so in each direction to get back to the covered path, out of the angle of the ravine.

"Who is it?" Randall says, breathing hard.

Kramer shakes his head. "Doesn't matter. We can't stay here."

Another ping of a bullet caroming off the boulder, stone chips flying over their heads.

"They're moving up the pass. We've got to make a run for it."

"Maybe it's a mistake," Randall says. "Hunters who can't see what they're shooting at."

But neither of them believe that.

"He's dead, Randall. Gerhard's dead. Hunters or not, they're going to have to finish it."

Randall's jaw muscles work; he runs a hand through his beard roughly as if to wake himself up. "Okay. Me first."

Kramer eyes him. "Whatever you say, buddy. Wait for the next volley."

The shots come in pairs, spraying calcite and dirt, echoing more loudly with each round. The shooters are coming up the ravine.

"Now!" Kramer says after a round of shots tear at the face of the boulder.

Randall lunges out of their cover, onto his belly, headed for the trail leading up the mountain. A shot kicks dirt, and Kramer grabs Randall's leg before he can begin scrambling, pulling him back behind the boulder.

"Not that way," Kramer says, after he manhandles Randall in back of the boulder once again. "Down the trail. They'll cut us off the other way. I'll take point."

Randall's eyes are wide and he says nothing, sucking air like it's a depleting commodity. Kramer waits for the next round of shots, dives from the boulder onto his belly, and begins scrambling, his shirt catching on rocks and roots in the path. A bullet smacks into the hard-packed earth a few inches from his head, but he keeps on scrambling, crawls in back of a smaller rock that provides some protection and then yells back to Randall, "Now!"

Randall obeys automatically, leaping a good two yards and

then scrambling on all fours, bullets flying over him. Kramer does not wait to see his progress, but makes an upright dash for it to the next protection along the path: a scrub pine not much wider than he is. He sucks in his belly, watching Randall make his way to the small boulder—their stations of the cross.

Who the hell are they? But he doesn't give his mind a chance to start working, or for fear to grip him. He's off, running and diving, the end of the ridge coming ever closer. Running and diving. Not giving them a clear shot. Zigzags won't help with profile shots. He keeps waiting for the shot that will bring him down, the shot that will tear into his flesh and splatter blood. But he also keeps moving, moving, his breath coming hard at this altitude. He reaches the end of the ridge and can hear nothing but the pounding of his heart for several instants, the grunting of Randall as he crawls along the dusty ridge, kicking up dirt like a dust devil. It takes Kramer that long to realize that otherwise, it is silent. The shooting has stopped.

He listens hard for loose rocks forming small avalanches as the shooters make their way up the scree. But there is nothing. Randall crawls the last feet to cover and continues lying on his belly, panting like an animal, unable to move.

Kramer listens to the sound of wind up the ravine; the goat bells; the rush of wings overhead as a hawk soars in an updraft. Then from far away comes the sound of car doors slamming, the revving of an engine, the whine of first gear.

Kramer edges cautiously back onto the ridge, moving toward where Gerhard lies like a pile of old clothes.

Randall looks up, reaches toward him. "Get back, Sam."

"They're gone, Randall." Down the ravine the vehicle is speeding away in the distance, leaving a parachute of dust behind it.

He now walks to Gerhard's lifeless body, looking down at it for a long moment, at the boots and vest and cummerbund. His oldest friend; not his dearest. There is a sour taste in Kramer's mouth: bile and the brass taste of blood and fear.

Flies circle the bloody wounds in the body, and Kramer shoos them away. He feels Randall coming up beside him.

"I'm going to find those bastards," Kramer says.

"We should get down to the car. Call the police. They might be back."

Kramer watches the car as it grows tinier and tinier in the distance, the cyclone of dust in back of it almost disappearing.

"Sam? You hear me? We've got to get to the police."

Suddenly, from above them comes a voice in Greek that makes both Randall and Kramer scramble for cover. Above them, from the impossibly steep slope abutting the trail, come three hunters in black shirts, carrying rifles. One has an ibex slung over his shoulders, its head lolling loosely, its purple tongue protruding.

They raise hands in friendly greeting as they approach, and Kramer comes out from behind the boulder, happier than he can ever remember at seeing another human. He looks back down the ravine; the car is no longer visible. But it must have been the sight of these hunters that scared the shooters away. That saved their lives.

The hunters come up to Gerhard's body and look from it to Randall and Kramer. Men in their thirties who, beyond their black shirts, wear none of the traditional Cretan garb. Levis and hiking boots for them. The one lugging the dead ibex has Nike Airs on. White against the blood-red dust.

"Dead?" one of them says in English.

Kramer nods. "They shot him." He points down the ravine at the last of the dust in the distance.

The men ask no questions, but the largest of them slings Gerhard over his wide shoulders like more bagged game, and they make their way down the trail toward Lourakia. Toward civilization.

"Your friend waved at the hunters, you say."

"They weren't hunters," Kramer says, but the police inspector from Timbaki is not listening. He's too busy fore-fingering information onto an incident report in the carriage of his typewriter.

They are sitting in the station offices later that evening. It's gotten chilly at night, but they're still wearing their perspiration-damp shirts. There are faded calendar prints of Greece on the walls, like a classroom in a primary school.

"We will go up Psiloritis in the morning to search for spent cartridges and for bullets," the inspector says, not look-ing up from his typing.

"There's one still lodged in Gerhard's body, if you're interested," Kramer says. "He took a hit after he was killed. Probably saved my life. The slug's still in there, I guarantee."

The inspector shoves his thick belly back from the desk, lifts the black-framed reading glasses up onto his forehead, and looks closely at Kramer, as if only now taking interest.

"Our forensics people will examine the body in the morn-ing."

"Just trying to save you a hike," Kramer says. "And they weren't hunters."

"How can you be so sure?" the inspector asks.

"They kept on shooting once they could see us plainly, that's how. We look like ibexes?"

Randall is sitting in a plastic chair, sipping on a demitasse of Turkish coffee. He tries to smile at Kramer's remark, but fails. It's been a long day.

The inspector lifts pudgy arms in a caricature of an Ital-ian shrug, "Perhaps they became frightened at what they had done on impulse. I am not trying to excuse the crime . . ."

"You have a funny way of doing that."

"Merely explaining how things like this happen in a land where most adult males own guns, even though they are illegal."

"These weren't Cretans, either," Kramer tells him. "They were northern Europeans."

"How can you be so sure?"

"The way they were dressed. The way they moved; heavy, like they had shit in their pants. Locals move over rocky terrain like they are goats. These boys were cows."

This makes the inspector smile in spite of himself. He turns back to the typewriter, flips his glasses down on the bridge of his nose, and begins hunting-and-pecking again.

"Identity unknown," he says as he types. "Perhaps European."

He turns back to Kramer and cuts his eyes to Randall momentarily.

"What were you three doing on the mountain?"

"Walking. Is that a crime?"

The inspector slams the carriage return home and scowls at Kramer.

"You have lost a friend. I am aware of that and truly sorry. But I do not like your tone, Mr. Kramer. Not at all. Neither do I like having to come into the office on a Sunday night when I have promised to take my boy to the movies. Or to have to speak English, which is a strain for me and for which I receive no recompense. Do you understand me, Mr. Kramer? You are annoying me. You don't want to do that. We will examine all possible clues in this unfortunate matter. Meanwhile, I suggest you both go and get some rest. And let me say that it is fortunate for you that those men witnessed the incident. Homicide is usually a family affair. Have you heard that?"

"It was one of those toy Land Rovers," Kramer says.

J. Sydney Jones

"What?"

"Their car. One of those little rent-a-car jobs that have four-wheel drive."

"I'll include that in the report."

"You do that, Inspector." Kramer gets up out of his chair. His legs are sore; every muscle in his body aches. His head, too. "Sorry to inconvenience you."

Kramer and Randall leave the cinder-block police station, going out into the fresh night air. A bright half-moon is out; Orion shines weakly just below it. Over the roofs of the houses on the opposite side of the road, Kramer can see the bulk of Mount Ida, a light gray against the darker sky.

Alexandros Kariakis is waiting up for them at his home on Odos Phaistos, a small replica of an Italian villa with a wrought-iron fence surrounding it, orange-painted wooden shutters, and the sweet scent of magnolia in the courtyard. He's got a *mezedes* for them of olives, stuffed grape leaves, chunks of feta, fresh tomatoes, and beans. He lives alone, has an old woman come in from the village to do his meals and keep the house tidy. Though Kramer's age, he looks and acts two decades older, like an aging roué with an eye forever roving over the young women of the town. He keeps scandal at bay with fortnightly visits to the brothels of Athens and is one of those men for whom the idea of marriage is as foreign as Swahili.

"We should wake the Chameleon," Kariakis says, fetching a dusty bottle of raki out of an old Venetian chest in the low-ceilinged living room. Heavy oak furniture, tapestries on the white walls along with reproductions of Oskar Kokoschka and Francis Bacon.

Kramer is still half-numb from the experiences of the day, but takes the proffered glass of raki gratefully.

"Was he Irish by any chance?" Kariakis asks, holding his glass up to toast with Randall and Kramer.

202

"Everyone's Irish when it comes to death," Randall says and throws back the drink in one gulp.

Kramer and Kariakis do the same.

"He was a funny one," Kariakis says. "I did not know him well, but I liked him. He had a heart."

Kramer sets the empty glass down on the oak table; Kariakis refills it.

"How long did you know him, Sam?"

Kramer looks at the full glass and then at the doctor. "We traveled here together in the '60s. Then went to school in Vienna. Both running from Vietnam. Keeping the student deferment intact."

But he finds he is no mood for a wake; revenge is more to the point.

"So who do *you* think they were, Randall?" he suddenly says. "Vogel's men?"

"Like the inspector said, Sam. Maybe they were just hunters who pulled off a stupid round when they saw something move on a distant hillside."

"You didn't believe that up on the mountain. You don't believe it now."

"Who is this Vogel?" Kariakis says.

"It's a long story, Doc." Kramer doesn't take his eyes off Randall.

"Okay," Randall finally says. "I don't think they were hunters. But it's plausible. I mean weirder things have happened. No sense jumping to conclusions."

"I don't think it's jumping to conclusions to figure that somebody shooting at you for several minutes—I mean seriously shooting—is trying to kill you."

"But kill who, Sam?" Kariakis says, smiling. "Did these people mean to kill all three of you or just you and Randall, or were they after Gerhard and you happened to be there?"

Kramer feels his heart leap into his throat; quite literally there is a sudden lump that prevents him from swallowing for a moment. His mind runs with what Kariakis has said, and he does not like the goalpost it's headed for.

"I hadn't thought of that," Kramer says. "Say we've rattled cages over Reni's death, over the missing memoirs. Say that whoever killed Reni finds out we're on their trail. So, okay, they get rid of us, right?" He looks at Randall.

"Right."

Kramer pauses for another moment, and then drinks off the raki.

"But why here? Why come all the way to Crete to do it?"

"Because it's out of the way," Randall offers. "No spotlights."

Kramer shakes his head at this. "Accidents can be arranged all over the world. Why a shooting in Crete? Why Gerhard?"

Kariakis refills the glasses once more. "If you do not mind an outsider offering an opinion . . ."

"Please," Kramer says.

"Perhaps Gerhard was, in fact, the target."

Kramer nods, then pounds the table with a clenched fist. "You've got it, Doc. And we led the sons of bitches right to him. He'd still be alive if we hadn't come looking for him."

"But what could he know?" Randall says. "He hasn't even been in Germany for months." He stops, looks down at his drink. "Duh. Pardon the slow synapses. Violence tends to disrupt my electrical system. Reni's confidant, right?"

Another nod from Kramer. "Right. If she was killed to suppress her memoirs, to eradicate memory of some incident, then wouldn't our killer want to track down the person closest to her for years, who maybe knows exactly what went into those memoirs?"

Randall sits up in his chair now, his eyes alert. "And Gerhard just happened to be nowhere available at the time. Off the face of the map. Until we came along and led them right to him."

They say nothing for a moment, and then Kariakis repeats his earlier question, "Who is this Vogel?"

This time, Kramer fills him in a bit more on the possible suspects, having already told him the broad outlines of the case yesterday.

"I do not think I would want Herr Vogel on the opposing side," Kariakis says after listening closely for several minutes.

"Not on your team, either," Kramer says. "The best place for him is in a zoo."

Suddenly, Kramer is taken back to the ridge this afternoon. He sees Gerhard looking down the ravine and waving to the men who got out of the car. And then he'd said something about Vogel. About not liking the coincidence.

Kramer snaps his fingers. "Gerhard knew something. Remember, Randall, just before he was shot, he said he'd have to go back with us. He had to talk with somebody. I'll bet dollars to doughnuts it had something to do with why Reni left me. Her big secret that he couldn't divulge, not even after her death."

Kariakis looks curious, but politely holds back questions. Kramer is grateful for this because he suddenly realizes he should not tell his old friend anything more. He understands that he and Randall are marked men now. There is no way the shooters can know that Gerhard did not tell them his secret. If his line of logic holds true, they will be the next targets, as well as anyone involved with them.

"We need to get back north pronto," he says to Randall. "Whoever's responsible for this is pulling the strings back there."

Suddenly, he remembers Gerhard's startling news about Maria; about Reni visiting her. *There's motive for you, as well,*

Kramer figures. If she was stuck in some Czech jail all these years, wouldn't she maybe have an ax to grind with those she felt responsible? Like whoever set her up with the car bomb? If Helmut finally tumbled to the bomb, wouldn't she as well, with nothing better to do than brood and kill bed bugs?

Two directions. One leading back to Munich, the other to Prague. Kramer thinks about it for a moment, remembering the advice of Kommissar Boehm. *Let the police keep tugging at Vogel*, he finally tells himself. *Meanwhile, we head for Prague to see Maria.*

But Kramer does not share this thought. Kariakis is one friend who's going to stay out of the loop.

"Kip time," Kramer says. "We've got some traveling to do tomorrow."

"What about the investigation?" Randall says.

Kramer stands and stretches. The raki has gone to his head, pleasantly.

"You heard the inspector. It was a hunting accident. I'm not contesting that. Not here. Not now. Murder's not good for tourism."

Kariakis corks the bottle, and Kramer shoots a grin at him.

"Doc, I'd advise you to keep a watch on your back for a time. Those were not nice fellows this afternoon. If they think we learned something from Gerhard, they may also wonder about anybody we talk to. Get the picture?"

Kariakis smiles broadly. "I stand warned. But I think those men, if they are professional at all, will be on a flight already from Iráklion, no? After all, Crete is an island. Large in the imagination, tiny in square footage. Foreigners still stand out, especially in the off-season. Especially if they buy weapons here. Which I assume they had to do. A person would be insane to try and travel with rifles through airport inspections."

"All the same," Kramer says, "I'd carry a gun for a while if I were you. You do have one, don't you?"

Another smile from Kariakis, "Am I not a Cretan?"

"What about tonight?" Randall says, rising now and yawning.

"We sleep," Kramer says.

"Very funny. I mean what if Doc here is wrong? What if our friends come back to finish the job?"

Kariakis has walked to a window, opens its shutter and looks out through the garden to the street beyond. He shakes his head as he turns back to them. "I wouldn't worry about that if I were you. Our inspector is perhaps not very friendly, but is very thorough, very civic-minded. He's posted a policeman outside."

CHAPTER SIXTEEN

It's cold and gray, and the Viennese look at Kramer's tan jealously as he paces in front of the Café Pigalle, checking the street up and down, keeping his eyes peeled for unfriendly sorts. The meet is set for four thirty. He looks in a window of the café at a clock over the bar: quarter to five.

One of the ladies sitting at the bar dangling a fishnet-stockinged leg sees him and winks.

Where the hell are you, Rudi?

"*Was gibts*, Kramer? What's up?"

Kramer spins around at the sound of the voice. Rudi Tourescu is smiling up at him, dressed nattily in a double-breasted camel-hair overcoat. He is hatless, his black hair plastered to his head like he's just stepped out of a mobster movie.

"Take it easy," Rudi says, seeing the alarm on Kramer's face. "It's a friend."

"I could use one," Kramer says.

"Trouble?"

Kramer nods. "Can we go somewhere to talk?"

They're in the Second District, near the Prater, hardly the

sort of place Kramer would have picked for a meet. But Rudi loves it; loves playing the hood with his pinkie ring and a caricature of a greaseball hairdo.

"We can talk in the car," he says, nodding toward a long black Mercedes limousine parked across the street and taking Kramer's arm in his tiny hand. "The only bugs in there are mine." He laughs loudly, gold teeth showing in front.

Kramer allows himself to be led to the car and climbs in the backseat. Rudi pushes a button on his armrest, and a window closes between the driver and them. The guy at the wheel never looks back.

Outside, women in short leather skirts and high boots are staking their places on the street. Offices will be closing soon; customers on their way.

"So what is it, Kramer?" Rudi says, straightening his slacks as he stretches out in the seat next to Kramer. "What's so urgent?"

"I need a gun."

Rudi pushes his palms at Kramer. "Hold on, there. I'm in software, remember?"

"This isn't bullshit, and I'm not trying to stick you. Strictly off the record. Someone's after me, and I need to be able to talk back in kind."

Rudi screws up his face. "You ever shoot a gun, Kramer? I mean, pardon the question."

His German is street; he smells like a flowerpot. Kramer met him a little more than a year ago after writing an article about the wave of new immigrants coming into Western Europe from the former Bloc countries. About how Western countries, Austria in particular, with its negative population rate, needed immigration, needed new blood and the optimism of immigrants. Not a popular article, especially for a country set on a course of kicking the refugees and immigrants out. But one day not long after the article appeared in translation in the local press—where it was ridiculed as more liberal hogwash from Amis who had no idea what the problems were on the ground—it brought him a visitor who had liked it. Rudi Tourescu took the article as a shot in the arm for the immigrant community. Kramer liked the young Romanian right off: spunky, enterprising and cocky. Tourescu treated him like a savior to his people, promised a favor in return.

It is time to call in favors.

"I know about guns," Kramer says. "And I know about your pirated software, too, Rudi. I've got nothing against the black market. How can I? I'm a capitalist."

"Exactly," Rudi says, smiling broadly. "It's the ultimate in free market enterprise. But a gun . . . that's a different matter. Who's trying to kill you?"

"The bad guys."

"You crack me up, Kramer. Know that? You want some help? I've got soldiers."

"I want a gun."

Tourescu nods, picking at a piece of lint on his black slacks. "Just one?"

"No. Make it two."

"Lots of enemies?"

"No. The other's for a friend."

"It's not easy."

"That's why I came to you," Kramer says.

Rudi's attention is diverted for a moment by a young woman on the street whose black hair is ridiculously coiffed and piled atop her head, wearing a black rubber raincoat and what look to be riding boots. She is positioning herself at the middle of the block in front of a cheap hotel that rents rooms by the hour. Rudi buttons down his window and beckons the girl in Romanian. She brightens when she hears her tongue, and sidles over to the car, licking her lips and propping her right hand on her hip as she moves.

When she leans in the window, Rudi says some quick, harsh words to her that Kramer cannot understand. Her eyes go huge and round, and she looks at Kramer with real terror. Rudi nods at her frightened eyes, and then pulls out a wine-colored calfskin wallet from the inside breast pocket of his overcoat, peels off a couple thousand-schilling notes and sticks them in her hand. He crumples her fingers around the bills, says something more, this time in a consoling tone, and she nods, glancing quickly at Kramer again. Finally, she backs away from the car and then moves off down the street, never looking back.

Kramer lets the silence go for a moment. Then, "What was that all about?"

Rudi is smiling to himself. "Nothing. My karma buy-off for the day."

"You told her I was the man, didn't you?"

Rudi turns to him with a mouth open to deny, then pauses, closes his mouth and shrugs.

"Maybe," he says. "But it was in a good cause. How old do you think she is?"

"Eighteen?"

"Guess again. She's fourteen going on forty. But I think I scared the shit out of her. She might even take the job I offered her."

"What? Selling stolen goods?"

"It's better than the streets, Kramer. Better than taking potluck with every kinky bastard in town." He looks hard at Kramer without an ounce of humor in his eyes. "I won't have our women selling their bodies. Playing the cheap Gypsy. Those days are over."

There's more silence as business picks up on the street; as the gray day turns to rain that pounds on the roof of their car momentarily, sprouting umbrellas outdoors.

"Anyway," Rudi finally says. "About that gun . . ."

"Guns," Kramer corrects him.

"A couple of nine-millimeter Walthers do you okay?"

Kramer grins. "If they're good enough for the police, they're good enough for me."

Rudi returns the smile.

"You are a smart guy, Kramer. Maybe even savvy. So how'd you get so dumb as to have somebody trying to kill you?"

"Just because I am so smart. I think I know something somebody doesn't want me to."

"Like what?"

Kramer snickers. "That's the problem. I don't know."

Kramer meets Randall at the Café Eiles just down from his apartment building. Randall's at a cozy window seat, sipping on a mineral water and reading yesterday's *Herald Tribune*. An empty plate, smeared with chocolate frosting, sits in front of him.

"It's about time you got here," he says when Kramer slides into the plush bench seat opposite him. "The boy was getting nervous."

Randall smiles a toothy grin at the waiter dressed in a tuxedo as he says to Kramer, "Bastard thinks I'm an indigent."

"Aren't you?" Kramer nods at the waiter to order.

"Not when you're around, Sammy."

Kramer orders a mocha and looks out at the hulking outline of the Rathaus filling the square across the road. It's raining steadily now, and the lights of the cars speeding along Landesgerichtsstrasse glisten off the pavement; the red-and-green pedestrian signs cast long glowing streaks of light on the wet, oil-impregnated asphalt.

"Sacher torte's good here, Sam. Why not have some?"

But Kramer ignores this, watching the street, checking for cars that come by too often.

"You think they followed us here?" Randall says after the waiter delivers the coffee and departs on squeaky shoes.

Kramer stirs in a cube of sugar. "It's a possibility. I didn't see anything or anyone suspicious today, though. But then, I'm not sure I'd notice."

"You going to tell me about the mysterious visit you had to make this afternoon?"

"In a bit." Kramer checks the clock over the cashier's booth at the entrance. "We've got to get home soon."

"Well, then, be that way, jerk. I thought we were in this together."

"You'll see."

They sit in silence for another ten minutes while Kramer finishes his coffee. He then pays for both of them and asks the waiter, Michael, how his oldest boy is. The kid has been undergoing chemo for the past six months.

"Not much change, Herr Kramer. But his spirits are up. I'll tell him you asked."

"Do that," Kramer says, leaving a generous tip. "It takes time, they say. They caught it early."

The waiter nods. "There is that to be thankful for." He scoops up the tip and places it in a separate compartment of the black leather change purse he carries strapped to his waist.

Kramer and Randall leave, stepping into the driving rain, and Kramer thinks again that there are many circles of hell to be investigated.

It's a jog and dodge of puddles and spiky umbrellas for the two blocks to his flat. Earlier this afternoon after returning from Crete, he and Randall stopped there only long enough for a shower and a change of clothes. But it felt good to be home, to be among his things once again. Seductive, the idea of security. But now, reaching the third floor with Randall panting alongside him, he immediately realizes that security is an illusion.

His door is open, lights on. He and Randall approach warily, and a door to his right flies open. Frau Bechmann stands backlit in the housecoat that she wears day in and day out, her hair covered in a babushka. They say she was once in the corps de ballet at the State Opera; she looks like a cleaning lady.

"You had some very rude visitors, Herr Kramer."

He nods at her, inching along cautiously toward his door.

"Did you hear me? They were so noisy that I had to come to the door and tell them to keep it down. *Petruschka* was playing on the first channel. I could barely hear. Regular barbarians."

She pulls the housecoat more tightly around her waist when neither Randall nor Kramer respond. They are too busy examining the damage from the doorway of the flat.

"Were they builders?" she asks.

There is not a surface or piece of furniture undisturbed. Papers litter the floors; clothing has been torn and scattered about like oversize confetti; chairs are broken and legs spread about like fat matchsticks. Kramer catches a glimpse of the kitchen floor covered with rice and pasta. The Tyrolean hope chest is ripped apart, its contents lying in a sodden heap next to the broken painted panels and empty liquor bottles. Directly in front of him, so close that he only examines it last, is the wooden Madonna from Hungary. They have driven nails into her eyes and breasts.

"Jesus, Sam!"

Kramer turns to Frau Bechmann. "You saw them?"

She looks at Kramer with silent suspicion.

"What did they look like?"

"I didn't get a good look at them," she says, pulling the housecoat tight around her neck, the veins on the backs her old hands bulging. "Only their backs. But they were quite large. Like movers."

"What did they say to you?" Kramer is persistent, but knows he is not going to get much out of her. She doesn't want to get involved; doesn't want to become a witness.

"They told me to mind my own business. I ask you, is that any way to talk to a lady?"

Kramer turns back, shaking his head at the destruction. "When was this?"

She purses her lips, looks upward in cogitation. "An hour ago, maybe less."

"We were at the café then, Sam," Randall says. "What if we'd come home early?"

Kramer ignores this. "Thanks, Frau Bechmann. Sorry about the noise."

"Well, I missed most of *Petruschka*, thanks to them." She turns and slams the door behind her.

"I guess we should clean it up," Kramer says.

"Aren't you calling the police?"

Kramer shakes his head. "What's the use?"

"The use is that the authorities are the ones to be handling this. Maybe somebody saw the guys come or go. Saw their car. How'd they get in, anyway, without a house key?"

"Just kept ringing apartments until someone buzzed them in without asking who was there," Kramer says. "Simple enough. And the police don't want to know about this, I guarantee you. I'll bet nothing's been stolen. Just damaged."

He traces fingers over the delicate carving of the wooden Madonna, feels anger rising like a black cloud over the horizon.

"No, this wasn't some breaking-and-entering goon. It's a calling card. A warning. We going to tell the police that? You think they'll understand?"

"Maybe we should take the warning, Sam."

Kramer looks at him hard. "You going to help me clean up?"

Fifteen minutes later, there is a knocking at the door and both Randall and Kramer tense. Kramer goes to the door, looks through the peephole, then unlocks it. Rudi's driver is standing there with a green Julius Meinl shopping bag in hand and gives it to Kramer. His eyes stray over Kramer's shoulder to the wreckage in the flat, go wide momentarily, but he says nothing.

Kramer thanks him and shuts and double locks the door, ignoring Randall's look of curiosity. The bag is heavy in Kramer's hand as he carries it inside to the kitchen, sets the pine table upright and then plops the bag on top with a dull metal clunk. He looks inside the bag. The guns are wrapped in tissue paper, along with several boxes of ammunition for each piece. A note accompanies this, and Kramer reaches in and pulls it out: *Call if you need help. Don't be too smart.*

Randall comes in the kitchen as Kramer sits at the table, unwrapping the guns, hefting them for balance, and checking the trigger mechanisms.

"I don't like this," Randall says over Kramer's shoulder. "Is this what you went out for this afternoon?"

Kramer says nothing, pulling the empty clip out of the pistol butt of one of the weapons, smelling the gun oil.

"You hear me, Sam? This is getting way out of control. It's not something we can play around with anymore."

Kramer looks up from the gun. "What do you suggest?"

"At least contact Kommissar Boehm in Bad Lunsburg. Let him know about Gerhard."

Kramer starts inserting bullets into the empty clip. "I did this afternoon."

"And what'd he say?"

"What you're saying."

"So what's all this about?" He jabs a finger at the guns.

"He also said he's getting stonewalled by the Berlin police. That people in Bonn are making noises about his investigating a case that should be closed."

"But with Gerhard's death . . ."

"Look," Kramer says, losing his temper, slamming the clip onto the table. "You want me to spell it out for you? Nobody wants to touch this. The Greeks are calling it accidental manslaughter. A hunting accident. The Germans don't want waves. So this is dead in the water unless we keep pursuing it."

"And we might end up dead in the water, as well," Randall says, looking around at the mess in the kitchen. Olive oil has been smeared into the rice and pasta on the floor.

Kramer says nothing for a time, trying to control his anger. Then, "Maybe you're right, Randall. Maybe this isn't something you want to be involved in anymore. I mean, Reni was close to me, and the whole thing with the memoirs seemed an incredible mystery. Like getting hold of a loose thread and unraveling the last twenty years of life. But you're right. It's not a game any longer. It's deadly serious. And I'm in it. Deep in it and there's no going back for me. I poked at the sleeping dog. I brought those killers down to Crete. They would never have found Gerhard if I hadn't led them straight to him."

"Give it a rest, Sam. We still don't know if those guys were after us or Gerhard."

"I'm sure." Kramer snicks the full clip into the pistol butt, jamming it home with the ball of his hand.

"So what do you plan to do? Go blazing into Vogel's offices and wreak vengeance? Get real, Sam."

"I'm not even saying it was Vogel. I just want to be able to fight back next time."

"You're crazy, you know that? I think you've been reading too much. This is real life, Sam. Not some detective novel. Whoever shot Gerhard means business. He, she, they are covering tracks from all sorts of potential crimes. If they put out a hit on you, you'll know about it after it's over. Period."

Kramer says nothing, which infuriates Randall.

"So what do you think?" Randall says. "It was Maria? She was paying Reni back?"

"She could be a player. And we know that someone else had access to that car besides Gerhard. Somebody else could have planted the bomb. Reni or . . ."

"Stop, Sam. This is no longer interesting to me, you know that?"

"Scared?"

"Yes. Aren't you?"

Kramer nods. "But angry, too. More angry than scared."

"Sam, you're a journalist, not a gun-toting cowboy."

"And what are you, Randall?"

Randall thinks a moment, shaking his head. "I'm not a violent man, Sam. Nothing's solved by it, only perpetuated."

"I'm not asking what you aren't."

Randall clamps his jaw. "I'm a global village idiot, Sam. That's my job. I come to spread the word of irresponsibility. To cheer and connect. I know my area of competency, Sam." He leans over and picks up one of the guns. "And this is not it."

Kramer takes the gun out of his hand, setting it gently back on the tissue paper.

"I'll see you around, Randall."

Kramer doesn't look up; begins filling the second clip from the part-empty ammunition box.

"Sam." Randall touches his shoulder lightly, but Kramer remains silent.

"Yeah," Randall finally says, removing his hand. "I'll see you around."

Randall manages to recover some of his things from the general mess and stuff them into his leather pack.

He is at the door when Kramer speaks next. "You're going to have to make a stand sometime in life, Randall. You know? It's just not worth it otherwise."

Randall starts to reply, thinks better of it, and smiles.

"Say hi to Maria for me," he says as he goes out the door.

Kramer sits in the flat for another two hours feeling the anger build to a palpable force, then gets his Barbour jacket, stuffs the guns into the pockets next to his passport and savings book, checks the hallway for visitors, and goes into the night.

The taxi drops him off in the Fourth District just behind the Karlskirche. He looks up at the apartment building on the corner, to the turret on the fourth floor with the huge rubber plant in it. Lights are on. Kate's still up.

He rings the outside buzzer and after a few moments Kate's intercom crackles to life.

"It's me," he says.

A pause from her, then, "Kramer? What the hell are you doing here?"

He doesn't much like talking on the street. A car draws slowly by the doorway to Kate's apartment. It's windows are tinted so he cannot see inside. A sudden panic grips him.

"Just let me in. I'll explain later."

"You drunk?"

"Come on, Kate."

She buzzes and the front door unlocks momentarily. He pushes and goes through, then closes it securely behind him. He's sweating, large drops trickling down his back and into the waist of his pants.

The red timer button for corridor lights is next to the door, but he doesn't push it. There are windows on the top half of the house door. *I'd be a perfect silhouette for a shooter*, he thinks.

He feels his way up the first flight of stairs, then hits the red button on the next landing, and the timed lights come on, dimly illuminating the tiled stairs, a pattern of irises in blossom along the bottom of the wall, purple against faded yellow.

He knocks on Kate's door twice before she opens it, wearing a terry cloth bathrobe the color of crushed raspberries and carrying a book. It's an old Harvard Classic edition in navy binding, and she clutches it to her bosom. He reads the title, *Anna Karenina*, but she mistakes the look and blushes, pulling the robe closer around her throat.

"Sorry to be bothering you so late," he says. "Thought I'd better check on the bureau."

"You'll see tomorrow," Kate says, not inviting him any further than the door jamb.

"Maybe not," Kramer says. "I'm only in town overnight."

She squints at him in the dimness of the hall, then reaches out and pulls him by the arm into her entryway.

"What happened to you?"

He follows her gaze to his forehead, feels the bandage. "That?" He shakes it off. "Happened last week. No big deal."

"You in trouble, Kramer?"

"Yeah. Sort of."

She looks at him with the eyes of a schoolmistress examining a truant.

"Marty's pissed," she says. "I might be next in line for bureau chief."

"That'd be great for you."

"You better come in." She looks out the door, up and down the hall.

Kramer has been at her flat once before, to pick up some copy on a day she was too sick to come into the office. He shows himself into the sitting room; all nineteenth century with heavy oak furniture, a carpet-covered sofa straight out of Freud's consulting rooms, dark oils in massive gilded frames on the walls, dusty green aspidistras and rubber plants wherever light is available. A secret side to Kate or just too lazy to change the decor of a rented apartment?

She nods toward a leather armchair. "Sit down. Drink?"

He sags into the seat with a sigh. "I'd love one."

"White wine okay?"

He nods. "Great."

A minute later, she is back with two glasses and no book for protection. She hands him his and sits on the sofa, curling her legs under her like a cat.

"So what's the deal, Kramer? You look like prey rather than predator."

"Like I say"—he takes a sip of wine; it is cool and tart and fresh tasting—"I wanted to check on things at the bureau. See if there were any problems."

"Umm." She says it like a contradiction. "Everything's okay, I guess. Marty's fuming, but there's no pink slip in the mail, if that's what's worrying you. We're starting a new series on the UN peacekeeping force—Blue Helmet Blues. Not bad, huh?"

"Your series?"

She nods.

"Good for you."

She almost smiles, then puts her glass down on a book-cluttered end table. "You really don't give a shit about this, do you, Kramer? You *are* in trouble."

"Could be."

"Is it that woman in Germany? The one who died?"

"I don't want to involve you."

She laughs. "Why come here, then?"

Why indeed? He thinks about this for a moment, about Randall's departure, about how he forced Randall to leave, actually. *Is that what you were after?* he asks himself. *To get Randall out of it, for his own sake?*

"I need a place to stay for the night, okay?"

She opens her mouth in protest.

"I don't mean that way," he quickly adds. "The sofa would

be great. Just someplace no one knows about." He checked on the way here in the taxi. No one was following. The cruising car at the entrance was just coincidence. Had to be.

"What do you say?" he asks after she is silent for a time.

"Sure. Give the neighbors something to gossip about over coffee." She smiles. "You sure you don't want to talk about it?"

"You've got the biggest rubber plant in Vienna," he says, rising and going to the turret window. He looks to the street below. No one is in sight.

"I get the message," she says. "How about a sleeping bag? Or do you want sheets?"

He turns, looking back to her. "The bag would be fine."

She gets up, all business and ready to get him organized.

"Kate."

She stops and looks at him.

"Thanks. I owe you one."

"One? Bullshit. Five or more if I have to cover for you at the office much longer."

He falls asleep to the musty smell of the old rug beneath the sofa, to the warm aroma of Kate from her sleeping bag. It's just before dawn when he awakens; gray light is coming through the turret window. A sudden urgency compels him to get on the road, to get to Prague. Maybe he should have gone last night? He scratches a quick note to Kate and leaves it on the end table; rolls up the sleeping bag; and departs the flat as quietly as possible. Near Karlsplatz, he finds a taxi rank. The dawn is turning pink on the horizon; there's a heavy smell of rain in the air. It's six thirty by the time Kramer gets to his Citroën garaged on Lenaugasse.

CHAPTER SEVENTEEN

One hour later, Kramer is still stuck in rush-hour traffic on the Gürtel, Vienna's outer ring road. The little Citroën Deux Cheveaux doesn't like stop-and-go; its temperature gauge is hugging the red zone even in the cold morning air. He's thinking maybe the airport was a better idea. Still not too late to turn around, but with guns in the carry-on, it's impossible. Then traffic starts moving a little faster, and he takes the Danube exit, crossing the river at the Praterbrücke.

Traffic is thinning out here; the commuters are coming into the center, not going to the suburbs. He hits the S3 above the Donau-Auen, heading northwest toward Stockerau and the agricultural plains above the city and the river. He's flying now, as much as his small car can approximate graceful motion; wide open, a four-lane autobahn, which he leaves in a half hour, taking the E84 north toward the Czech border. It's raining steadily, and the passenger-side wiper does not work; the one in front of him has only one speed—slow. The heater died long ago in the car, and the defrost is an open window.

The next hour through the gently rolling farm country of Lower Austria is a cold one. Rain splatters in the barely open window; his hands turn white on the steering wheel. In Hollabrunn, he makes a quick stop for a cup of tea and rum to thaw out. The inn is smoke-filled at nine in the morning. Local farmers in gray woolen *Trachten* with green piping trim look at him suspiciously as he stands at the bar and swills his tea. They have glasses of red wine in front of them; nicotine stains on their index and middle fingers. Not much happening in Hollabrunn in the late fall. No fields to plow or grapes to harvest. It'll be a long winter, Kramer figures, looking at the farmers' red cheeks and road-map eyes.

He's forgotten to fill the Deux Cheveaux up in Vienna so, after leaving twenty schillings on the bar, he goes to his car and hunts out the nearest petrol stop. There's the green-and-yellow sign of BP on the northern edge of town. He has a young, pimply kid fill it up at eleven schillings per liter, thanks very much, and is off again, realizing five clicks from town that he's famished.

Kramer has to apply the brakes and swerve to avoid a couple of sodden cows that have wandered out onto the road. The cows do not even stop munching as his tires squeal around them.

An hour later at Unterretzbach, the border guard waves him on, not bothering with even a passport examination. One look at the Austrian plates is enough; they're desperate for foreign currency to shore up the sagging crown. Kramer pats the Walthers he's carrying in each pocket of his oilskin. *Thank God for currency problems*, he thinks.

At Jihlava, he hits the E14 freeway, heading almost due west for Prague. The road is one of the last of the old Soviet projects, and drives like it. The multitude of cracks in its surface makes a steady rhythm on his tires, almost lulling. The rain abates somewhat; the countryside to both sides of the four-lane freeway is lush, green, rolling hills with copses of linden and sycamore tucked into the folds. Some of the sweetest-looking country in the world, Kramer has always thought. And for all of his life, save the past several years, it has been an occupied land. He expects to see Soviet troop transports; cannot escape the after-image of the Cold War.

Prague has always been a black-and-white photograph for him. A beautiful old city of cobbled lanes and streets empty of traffic; of church spires and Gothic arcades. Somber and stately, but in no way depressing as so many of the former Eastern Bloc capitals are. But now Prague is most definitely in color. Technicolor. The baroque facades have been painted a rainbow of pastels; there are red-and-white Coca-Cola umbrellas and white plastic chairs and tables out on the Old Town's main square, Staroměstské Náměstí, despite the biting cold. Even a few youthful foreigners gathered there with rows of empty beer bottles in front of them, laughing loudly. The rain has stopped, but these intrepid al fresco drinkers are bundled in bright red and yellow slickers or in the puffy Michelin Man down jackets of a generation earlier. Kramer is suddenly reminded of Amsterdam in the '60s, of all the hips and proto-hips gathered there. The Levi brigade. These are the remnant of the thousands of young tourists who flocked to Prague directly after the fall of the Soviet Union, when the living was cheap and the city was still in black and white. But now prices have soared and civic pride wishes for the tourists to return home. The Czechs want their city back.

Kramer has put his car in a subterranean car park at the edge of the Old Town, hoofing it under the Prasna Brana and down Celetná Ulice to the main square. He's just in time for the tolling of the hour at the astronomical clock on the Stará Radnice. Christ and the Apostles show themselves, but the drinkers in the square do not notice. Death tolls the bell, but the tourists keep on drinking.

He's headed for Kaprova Ulice, just beyond Kafka's birth

house. The narrow, cobbled streets are packed with fiddlers, guitarists, even a fire breather. It's like a carnival, but has the down side of a festival atmosphere, as well: the desperate revelry, panhandlers working the streets. One young, stringy-haired blonde girl comes up to Kramer.

"*Prosím*. Please," she says, a tiny dirty hand held palm up.

He looks into her eyes, is about to tell her to wire her parents if she needs money, but then on impulse digs out some schillings from his pocket and lays them in her hand. She smiles at him and runs off.

Moving on, Kramer hears a high, happy American voice behind him, "Did you see? He actually gave me money. Cooool."

Kramer shrugs and moves on toward house number 12. It's been fixed up since he was here last: a fresh sand-blasting job to reveal honey-colored sandstone; the incised frog over the door—At the Sign of the Frog—has a light shining on it. Prague has discovered itself. Not such a big step from quaintness to kitsch.

The courtyard is arcaded with ivy growing up the walls. Enclosed porches surround it, one on each of the three stories. Kramer crosses the courtyard to the huge doors of the old stalls and uses a wrought iron clapper to sound the wood. There is no response, and he uses the clapper again, this time louder. Finally, from inside comes a muffled sound, silence, and then a voice shouting, "*Dále!* Come in!"

Kramer does. The half basement is as he remembers it: dark in the middle of the day, musty-smelling like a wine cellar, and brick lined. Jiří Vaslov is sitting at an enormous old desk under one of the street-level windows. His white hair is sticking straight up as if he just got out of bed. On the table near his bed alcove is the Gestetner mimeograph machine that Kramer arranged for him to get in the late '70s. It's the best cared for object in the whole place. An armchair with stuffing coming out of the back sits lopsided with a leg broken; clothes lay crumpled over a bookcase; old phonograph records out of their sleeves litter the floor in front of a stereo that must be thirty years old.

Jiří Vaslov turns in his chair, squinting over the tops of half-frame reading glasses. He's wearing a camel-hair smoking jacket over a purple turtleneck sweater, baggy gray woolen pants, and ancient house slippers with pointy toes. He could be a caricature out of a nineteenth-century painting: *The Bookworm*.

"How you doing, Jiří?" Kramer says, coming down the three steps into the room. There are books everywhere and manuscript pages littering every surface.

Vaslov gets up from his desk, smiling now.

"Kramer! I thought you'd forgotten us now that we're no longer news."

Vaslov is a thin, short man with a Roman nose and skin as white as paper. He rubs his hair bashfully, as if not knowing what to say. It is this continual rubbing that makes his hair stand up so oddly, Kramer now remembers. Vaseline, the other writers in the union used to call him. Vaslov put out some of the most widely read *samizsdat* (literary "magazines") during the Soviet occupation, using the mimeograph enshrined by his bed. Except that back then, the duplicator would be hidden in an alcove in back of a wardrobe and only brought out for the printing late at night.

They do not embrace; Vaslov is much too reserved for that, but the handshake is warm and welcoming.

"This calls for a drink," Vaslov says and goes to one of the bookshelves to fetch a bottle of plum brandy. He pours out two double shots in finely etched crystal shot glasses, and they toast each other. The liquor burns down Kramer's throat, warming his stomach. He can use it, but feels suddenly light-headed. He still has not eaten today.

"Sit, sit," Vaslov says, taking a bundle of papers and some clothes off the lopsided armchair and tossing them into a corner. A cat is in the clothing, and spits as it lands on the floor. Kramer sits lightly in the chair and Vaslov draws up a straight-back one.

"Good to see you, Kramer."

"You, too." Kramer finishes the drink.

"Another?"

Kramer shakes his head. "I've still got work to do today."

"You're on assignment? Good. I heard you weren't writing so much anymore."

Kramer doesn't want to talk about that; decides on the direct approach.

"I need some information."

"As usual, I've got more questions than answers."

"This is an easy one. I'm looking for a publishing house here called something like Kareesia."

Vaslov finishes his drink and sets it down on the floor. The cat has come back now and sniffs at it.

"You make me feel like a knowledgeable person, Kramer. Here is a question for which I have an answer. I imagine it is Keresya Publishers you're looking for. They've got an office a couple blocks from here, near the Starý Židovský Hřbitov, the Old Jewish Cemetery along the river. But why them? A terrible bunch of reactionaries. The romance of the land, folktales of Bohemia, fancy picture books of village costumes. That sort of neo-nationalist pap is what they publish."

"I'm not interested in their list, Jiří, just one of their editors."

"Who?"

"Maria Dalibor."

Vaslov grins. "Ah-ha. Now I get the lay of the land. I would like to bed her myself, but they say she only sleeps with books. Save her, Kramer. Save her from that insufferable house she works at. They only took her on because she was a sort of icon. When the Bastille fell, there was our poor Maria, still incarcerated. They've got a lot of mileage out of her at Keresya, I can tell you that. Good weaponry for bashing the Left. You know her?"

Kramer nods. "A long time ago."

"All the more reason then to save her from the Fascists. I'm sure she doesn't know she's being used. Much too ethereal for that is our Maria." Jiří looks at the mimeograph machine gathering dust. "You know, I hate to say it, Kramer, but I rather miss the old days of repression. The Soviets made such good people to hate. Prague was a united city then; united against the common enemy. Now we only have each other. Examining credentials of what one did or did not do in 1968. Whether one tried to reform the system or tear it down. Terrific lot of right-wingers running around today posing as nationalist heroes. Prague isn't what it was."

Kramer rises to go. "I've got to see her as soon as possible. You understand?"

Vaslov stands, too, rubbing a hand through his hair. "Of course. Follow that story, Kramer. We writers are yesterday's news. We made the country safe for Coca-Cola and *Time* magazine. Clever of us, wasn't it?"

Kramer follows Kaprova Ulice toward the Vltava river, smelling it before reaching it. The publishing house is in Náměstí Jana Palacha, a square named after Jan Palach, who set himself alight to protest the Soviet invasion in 1968. *Appropriate for Maria to be working here*, he thinks. Her publishing house has a fine old baroque facade with offices on every floor. Kramer goes up to editorial on the third and asks the young man at the desk for Maria Dalibor's office. The guy wears his hair short and a white shirt with a string tie from a folk costume. The wall in back of him is covered with brightly colored book jackets. He doesn't bother to call ahead, but directs Kramer down a corridor to the second door on the left. There are framed book jackets along the corridor as well, new carpeting on the parquet. Kramer comes to the door, knocks once lightly and a female voice from inside tells him, in Czech, to enter. He opens the door, and she is sitting in back of a modern desk of Scandinavian design wearing a green cardigan over a white blouse. Her hair is cut short and is graying; the skin of her face is as translucent as ever; the cheekbones high and fine. Her eyes smile at him.

Then out the corner of his eye, half-hidden by the door opened inward, is a denim-covered leg dangling over a knee. The shoes are red Converse high-tops. Kramer opens the door completely to reveal Randall sitting in a low-slung leather armchair, smiling at him.

"What took you so long, Sam? Maria and I have been waiting all morning."

CHAPTER EIGHTEEN

"What are you doing here?" Kramer says to Randall.

Maria gets up from her desk and moves around toward Kramer.

"Aren't you even going to greet me, Sam?"

She holds out frail-looking arms to him.

"Of course. Randall surprised me, is all."

Kramer meets Maria halfway around the desk and embraces her, keeping an eye on Randall who is still slouching in the armchair, grinning like a magician who's just pulled the bunny out of the hat.

There is nothing frail about Maria's grip; her arms are strong and firm, and she pulls him into her front, not holding back the pelvis. Their bodies wrap together seamlessly for a moment, and Kramer smells a scent, subtle like early morning in a garden. He feels his body respond automatically to the embrace and kisses her hair. She holds him back from her suddenly, two hands on his shoulders squeezing. Red spots show at her cheeks, her mouth is partly open, eyes dilating.

"Whoa!" Randall yelps. "Got to watch old Sammy. Gets you in the ropes, and he won't let up."

She pulls her cardigan down primly, smiling to herself.

"Sorry," Kramer manages to mumble.

She half shakes her head, pursing her lips. "Don't be. It was nice."

"Maybe I should just leave," Randall says, making as if to stand, but getting no further than hands on knees.

"Good to see you again, Maria." Kramer means it.

She nods. All her movements are slight, as if anything more would be too showy.

"You, too."

Kramer turns to Randall.

"I repeat. What are you doing here? I thought you'd be in Switzerland by now, leading a group of geriatrics in the wonders of Kundalini."

Randall slumps back in the chair. "You hurt me, Sam. Know that? Making light of my teaching ability. Hatha, not Kundalini, for your information."

Maria smiles at Randall. "We were just talking about the time we all tripped in the Vienna woods. Remember, Sam? Randall brought all that lovely hash back from Istanbul, and we ate Suchard chocolate bars to get the aluminum foil to make pipes. We took our clothes off like innocent children and played in the golden leaves."

The memory comes back to Kramer in a flash. One not dredged up ever before. Yet it is lodged there, replaying itself as if no time has elapsed between then and now. It was early fall, a warm day with dappled sunlight coming through the birch trees, and they had skipped like children, kicking up leaves. Everyone except Reni. She sat and watched, Kramer now remembers. Watched as an anthropologist might do, or a visitor to the zoo.

"I remember," he says. "Apropos of what?"

"Yoga." Maria laughs out loud. "Don't you remember? That's when Randall sat cross-legged and did the *om* chant for us. And finally the wild boar came out of the underbrush, ready to mate with him."

Kramer and Maria laugh until tears come. Randall sits in his chair, scowling.

"Very funny," he finally says. "That wart hog could have caused me permanent psychosis, not to mention giving me a dose of porcine clap. But go ahead and laugh. I am here on Earth to amuse."

"Come on, Randall," Maria says, holding her mouth with a delicate white hand to hide her laughter. She goes to his chair, leans down over him and kisses the top of his head. "We love you," she says.

It's what the seven of them would say to each other. Kramer wonders who the "we" is now.

Randall pulls her down onto his lap and tickles her. She shrieks and squeals, trying to get out of his grasp. A moment later, a knock comes at the door.

"Maria?"

She gets up from Randall's lap, straightens her skirt, brushes back her hair with her fingers, and opens the door.

It's the young man from the reception desk. He looks into the room past Maria, suspicion in his eyes. "Excuse me," he says in stilted English. "I heard . . ."

"It's okay, Pavel. Old friends." She pats him on the shoulder and begins giggling again before getting the door closed. She turns to them, her back to the door, and sighs loudly.

"God, it feels so good to laugh again. I don't get much chance for it here."

"Maria," Kramer begins, "we didn't know what happened to you. I tried during the '70s . . ."

She holds her hand up, closes her eyes. "It's over now, Sam. Let's not talk about it. I know you cared. That you did what you could."

"But we've got to talk about it," he says. Then he glances at Randall who is looking down at his hands folded in his lap.

"Didn't you tell her?" he says to Randall.

He shakes his head, not looking up. "I was waiting for you." Then Randall looks up, finds Kramer's eyes and locks on him for a moment. "You were right, Sam. You've got to make a stand sometime."

"Tell me what?" Maria says.

Kramer turns to her. "Maybe you've already heard. Reni is dead."

She puts her hand to her mouth again. "No." This time when she shakes her head, it is violent enough to make her short hair sway back and forth. "I hadn't heard. I've been so busy lately . . ."

"And Gerhard. Someone killed them both to keep them from telling a secret."

"Oh, Jesus!" She stands stunned at the door for a moment, then slides down it slowly, to sit hunched and blank-faced.

"Nice work, Sam," Randall says, getting up from the chair and rushing to her. Kramer is there, too, and they both help her to the armchair, sitting her down gently. Kramer runs his hand over her cheek.

"Can I get you something? Water? Brandy?"

She says nothing for a moment, her eyes focusing beyond them both, to the window of her office that gives off onto a bare plane tree in the courtyard of the building, its branches like a black tracery on the other side of the glass. Finally, she shakes her head at his suggestion.

"It's never over, is it? I mean, once the Soviets left, you would think the nightmare would be finished, wouldn't you?"

"I guess so," Kramer says.

She bites her lower lip, starts rocking in the chair. "But it never ends. Not even with death."

"Easy, Maria," Randall says, putting an arm around her shoulders and scowling at Kramer.

She sits rocking herself for several moments, then finally pulls her body upright and takes a deep breath. "She came to visit me a couple of months ago. Did you know that?"

Kramer nods. "She mentioned it to Gerhard. How did she know where to find you?"

Maria runs her hand through her fine hair. "She didn't. I got in touch with her."

She looks frankly into Kramer's eyes. He crouches at her side and takes her left hand in his. Randall is kneeling on the other side of the chair, his arm still around her shoulders.

They look at each other momentarily across her.

"Why?" Kramer says. "How?"

"Oh, the how is easy enough. Fancy my surprise getting out of prison after all those years to discover one of us was famous. Even if at the end of a career. The newspapers were full of her defeat. But I waited. I didn't want . . ."

She pauses, taking her hand out of Kramer's and looking at him. "She said you two were together for a time."

"For a time," Kramer says. "It didn't work out."

"No," Maria replies. "I never thought it would. You two were light-years apart. Reni has . . . had a worldly type of ambition that precludes real closeness. The type of person to have connections rather than friends."

Kramer says nothing, waiting for her to continue. Randall pats her shoulder consolingly.

"But that is unkind," she quickly adds. "Reni was good enough to come and see me when I requested it. Though there was trepidation in her eyes. I could see that when she came in here."

"You waited a long time to get in touch with her," Kramer says.

"Yes." Maria holds her head between her hands for a moment, then looks up, first at Randall and then at Kramer. "I didn't want to get in touch with her; with any of you, truth be told. The memories were too painful." She fixes Kramer in her gaze. "Gerhard is dead, too? Together?"

Kramer shakes his head. "Reni was killed in Germany. Gerhard was shot a couple of days ago in Crete. I'm sure it's the same person behind both deaths."

"Poor lovable Gary," Maria says. "He was harmless, really. If he knew anything, it was quite by accident, you can be sure of that." She sits back in the chair, saying nothing for a time.

"So why?" Kramer persists. "What did you want to talk to Reni about?"

She ignores this, taking the story at her own pace. "I didn't want to dredge up the past, you see. I really just wanted to get on with a new life. So many years wasted. I felt like Kaspar Hauser coming out of the root cellar into the light of day. But it wouldn't work. To put the past away, I had to settle things finally."

"The car bomb?" Kramer says.

She jerks her head to him. "So you knew?"

"Helmut suspected it might be something like that. But that's only recently."

"Helmut." She says his name softly. "He left me there. Police swarming all around." She goes into herself for a moment, then sighs again. "But there was nothing he could do but try and save himself. They knew, you see. The police here. Somebody had told them. And somebody had set the bomb under that car, timed to go off in Prague."

"Who?" It is almost a scream from Kramer.

She moistens her lips, looking straight ahead.

"Reni, of course. That's why I called her. I had to confront her with it. To get it out of me once and for all."

Kramer thinks of this for a time. "How could you know it was her?"

"I overheard them, you see. Sorry. I don't mean to sound so mysterious. It's just that there were so few people in my life for so many years, that I got accustomed to referring to them by pronouns. I mean my warden, my interrogator, the man who handled my case from the beginning. I heard him talking once early on in the questioning. He was German and spoke to a colleague over the phone, thinking I wouldn't be able to make out his language. And he said quite clearly, 'Müller set it. We have that all taken care of. It's all been arranged. Absolute secrecy on that front.'"

"But that could mean anything," Kramer says.

"No, Sam," she replies. "Not anything. It was at a crucial part of the interrogation. I got the feeling that my warden's masters were getting nervous. That they thought this might backfire into some sort of international incident against the Prague regime, rather than against the West. My interrogator was convincing him not to worry, that Müller was the one who set it. That Reni could be trusted to keep her mouth shut."

"But why?" Kramer asks. "What would have been in it for her?"

Maria shakes her head. "We were all great leftists then. Maybe Reni actually believed the party line."

"No way," Kramer says. "I lived with her, loved her. I knew her." But Eva Martok's revelations have already made him question how well he knew Reni.

"Well, whatever Reni's reasons, it was her," Maria says. "I'm sure Gorik said 'Müller' over the phone."

Randall and Kramer blurt out together, "Gorik?"

"My interrogator. The one who let the name slip. He was with East German intelligence, but was posted in Prague. I would see him from time to time. You see, I never confessed. I think it was a point of pride with him that he could force a confession out of me. Nothing so crude as physical torture, though. Only the carrot of freedom dangled in front of me if I would invent a confession for the world."

"Gorik's dead, too," Kramer says. "Hit-and-run in Berlin."

She does not respond to this; it is as if the news of deaths have numbed her momentarily.

"What did you say to Reni when you saw her?" Randall suddenly asks.

Maria thinks about this for a moment. "Well, the truth, I guess. I mean we talked about old times for a bit, picking up the traces. But then I just couldn't stand it any longer. I had to tell her I knew. That I had overheard Gorik use her name in a phone conversation."

"What did she say?" Kramer says.

"Nothing. That was the strange thing."

"She didn't deny it?" Randall says.

"No. But her eyes . . . they were terrified. It was like the bottom had fallen out of her world. As if her last idol had failed her."

She looks from Randall to Kramer. "Don't worry. I didn't kill her or have her killed. The need for vengeance was drained from me by my tenth year in prison. I had to dream of positive things in order to survive. A love of revenge would have dried me up, would have killed me, boxed up like I was in prison."

But it doesn't make sense to Kramer. Okay, say Reni set the bomb and that Maria's knowing it and confronting her with it drove her to suicide. How to explain Gerhard's death then? No, whoever was eliminating witnesses or memory is still a player, Kramer figures.

"Anything else about her visit that you can remember?" Kramer says.

She shakes her head. "Just those eyes, empty and terrified. I told her it was okay; that I wasn't interested in retribution. I just wanted to know why she did it, but she wouldn't respond. Finally, she left. One thing she did say—'I'm so awfully sorry I can't give you the years back, Maria.' Something like that, anyway. It was the closest she came to an apology. The closest Reni could come."

They huddle together in silence for a time, thinking their separate thoughts. Kramer steals a glance at Randall.

"It really doesn't make any sense," Randall says, looking up suddenly and catching Kramer's eyes. "Reni was not my favorite person, but I can't see her setting a bomb and sending a good friend to prison, all for the sake of some dubious propaganda coup."

"I'm sure I heard Gorik right," Maria says. "I didn't want to believe it, either."

"And that was the last time you saw Reni?" Kramer asks.

"Yes." Suddenly, she leans forward in the chair and then rises. "But not the last word I had."

She crosses to her desk, goes around to the drawers, and opens the top one under the writing surface. Her hand comes up with an orange envelope.

"You see, I was expecting you," she says to Kramer. "Reni told me to. In the event you came here, I was to give you this."

She hands the envelope to Kramer. He takes it and feels a weight heavier than paper in it. Looking inside, all he sees is a key, short and fat. Turning the envelope on end and shaking the key out, he sees it has a few simple notches cut in it and the number 301A etched on the grip end. A white paper tag attached by a string through the hole in the top of the key has an inscription: *Bank Austria*.

Kramer holds the key in his palm for a moment, realizing with a thudding heart that it might well unlock the mysteries of this case. Randall looks over his shoulder at it.

"Looks like it belongs to a safe-deposit box," Randall says.

J. Sydney Jones

"No other message with this?" Kramer asks Maria.

She stands, her fingertips on the desk. "Only a note telling me I should give this to you when I see you."

Kramer looks at the postmark on the envelope. It was mailed October 23. Just about the time of Reni's death. He begins to get the uncomfortable feeling that Reni had been scheming one last time; had set one of her elaborate plans for them all. Got you last.

"Looks like we need to get back to Vienna, Sam," Randall says.

Kramer nods, curling his fingers over the key and then shoving it into his right front pants pocket along with his car keys.

"You can't stay the night?" Maria says. "I have a tiny apartment, but there are a couple of extra sleeping bags."

There is nothing more that Kramer would like to do at the moment. Looking at Maria with the light in back of her shining golden through her hair, he would love to fold her in his arms and lie with her forever; to be at peace for once. Before, he's always looked for excitement in women; with Maria he senses the calm that he longs for.

"We can't," he says. "But I'll be back. I promise."

She smiles, lifting her hands from the desk and folding her arms over her breasts, hugging herself.

"Sure."

"Believe me, okay?" Kramer searches out her eyes, but she is looking down at manuscripts on her desk.

Kramer and Randall leave the building and cross the square by the Starý Židovský Hřbitov. The smell of water from the river is strong; a sharp wind has come up, cutting through Kramer's jacket. He still has not put the wool liner in.

Looking at the tumble of stones in the cemetery for a moment, Kramer remembers it is said that there are more than a dozen layers of burials there, and he believes it the way the ground on top has subsided. Tombstones lean against one another under the bare trees like broken and plundered megalithic tombs. Someone has painted a red swastika on the entrance.

Suddenly, his eye is struck by something else. A purple car turns into the square, cruising close to the curb, headed straight for them. It bounces up onto the sidewalk, and Kramer just has time to shove Randall out of the way, both of them falling against the entrance to the cemetery as the car speeds past, narrowly missing them. It stops only yards away, and Kramer does not waste time seeing who gets out. He's up and running, Randall in back, into the cemetery.

Not again, he thinks, running along the dirt path between stones. *Not bloody again.*

A spray of dust and chips flies off a stone to his right; he can hear Randall's feet in back of him, his heavy breathing getting further and further away. Another spray of stone chips to his left and suddenly he realizes they're shooting. But he hasn't heard shots. He dives off the path into a clutter of tombstones that lay tumbled against one another like a child's building blocks. Randall has tripped on the path, then scrambles to the other side, protected by stones. Kramer can see the two men moving toward them, the barrels of the pistols in their hands elongated. *Silencers*, he thinks. *That's why they dare to come after us in the middle of the day. Silent death.*

But you don't have to be a victim this time, he tells himself. *Don't have to be the fox running from the hunters.* He feels a knot in his stomach. Another fusillade of shots rips through the bushes near his tombstone, tears at the rock surface, and pings off the metal fence in back of him. He shuts down his mind as he pulls a Walther out of his coat pocket, flicks the safety off. Keeping his head well below the top of the stones, he rolls right. He holds the pistol in both hands ahead of him, elbows steady on the wet ground, then pulls off two quick shots that buck the gun up in his hands and set his ears ringing. The shots are wide, but they make the shooters take cover. Pigeons flap away at the sharp report as Kramer rolls back to safety.

"Sam, did you bring the other gun? Toss it to me."

Randall is huddled in back of a griffin-surmounted tombstone. His voice gives his location away. A shower of rock splinters fills the air and silenced bullets rip through brush on both sides of him.

"Sam? You hear me?"

Kramer rolls to his right again, but this time they're waiting for him. Bullets thud into the earth in front of him, and he scrambles back to cover behind his stone.

Kramer takes the second pistol out of his pocket, snicks the safety off, and then tosses it across the path. Randall bobbles it, finally catching it against his stomach.

"How do I use it?" he says.

"Pull the trigger," Kramer yells.

"Isn't there a safety or something?"

"It's off."

"Jesus! You trying to kill me, Sam?"

Kramer rolls left this time, toward the path; shooting wild, but shooting. Making enough noise to be heard above the growl of traffic outside the cemetery. He sees Randall examine his gun, then has no more time for thinking as bullets kick mud at him and he rolls for cover once again. Shots ring out from Randall's position now. Kramer looks across the path; Randall is opening and closing his jaw as if to make his ears pop.

"Keep shooting, Randall!" Movement to his far right makes Kramer swing around toward the fence, nearly pulling off a quick round at a small boy with big eyes, wearing jeans and a University of Prague sweatshirt, who is watching him like a television. Kramer waves him away, out of the line of fire. The kid doesn't move.

Kramer makes a dive across the path to take the trajectory of bullets away from the kid. He lands hard, knocking the breath out of himself. Bullets rip leaves over his head and more shots ring out from Randall's position only yards away. Kramer shoots and rolls for cover and then hears a metallic clicking to his left, from Randall's position.

"Any more bullets, Sam?"

Plenty, Kramer thinks. *All in the car. Well done.* He pokes his head up momentarily, pulls off another round, then hears the sickening click of his own empty chamber with the next.

He's down and covered, his back to the tombstone. It's cold as death and he wonders what to do now. He's about to start using his vocal cords when he hears the high wail of a siren in the distance. Another round of silenced shots tears through the foliage between him and Randall as the sirens get closer and closer. Kramer hears rustling in the brush from the shooters, a scrambling of footsteps. *Here it comes*, he thinks. *Coming for us to finish the job.* The gun is warm and useless in his hands. He looks to Randall who is still working his jaw, trying for hearing.

But the sound of steps is not coming toward them. Kramer looks around the side of the rock just in time to see the backs of the two men racing out of the cemetery and heading for their car.

"Come on, Randall."

Kramer is up, but Randall stays huddled behind his tombstone. Kramer goes to him and shakes him. Randall looks up with wide eyes.

"You okay?"

Randall shakes his head, taps at his right ear with the palm of his hand. "My ears."

"Come on." Kramer hears the car start. "They're getting away."

But Randall stays put. "I rather think that we should let

them." He aims toward the sky and pulls the trigger of his empty pistol again.

The sirens grow louder and louder; clearly they are headed for the cemetery.

The squealing of tires comes from near the entrance as the shooters' car pulls away.

"Time we get lost," Kramer says. "I don't feel like explaining to the Prague police what we're doing holding a shoot-out in their town."

Kramer pockets his gun, wiping the dirt from his jacket. Randall gets to his feet and does likewise. The kid is still staring at them as they leave the cemetery, and Kramer puts his fingers to his lips, smiling at the boy. The kid looks at him once more, then turns and races out of the square. Kramer and Randall do the same, running past shocked-looking pedestrians coming out of hiding places in doorways; one step ahead of the police cars converging from two directions. They stop running after two blocks and blend into the other pedestrians of the Old Town, a couple of day-trippers ogling the sights.

CHAPTER NINETEEN

The train pulls into Franz-Josefs-Bahnhof at 6:12 the next morning. As the brakes screech, Kramer opens the curtains on his sleeping compartment, one of only four on the slow milk-run from Prague. He casts bleary eyes at the huge, gray, unbroken mass of the Karl Marx-Hof apartment complex across the tracks, then makes his way to the exit. Kramer looks back and forth along the short concrete platform before descending: no waiting party.

He left his easily traced car with Randall, who stayed in Prague at Maria's in case the goons decided to come back. But Kramer doubts they will. *Like me*, he figures, *they must feel the search drawing to an end.* They must know the lines are converging. As he walks briskly along the platform, Kramer taps his pants' pocket. The key to the safe-deposit box is there.

Another look along the platform; no suspicious-looking people, only the station master in a long blue cape and red-tipped signal baton looking like a kid dressed in play clothes. In the main hall, the station coffee shop is open, and Kramer ducks in for a quick cup. He's got time to kill before the bank opens; no going home or to the office.

They know my routines, he tells himself as he sips on the mocha he ordered, standing at the bar. *They know my addresses and friends.* So all the old familiar haunts are off-limits.

He finishes the coffee and notices some fresh brioches under a plastic lid on the zinc counter and orders another cup and a roll to go with it this time. The night train has given Kramer plenty of time to think; plenty of time to try to put things together. The killers, for instance. He thinks he recognized one of them yesterday—the huge no-neck bodyguard in civvies at Vogel's headquarters. The one who had frisked him.

Was he the same one in Crete? Kramer wonders. He can't be sure, for there it had all been surprise and terror. Distances were greater, as well. But he figures it's a safe working hypothesis to assume the man was one of those who killed Gerhard. Which would place Vogel right in the center of things: Reni's murderer; Gorik's, too. But why?

The connection to Reni is obvious enough. Protecting his patronage and membership lists. Gerhard fits in there, also. Someone close enough to Reni to have access to such information.

How was Vogel to know they were estranged? *Then Randall and I come snooping around. Maybe we know something, too. Maybe we'll even trace Reni's murder back to Vogel. But where does Gorik figure in? And why bother following me to Prague? Why not just get rid of me in the car? Am I still being used as somebody's bloodhound sniffing out loose ends? In which case, that could mean Maria. But why? What part could she play in all this? More questions than answers.*

Kramer finishes the pastry and coffee, feels again in his pocket for the bank key. Maybe the answers will lie in this, he thinks. Maybe Reni has played the games master one last time.

It's just after nine when Kramer enters the large front doors of the Bank Austria on Am Hof in the middle of Vienna's Old Town. It's all marble pillars and mahogany counters in here: old money, old secrets. He has no idea where the safe-deposit box is, but figures that there must be some code on the key to identify the branch. He crosses the stadium-size main hall to the proper window and is the first in line for today's business. The clerk is a young woman with a beauty mark on her upper lip that is in no way beautiful; it sprouts hairs. She has on a black suit and too much perfume. Her hair is cut severely in a V with long bangs in front. Kramer hands her the key without saying anything, and she examines the serial numbers, sniffs, then pushes a pad and pen across the counter to him.

"Name, please," she says.

He hadn't figured this far ahead. Stupid of him, but there it is. Of course the box is going to have to be in someone's name. Kramer thinks about this for a moment, hesitates with the pen hovering over the paper.

"This is your key, isn't it?" she says, rapping her fingers on the counter.

He gives her a scrunched eyebrow look that's supposed to convince her of his proprietorship, but only draws her attention to the bandage on his forehead.

He's about to scribble "R. Müller" on the pad, then puts himself in Reni's mind. *If she left the key for me, in my city, she's damn well going to take care of the identity.* He signs his own name, shoves the pad across to the clerk, and she examines it against the signature on file.

"They look different," she says, looking up at his bandage again.

"I'm a little shaky today," he says, drawing out his passport and Austrian visa. "Too much wine last night."

She looks at the identification closely, sucks air, and finally nods her head.

"That's you, I guess. Follow me."

He retrieves his identification, and she buzzes him through a half door back to the vaults, flicks the timed combination expertly, and opens the large barred doors. It's cold in the vaults, like a wine cellar. They find the proper number after a bit of searching. The box is low, one row from the bottom, and they must both bend down to insert the two keys and open the lock. She has good knees bending down, but catches his glance and puts a hand on them, standing quickly.

"Will you be needing a room, Herr Kramer?"

Kramer pulls out a double-wide box. By the heft of it, he knows there's a fair amount of stuff inside.

"Yes. That would be very helpful."

His heart is racing; he feels that he may be nearing the end of all this mystery. But he forces himself not to look inside the box until the door to the tiny cubicle with a table and chair closes behind him. The overhead light is incandescent; there are no windows.

He opens the metal box slowly, almost reverently. He sees a sheaf of papers inside surmounted by an envelope. He pulls the envelope out first: it's addressed to him, typewritten. He tears it open, fumbles the letter out and unfolds it, his hand trembling:

> Dear Sam,
>
> I'm sorry to have sent you on such an Easter egg hunt, but it was the only way I could tell the world. Believe me, the only way. It all began in 1974 when I came back to Germany from Crete . . .

The War Crimes Commission is housed near Bonn's Bundestag in an aluminum-and-glass structure from the 1950s. It's late afternoon now. Kramer just managed to catch the midday flight from Vienna. He goes to the visitors' reception and flashes his press card to gain admittance to the library. Rows of somber desks fill the large reading room; blue- and red-bound reference volumes line the high walls. Kramer goes to the call desk and hands a white-haired civil servant, who is in no way civil, his press ID along with a printed request: the folder on SS-Oberleutnant Arno Semich. The librarian adjusts his half-frame reading glasses, peering down at the request slip, then looks over the frames at Kramer. His eyes are filled with liquid; white guck like farmer's cheese clots the rims of his eyelids. He sniffs once, wordlessly, and turns back to a younger colleague who does the fetching. They are all dressed in blue lab coats, as if this were a pharmacy. The younger man disappears behind double doors, and Kramer catches a glimpse of a warren of metal floor-to-ceiling cases filled with gray cardboard file boxes. No luxury of computers here. The mandate is soon to run out, anyway; the statute of limitations on war crimes set to expire. You can only chase the past so long, Kramer figures. Go hunting for the Nazis in the old folks' home too ardently, and you'll only miss those who are taking over the country currently.

Kramer sits on a Naugahyde-covered bench opposite the call desk thinking about Reni's letter, about the sheaf of documents in the safe-deposit box.

Her memoirs. A xerographic copy of them, at any rate. And just as Pahlus described it, the document is political dynamite. Kramer did not have time to go through it thoroughly this morning but could see Reni was obviously an ardent diarist.

Not only did she detail shenanigans in Bonn's corridors of power, but in the city's bedrooms, as well. And in her concluding section, he found the secret list of Vogel's members and sponsors. A quick perusal made Kramer give a low whistle. So-called liberals and conservatives alike, all stripes of the political spectrum were included there. They were doing what politicians do best in a volatile time of change: hedging their bets. This time on the neo-Nazis.

Quickly leafing through the other typed pages, Kramer found the name Gorik, and along with that, another name: Semich. SS-Oberleutnant Arno Semich. A name that brought him to Bonn and perhaps to the end of the long trail.

Maybe you'll become a real journalist again, Sammy, Reni wrote in her letter to him. *Fit the last piece to this puzzle, and you'll have a fine little picture of corruption.*

Kramer thinks he knows what that final piece will be, for things are clicking in his head; little things he's noticed but not remarked on. They make sense, however, now that Reni has given him the name.

Fifteen minutes later, Kramer's name is called. He goes to the desk, retrieves the file, and takes it to one of the rows of desks, each with a green-shaded brass lamp attached to it. He turns on the light and pulls the contents from the cardboard file box. There is very little documentation. Semich was born in 1918 in Munich, joined the Hitler Youth in 1934, the SS in 1939, earned degrees in law and economics from Heidelberg. During the war, he headed a battalion of Einsatzgruppen, mobile killing squads, that was responsible for the deaths of 5,200 Serbs and Muslims in and around Sarajevo. A wanted war criminal, Semich was initially arrested by the advancing Fifth Army near Innsbruck and held in an American detention camp until the morning of June 16, 1945, when he escaped. He has not been heard of since.

Kramer quickly thumbs through the affidavits of dozens of witnesses and the report of the commission on the attempts to trace him. The final page bears a stapled photo of Semich as a young SS officer astride a horse. There are two noncoms with him, their hands on the flanks of the tall animal. Semich has his death's head cap pulled down low over his eyes and smiles arrogantly at the camera. Kramer squints at the photo, then gets up, goes to the call desk, and requests a magnifying glass. The rheumy-eyed assistant looks at him dumbly for a moment as if he has not heard, then lazily opens a drawer behind the counter and fishes out a small square magnifier, the type used for examining photographic proof sheets. Kramer takes this back to his desk. He jerks the glass unsteadily over the photo at first, and the image of Semich is unclear. Then he settles the magnifier firmly over the face, and the features leap out of the surroundings with distinct clarity. The black and white dots separate for an instant and then fuse again as his eye adjusts. There the nose is, hawklike, and predatory. The same eyes; the thin tight lips fixed in an ironic smirk.

Kramer looks up and out the high windows to the gray day. He takes a deep breath. Suddenly, it all makes sense to him. All the disparate facts come together for him like the black and white dots of the photograph, which suddenly form a picture.

Later in the day, he will pay a visit to Bad Lunsburg and see Kommissar Boehm, but for now he returns the file, gets his press pass back, and then goes out for a pint of beer to sit and think. To make sure the dots hold; that the mosaic is set.

There are no lights on in the villa, but Kramer buzzes anyway. The time was agreed on; he should be home.

A voice talks to him out of the microphone grating of the house intercom, "That you, Sam?"

He tells him it is.

"Come on through to the back. I'm in the pool." The lock clicks open, and Kramer enters the vestibule, being sure to leave the door partly open behind him. He follows the wood-cobbled vestibule out to another door leading to the gardens and the glass-covered pool. Green light shimmers eerily in the darkness and Kramer follows it. Underwater bulbs, like a marine world.

He enters the pool house, steam hovering over the chlorinated water like a drift of fog. Müller is doing laps again, long, smooth strokes cutting through the thick water almost soundlessly. Kramer stands for a time by the open door, then slides it closed, watching Müller some more. Finally, the man stops swimming, holding on to the edge of the pool at the deep end and blowing water.

"Come on in, Sam, if you like. I've got extra swim wear in the changing room."

"No thanks." Kramer looks around the pool room; they are alone. A white towel lays crumpled by a chaise longue; a drinks cart stands close at hand.

Müller pulls himself out of the water.

"And what is so urgent that it must be discussed tonight?" Müller says, picking up the towel, drying off, and then wrapping it about him like a toga. "Drink?"

Kramer shakes his head.

"Well, I believe I will," Müller says. "I've earned one." He goes to the drinks cart and pours a couple of fingers of single malt whiskey in a tumbler, turns to Kramer, and holds it up to him. "Cheers."

"Long life," Kramer says, his eye going to Müller's left arm as the man tips the glass to drink. Kramer cannot see underneath the arm, but remembers clearly the bit of scar tissue there.

"You're still at it then," Müller says, stretching out on the chaise and crossing his thin legs at the ankles.

"Pretty much," Kramer says. "Your word in the ear of the local police didn't scare me off, if that's what you want to know."

Müller looks at his drink philosophically. "Sorry about that. But it's better letting things just lie, believe me. Reni would not want her name dragged through any more mud. She was tired of the fight. Tired of all the turmoil. She just wanted a bit of peace."

Kramer looks down at Müller lounging so complacently and has the sudden urge to tip him over, to kick him in the face, and wipe that arrogance off his features.

"That's what she wanted, is it?" he says instead. "Just a little peace."

Müller nods, finishes his drink, and then looks hard at Kramer. "Do I detect irony? Is that why you've come, to be ironic with me? At this hour?"

"No. That's not why I've come. I want to ask you about a man named Semich."

Müller squints at Kramer for an instant, then forces a smile.

"Semich? Am I supposed to know him?"

"I think so," Kramer says, nodding slowly. "The Hangman of Sarajevo, he was called. Nice enough guy they say, but he took his job too damn seriously. Too successful routing out impure racial elements."

"Sam, I don't follow you at all. Who is this Semich fellow?"

Müller gets up and goes to the drinks table once again, pouring a stiffer shot of whiskey this time.

"He's a war criminal. One of the last big ones unaccounted for."

Müller has his back turned to Kramer as he speaks, "And what has he got to do with me?"

"Gorik found out, didn't he? And he blackmailed you."

Müller tosses off the drink in one gulp. When he turns to Kramer, he is holding an automatic pistol in his right hand, aimed straight at Kramer's midsection. Kramer takes a slow breath; feels his mouth go dry and his stomach knot.

"You're much too curious for your own good, Sam. You know that?"

"It's true, isn't it?" Kramer says, finding it difficult to speak with his tongue sticking to his suddenly dry palate. "You're Semich."

Müller looks at him with cold eyes, betraying no emotion. "There have been a lot of burglaries in this neighborhood lately. Did you know that, Sam? A man can't be safe even in his own house any longer."

"You are Semich," Kramer forces himself to repeat it.

Müller's thumb creeps up the side of the pistol, flicking the safety off.

"You seem to have all the secrets," Müller says. "Why don't you tell me?"

"It all fits," Kramer says. "You were a wanted war criminal and changed your identity. No huge difficulty there," Kramer says, looking around the pool room, trying to buy time, to keep the dialogue going. "There were plenty of poor bastards who never came back from the war whose identity you could take over as easily as slipping on a new suit. So Arno Semich disappears amid the flood of refugees returning from all over Europe and Russia, and Karl-Heinz Müller takes his place. He erases all trace of his past, even the SS identification under his left arm, the tattoo of his blood group, though he cannot avoid the ensuing scar."

Müller momentarily looks down to his own left arm, then quickly back to Kramer.

"He hides out where he is least likely to be discovered," Kramer continues. "Smack in the middle of the American denazification program, and makes a lucky marriage to an

American woman with enough money to finance his invest-ment schemes. They have a daughter together, business pros-pers during the postwar miracle of Germany, and everything is going beautifully until one day . . ."

Kramer stops, swallows hard, and stares down the barrel of the gun.

"Go on," Müller says, waving the gun. "This is quite good. I find myself enjoying the story. Most entertaining for a com-mon thief breaking and entering my villa."

Kramer's mind is racing, but there is no way out. He can only keep talking, spinning out the story, buying time.

"Until one day, he is contacted by a nasty sort of man, a representative of East Germany, as a matter of fact, who has learned the dirty little secret of Karl-Heinz Müller and offers a Faustian bargain to him. In exchange for not being turned into the authorities, Müller, or rather Semich, must act as an agent for the East. That is where Gorik fits into the mosaic. He becomes the controller of Semich/Müller. It is doubtful we will ever know what useful secrets Gorik received from his unwilling spy, but one certain result is a car bombing in Prague that was calculated to cause embarrassment to the West and take the heat off the Soviets."

"No!" Müller's face is contorted in anger. "She said she had told nobody. That she could not betray me, could not turn against her own father."

"She didn't," Kramer says. "She never would have. Reni left it to me to piece things together. To follow the clues she laid for me. She said I would understand why she had to leave me in 1974, after I researched the identity of Arno Semich. And she was right. Reni found out about you in 1974, didn't she? About your Nazi past, at any rate. And being Reni, she couldn't turn you in back then, could she? And she could no longer face me if she didn't. She couldn't live that close to a lie."

Müller shakes his head. "No. Sweet little Renata. She

loved her father so. We were an unstoppable team, she and I."
Suddenly, his shoulders slump. "Something's been lost for me
with her death, Sam. I don't care much anymore."

"Then put the gun down. We can talk about it."

Müller jerks himself upright again, gripping the gun
tightly.

"Sure. With you and the police. Is that it?"

"Reni's dead. It's over, Herr Müller. All over."

"No, Sam. Perhaps for you it's over, but not for me. No
one will fault me for shooting someone who broke into my
home. Self-defense."

"You don't want to know how I traced you?" Kramer asks
hurriedly.

"Does it really matter?"

"To me, it does. If I'm going to die for my troubles, I'd at
least like to know if I figured it right."

Müller waves the gun impatiently. "So?"

"So Reni never knew about your involvement with East
German intelligence. Not until lately, that is. Until she got
word from an old friend who believed Reni was responsible
for the Prague car bombing. You see, this friend overheard
Gorik on the phone to his master one time, saying that Müller was the one who had done it. Müller could be trusted. But
Gorik didn't mean Reni, did he? He meant you."

Müller is silent; the pool heater kicks on, filling the room
with a low hum.

"Reni confided in you, didn't she?" Kramer hurries on.
"Back in 1968, before she knew anything about your past,
she came to you one weekend with a rented car and told you
about a silly, noble scheme to throw leaflets from a building
in Prague. And you told Gorik about it. You were the one she
drove to; you whom she trusted."

Müller's eyes close slowly, then re-open. There is moisture
in them.

"She was a little fool, Sam. Bound to take a fall with all her radical politics. She never understood the cynical realities of the world. Survival is the name of the game. Survival at any cost. Under any system. That's why I did it. I wanted to teach her a lesson. To scare her away from this peace and freedom nonsense. Instead, the bomb drove her even further away from me, radicalizing her even more. You were just playing at life, all of you. I wanted to save her, protect her."

"Regardless of whose lives you ruined; of what innocent bystanders might be killed."

"She was my daughter. She came first."

Kramer can see Müller's finger tightening on the trigger.

"And so she killed herself to keep from having to turn you in. Does that make you feel proud of your daughter? Proud of her love? Or sick at the cost you made her pay?"

He thinks he has gone too far, for Müller's finger tightens even more on the trigger, his eyes close down to slits.

"That is what happened, isn't it? After learning about you and Gorik, and faced with protecting you a second time, she could no longer live with herself. She was caught in the ultimate dilemma: her love for you versus her love of justice. For what is fair. The only way out for her was to kill herself and leave a trail of clues that someone might follow back to you. That way it wouldn't be her turning you in, but instead blind justice working its path to you."

Müller clenches his jaw, then slowly nods. "She was cold by the time I arrived. The memoirs were there. She left instructions for me to dispose of them as I saw fit. Does that satisfy you, Sam? Does that clear up the last mysteries before you die?"

"Why Gorik?" Kramer asks quickly. "Why kill him?"

A sudden grin crosses Müller's face, "The fellow was double-dipping, wasn't he? I assumed it could only be from him that Reni learned of my little secret. He was a paid informant for her memoirs. Yet, since reunification, I've been paying him quite handsomely to keep such secrets to himself. So, you see, Herr Gorik earned his death, Sam. I have no regrets there."

"No regrets about Gerhard, either?"

Müller looks at Kramer quizzically for a moment.

"Did you have him killed to keep your Nazi past a secret? What did you do, hire some of Vogel's goons to do your dirty work for you?"

Müller continues to stare dumbly at Kramer, and suddenly a shout breaks the silence.

"Dive, Kramer!"

Kramer hesitates a moment, but does not need to be told twice. Müller's eyes are averted toward the voice momentarily and Kramer throws himself into the water. Dull explosions sound above the surface; spears of foam and bubbles crisscross his head as bullets rip past him, their trajectory skewed by the water. Kramer holds his breath as long as possible, hearing more distant explosions in the pool room above. His heart thumps in his ears, and his lungs feel about to burst. Finally, he can stand it no longer and exhales a stream of bubbles, but his oilskin jacket and the weight of the useless pistol in the pocket hold him down. He sees black dots before his eyes, thinks that he must surely die before finding air again, and then his head suddenly breaks the surface, and he is flooded in light and the loud hum of the pool heater. A pair of legs in blue worsted slacks stands above him at the edge of the pool. A quick look to the other end shows him Müller still draped in the white towel, though now it has turned crimson. He is sprawled next to the water, one hand drooping over the edge, leaking blood into the water.

"Come on out, Kramer. It's safe now."

Kramer has trouble pulling himself out, for his clothes are weighted with water. His tweed cap is slowly sinking at the far end of the pool. Kommissar Boehm reaches down and gives him a hand out of the pool.

"He's dead?" Kramer asks, dripping water onto the tile floor.

"Afraid so." Boehm's face is pained.

"I thought the deal was we take him alive. I get him to talk, then we take him."

"Some things don't work out the way you plan, Kramer. He didn't give me much choice. Where I was standing, he looked about ready to empty his pistol into you. But don't thank me for saving your hide. It would be out of character."

Kramer looks over to Müller's crumpled body, smells the cordite in the air through the chlorine.

"It's over, Kramer," Boehm says, looking at the crumpled form of Müller now. "Over and done with."

CHAPTER TWENTY

"So you're back?" Kate doesn't take her hands off the key-board as Kramer enters the door to the office.

He hangs his cap and jacket before saying anything. "I still have a job?"

Kate smiles, then nods. "I got your story out this morning to Marty. He thought it was, quote 'fucking marvelous' unquote."

Kramer stands with his back against the door and hands in the pockets of his bagged out cords. "Thanks, Kate. I mean it."

"Jesus, don't get maudlin first day back. It was a good story. The last of the war criminals brought to justice and our bureau chief in on the kill. Marty figures we'll increase circ by four or five points on the strength of it."

"Great."

"Come on, Kramer. Why so glum-looking? It's over. You can go back to fudging stories from CNN now."

He forces a smile; there's still a sour taste in the back of his throat. One way to get rid of the past: kill all the players off.

"Too bad you couldn't pin anything on that Vogel creep," Kate says. "I'd love to see his slick ass in jail."

"Nothing to pin, it turns out," Kramer tells her. "I've got a follow-up, but it's a sidebar. Not the main story. Müller was our man all along. The thugs he hired to do his dirty work have probably done a scamper to Iraq by now, though."

He looks around the office. Nothing's changed. Palms and fancy new furniture look just the same as they did before he went tilting at windmills, though *he* feels fundamentally altered. Reni's final legacy—he cares once again. He's not sure what he cares about, but at least the facility is there, functioning.

"I imagine my desk is swamped," he says, heading toward his office. And he is right. He spends the next few days crawling out of the mountain of paper on his desk; stories from stringers and news wires all sorted neatly by Kate into urgent and less urgent mounds. He rails at it at first, but soon settles down to the task. It keeps his mind from wandering where he does not want it to go just now. Focuses himself on a job. He knows he has to make a decision about Reni's memoirs soon, but not now. Not until things have settled, until he can see clearly again.

Two weeks later, Kramer raises a glass of beer in a toast: "To Reni and Gerhard."

The others do the same, saying the names with a hushed reverence as if not wanting to invoke spirits or remind themselves too profoundly of the reason for this gathering. Glasses and steins are knocked together, the beer drunk. Then there is a good thirty seconds of uncomfortable silence.

"They going to feed us sometime?" Margit looks around the crowded Viennese gasthaus, trying to spot a waiter.

Kramer is suddenly happy Rick decided to bring her along.

"They're going to serve it family-style in a few minutes," Kramer explains to her. "It's all arranged."

"You mean I don't get to order?" She glares at Rick. "I hope you told them I'm a vegetarian."

Kramer and Maria exchange amused glances; his stomach does a minor flip-flop at her smile.

"This is not exactly tofu heaven," Randall says by way of warning.

Rick pats Margit's hand. "I'm sure there will be something for you to eat."

She grins at him lasciviously. "I love it when you talk dirty to me."

No more muffled speech for Rick. His bandages are off, but the scars look like ridged pink worms on his face and hands.

Helmut sits quietly through all this, Kramer notices, peering at them through his round glasses, just as he used to back in 1968.

"It's too bad Katia couldn't make it," Kramer says to him.

Helmut shrugs and settles back in his chair. "To be frank with you, she did not want to come. Nor did she think that I should come. Why have you brought us all together, Sam?"

Maria looks at Helmut out of the corner of her eye. They have not said a direct word to one another yet.

"It's called a reunion," Randall says, preempting Kramer's response. "The idea is to have fun. You remember that concept, don't you?"

"You know," Margit says, staring at Randall, "you're sort of cute. Weird, but cute."

Randall nods to her. "Your lady friend has excellent taste, Rick."

"I think Sam wants us all to like one another again," Maria suddenly suddenly, looking straight down at her glass of beer. "He's a sentimentalist."

She looks up at Kramer with those liquid eyes of hers, and he thinks he might agree to anything she says.

"I've been accused of it on occasion," he says.

Maria turns to Helmut. "I imagine he thinks it is a pity for old friends to lose one another in a highly unfriendly world. I feel the same way."

Helmut cuts his eyes from Maria's for a moment, then looks straight at her, returning her open smile. Randall is sitting between Maria and Helmut, but they manage to link hands across him.

"I'm sorry, Maria . . ." Helmut begins.

"No," she says. "Nothing to be sorry for. You couldn't have helped me in Prague. It was all arranged. All set up."

Helmut holds her hand as if reluctant to let it go. Finally, their hands drift apart and Randall leans forward again, elbows on the table.

"What I don't get," he says, "is the purple car."

The others look confused for a moment, and then the waiter brings a platter of golden, flaky schnitzels, setting it in the middle of the large, round table. A cloth covers the dark wood, stitched in golden threads representing hops. A heavy wrought-iron chandelier is overhead; dark wainscoting on the walls. The pleasant hum of voices and click of silverware against dishes comes from other tables.

Margit looks disappointedly at the platter of schnitzels for a moment, "I hope those aren't veal. You ever see how they raise calves?"

Then the same waiter brings more platters of deep-fried mushrooms and cheese, and a huge bowl of salad made from fresh butter lettuce from Israel.

"That's more like it," she says, reaching a blue-fingernailed hand out to retrieve one of the crusty, steaming mushrooms and plop it into her mouth with sexual ferocity, nostrils flaring and eyes rolling as if in orgasm.

Rick doesn't seem to notice or, if he does, is only amused while the rest of the men look on in a sort of dumb, numb awe.

"What purple car?" Rick says as they all begin helping themselves.

"You explain, Sam," Randall says as he spears a hefty schnitzel with his fork.

"I guess it's our red herring," Kramer says, looking at each of the other five in turn; Maria to his immediate left, then Randall, Helmut, Margit, and Rick to his right. "A bad color scheme, I know, but it kept us diverted enough so that we never focused on Reni's father."

"Could you perhaps take it from the beginning for those of us unfamiliar with the players?" Helmut says in his stilted English. "So Reni really did kill herself?"

Kramer nods. "Right. That's where it all started for me." He looks to his left. "And for Randall. She killed herself because she couldn't bring herself to turn her father in for his Nazi past or for his spying for former East Germany. But she left tantalizing little clues around for me to follow. She even left a message for Randall so he would come knocking on my cage if I was too lazy to self-start."

"It's like she was still here," Rick says. "Like she stage-managed the whole thing, even tonight's reunion."

"Maybe," Kramer allows. In fact, it was one of her last wishes, expressed in the letter to him, that he gather the old gang one last time.

Margit cuts a large section of baked cheese, wrapping melted tentacles of it around her fork and stuffing it into her mouth, chewing happily. She swallows and looks skeptically at Kramer.

"She loved her father that much?" she says. "After learning all she did about him?"

"I don't know if it's love we're talking about here," Kramer says. "More like an obsession."

He can still see the wall of photos at Inheritance, the minute recording of her life with her father, the paucity of photos with the other men in her life.

Margit drinks some beer, wipes the foam from her mouth

with her wrist. "I would have turned the bastard in." She looks at Maria. "He ruined your life."

Maria is about to speak, thinks better of it and merely smiles at Margit.

"So all right," Helmut says. "Reni finds out about her father twice, cannot deal with it, ends her life, but leaves clues that might lead you," he nods at Kramer, "to Herr Müller. But what about this purple car?"

Kramer is still looking at his mental picture of Reni's photo wall.

"Sam?" Helmut says again.

Maria touches his forearm, bringing him back to the discussion at hand.

"Sorry. The purple car. It kept turning up everywhere we searched. It was a purple car in Berlin that killed Gorik, Müller's East German control. One may have been parked outside Reni's house around the time she . . . died. A similar car almost ran me down in Bad Lunsburg. But it turns out that they were all coincidence. Kommissar Boehm even tracked one to Vogel."

"Who?" Margit asks, setting her fork down hard.

Kramer repeats the sentence.

Margit sucks her lips, looking at Rick and running a forefinger up his arm playfully, then finally looks back to Kramer.

"You mix with very strange company, Kramer," she says.

Two hours later, after finishing the heavy meal and consuming several pints of beer and a couple of thimbles full of Hungarian peach brandy each, the six of them gather outside the gasthaus, under the glow of a streetlamp.

"We should have gone Dutch," Helmut is still protesting.

"You pick up the tab next time," Kramer says. Tonight has pretty well topped out the plastic, but what the hell. Cost accountancy has never been his strong suit. He figures it was worth every groschen the meal cost to get old friends together again.

"It was great, Sam," Margit says, grabbing him in her strong arms and squeezing him like a melon she is testing for freshness. "We must do it again. Munich next time. Right, Rick?"

Rick is feeling the effects of the booze after a long period of abstinence and can only manage a nod of his head.

"Come on, lover." Margit grabs his hand. "Time to tuck you in."

Helmut shakes hands all around, pecking Maria's cheek lightly. "Time for me to sleep, as well. I've got an early flight tomorrow." He is about to hurry off after Rick and Margit, who are headed up the street to the pension where Kramer has booked rooms for them, but stops and flashes a broad smile. "It really was great seeing you again. We'll stay in touch, right?"

"Right," Kramer and Randall say in unison, and then they all laugh.

"Seriously?" Helmut says.

"Most adamantly and seriously," Maria answers him in an all-business tone of voice.

Helmut jogs up the street to catch Margit, who is swaying as she tries to guide Rick along the pavement. Kramer, Randall, and Maria stand silently for a time, watching as Helmut catches the others up and swings Rick's left arm over his shoulders, helping to half-carry him along.

"He ain't heavy," Randall begins singing the old song.

Maria, between the two of them, suddenly wraps her arms around their shoulders. "I want to sleep at your place tonight, okay, Sam? It's too lonely at the pension."

"Sure." Kramer likes the feel of her thin arm draped over his shoulder. "I'll take the couch. Randall, you get the floor."

"Hey, we toss for it," Randall says.

Maria looks up into Kramer's face. "I mean with you, Sam."

"Whoa," Randall says, and whistles lowly.

A mischievous grin passes over Maria's face. "Aren't I awful? The brazen hussy. But if there's one thing I learned from all those years in prison, it's to not wait for what you want. Life is long, desire short."

"A philosopher," Randall jokes.

Kramer is looking into her face, searching out her eyes, trying to examine his own feelings, trying to figure out if he really wants the roller coaster of emotional attachment to begin once again.

"I'd like that," he finally says. Then to Randall, "And no jokes."

"I wasn't thinking of any," Randall says. "Looks like I'll be using that pension room."

He has the flat back in a semblance of shape; even dug the nails out of the wooden Madonna in the hall. Maria scampers off to the bedroom while Kramer uses the facilities.

She is already under the eiderdown when Kramer enters the darkened bedroom. The streetlight outside plays on the white coverlet like a harvest moon.

She wriggles her feet under the covers. "Hurry, Sam. The sheets are freezing."

He strips quickly, his back to Maria, then jumps in beside her, feeling a pocket of warm air and then the velvety smoothness of her thigh against his. She is on her back, eyes closed and smiling up at some secret images or thoughts. On his left side, he props his head in his hand and looks down at her face. There is a lovely luminosity to it, as if the hard years only worked to soften her, to complete her.

Bullshit, he tells himself. They were miserable, lonely, terrifying times for her. Don't confuse romance with Romance.

She is looking up at him suddenly. "They say it's like riding a bicycle. I'm not so sure, though. Touch me. Remind me."

She takes his hand and places it under the quilt on her breast. The nipple is hard; he can feel her heart pounding beneath the flesh and tissue. It's as if he has a primal attachment to her—as if he's part of her body, of her pulse. He leans over, brushing her lips with his, lightly, tenderly, smelling the sweet aroma from the apricot brandy. There is a sudden swelling of tenderness in him that brings tears to his eyes, a sudden expansion in his chest. It's the same feeling he sometimes experiences listening to choral music in the Stephansdom or looking at the play of light in a Monet painting. He kisses her again, but this time their lips hold; he feels the flicker of her tongue and the sudden jerk and catch of eroticism in his groin.

"I think it's coming back to me," she whispers, her hand tracing down his flank, inching toward his sex, and then holding him, squeezing, caressing. With her other hand, she pulls him on top of her, guiding him inside, giving a little shudder when he is fully in.

They make love slowly, neither eager for the climax. It's all in the journey. Kramer kisses her deeply as they move together. Her hands press him into her, as if she can't feel him close enough, gripping at the small of his back, fluttering over his shoulder blades.

Kramer awakes in the middle of the night. Maria has been watching him sleep, brushing her hand lightly over his cheek.

"Want to play some more?" she says, the same mischievous grin on her face.

He breathes in her scent; snuggles his face into her warm breasts.

"Sam?"

"Mmm." He is nuzzling her nipple, rolling his tongue about it.

"You don't really think it's over, do you?"

He pulls back from her, wiping a hand over his face to wake up fully.

"What's over? I thought you wanted to play."

She sits up in bed, propping the pillows in back of her, drawing her knees up and the eiderdown over her breasts.

"Be honest," she says.

Kramer sits up too, wishing for the millionth time he hadn't given up smoking, badly needing not only the nicotine rush but also the distraction. He stares at the foot of the bed, not looking at Maria.

"You think there are loose ends. That's why you're holding back the memoirs, isn't it?" Maria asks.

He nods slowly, making the bed springs sound.

"What are we going to do about it?"

He turns toward her. "*We* aren't going to do anything."

"Please don't get protective on me. I would hate that."

They sit in silence some more, then she reaches over and touches his cheek. "Did she really kill herself?"

No need for names; they both know who *she* is.

Kramer turns to Maria again, putting his hand on her stomach under the quilt. "That's the one sure thing in all of this. Reni killed herself. She made that clear."

He sees the letter again.

If you are reading this, dear Sammy, then I am dead and I can tell you what I could never tell you before. I love you. I have always loved you. As much as it is in me to love any man.

"Then what?" Maria says.

He thinks of Reni the games master, setting the rules of the hunt. But she had no idea her game would take the lives of Gorik or Gerhard; that her father would track both of them down.

And then he remembers something.

"That night at Müller's," he says, "when Boehm saved my life . . ."

He pauses, sitting bolt upright in bed, trying to recapture the scene.

"Yes?" Maria says.

Suddenly, he sees it clearly and feels a racing of his pulse. "It was Müller's face. Absolute surprise when I mentioned Gerhard's death. I don't think he was faking that. No need to."

Maria says nothing, waiting for him to continue.

A car rattles along the cobbles below, headed away from the inner city.

"And?" she finally says.

"I've been a fool." He turns to her. "Don't you see? If Müller didn't have Gerhard killed to protect his Nazi past, then who did? It's not much of a reach to point the finger at Vogel."

"But why?" Maria says.

"The lists." He should have seen this earlier. "It all comes back to the donor lists to his party. Vogel must have assumed Gerhard was privy to whatever Reni did. He couldn't take the risk of letting him live."

"And the hired killers were the same ones who attacked you in Prague?"

Kramer nods and sinks back down against his pillow. They sit in silence a while longer. "But it doesn't make sense," Maria says. "If these lists are so important, why hasn't anybody made a move to get the duplicate ones from Reni's safe-deposit box?"

Kramer laughs without humor. "That's an easy one to answer. Because I never told anyone about them. Only about Reni's letter. Even when I enlisted Boehm's help, I only divulged the trace of Semich to Müller."

Maria suddenly bends over and kisses his cheek. "That's why I'm in lust with you, Sam. You're such a clever old dog."

He allows the compliment, even though he hasn't earned it.

And Sammy, Reni added as a caveat postscript to her letter, *think long and hard what you intend to do with the memoirs, with the list of names. To publish or not to publish, that is the question. And you see how I answered it for myself. Don't make any leaps; don't tell anyone of their existence until you are ready to act. There is too much at stake.*

Maria snuggles next to him. "But this might just be three-in-the-morning talk, right?" she says. "Paranoia. There's no real proof for any of it. Maybe we should just let things lie."

He doesn't respond to this one, but pulls her on top of him, feeling the heat between her legs. When he slides inside of her, she looks down at him with narrowed eyes, her breasts dangling over his face.

A whisper comes from her, "Wouldn't it be nice if we could just play like this forever?"

She folds herself over him, blotting out the world, blotting out everything for the moment but the heat between them and the slow movement of their hips.

CHAPTER TWENTY-ONE

The elevator doors open slowly, and there are two carbon-copy goons just as before, all dolled up in brown and black uniforms with submachine guns. He can't tell if they're the same ones, but it's a dead cert that the frisker standing in back of them in civilian dress is new. No-Neck, who followed him to Crete and to Prague, is nowhere to be seen. Kramer passes between the two uniformed guards, coming up close to the new frisker, a short, stocky guy with dead white skin and stylishly long hair, wearing a baggy tweed jacket. Kramer reaches into his jacket pocket and brings out the Walther. He is so close to the goon that the others don't see what's in his hand, but the frisker does, and his eyes bulge. Kramer pauses a beat, then reverses the pistol, handing it over butt first.

"I want it back after I talk with Vogel."

The thick-necked goon finally finds his voice. "Who says you're going to see him?"

He roughly frisks Kramer, the two other guards grinning like hyenas.

Satisfied that Kramer is clean, the frisker passes him on to the reception desk with a cynical bow.

There's the same secretary as last time, her voice every bit as hard as before, her manner just as officious. Hearing Kramer's request, she shoots him a disapproving look across the massive oak desk.

"Herr Vogel is otherwise engaged. You have no appointment?"

"I think he'll see me. You might just mention Article 129a."

She looks at him with cold gray eyes for a moment, then in back of him to the guards. For a second, he thinks he has overplayed his hand, and his stomach knots in anticipation.

Finally, she reaches for the phone. "Very well. But this is most irregular."

Kramer lets out his breath. She relays his name and message; there is a pause on the other end, then a small distant voice says something and she hangs the phone up.

"He will see you. But for only a short moment. There are others waiting."

The only others in the hall are goons, but Kramer says nothing, nodding his head politely at her as if she were the receptionist at a doctor's office who had just allowed him to jump the queue.

He passes down the long corridor covered in red carpeting, guards at attention at ten-foot intervals. The young guard from the Hitler Youth cartoons is on duty again at Vogel's door and ushers him into the "Führer's" office.

"Sam." Vogel sticks out his hand as the door opens, a phony smile on his lips. "Good to see you."

Kramer enters and shakes hands with him limply, taking in the gray wool Bavarian country suit trimmed in forest green that Vogel's wearing; the pink tie against a sparkling white shirt.

"I wish you'd given me more notice. As it is . . ." Vogel shrugs with his hands to indicate how pressed for time he is. "But sit. What is this cryptic message you had my secretary deliver?"

"Hardly cryptic." Kramer does not sit, and Vogel remains standing as well.

"What is it you want?" The false smile disappears with the question.

"We're talking about the Grundgesetz, the Basic Law," Kramer says. "Specifically about Article 129a, which states . . ."

"Yes," Vogel flutters a hand at him to interrupt. "We all know what it says. It is against the law to belong to terrorist organizations such as the Red Army Faction."

"Or a Fascist party," Kramer adds. "The law as written decrees membership in both right and left terrorist organizations to be illegal."

"One can hardly compare us with the leftists, Sam. They want to destroy Germany as we know it, to replace it with some foreign-dominated criminal state. We—all of us on the right—want to revitalize the German national spirit; to make Germans proud to say they are Germans after so many years of forced guilt feelings and shame."

Kramer listens as Vogel warms to his topic, saying nothing, betraying no emotion on his face.

"We are fundamentally different from such organizations, and the courts have been recognizing this difference," Vogel continues. "It is not we who are the target of the antiterrorist squads. In fact, if asked, we would gladly aid the government in its efforts to finally squash the RAF."

Still nothing from Kramer, and Vogel stops, looking straight into his face.

"Why have you come here?"

"I've got a deal for you. I want the goons who killed my friend in Crete. The ones who tried to kill me in Prague."

Vogel puts on a shocked face. "Sam, what is all this about?"

"You know what it's about. Müller did a hiring job, recruited some of your volunteers for a hit."

Vogel is about to protest further, but Kramer pushes on.

"I'm not interested in anyone but those two goons. Not accusing you of having anything to do with it, either. All I'm after is simple vengeance."

"I know of no such men."

"He frisked me last time I was here. I recognized him. The other one was unknown to me."

"This is absurd."

"I'm willing to do a trade."

"There's nothing to trade for. I don't know what you're talking about."

"The Basic Law says it's illegal to belong to terrorist organizations, yet you have boys from the Bundestag paying dues here. I wonder what the press would do with a list of those old boys."

Vogel tenses. "This is the second time you have come to me with preposterous suggestions. I told you then I would tolerate no further such inquisitions."

"I've got the list, Vogel. Copies of it are stamped and ready to be mailed in case I suddenly die. All the names are there. All the ones Reni Müller gathered. But I'm willing to trade. The list for the two goons. Alive and slightly incapacitated. I want to take care of them personally."

Vogel says nothing for a moment, his eyes sizing up Kramer, squinting and making his face take on a porcine appearance. There is a twitch at his left eye, a moment of weakness. Then, "I haven't the faintest idea what you're talking about, Herr Kramer. I believe this interview is finished. You are no longer welcome at our headquarters. I hope I make myself clear."

He pushes a button built into the top of the metal tube of one of the chrome and leather chairs, and the huge oak doors open quickly, the young guard looking alert.

"Show Herr Kramer out, please."

Kramer stands his ground. "I'll give you two days to consider the offer. Then I publish. Think about it hard, Vogel."

Vogel does not look at him as Kramer passes to the door. The guard is about to take his arm, but Kramer pulls away from him.

"I can manage by myself, thanks." He looks back at Vogel who has turned to the window giving out onto the main square. "Two days," Kramer says to his back. Then to the guard, "I'll take my gun back now, too."

"How wise do you think that was, Kramer?" Kommissar Boehm's face is largely impassive after hearing of Kramer's visit to Vogel. A half-empty bottle of Polish vodka sits on the desk, one glass next to it.

"Not very wise," Kramer says, eyeing the bottle. "But it should get the hive stirring."

It's been a long day for Kramer. He wants only to get something to eat before catching the late-night flight back to Vienna.

"You sure you want to get these bees angry?" Kommissar Boehm says thickly, looking old and tired suddenly.

Kramer wonders how much of the vodka Boehm has had, then gets up abruptly. "You going to let the bastard get away with it? Just let him walk? I thought you wanted to nail him. Stick him so deep in prison they'll have to shotgun his lunch to him."

Boehm sits impassively behind his desk, his eyes never leaving Kramer's.

"So why come to me?" Boehm says finally. "I can't protect you night and day."

"Who's asking you to? Besides, Vogel's not going to do anything too stupid." Kramer goes to the window, looks down at the streets of Bad Lunsburg. The lights are just coming on in shop windows. Then he turns back to Boehm.

"I told him I had postmarked copies of the list ready to go out to major newspapers if anything happened to me. It's the kind of insurance that works. I figure I'm in a win-win situation. Even if I can't get to Vogel, I'll get the goons. Then we make them talk." He smiles.

"You've got it all figured out," Kommissar Boehm says. "And what about legalities?"

"What about your daughter?"

Boehm's jaw flexes; he taps thick fingers on his desk blotter.

"Sorry," Kramer says, but Boehm does not respond for a moment.

"You ever feel so tired out that you wanted to crawl in some hole, Kramer?" Boehm looks at the desk blotter as he speaks, then lifts his eyes to Kramer's. "I mean in here." He taps his chest over his heart with a thick forefinger. "It's all a waste of time. Know that? We catch the criminal, and the sociologists and psychologists sob about the poor guy's battered childhood, about lack of love in early developmental stages, and the lawyers get the bastard off. No more cause and effect; no more punishment for crimes. No more leaders, just managers . . ."

Boehm's eyes cut from Kramer again as if he realizes he has said too much. The booze has opened too many interior doors. Kramer says nothing.

"Christ," Boehm finally says. "Listen to me going all maudlin. Maybe it's time for me to call it quits here. Retirement sounds pretty good to me right now."

"And what about Vogel?" Kramer says, thrusting reality in Boehm's face once again.

Boehm looks at Kramer hard. "I don't think we've had this conversation."

Kramer pauses for a moment. "Okay," he finally says. "If that's how you want it."

"I could demand you turn over these documents as state's evidence."

Kramer shakes his head. "I don't think so, Kommissar. First, the state hasn't got any investigation going. Second, I'm literary executor. Remember?"

"And you expect Vogel to trust you?"

"I guess we'll find out how desperate he is. You should see the names on the list."

Boehm stops tapping his fingers, closes his eyes momentarily and then opens them, looking straight at Kramer.

"You've come all the way to Bad Lunsburg just to tell me this?"

Kramer shoots him a wry smile. "I was hoping maybe we could work together." He shrugs. "But we never had this conversation."

Boehm shakes his head and lets out a sigh. "And what if he calls your bluff?"

"I publish."

"No," Boehm says, a tight smile on his lips. "About the insurance. What if he has you eliminated?"

Kramer grins. "Then I get a posthumous Pulitzer."

"Kramer, you've got a death wish. Know that?"

"Just stirring up the bees, Kommissar."

Kramer is woken out of a sound sleep by the phone on his bedside table, and he grapples for it, half-asleep, knocking his clock off the table in the process.

"Yeah?" he says groggily.

"Herr Kramer. Sorry to wake you."

Vogel's voice makes Kramer sit up in bed, instantly awake.

"You ready to bargain?"

"Oh no, Herr Kramer. I think perhaps it is you who will be ready to bargain now."

"You've got a day left, Vogel," Kramer says, then hears muffled sounds on the other end, and a new voice.

"Sam."

His body goes cold and rigid.

"It's me, Sam. Maria."

"You okay?" he says, feeling anger sweeping over him and losing himself in it.

"I'm okay." Then she hurriedly says, "Whatever they want, don't give it to them, Sam. Don't give in . . ."

More muffled sounds on the other end and then Vogel's voice is back on the line.

"You still there, Kramer?"

"I'll have your heart on a plate for this, Vogel. You hurt one hair on her head . . ."

"You're the one who is hurting her, Kramer. You turn over the list you were speaking about, and all copies; then we can talk about your girlfriend."

The anger brings bile into Kramer's throat; he cannot respond for a moment.

"Do we understand each other, Kramer?"

"Where?"

"You just sit tight. I'll be getting back to you this afternoon. And no police. I get word of police activity on this, and I cut my losses. Understand? Meanwhile you figure out how you can assure me there will be no lists published. Ever."

There is a clunk and then the dial tone. Kramer sits in bed, holding the receiver for moments, listening to the tone as if it were a mantra.

He doesn't sleep again. The night seems to go on forever as he sits and thinks, or wanders the apartment, cursing himself for his arrogance that has brought this on Maria.

They've obviously been following me, he figures. *Saw Maria come and go from here; followed her back to Prague.*

But it doesn't matter how they got to her, only that they

did. *Her life is on the line because you got cute, Kramer. Because you were playing hardball in a league way over your head.* He wants a Scotch but knows he has to keep his head clear.

By first light, Kramer's anger has hardened into purpose. He fixes coffee and a day-old *Semmel* with marmalade and forces himself to eat. Then he gets the Walther from the third drawer of his dresser, out of the cloth sack he has stored it in tucked under a level of socks, takes it back to the kitchen, and cleans it methodically. He has half a box of ammunition left; he fills one clip and shoves it into the grip, then loads a backup clip, making sure the spring mechanism is in working order. He'll carry the rest of the bullets loose.

By eight thirty, he's on the phone to Munich. The receiver is picked up on the fourth ring.

"Bitte?"

The voice is low and thick. Still in bed, Kramer figures.

"Sorry to get you up, Rick. Kramer here."

"Hey, Sam." Rick's voice brightens. "You always get up this early?"

"Sure," he says. "Margit there? I'd like to talk to her for a second."

"She's sleeping."

"Wake her, will you, Rick?"

"You okay, Sam? You sound sort of stressed."

"Just wake her, all right?"

"Yeah, sure."

Kramer waits for what seems hours for Margit to get up and to the phone.

"Hello, Sam," she says. He can hear the sleep in her voice, too.

"Margit." He pauses. This is a hunch. Instinct. A place to begin. Vogel is in the skin trade; perhaps Margit, with her Munich connections, knows something about him. And there was that comment she made the night at dinner in Vienna when he was talking about the car traced to Vogel: *You mix with very strange company, Kramer.*

"Look, I need some information. You know anything about a guy named Vogel?"

"What's wrong?"

"Nothing. I just need information."

"Like for example?" Her voice is suspicious, on guard.

"Like where he might go if he wanted to hide away. Some little country retreat."

She pauses. "How important is this?"

"Life and death."

Another pause and then he hears her voice away from the receiver asking Rick to go make some coffee. Then, into the receiver once again, "This is between you and me, right, Sam?"

"This is all the further it goes."

"Okay. It's just I wouldn't want Rick to know. A couple of months ago, Vogel was recruiting some of the girls from the district for a big party out at his training grounds. We were supposed to be the prizes for a bunch of recruits who just finished basic training. It was a fucking zoo scene with about five men to every one of us." There is emotion in her voice, a tremor, the catch of breath.

"I only want to know where it is," Kramer says.

"I know. It just all comes back when I think of it. You going to nail that little prick?"

"I hope so."

"You take some friends along, Sam. He's got a permanent staff out there. Five, six men."

"Margit. Where?"

"It's just over the border," she says. "In Austria, so the German police don't bother him. Near the lake district."

She gives him exact instructions; he knows the area, has hiked it before.

"You want some help, Sam?" she says finally.

He thinks about it. "No. But there is one other thing. That night at the restaurant in Vienna, you said something that maybe I didn't understand."

They talk for another few minutes, and Kramer makes the final connections in the puzzle. It all fits together for him. He knows now what he has to do. There is no other choice.

"Thanks, Margit," he says. "Give Rick a hug for me."

"We'll see you soon, right?" she says.

"Right."

He gets out some topographic maps for the lake district, which he keeps in the bookcase next to his work desk. The one he needs is torn from when the goons turned over his apartment, but he repairs it with Scotch tape and spreads it out on his desk, examining the area. He sees the symbol for the disused forestry station just where Margit described, puts a finger over it and jabs it once, twice.

Then he takes his old portable Olivetti that he retrieved from Inheritance out of the drawer of the desk. It's dusty, but the keys are okay and the ribbon fresh enough. Reni used it for the memoirs. He inserts a sheet of plain white paper and begins typing.

The sound of his doorbell startles him. He waits for it to sound again, then gets up, goes to the kitchen, and gets the automatic. The doorbell sounds a third time when he gets to the door. He jerks the door open suddenly, holding the pistol straight out in front of him.

Randall is standing in the door jamb looking distraught. His eyes go down to the pistol aimed at his stomach.

"So you know," Randall says.

Kramer lowers the gun, looking both ways along the hall before closing the door behind them.

"Know what?" he says.

Randall wastes no time, crossing to the repaired Tyrolean hope chest recently resupplied with booze. He opens it, takes out a bottle of Scotch, and drinks straight out of the bottle, replaces the cap, and puts the Scotch back in the chest.

"Come on, Sam. Why else the gun? You must know."

"You tell me." Kramer puts the gun down on the foyer table next to his wooden Madonna.

"Look. I've been in Prague for the past week staying with Maria. When she didn't come home last night, I called and called here to see if she'd come to pay you a surprise visit. When no one answered, I got worried and hopped the early-morning flight. By the looks of you, she's not here, either. So what's up?"

Kramer is about to lie, then thinks better of it. "Vogel's got her."

"Vogel? What the shit for?"

"I was putting pressure on him, doing a trade for some information Reni left me."

Randall squints at him, bobbing from foot to foot as if he has to use the john. "So he kidnaps Maria?"

"Upping the ante," Kramer says.

"We've got to call the police."

"No!" Kramer hears the panic in his voice and does not like the sound. "No police. He warned about that and there's no telling what kind of contacts Vogel has."

"So what does he want?"

Kramer goes to the liquor chest and takes a swig of the whiskey himself, straight from the bottle. It tastes of peat bogs and burns all the way down.

"Assurance that I give him back all copies of the lists; that I never publish them."

"So okay, give them to him."

Kramer shakes his head. "Maybe it's not that simple."

Randall looks at the gun on the table in the foyer.

"So you're playing cowboy. You're going after him, aren't you?"

"Maybe."

Randall grabs his shirt, shakes him. "You're playing dice with Maria's life, you shit."

Kramer takes Randall's hands off his shirt, steps back, holding his rage in. "It's not so simple," he says again. "You've got to believe me on this one. She's dead if we don't do something."

Randall looks at him for a long moment, then slowly nods. "You know where she is?"

"I think so."

"So," Randall says, "when do we leave?"

Kramer is about to protest, then stares back at Randall and knows it's no use.

"Okay," he says. "We leave soon. First I've got this to finish," he gestures toward the typewriter on his desk, "and then I have a call to make."

They leave the back way, just in case Vogel has men watching the flat. Kramer carries a copy of the memoirs in an old leather day pack, the gun in the pocket of his coat. At the Landesgerichtsstrasse, he flags a taxi and has it take them across the Donaukanal into the Second District.

"This isn't the way out of town," Randall says, looking out the window to the brown-green water below as they cross the Aspernbrücke.

Kramer says nothing, keeping a watch behind them to make sure no one is following. The taxi drives up Taborstrasse into the heart of the Second District and finally stops on a side street not far from Praterstrasse. Kramer pays the driver, and he and Randall walk the two blocks to the address he got over the phone.

Randall asks no further questions, not even when Kramer stops at a large villa near the Augarten with the huge bulk of the World War II antiaircraft tower visible through leafless branches in the center of the park. A butler in eighteenth-century livery answers the door and nods politely at them.

"Herr Kramer?"

Kramer nods back in affirmation.

"He is waiting for you," the butler says, and leads them through a gaudy marble-floored foyer, up a grand staircase under a crystal chandelier to the second-floor suite of rooms, and into a library with floor-to-ceiling bookcases. In front of a fireplace blazing with three-foot logs stands Rudi Tourescu, decked out in elk-hide knee britches and a heavy sweater, his hands behind his back and a smile on his face.

"You are ready, my friend?" he says. "But first, tell me. This Vogel and his Germany United you mentioned on the phone. They think it's fun to burn immigrant hostels, beat up foreigners?"

"Among other pastimes."

Rudi looks squarely at Kramer, his dark eyes, usually playful and smiling, are now hard and appraising.

"So it is not just a matter of private vendetta. This is a payback for Rostock and Solingen and how many other insults and atrocities. You see, Kramer, I would help you no matter what. I sense a good man inside you, someone sympathetic to the underdog, the outsider. Maybe because you feel like one yourself. But to involve my other men, then there must be something bigger than personal vengeance. They are professionals; they know how to handle themselves and have proved it. But they are not simply soldiers of fortune to be aimed at a target. They trust me to use them in the right cause, the proper cause."

It's the first time Kramer has seen this side of Rudi—the calculating, responsible leader—and he's happy for it.

They travel in two Range Rovers, new models worth at least forty thousand dollars each, and with five extra men. Kramer doesn't get a good look at the men in the second vehicle, only at the leather-encased arsenal they're carrying. Hunters off to the hills.

Rudi keeps the CD player going the whole way: Jussi Björling belting out Verdi and Puccini.

"The way he hits that high C in 'Nessun dorma,' now that is artistry," Rudi says just as they are approaching the industrial outskirts of Linz.

Kramer has said nothing since leaving Vienna. They're making time on the E5 autobahn, in the left lane all the way, leaving Mercedes-Benzes and Audis behind. The black Range Rovers hold close together and other drivers make way, as if sensing their purpose. But still Kramer keeps his peace. As they head southwest past Linz toward Gmunden he looks at the digital clock on the wooden dash: 11:13.

Björling is melancholy and lost, and Kramer finally notices the music, picking up the mood from him, feeling the welling up of anger and regret, seeing for the first time that the cycle of history is repeating itself. Plans and schemes have once again put Maria in harm's way, made her the victim of others' machinations. Easy enough to blame Reni for all those years; harder now to face the blame himself. But he knows it is no use playing "should have, could have." There's only one thing that can save her now.

Rudi is sitting in back with Kramer; Randall is up front with the driver, Georges.

"So that there is no misunderstanding when we arrive," Rudi says, looking at the scenery, "what is it you want, my friend?"

This is an easy one for Kramer.

"To get Maria out of there alive."

Rudi nods his head slowly, ruefully. "That may be a lot to hope for."

CHAPTER TWENTY-TWO

They fly past Bad Ischl doing a hundred miles per hour, turning north again past the Wolfgangsee.

"Here it is," Kramer says as they approach the exit to the secondary Route 154.

Georges hits the turn signal but does not slow for the exit, and soon they are at the Mondsee, all green and blue under scattered clouds like a calendar picture, but there is no tranquillity in it today. Kramer's stomach is in knots. Rudi finally has Randall switch off the CD player, and now there is silence but for the tight hum of the engine. In another ten minutes, they cross Route 1 and Kramer pulls out his topographic map.

"The turn should be soon," he tells Georges. Out the window, he sees signs for Lengau. "There, to the left."

The Range Rover bumps onto a narrow country road cutting through rolling hillsides, some of them in winter wheat, others covered in pine and deciduous forest. The second Rover is close behind, its hood picking up mud from them. They drive deeper into the wooded countryside, passing no other vehicles. Kramer hopes for the hundredth time that his instincts about Vogel are right; that he has crept off to a country hideout with Maria and is not in Munich, holed up at his headquarters. If she's not here, Kramer will have to make it back to Vienna in record time to get Vogel's afternoon call.

She'll be here, he tells himself. *She'll be here.*

Soon they pass the forestry road going off to the right, just as shown on his map. A guard stands at the gate dressed in hunter green, smoking a cigarette and trying hard to look nondescript. Kramer crouches forward in his seat as they pass by the guard, not wanting to be seen, and is thankful for the tinted windows of Rudi's truck. They continue another mile past the turning to the forestry road, around a bend and out of sight of the sentry, and Kramer tells Georges to pull over. The second Rover parks in back, and they get out into the brisk fresh air. Kramer takes in a couple of deep breaths. It is midday, but now he is no longer so concerned about time. She is there, all right, he tells himself. Why else post a guard?

He has to risk gambling that Maria is being held at this camp; has to use the element of surprise with Vogel, the best weapon he has and the best chance to get Maria back alive.

"So that was it?" Rudi says.

"That was it."

Rudi is at the back of the truck pulling out leather scabbards, unzipping them and extracting Mannlicher rifles. Kramer can smell the fresh gun oil on them.

Randall wraps his arms around his chest, shivering. "Anybody remember to pack a lunch?"

"Maybe Vogel will have something for us," Kramer says.

Randall considers this. "Maybe so." Then nodding at the rifles, he asks Rudi, "You got one of those for me?"

"Most assuredly," Rudi says, unzipping the last of the scabbards.

The four men from the second vehicle, and Georges busy themselves with ammunition, then hump on protective vests before putting NATO jackets on over them. Kramer looks at the vests, and it hits home that this is for real; this isn't playing cops and robbers.

Rudi is at his side suddenly, one of the flack vests in hand. "I recommend you wear this."

Kramer takes it gratefully. "Thanks. Thanks for everything."

"Save it for later. Until we know what we have to be thankful for."

It's not so much a plan as a maneuver Kramer has in mind. He pulls out the topographic map and shows the location of the three converted forestry huts, explaining the situation to the men at the same time. They all listen closely, Georges nodding his head at intervals. The other four appear just as Rudi said: proven soldiers. There is that faraway look in the eyes that Kramer has seen before in soldiers going into action: a sort of stoic fatalism and a turning inward before battle. They're all sizes: a large, raw-boned one with a kid's rosy complexion and the eyes of an old man; a shorter wiry one who cuts his eyes between Rudi and Kramer; and the other two who are about the same size and weight, almost interchangeable. They could be brothers. Kramer has no instantaneous make on them; hopes only that they are competent.

"We may have fire power in our favor," he says to them after detailing the layout. "But it means nothing without surprise. That's our real tactical weapon. With Maria under guard inside, we can't afford to lose the element of surprise."

Georges nods at this knowingly, the others simply keep focus on that invisible distant point. Rudi gives a thumbs up blessing to the mission, and then the eight of them sling rifles over their shoulders. Kramer takes along his day pack for good measure. There is a path parallel to the road that leads back toward the forestry road. They walk single file along the path for several minutes, Kramer taking point. The others have been around too long to complain about someone else taking the lead.

The path is densely overgrown, and Kramer picks slowly through the undergrowth, careful not to break twigs underfoot or catch his rifle on a branch. Despite the chill of the day, he is soon sweating. The sound of the hitch and jostle of weapons against bodies is hard to muffle. Randall stumbles over a root and falls in a clatter onto the side of the path. A covey of larks is startled, flapping overhead and calling out. Then the forest is quiet again, deadly still.

"I need two volunteers," Kramer whispers, realizing that this travel en masse is absurd. "The rest stay behind until we take care of the guard."

"Marco, Peter. You go with him," Rudi says to two of the men.

"Volunteers," Kramer says again.

"That's us," Marco, the slight, wiry-looking young man, says. He moves like a cat through the woods; Kramer senses he is a good man to have on your side. Peter simply nods in assent; he's the bigger one, with hands large enough to crush melons. He reminds Kramer of some of the kids he grew up with in Oregon, big and rough and born to work in the woods, the kind you didn't want to meet Saturday night in town after a few too many beers.

"Okay," he whispers. "But my way. We don't kill unless absolutely necessary."

Marco and Peter glance at Rudi who blinks his eyes in assent.

This time, Marco automatically takes the lead, and it's Kramer's turn to make no complaints. They move on slowly for several more minutes, and suddenly Marco slashes his right hand upward. They stop, craning their ears. A faint humming is coming from the path ahead of them. They move on, hunkered over, peering through the lush greenery and the humming grows louder, finally attaching itself to a body only fifty yards ahead of them.

The guard is pissing against a tree, humming some pop melody out of tune. His urine flows in a golden arc, illuminated by a sudden ray of sun penetrating the thickness of the forest. Marco looks back at Kramer and smiles. Without warning, he strips off his rifle, hands it to Kramer, and begins sprinting down the path. The guard is shaking the last drips, still humming to himself, when finally, too late, he hears movement behind him.

Marco dives onto the guard, knocks him to the ground, and thrusts his forearm over the man's mouth as he drives his knee into his groin. The guard curls into a fetal ball and a sharp crack to the side of his head from Marco's pistol stops him groaning. Peter and Kramer rush to the scene and help pull the guard behind a thick stand of trees. Peter takes strong nylon twine from his NATO jacket and binds the guard to the tree, then rifles the man's pockets, finds a soiled handkerchief, and stuffs it into the man's mouth to keep him silent.

Kramer sends Peter back for the others while Marco and he stand for a moment in silence waiting. He feels his heart pounding blood in his ears. "Next time, wait for my orders," Kramer says finally.

"It was opportune," Marco replies, looking down the trail.

"Yes, but there may be more than one opportunity."

Marco turns his eyes on Kramer, blinks once slowly, then nods. "As you like."

The other six come through the brush.

"He's sure to have periodic call-ins," Kramer says, nodding toward the tree where the guard is bound. "We have to move quickly now, or his silence will tip the others off."

One direction to move: down the trail toward the huts. They fan out: Marco, Randall, and the twins on one side of the narrow dirt road and Kramer, Rudi, Peter, and Georges on the other, all keeping as close to the tree line as possible. At one point, they hear a car engine start up, its engine revving. Kramer halts and scatters them into the foliage at the roadside, but then the engine is turned off. Birds are singing, unaware of the silly games men are playing below. They set out again.

The first hut comes into view in a little clearing before Kramer expects it. He pulls back away from the road, motioning the others to do so as well. Luckily, no guards are posted on the perimeter. Suddenly, the door to the little hut opens, and a heavy-set man in a brown and black uniform comes out, zipping his pants and buckling his belt.

Outdoor crappers need no guards, Kramer thinks.

This man heads back to the left toward what Kramer sees now to be a second hut. Parked next to it is a purple Mercedes, its hood up and another man leaning over the fender, his torso lost in the guts of the car. A voice calls from inside the hut, "Is that fixed yet?"

The man under the hood mumbles something Kramer cannot understand, and then Vogel walks out of the second hut, dressed in a town suit with a heavy overcoat on.

That's three of them, Kramer tells himself.

The goon from the toilet comes up to the car and peers into the engine now, then slaps the man with his head under the hood on the back. "Christ!" he says, grinning at Vogel. "Max is a regular mechanic, all right. Got grease up to his eyeballs and a dead engine."

He laughs loudly, taking great delight in his own banter.

"Get the damn thing fixed," Vogel hisses. "I've got to make that call soon." He turns in a huff and goes back into the hut.

The headless mechanic stands up suddenly, stretching his back, hands on hips and a pained expression on his face.

No-Neck. The one who killed Gerhard.

Kramer watches him as he gets the kinks out of his back, then bends over his task once again, the other guard watching over his shoulder.

Rudi has come up to Kramer's side now. "There are only three of them," he says.

"That we can see," Kramer says in a low voice, never taking his eyes from the huts.

His eyes jerk to the right at the sound of a door slapping shut. In the opposite corner of the clearing is the third hut, partially hidden from view by the foliage surrounding Kramer. Parked near it is a tan Volkswagen van. Kramer sees a uniformed man making his way from the third hut to the crapper, but can't make out the features through the underbrush until the man gets to the door. It's the blond Hitler Youth look-alike from the Munich headquarters.

Old home week.

"There're the rest of them," Kramer says, nodding toward the third and larger hut. It looks like it may be the bunkhouse for the camp, but without windows there's no telling. A second guard comes to the door of this hut and flicks a burning cigarette out onto a large, round charcoal pit in front.

At least five of them, Kramer thinks. And no telling where Maria is—with Vogel or with the Hitler Youth.

"What now?" Rudi says.

"We wait a little. See what we can see."

He tries to make his voice sound calm, but he does not feel that way. The anger eating at him cries for action, but he knows he has to rein that in.

Vogel comes out once again, drawing Kramer's attention back to the huts. He leans over the car, looking at No-Neck's work, shaking his head impatiently. Then he stands upright, blowing vapor bubbles into the cold air. The first guard is still standing by the car, getting a kick out of it all.

Behind them, a sixth figure is suddenly standing in the door of Vogel's hut. Kramer makes him instantly: No-Neck's partner.

"She says she's got to take a piss," he yells to Vogel.

Vogel jerks his head back to the door. "Then take her to the fucking toilet, you idiot. Do I have to do everything around here?"

The man in the doorway flexes his jaws, but says nothing. He goes back in the hut and returns a moment later, guiding Maria out of the building. Her hands are bound behind her and a white scarf covers her eyes, but she looks unharmed.

Kramer feels his heart soar.

"That her?" Rudi whispers at his side.

"Yes."

"I think it's time to dance, then," Rudi says.

Kramer closes his mind down, channels the anger. He glances across the road. Marco is checking it all out, his eyes narrowed to slits, his jaw set. He turns to look at Kramer, and their eyes lock for a moment. Kramer jabs his finger to the left, and Marco nods. He, Randall, and the other two men begin fanning out around the huts to the left, hidden in the bushes. Kramer and his three move ahead on their side of the road to circle to the right. He keeps his eyes on Maria and the goon as they slowly proceed toward the outhouse. The brush tears at Kramer's face. He thinks he and the others must be making enough noise to wake a drunk, but no one in the clearing appears to notice.

Thirty yards from the toilet, Maria stumbles, and the goon bends over, grips her arm, and roughly lifts her to her feet. Peter is at Kramer's side, whispering as they move forward bowed like old men, "I'll take care of the guard once they're at the outhouse."

"I'll take care of him," Kramer says, not bothering to look at Peter.

BASIC LAW

"It's got to be silent, or you'll alert the rest of them," Peter says, lightly touching Kramer's arm. "Marco and his men won't have time to get in position."

Kramer stops, wetting his dry mouth to speak. His angle of vision is better now. He can see that the three buildings form a rough triangle in the clearing, with the outhouse at the apex closest to him. Its door is facing the road, out of sight of the other two huts, and the woods come up to within a few feet of it. Still, he knows taking out the goon will require a pro. No on-the-job training with this one. Not only Maria's, but the lives of Randall, Rudi, and the other men are in the balance. Muff the job and there's no second chance.

"All right," Kramer says. "I don't feel good about it, but okay."

Peter squeezes Kramer's biceps lightly. "There will be enough action for everybody," he says.

"But she's not your fight."

Peter shrugs. "A fight's a fight."

They move on silently, nearing the tongue of wooded land that juts out into the clearing by the outhouse. Rudi and Georges take up positions further to the right, their field of fire concentrating on the bunkhouse; Kramer and Peter lie in the brush nearest the outhouse. Kramer silently takes off his leather pack.

Out in the clearing, Maria falls again on the uneven ground, and the goon stands over her for a moment, shaking his head in disgust before bending over to help her up again.

"Wish me luck," Peter says, and begins crawling out of the brush toward the outhouse, using Maria's unintentional diversion to conceal his movements.

Kramer covers him. By the time the goon gets Maria up and they are on their way again, Peter is hidden from their view by the outhouse. He moves quickly and effortlessly for

295

such a big man and is almost at the outhouse when Kramer
realizes they've made a terrible mistake.

The Hitler Youth kid is still in the john.

Kramer frantically searches the leaf-covered forest floor
for a stone or twig to toss at Peter, to somehow get his attention. The door of the outhouse opens before he can find anything. Hitler Youth steps out, adjusting his brown tie, and
Peter is almost at his feet, his rifle cradled in his arms.

They both jerk to a stop, frozen like snakes about to strike.
Kramer looks beyond them to Maria just approaching the
outhouse, so close to them. The goon is behind her, partially
blocked by her body.

"They've come! They've come!" the kid yells before Peter
can silence him.

Kramer has the goon in his sights, but Maria is startled by
the kid's screams and jumps into the line of fire.

The rest happens like a slow-motion pantomime. Kramer
tosses the rifle aside and is up and running, only vaguely aware
of shots coming from both sides. The kid falls at his feet, lev-
eled by a blow to his shins by the barrel of Peter's Mannlicher.
Kramer leaps over the sprawling body.

"Down, Maria!" he yells as he tugs the pistol out of his
jacket pocket.

She automatically does as he says, and the goon is caught
off guard, scrambling to get his pistol out of his shoulder hol-
ster. Kramer shoots as he runs, the first shots going wide, and
hears high and piercing screams coming from Maria. The
goon has his pistol out now, and Kramer lets off another quick
round that misses, the gun recoiling heavily in his hand. The
goon is smiling as he sites Kramer, but the front of the man's
tan jacket turns crimson suddenly, and he lurches backward
as if struck by a board. A second shot rings out from behind
Kramer, and the goon's pistol hand shatters like meat under a

cleaver. He looks at his ruined hand, then touches the blood on his chest with his good hand, and crumples to the ground on top of Maria.

Kramer looks over his shoulder and nods a thanks to Peter, just lowering the rifle from his shoulder. More shots sound from the compound, and Kramer rushes to Maria. She is screaming hysterically by the time he pulls the guard off her. The man is breathing raggedly, blood coming from his mouth.

"It's okay," he says, scooping Maria into his arms. "All okay now."

"Sam?"

He runs with her in his arms to the cover of the outhouse, sets her down momentarily, pulls her blindfold off, unties her wrists.

"God, Sam!" She throws her arms around him.

He holds her with one arm, the pistol held up at the ready. Peter has pulled the Hitler Youth kid back into the foliage, and Kramer and Maria make a dash for its cover as well. Bullets rip into the outhouse in back of them, splintering the sides and spraying wood chips. Maria and Kramer dive into the brush, and more bullets rattle through the branches over their heads. The kid is lying on the ground near them, gripping his leg and groaning.

"You broke it," he says, rocking on the ground, glaring at Peter next to him.

Kramer looks closely at Maria, tries to smile, but his lips won't allow it. "You okay?"

She forces a grin; there is moisture in her eyes. Then she nods quickly.

"My leg," the kid whimpers.

Maria crawls over to him and pulls the khakis out of his black boots, examining the contusion. The kid yelps when she touches it gently.

"You'll live," she says dispassionately. "It's only a slight fracture."

Kramer hands her his pistol. "Keep him covered."

The discarded rifle is lying nearby, and he pulls it to him, taking stock of the situation for the first time. Peter scuttles over to his side. Shooting has stopped for the moment but the heavy stink of cordite fills the clearing. No forest noises can be heard, only the rattle of breath from the dying man near the outhouse and the kid's groans.

The windows of the Mercedes have been shattered; jagged ends of glass are left on the frames. Pockmarks of bullet holes show in the doors of the car and on the wooden sides of both the other huts. In front of the hut to the far right, a body lies sprawled and motionless.

"Marco!" Kramer yells.

There is an instant of silence, then Marco's voice calls out, "We're okay. One in the hut, two under the car."

Kramer looks closely. He can see No-Neck's feet barely sticking out from under the car. They are rapidly pulled back in at this declaration.

"Rudi?" Kramer calls out.

"Okay here," Rudi shouts back. "One down. One or two in the hut."

Kramer watches as Peter opens his NATO jacket and unhooks two grenades from cloth loops.

"No," Kramer says. "We got what we came for."

"What you came for," Peter says. "I had a sister burned out in Rostock. The score isn't quite even yet."

Maria looks at him and Kramer puts a restraining hand on Peter's shoulder. "Let me try it my way first," he says.

Peter hefts the grenades in his hands, takes a deep breath, and lets it out. "Okay. But if it doesn't work, these will."

Kramer looks back at the kid. "You know what this is all about?"

The kid continues to rock, gripping his broken leg in his hands.

Kramer scoots on the ground over to the kid, laying a hand on his shoulder. "I asked if you know what this is about."

The kid looks up at Kramer, and his eyes close to narrow slits emitting hate and fear. He shrugs Kramer's hand off his shoulder.

"I am prepared to die for the Fatherland."

"Give me a break," Kramer says. "You know you don't want to die. Not for this piece of real estate, anyway. What did Vogel tell you about the kidnapping?"

The kid stares at him for a moment, then says defiantly, "That you have member lists and were blackmailing him."

Kramer laughs. "That's his story, is it?"

"I heard you threaten him," the kid says. "Yesterday at headquarters when he summoned me. You said that in two days you would publish."

"That's right," Kramer says calmly. "But it's not member-ship lists I threatened him with. Those good old boys on the lists are already lost to you. They went scampering for the high ground once a man named Müller was killed. You might have heard of Müller, actually a guy named SS-Oberleutnant Arno Semich. A wanted war criminal from World War Two. It was in the papers."

"Victors' justice," the kid spits out.

"Yeah, sure," Kramer says, "the party line. But plenty of the powerful in Bonn knew who he was. They were protect-ing him all these years. And they're not risking their careers any further. You'll have to find other sources of income. That's a done deal. So, no, this isn't about some lists."

The kid makes no response, remembers his pain and rocks sitting up now.

"You're a smart kid," Kramer says. "Want to know the truth?"

"Screw you," the kid says through bared teeth.

Kramer scoots back to his original hiding place, grabs the leather day pack, and crawls back to the kid.

"Kramer!" It's Vogel, from the small hut.

Kramer ignores him for the moment, opening the pack, and pulling out the copy of Reni's memoirs.

"This is what your fearless leader is after," he says, dropping it in the kid's lap. "I suggest you read pages 133 and 134."

The kid looks at the papers suspiciously at first.

"Kramer!"

Kramer looks toward the hut.

"How you doing, Vogel?" he yells out.

"We had a deal."

Kramer smiles. "I didn't like the terms." Then to the kid, "Read. You might learn something."

The kid flips through the pages, finding the ones Kramer told him about—the ones he inserted in the manuscript just this morning. The kid reads them quickly, then takes the pages out, and compares the typing on them to other pages in the manuscript.

"Lies," he finally says, setting the sheets back down in his lap and wincing at another jolt of pain.

"Kramer!" Vogel yells again. "You got what you want. Just leave. We're square."

"You don't want the documents?" Kramer calls out, and looks at the kid with savvy eyes.

Silence from Vogel's hut for a moment. Then, "You brought them?" A hint of eagerness in the voice.

"Sure," Kramer yells, never taking his eyes off the kid. "But you didn't give me a chance to trade. Look, I leave the documents, and you and your organization forget all about me, okay?"

In the intervening silence, the kid picks up the memoirs again and rereads the passage Kramer had written this morning, substituting Vogel for Müller as the spy who had worked for the East to get money to fund Germany United.

"Okay," Vogel calls out. His voice sounds reassured once again, in control.

"You're full of lies, just like all journalists," the kid says.

Kramer shakes his head at him. "You know it's true. Why else would Vogel take chances eliminating a washed-up intelligence agent like Gorik?" He gives it a moment for the name to sink in. "Gorik was his East German handler, and Vogel didn't want any traces of his former employment."

The kid considers this for a moment, his eyes opening a fraction.

"Kramer?" Vogel calls. "You got a deal. You hear?"

"I want guns thrown out first," Kramer yells to him. "Nobody follows us."

"You're crazy," Vogel screams from the hut.

"You've got to trust me. I don't want a war with all the right-wingers of Germany. I just want to peacefully withdraw from here. Don't force me to use the heavy shit. I've got men here. They would just as soon start lobbing grenades, understand?"

Silence.

The kid looks hard at Kramer. "Why tell me this?"

"I like to see justice done. Know what I mean? And I don't much like your fearless leader. Maybe it's time for a change of leadership. You know my reputation. I've always covered you folks fairly. *We* could work together in the future, but Vogel . . ." He looks toward the huts. "Maybe he's outlived his usefulness to your cause."

The kid squints at the pages again, and Kramer can almost hear his brain working, the simple calculus clicking through the boy's mind. *Get rid of the traitor Vogel, and there is one less person between me and the center of power.*

"You give those pages to Vogel," Kramer says, taking the

rest of the manuscript from the kid. "That's what he's after. I'm keeping my end of the bargain."

Then, looking at the hut by the Mercedes where Vogel is holed up, "What about it, Vogel? Do I need to start counting? There's some pretty pissed-off men at work here."

"Okay. We're throwing down our weapons. No tricks."

"No tricks," Kramer says. Then to the kid, "Your man under the Mercedes might be interested in learning why Vogel was having him risk his life knocking off the opposition. Might be interested to know just what noble cause got his buddy out there shot to hell."

The kid considers this for a moment.

"Something to think about, huh?" Kramer says, and the kid nods slowly.

CHAPTER TWENTY-THREE

Rain is washing along the gutters of the town by the time they arrive. The dash clock reads 22:30. Maria is sleeping with her head on Kramer's lap and Randall is slumped against the passenger door next to them. In front, Georges and Rudi are speaking softly in Romanian. The swish and slap of the wipers sound like a metronome; puddled water explodes underneath the Rover's chassis. Rudi puts an arm on the back of his leather seat and swivels to Kramer. "You sure you got to see this guy tonight?"

Kramer nods. "I'm sure." He pats Maria's head absently, liking the warmth of her next to him. "It's the next left," he says to Georges, and makes eye contact with him in the rearview mirror, Georges's face illuminated by the dash lights.

They pull up in front of the municipal building. The final stop; the last piece to fit into the puzzle. The second floor is mostly in the dark, but one office remains lit.

Randall awakes as the engine is turned off. Kramer has to gently nudge Maria to wake her.

"What . . . ? No . . ." she begins, but he pats her consolingly.

"It's all right," he says, lifting her by the shoulders. "I've got a little errand, and then we're homeward bound."

She is disoriented, and Kramer gives her no time to get her bearings, to ask difficult questions. She leans against Randall and closes her eyes. Kramer and Randall exchange smiles.

"You sure you don't want company?" Randall says.

Kramer opens his door. "Not this time. I'll be back in a sec."

"And if you are not, Kramer?" Rudi says.

The cold damp air sweeps into the car from the partially open door. Kramer considers this. "Give it ten minutes. If I'm still in there, you better call the police."

"Most amusing, Kramer," Rudi says.

Kramer slides out of the car and dashes through the rain to the front door of the building. The front desk is manned by a noncom. It's a slow night in Bad Lunsburg; most of the uniformed officers have gone home.

"I've got an appointment with Kommissar Boehm," Kramer says to the young noncom. The evening paper is open on the desk, the sports page announcing that the German team has been eliminated in World Cup competition.

"Yeah, good," the policeman says, barely lifting his eyes from the paper.

Kramer passes through the empty interviewing area, its desks tidied up for the day. A light burns in a back office. Kramer goes to the emergency stairs and climbs a flight to the second floor. Boehm's office is to the left of the stairs, the light still on.

Kramer taps on the frosted glass, then eases the door open. Boehm is sitting at his desk, his head bent, looking at his green blotter. A lamp washes the desk in light, leaving the rest of the room in shadows. Boehm does not look up as Kramer enters; does not stir as he crosses the room and takes a seat across the desk.

They sit for a moment in silence. Finally, Boehm raises his head. Kramer sees the photograph of the Kommissar's daughter on the blotter.

"What have you been up to, Kramer?"

Kramer sits silently for a moment, staring at Boehm. "I think you know," he says.

Boehm forces a smile. "We are going to be cryptic, are we?"

Kramer shakes his head. "No. There are no more secrets or hidden codes." He looks at the picture. "She was a pretty girl. How'd she really die?"

Boehm squints at him. "I told you."

"I don't think so, Kommissar."

"What are you getting at, Kramer?" Boehm slouches back in his desk chair; the leather squeaks under him. "And what's happening with Vogel?"

"I'm sure you've had a call about that," Kramer says. "But then again, maybe not. Maybe Vogel's in no shape to be making calls."

Kramer can still see Vogel's face this afternoon going red as he screamed at him, demanding the lists, accusing him of treachery after the neo-Nazis had thrown down their guns.

He had a point, Kramer must admit. Kramer demanded one more little favor before handing over the memoirs. So, after speaking clearly into the microphone and signing a statement, Vogel had reason to be fuming when Kramer did not come through with his part of the bargain. But those watching the interview had no way of knowing the memoirs were altered.

"Instead you give me this . . . this pack of lies. We'll get you for this, Kramer. No matter where you go, we'll be there."

"I'm just the messenger here, Vogel," Kramer told him. "You don't like the message, too bad. And if I were you, I might think twice before doing something dumb. My friends here"—he nodded at Rudi and his gang—"have long memories. You might watch out where you step, yourself. There's dog shit enough to go around for everybody."

Kramer isn't worrying. The Hitler Youth kid, leaning on

a broken branch as a makeshift crutch, was watching it all, his face cold and dispassionate, his eyes full of suspicion. No-Neck didn't look any too happy, either, once he took a look at the pages. Kramer knew there would be a change of leadership at Germany United very soon. Vogel would meet with an unfortunate accident, perhaps en route to Munich.

"Straight talk, Kramer," Boehm says, jarring him back into the present.

Kramer fixes his eyes on Boehm again. "Okay. Straight talk. Before Renata Müller killed herself, she let her father know about her memoirs. So he came and tidied up things. And then he called the police."

Boehm sits forward in his chair about to protest, but Kramer waves a hand at him. "Just let me finish. Then we can talk. So he calls the police. It's late at night. Later than tonight, but someone's on duty. Someone who works late, who doesn't have much of a home life. Someone who even understands what it might feel like to lose a daughter. So our policeman goes to the scene and immediately sees what Müller has not: a list of prominent politicians who are members of a certain right-wing party."

"You got a crystal ball, Kramer? Where'd you hear this? Where's your witness?"

"Let's imagine," Kramer says. "Humor me."

But it was the last piece of the puzzle handed to him by Rick's girlfriend, Margit. That night at the gasthaus in Vienna when Kramer was talking about how the purple car was traced back to Vogel, he mentioned that it was Kommissar Boehm who tracked it. *You mix with very strange company, Kramer*, Margit said then. But it was not just Vogel she was referring to. No. He confirmed that when he talked with Margit earlier this morning to try and find Vogel's hideaway. Margit meant both of them; Boehm was in attendance at Vogel's party for the graduates of basic training. An honored guest, she told him.

"Just humor me," Kramer repeats.

Boehm snorts. "Okay. So what the hell would some cop care about membership lists?"

"That's simple," Kramer says, forming a steeple with his fingers and touching his lips with the forefingers. "Because our policeman is also a member of this right-wing party. Secretly, of course. He figures his name won't show up on any membership lists. He's much too smart for that. But he cares about protecting the party; protecting the membership and contributor lists."

Boehm leans forward, hands on the desk. "Continue, please. I'm all ears."

"Our wise policeman must have known about Müller's Nazi past. The old boys' network would see to that. Though he certainly did not know about Müller's activities on behalf of the former German Democratic People's Republic. So he plays a double game. He enlists Müller's support; tells him he knows how it feels to lose a daughter, that he can help to tidy things up. And Müller agrees. What our smart policeman doesn't know, though, is that Müller is playing his own double game. But we'll get to that in a moment."

"I'm sure we will," Boehm says. "You've got a very active imagination for a journalist, Kramer."

Kramer ignores this. "Our policeman needs time. Time to investigate further. If Renata Müller had membership lists of this right-wing party, what other incriminating bits of evidence might there be tucked about the place or given to friends and relatives? Solid deductive reasoning," Kramer says, "because our policeman is not just somebody on the beat, but a well-trained, thorough detective. So Müller goes home with his bit of misery, the memoirs. And our policeman calls in help from the right-wing party itself. A car arrives in the middle of the night all the way from Munich. A purple car that turns up in many different places in this case. Inheritance is turned over; every nook and cranny searched for further incriminating evidence. It is only then, in fact, that the leader of this right-wing party learns he has been infiltrated by Ms. Müller. Most unsettling. Who else might she have confided in? Isn't there a husband? But he is nowhere to be found."

Kramer pauses momentarily. Rain streams down the office window, back-lit by sodium streetlamps, and reflects on the interior wall opposite: an orange, flowing light show.

Boehm still hunkers over his desk like a caged bear.

"So the suicide goes unreported," Kramer continues. "Renata Müller is left to molder until her stink arouses neighborly curiosity. Meanwhile, time is bought to ensure there are no further copies of the list. There is no sign of the husband, but Herr Müller very helpfully—too helpfully, in fact—furnishes a lead. A certain Herr Gorik who lives in Berlin has been in touch with Reni. Gorik subsequently has an accident, and his place is completely cleaned out. The policeman and the Nazi leader hope that all is taken care of. Renata Müller's body is duly discovered and buried, but then comes a journalist and former lover of Renata Müller's asking unfortunate questions, making people nervous. Instead of simply getting rid of the journalist, it's decided that he should be used to trace the wandering husband. And in order to do that, he has to be won over by the policeman, made to think they are playing the same game and are after the same prize. He has to be convinced that the policeman hates the Nazi leader—let's call him Vogel, shall we?—as much as the journalist. So the cop gives the journalist a heartbreaking story about a daughter who got lost in drugs and the skin trade. But like everything else the policeman said or did, this story, too, was phony. The journalist did some checking late this afternoon in Munich, see, and found out the policeman's daughter died in a car accident. The other driver was a Nigerian who'd been drinking."

Kramer pauses a moment before continuing, his voice

hard and cutting now, "Is that what sent you into Vogel's arms, Kommissar? What made a secret Nazi of you? That and your frustration at a legal system that prevents you from being cop, judge, jury, and executioner all in one?"

Again Boehm leans back, exhaling a mighty breath. He scratches his eyebrow, rubs his nose, and smiles at Kramer. "Interesting," he says.

"So you used me," Kramer says, keeping his hatred on low fire, controlling his voice. "You did some computer searches on Gorik and gave me some information about a parked car, which led to Vogel. But these were trails that I was on the verge of discovering anyway. And you won me over. You spoon-fed me Gerhard's credit card information and then turned me loose like a trained bloodhound to sniff out the husband for you. Your goon killed Gerhard, and then I had outlived my usefulness. The goon's next job was to get rid of me, too. But suddenly, the trail led back to Herr Müller in ways you never expected. When I told you that Müller was actually a wanted war criminal named SS-Oberleutnant Arno Semich and that he was a spy for the East Germans, this changed the game. Only then did you understand how Müller had set you and Vogel up; how Müller had used you to do his dirty work eliminating Gorik. So you decided to kill Müller instead of me and thought that would be an end of it. That everything could be pinned on Müller if he were dead, and that I would go off to Vienna and play reporter again and you and your friend could get on with your work undisturbed."

Boehm makes no response to this, merely shaking his head.

"And then you used me one last time after I discovered the true identity of Müller, telling me that no judge was going to convict on the strength of a blurry, forty-year-old photo of SS-Oberleutnant Semich. What we need is a confession, you told me, and I bought it. I agreed to be the stooge, going to

Müller and getting him to talk, with you waiting outside to clap the handcuffs on. But instead, you waited long enough for Müller to threaten me—you knew he would. And so you came in blazing away like a cowboy."

"Is that all?" Boehm says. He's got the photo of his daughter in his hand now.

"No. One last thing. It's time for you to retire."

"You wouldn't be wearing a wire, would you, Kramer? Trying to pull on me what we did to Müller?" He sets the photo down and eases his hands off the desk.

"Nope. No wire. Just a carload of heavily armed friends waiting downstairs for me."

Boehm's hands stop wherever they were going, coming back to the top of the desk. "Why would I want to retire?"

"To keep your pension. Once word of your involvement with Germany United gets out, I doubt there will be any retirement party for you. No gold watches."

"It's a pretty story, Kramer. But that's all it is. A story. You've got no proof for any of it. You get witnesses or hard proof, you bring them in. Until that time, don't bother me."

On cue, Kramer brings out the digital recorder he carries in the inside pocket of his oilskin. He sets it on the desk, clicks it on. Vogel's resonant tones fill the room.

This is to confirm that Kommissar Reinhard Boehm of the Bad Lunsburg Police is a dues-paying member of Germany United and a long-time supporter of our cause.

Kramer snicks the switch off, puts the device back in his pocket.

"Crap. Could be anybody's voice."

"I've also got his written testimony. He was quite anxious to shop you and save his own skin."

"I thought you told me Vogel might not be around anymore."

"Last will and testament, you might call it. There are plenty of witnesses to back up the authenticity. We'll be running it as an update to my story in the *Daily European* tomorrow."

"Unless . . ."

"Yeah. You've got the idea. Unless you retire first. Write the letter tonight. You've put in your years. Save the pension. It's too late to save the asses of the folks in Bonn who've been playing sweet with Germany United. They're going down with the publication of Reni's memoirs. And that manuscript is in the publisher's hands as we speak. But you? At least you get your country house and plot of ground to plant petunias and zucchini."

"And you're doing this because . . . ?"

"Because I'm a realist. Same reason I left them standing at the Germany United camp today. You're my insurance to continued good health. I'm sure you've got connections in the force, here and in Austria. I don't want you using them against me. I'm not a crusader. Publishing Reni's memoirs was what I was tasked with. That's happening. Those boys in Bonn got a problem with it, they can take it up with the writer, but she's already dead. Me, I've got to live afterward."

"Very heroic, Kramer."

"I leave the heroics to you folks, Boehm. Retire. Take it easy."

"You say I'm a killer. You going to let a killer go?"

"Müller was going to live out the rest of his days in a prison cell anyway. You did him a favor."

"You've got this all figured out, don't you?" Boehm says. "Nice and wrapped up. It's what a rational man would do, right?"

"Right."

They stare at each other in the murky light for a moment.

"Think about it," Kramer says. "You have until tomorrow. But nothing cute, okay?" He smiles at Boehm as he opens the door. "Those friends of mine in the car? They've got a penchant for violence. Ask Vogel."

He looks at Boehm for a silent moment, sees the doubt in the Kommissar's eyes, and then leaves, closing the door behind him without waiting for a response. Suddenly, he feels drained, as if he has not slept in weeks. He makes it downstairs and past the guard at the desk, who is still on the sports section but looks up to give Kramer a nod as he passes. He reaches the car in a daze.

"We were beginning to wonder," Randall says as Kramer climbs in.

Maria is still sleeping curled up against Randall, and now he shifts her weight to Kramer's lap.

"So?" Randall finally says.

Kramer shrugs. He looks down at Maria's head, at the throbbing blue vein at her temple. "I think it's over," he says.

From the office above comes a muffled popping sound. One short explosive noise like the backfire of a car. Randall looks at him.

"A *rational* man," Kramer says.

Then to Rudi in the front seat, "Maybe it's time we go home."

ACKNOWLEDGMENTS

Thanks go first to MysteriousPress.com founder Otto Penzler and associate publisher Rob Hart for turning this project into a book.

Folks at Open Road Integrated Media have also earned my gratitude. Lauren Chomiuk, associate managing editor, and Joan Giurdanella, copyeditor, have once again teamed up to help make this a much better novel by catching inconsistencies, tracking down and eradicating historical faux pas on my part, and generally making the narrative read more smoothly. Randle Robinson Bitnar's meticulous proofread is also much appreciated.

A big thanks to this fine group of professionals.

And finally, thanks as usual go to my family, my sine qua non. Love you guys.

EBOOKS BY
J. SYDNEY JONES

FROM MYSTERIOUSPRESS.COM
AND OPEN ROAD MEDIA

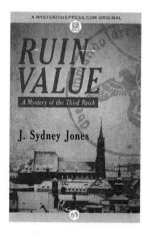

Available wherever ebooks are sold

MYSTERIOUSPRESS.COM

Otto Penzler, owner of the Mysterious Bookshop in Manhattan, founded the Mysterious Press in 1975. Penzler quickly became known for his outstanding selection of mystery, crime, and suspense books, both from his imprint and in his store. The imprint was devoted to printing the best books in these genres, using fine paper and top dust-jacket artists, as well as offering many limited, signed editions.

Now the Mysterious Press has gone digital, publishing ebooks through **MysteriousPress.com**.

MysteriousPress.com offers readers essential noir and suspense fiction, hard-boiled crime novels, and the latest thrillers from both debut authors and mystery masters. Discover classics and new voices, all from one legendary source.

FIND OUT MORE AT
WWW.MYSTERIOUSPRESS.COM

FOLLOW US:

@emysteries and Facebook.com/MysteriousPressCom

MysteriousPress.com is one of a select group of publishing partners of Open Road Integrated Media, Inc.

THE MYSTERIOUS BOOKSHOP, founded in 1979, is located in Manhattan's Tribeca neighborhood. It is the oldest and largest mystery-specialty bookstore in America.

The shop stocks the finest selection of new mystery hardcovers, paperbacks, and periodicals. It also features a superb collection of signed modern first editions, rare and collectable works, and Sherlock Holmes titles. The bookshop issues a free monthly newsletter highlighting its book clubs, new releases, events, and recently acquired books.

58 Warren Street
info@mysteriousbookshop.com
(212) 587-1011
Monday through Saturday
11:00 a.m. to 7:00 p.m.

FIND OUT MORE AT:

www.mysteriousbookshop.com

FOLLOW US:

@TheMysterious and Facebook.com/MysteriousBookshop

Open Road Integrated Media is a digital publisher and multimedia content company. Open Road creates connections between authors and their audiences by marketing its ebooks through a new proprietary online platform, which uses premium video content and social media.

Videos, Archival Documents, and New Releases

Sign up for the Open Road Media newsletter and get news delivered straight to your inbox.

Sign up now at
www.openroadmedia.com/newsletters